Thin Air

Storm Constantine

WOODMILL HIGH SCHOOL

WARNER BOOKS

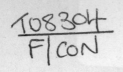
A *Warner* Book

First published in Great Britain by Warner Books in 1999
This edition published by Warner in 2000

Copyright © Storm Constantine 1999

The moral right of the author has been asserted.

A CIP catalogue record for this book
is available from the British Library.

ISBN 0 7515 3032 8

Typeset by Palimpsest Book Production Limited,
Polmont, Stirlingshire

Printed and bound in Great Britain by
Mackays of Chatham plc, Chatham, Kent

Warner Books
A Division of
Little, Brown and Company (UK)
Brettenham House
Lancaster Place
London WC2E 7EN

This book is dedicated to Paula Wakefield,
for her help, support, inspiration and friendship.

Part I

The Sea

On the day he disappeared, the sky was silver. He stood beside the sea, looking down at the beach from a car park, gripping a black metal hand-rail, gazing out at infinity.

It had begun already.

People walked across the damp Tarmac behind him, wreathed in an almost invisible steam. They paid him no attention. Children shrieked and seagulls scattered. The sands were pearl below. He felt so insubstantial. Perhaps it would not be necessary to carry out the plans. Perhaps, if he concentrated hard enough, he could be absorbed by the silvery ether.

Summer time. He thought of childhood, of those snap-shot days in sunlight. He did not mourn them, but examined the memories with a distant nostalgia. The film of his life. Where had it changed? When?

For a moment, he turned round and looked up at the hills behind him, where seaside residences perched pink and white among the sycamores. This town held so many memories, but none of them were his. There was something odd about resorts, he realised. They were ephemeral. They had a virtual life. Full of ghosts. Like he was.

Back to the sea. It heaved in the distance, listlessly; a goddess in repose. Now that he had made the decision, it was difficult to proceed. He might be wrong.

The sky was clear of rain now. All tears were shed. He was surrounded by the smell of the Tarmac, by the rank aroma of the beach, mixed with a synthetic vanilla reek from a nearby doughnut stand. It was unremittingly ordinary, the most concrete of illusions.

Would his disappearance be as simple as making a decision? He had believed it so, sitting alone in a hotel room, able to see through the illusion. Reality does not exist. You can step

3

out of it. So easy. Two hundred and fifty thousand people disappeared every year. Where did they go? How could such a vast number be so invisible? How many of them felt as he did now?

He imagined it would be like pushing through a membrane, slight resistance at first. He looked down at the beach, at the buzzing masses of energy: human beings, beach towels, sand. I do not believe in it, he thought. Not any longer. And the sky continued to burn above him. A hundred tiny hands reached from the top of his head towards it. He felt weightless.

The sea, the gulls, the sand. It was all empty. Elemental. He fell.

Chapter One

If he was dead, she was sure he'd make his presence felt to her somehow. She wasn't a great believer in the paranormal, but surely, if he was no longer part of the world, there'd be some subtle indication in her heart? She didn't feel it, but perhaps that was because she didn't want to believe he was dead. If she imagined it hard enough, would he come walking in through the door as if nothing had happened?

The flat was quiet in the afternoon, almost too quiet, but its stillness didn't seem watchful, just empty. Dex wasn't there. In a sense, he'd never been there.

The phone lay in two pieces on the floor, its wire and cord trailing like entrails. She'd savaged it the night before, unable even to bear the click of the answering machine as it fielded all the calls.

Jay padded barefoot out into the kitchen where the refrigerator hummed reassuringly. The sun didn't reach here in the afternoon; all was in shadow, but warm. Inside the fridge were three bottles of rum, one white, one spiced, one dark. Today, it was white rum, for clarity. Jay took down a clean glass from the cupboard overhead, filled it with ice from the freezer. Then she poured the white fire over it, cracking the ice, releasing its potency. Sometimes, Jay would put flower petals in the glass, or leaves from her house-plants, or threads of her own hair. All of these rituals were meaningless, because she had lost the focus of her life, and no omens existed to herald its return. Everything had changed. For ever.

As she sat drinking, with the curtains drawn across the windows, filtering the light to the colour of cinnamon, Jay realised that in her shock and sorrow, she was somehow cleansed. All that existed was a raw form of herself, perhaps without identity, but primal. For five days, she had shut out the world, because it was trying so desperately to get in. Even with the curtains pulled close together like stubborn lips, she still crawled across the floor when she had to pass the windows. Not even her shadow would fall upon the world outside. Perhaps they had all gone; the fans, the reporters, the photographers, and those other people, who were drawn to sites of human drama like carrion-eaters. Jay hadn't checked since early yesterday morning. She had been acquiescent at first, warmed by the attention. It felt as if everyone shared her bewilderment. Images of herself, pale-faced and disguised by sunglasses, were strewn about the room; on the newspapers she'd trampled over, rolled in, wept on to. Her skin was dappled with smeared print. Now, she felt like a spectacle, something to be gloated over. Who cared, really?

There was no way forward from here. This was the end, and it was endless.

Jay had met Dex at a party for someone's new CD release, a band who were on Sakrilege, the same label as he was. She was covering the event for her column in *This* magazine, accompanied by a friend, another writer named Grant Fenton. Both Jay and Fenton were regarded with awe and fear by the bands whose fate they could decide in print. Jay never pulled her punches: most of what she heard and saw in the music business irritated her. But, despite this, it had become her natural habitat. Dex's presence had inevitably touched Jay's world already on a number of occasions, but with little impact. She saw him as nothing more than a product, embarrassing in his bravado. He was also very famous, and would undoubtedly treat her with little respect, so she'd avoided any confrontation. Jay was careful to mix only with people who appreciated who and what she was. But that one night in the summer of 1988, coincidences had aligned, bodies had been strategically placed upon the board of the social gathering and by ten to midnight, Jay and Dex were enclosed in the same group of people, who were all gabbling rubbish inspired by too much champagne. At just the right moment, when Jay in her private world had been wondering what she was doing there, Dex had caught her eye and a knowing smile had been exchanged. Somewhere, a light turned on. Jay saw a kindred spirit in this unlikely figure before her. For a fleeting second, she knew they had both been aware of the travesty of the party, the superficiality of its participants, the silly, delusional egotism of the whole scene. It was not love at first sight by any means, simply a feeling of relief. They went outside together.

The balcony hung high above the river and the lights of London vibrated through the warm air.

Jay put down her champagne glass on the balcony rail, and brushed her fingers through her hair. 'God, those people are just awful.'

'Twats,' Dex agreed succinctly.

'I don't know why I come.'

'Free booze.'

'It's not worth it.'

'No.'

She inspected him for a moment, eye to eye, without the media screen. He was shabby, rather goofy in appearance, but with interesting eyes. She suspected his hair could do with a wash, because she could smell it, but the smell wasn't unattractive. His hands were sensitive, with oddly aligned thumbs. This was the man whose image was enshrined upon the pages of every teen magazine in the country. Thousands of little girls wanted to touch him, and here she was, on a balcony above the Thames, close enough to smell his hair. The thought made her smile, and he just smiled back, didn't ask why. She liked that.

'So what are you here for, then?' he asked her. 'You work for Sakrilege?'

Ten minutes before, Jay would have been offended that he didn't know who she was, but now the feeling was liberating. She shrugged. 'No. I'm supposed to write up the edifying experience for a magazine. People want to read bitchy things about their friends.'

'You're a writer.'

'I write, yes.' She pulled a face. 'Pays the bills.' She waited for him to ask if she'd ever written about him, already formulating a suitable reply.

7

'Words are the most powerful thing in the world,' Dex said. 'People who work with them are warriors.'

She glanced at him sidelong, resisting the urge to laugh at these earnest words. 'In that case, I have a veritable arsenal about tonight.' She paused. 'I'm Jay. Jay Samuels.'

His smile widened with private amusement. He'd heard of her all right, and from the look on his face had read what she'd written about him. 'I've seen your weaponry draw blood on occasion.'

'Nothing too fatal, I hope.'

He shook his head. 'No, it's funny. Makes me laugh. That's why you do it, isn't it – to make people laugh at other people's expense?'

She narrowed her eyes. 'Are we arguing about this?'

He shrugged, stuck out his lower lip. 'Don't think so. Are we?'

No, they weren't arguing.

'So, come on then, tell me about yourself,' he said. 'Where are you coming from, Ms Samuels?'

She told him. Dex did not listen with the ingratiating air she had become used to from musicians, those who were afraid she would destroy them with words. Dex did not care about such things. He just wanted to know her.

She described how she'd hung around the music scene since she'd been a precocious fourteen-year-old in the late Seventies. 'They were the times though, weren't they,' she said, then frowned a little, 'or are you too young to have been around then?'

'I wasn't around your scene,' Dex said, 'I'm a foreigner.'

'Excuse me?'

'Up north. Foreign. Cloth cap and whippet. You know.'

She smiled. 'Not everyone thinks that civilisation ends at Watford.'

'But you do – perhaps until now, anyway. I know what you London people are like.'

'I wasn't born in London. I come from Hampshire actually.'

He raised an eyebrow. 'I was just a kid in your time, but

8

not much younger than you. So how did you get into it all? Bet you were in a band.'

'No. I was never musical myself. I got into it through my art.'

'Not writing?'

'No, that came later.'

As an eighteen-year-old, Jay had gleaned enough skill from a brief art school experience to create record covers that aptly reflected the time. Startling pinks and scratched black mutated slowly into the abstract art of textures; mottled backgrounds and carefully placed artefacts; a rose against degraded rock; the skull of a bird upon a collage of grainy hieroglyphs. She'd never spent that much time on her work, being too fond of parties and bored by sleep. Jobs had been rushed, but eerily competent. She'd taken her environment so much for granted, unaware that things inevitably change, and so they did.

'One afternoon, I woke up with a hangover. I was lying in the bath, throbbing with various pains from head to foot, and then I realised. The life I'd led had disappeared. The people were gone, the young had changed, and I couldn't really call myself young any more.'

'That must have pissed you off.'

Jay twisted her mouth to the side, thought about it. 'I suppose the demise of my world grieved me, but I've always been adaptable. I just cut off the spiked black hair, changed my wardrobe, and became someone else. There was a new mood in the air. Music had fragmented, had somehow condensed. It was less about hedonism and release and more about money. It was the world that created you, Dex.'

He turned away from her, leaned against the balcony rail. 'I existed before that, sweetheart.'

'I didn't mean to sound insulting. You know what I mean, though, you must do. The music business has always delighted in creating people. It's a sort of Pygmalion thing. Let's face it, you were certainly the right raw material.'

He glanced at her and she was no longer sure what he was thinking. Had he taken offence? But she was quite sure he

9

understood her. His background had been suitably impover-
ished, his manner pertinently abusive and self-assured. He'd
had no education to speak of, yet possessed the ability to
work magic with words and music. Read separately, his
lyrics seemed almost banal, which was why they'd never
been printed on the CD covers, but once they were given life
by his voice, and set to the haunting yet powerful cadences
of his music, they became filled with meaning.

'I'm not what you think,' he said. 'You don't know everything.'

'I didn't mean to imply that. God, Dex, I know your success
is just as much to do with your work, as any favours from the
suits. You sing about the details of existence with a clarity
that touches people. It's like you can see around the corners in
people's lives and illuminate the dark spots.' She was amazed
at her own eloquence, given the amount of champagne she
had consumed.

He laughed, but she could tell he was flattered. 'Sounds like
you're working now! Funny. I never saw you write anything
like that about me.'

'You haven't read everything, you know you haven't. I don't
think you read my work very much at all. You don't like it.'

'Maybe. In that case, what do you think of mine?'

She paused. 'To be honest, it's a bit too commercial for me.
Remember, I was reared in the grimy alleys of the alternative
nation.' She smiled. 'As you know, I'm renowned for scorning
anything that gleams with popularity, but that doesn't mean
I can't appreciate its qualities.'

'Privately.'

She stared at him a moment. 'Yes, privately.'

'So what happened next, then? How'd you get to be a
hack?'

She let that ride. 'Let's just say I graduated from doing
artwork for independent labels – most of them were gulped
down whole by larger companies. I work for *This* magazine
mainly, with the odd other job here and there.' She wrinkled
her nose. '*This* is a bit self-conscious, I know, but it has a
good pedigree.'

Dex nodded. 'I can remember when it was still a fanzine. Black and white smudged photocopying.'

'Yeah. But it's survived, perhaps through luck more than judgement. It's respectable now.'

Dex laughed. 'Well, let's face it, your safety-pinned punk anarchists have all got electronic Filo-faxes now, talking about "windows" in their diary.' He pantomimed an affected voice. 'Oh, we're radio DJs and TV presenters. We have our little shops, restaurants and recording studios.' He uttered a sound of derision. 'They've become fat and complacent, but still think they're trend-setters.'

Jay grimaced. 'Harsh, but accurate.' She didn't want to say more, because she fitted comfortably into that world, writing a scathing column in *This* once a month that attacked anything that promised controversy. Still, she was aware that the youth of the country burned with different fires now, and perhaps her writing spoke only to her contemporaries, who lived in a time bubble of when anything had seemed possible.

She took a breath. 'So, what about you, then?'

He laughed bitterly. 'You know about me.'

'I'm not stupid, Dex.'

He studied her. 'No, I can see that.'

Later, Jay went back inside alone. Dex had uttered a friendly goodbye and left. She was slightly disappointed he hadn't suggested they go on somewhere else together, but was amused by the quaint way he'd formally asked her for a date. They would meet tomorrow. She smiled to herself as she moved through the twittering crowd of the party, mentally replaying details of their conversation. His ego hadn't been painful, he'd really listened to her, he'd been interested in what she had to say. How long had it been since she'd talked to someone like that?

Eventually, Jay came across Grant Fenton in a corner, draped drunkenly over a scantily clad giggling girl.

'Hey, Jay!' Grant drawled. 'Where've you been?'

She sat down next to him, aware she felt light-headed, excited. She hadn't felt like that for a long time. 'Grant,' she said. 'I've just met the most amazing man.'

* * *

Perhaps, if Jay had met Dex five years before, they wouldn't have been that different, but now they seemed like opposites; she articulate, groomed and sharp; he mouthy, scruffy and often insulting. He never insulted her, though. She wondered what they saw in each other, and whether other people thought they made an odd couple. Because they did become a couple.

He treated her from the start with a puzzling familiarity as if he couldn't see the exterior she'd constructed for herself. There was something about her he liked or needed. She wasn't a career girlfriend, like so many other women who fluttered desperately about the music scene. She didn't measure her own worth in terms of who she could persuade to sleep with her. When she met Dex she hadn't really wanted a regular partner. Romance was great, lust exhilarating, but after the gloss had dimmed, men, in Jay's experience, tended to become unfaithful, demanding or cruel. Dex became none of these things. She often hated him for the things he said and did to other people, and detested the public persona he'd created, but at home he was her soul companion. They'd infiltrated the scene and had found each other. They knew the truth of the music industry, but milked it for all they could. It was their secret. They could laugh about it.

For their first date, Dex took Jay to a riverboat restaurant on the Thames. She wasn't sure whether this was because he thought she'd expect something like that or a natural choice on his part. Throughout the meal, he was attentive and amusing. Conversation flowed easily between them. As the evening went on, Jay was conscious of a mounting sense of surprise within her. Dex seemed too good to be true. Could she dare believe in what she was being shown?

Later, as they left the boat and went to hail a taxi, a couple of kids came running across the road. One of them screamed Dex's name. Jay wasn't sure whether they were male or female. It all happened so quickly. The snarl that Dex turned on them was frighteningly loud; the roar of a maddened lion. 'Fuck off! Give us some respect, man!' His teeth were bared, his eyes dark with the emptiness of hate. Fortunately, before the stunned fans could respond, a black cab swung to a halt beside them. Dex hustled Jay in through the door. She lay back against the seat blinking, feeling dazed. Dex took her hand, smiled at her. 'Sorry,' he said. 'I just like privacy at times like these. People can't get their heads round that.'

She glanced at him. His face was serene, his eyes warm. Should this be a warning sign? She swallowed. Would a time come when she'd be crouched in a corner somewhere, her arms over her head, afraid?

That night, she seriously considered not seeing him again. She'd had abusive lovers in the past and certainly didn't intend to have one again. She was too wise for that now. But, the following morning, when Dex called her, she again felt a strong rapport with him. Perhaps she'd been too judgemental. It must be hell to live under public scrutiny all the time. She agreed to meet him again. They were rarely apart afterwards.

Jay would have understood if Dex had wanted her to remain in the background of his life – permanent women were often seen as something of an embarrassment to stars whose main audience was a host of adoring females – but Dex wanted no such thing. He was proud of Jay and wanted her sizzling in the limelight alongside him. She knew Dex's backing band were not wholly happy about it, but no one would dare voice their complaints. She knew, and so did they, that her presence in Dex's life had transformed him. There were fewer temperamental displays, and when they did occur, they were not as unpleasant as they had been before Jay had come into his life. The band were really just backing musicians. When Dex went on tour with them the posters never carried anything but his own name. Still, Jay made a point of getting to know the band girlfriends and organised social events that they could all attend. Dex pulled a face about that at first, but Jay explained that she didn't want to be seen as a pushy rock wife. She was her own person, who could make her own friends. Gina Allen, the wife of the bass player, Dan, was the last to crack beneath the pressure of Jay's relentless friendliness, but they eventually became close friends. Jay told herself that the friendships which took time to develop were often the most enduring.

Jay felt that Dex saw his life with her as a sanctuary. He had chosen her deliberately, and had perhaps been looking for someone like her for a long time. Maybe he thought the right woman would hold him together. She managed to influence his appearance to a large degree, realising his scruffiness came from self-neglect rather than choice. They moved into the ranks of the beautiful people, photographed smiling in airport terminals, laden with bags from L.A. During the first year, Jay's life became a hurricane of activity. Her own work had to be slotted in between media events and rushed trips abroad, but she did not feel it was taking a back seat to Dex's career. There were just so many good opportunities for travel and meetings with celebrities she could not miss, and anyway she could always write about them for *This* afterwards.

Every year, Dex scooped up trophies at the MTV Awards and the Brit Awards, as well as other ceremonies in America and Europe. Each time, the spotlight would sweep across the audience to Jay, who would be wearing exquisite designer gowns, her hair a sleek cap curling around her shaded cheek-bones. On one occasion, Dex even dragged her up on stage to tell the audience she was his greatest inspiration. Jay kept a firm control over these situations, exuding the right blend of self-effacement and pride in her partner. No one could accuse her of hogging the limelight, or of using Dex as a vehicle for her own ascension. She made sure of it.

Every summer, Dex and his band would play at one of the big music festivals. Jay would make one or two appearances back stage, haloed by camera flashes. She spoke to the press more than Dex did. She knew the ropes, and could appear to speak freely without actually saying much. At home, she was interviewed for women's magazines, where she spoke warmly of the harmony in her home. Dex might be a wild man of popular rock, but to her he was a loving and considerate partner. 'But what about his reputation?' the bravest of the journalists might ask. In their eyes would be the other questions: 'Doesn't he drink at home? Doesn't he throw tantrums? Aren't you sometimes afraid?'

Jay would smile tolerantly. 'You shouldn't believe all you read in the papers,' she'd say. Her glance would not even flicker.

Dex reserved a part of himself solely for Jay, which she loved, but it was only a part, and her commitment and trust were not enough to sustain him. She always knew the cracks were there, even though he tried to hide them from her. People speculated how difficult he must be to live with, but he wasn't. The problems arose when Jay wasn't there.

Twelve months after they'd met, Jay decided the honeymoon period was over, and she would no longer accompany Dex on tour. She did not enjoy life on the road. Hotel rooms held no appeal for her and she found it difficult to concentrate on her writing in them. Increasingly, she found herself yearning for the smoky cosiness of her small office at home. When she informed Dex of her decision, he was disappointed, but understood her feelings. The first time he went away without her, more than one friend asked her how she could bear to let her man travel alone, exposed to the fleshly temptations that lurked in the wings of every stage. Patiently, Jay would explain that she and Dex were not possessive with one another. She didn't feel she needed to keep an eye on his fidelity. If the occasional indiscretion did occur, Jay didn't want to know about it. She trusted his heart, which was enough. But despite this faith, Dex couldn't always control himself. Women were the least of the problems. Sometimes there were scuffles and arguments, punches thrown at photographers, broken furniture in hotels. Music press headlines screamed gloatingly about his exploits. He drank a lot, before and after gigs, picked fights with his band, went on the rampage, sometimes disappeared for days at a time. Only Jay's presence, during what the band came to view as that one idyllic year, had kept Dex's less savoury characteristics at bay.

Jay was used to getting frantic calls from the band's manager – often in the middle of the night, when she was red-eyed at the computer trying to meet a deadline – despairing of how to cope with Dex. Only Jay could control him, and she was honest enough with herself to know it wasn't even that. Her presence merely soothed him, quieted his demons. But Dex was an adult; she could not be constantly at his side like a mother. Initially, she had dropped everything and flown out to deal with the situation, wherever he was. Whenever she walked into the hotel room, or the bar, or the venue, she would find him subdued, sheepish, but grinning. He was always pleased to see her. Jay did this rescue act precisely three times, but knew it would have to stop. She and Dex talked about his difficulties and how he should take responsibility for his own actions. That was the sort of relationship they had. She did not approve of his binges, but neither would she continue to stride in and interfere. Really, his behaviour on tour did not touch her life, for she never witnessed it firsthand. In her heart, she did not wholly believe the stories of mayhem and rage, and thought they were exaggerated. As a writer herself, she knew how the creative mind could shape mundane real events into dramatic fiascos.

She knew his pattern. When the world Dex moved in became too overwhelming, he would find a bolthole and hide for a few days, getting drunk and smoking dope with people who were only too glad to take him in. He didn't always call her, but she never worried, confident that Dex knew his own limitations and when it was time to withdraw and recuperate.

So, when he disappeared again, late in October 1995, Jay was not unduly concerned. She received the call on a Sunday morning, while Dex was on his 'Vanishing Light' tour in the north of England, doing some warm-up gigs for the release of his new album, *Songs to the Shadow*, early in the following year. She'd had friends round the night before, who'd left quite early at two a.m. and had then worked through until five on her monthly column, which if it wasn't delivered by Monday would be late. At nine-thirty the phone rang. Jay woke up, groggy, and lay there ignoring it. Presently the answer-phone clicked in and as the volume was turned down, Jay couldn't hear who was calling. Whoever it was could wait. She put the pillow over her head, and turned on her side, determined to sleep on at least until one.

The phone rang seven more times in the next half hour. She stubbornly ignored it. It must be the same person trying to get through, perhaps even Dex, although he was never the urgent type. Finally, cursing, Jay picked up the phone on the eighth call.

'Jay!'

She recognised the cigarette-cracked tone of the band's manager and her heart sank. 'Tony, it's the middle of the fucking night! What do you want?'

'Sorry to ring so early, babe. We've got problems.'

At this moment, some celestial agent should have touched Jay's shoulder, warned her with a wave of intuition. She reached for her cigarettes on the bedside table. 'Oh, for fuck's sake, Tony! Sort them out yourself. I'm not coming up there, no matter what, so . . .'

'Jay, he's gone.'

'He's always going. What pissed him off this time?'

'He didn't even play the gig last night.'

Jay paused. That was unusual. No matter what temper he was in, nor how much he wanted to murder any members of the band, Dex delivered when it was needed. He was not an absconder in that sense. 'What happened?' She inhaled unwelcome smoke into lungs that had smoked too much the night before.

'Well, there was a row at the sound-check.'

Jay groaned.

'It wasn't the usual row. It was weird. Sammy had let some kids in – fans who'd been hanging about outside, and Dex went crazy – quietly. Not him, right?'

'Sammy's an idiot sometimes. He should've known Dex'd go spare.'

'He just muttered something and walked out. Didn't even kick down a door on the way. That was the last we saw of him. We had to cancel the show, which pleased multitudes.

Jay, this is all going too far. He needs help or something. I can't afford this prima donna stuff.'

'What do you want me to do about it? Dex isn't *here*, Tony.'

'You just talk to him when he shows up, that's all. And let me know if he calls. It's every time now, Jay, every fucking gig there's a problem with him. We're all treading on egg-shells. We've got another show scheduled for tonight and—'

'Then find a new band.' Jay slammed down the phone and laid on her back, pulling the pillow over her head once more. This wasn't her problem. She wouldn't let anyone make it hers.

She eventually went back to sleep and dreamed she woke up and Dex was there in the room with her. They had a measured conversation about what had happened, and she persuaded Dex to call Tony. Everything was resolved. Jay and Dex made love with exquisite tenderness, then Dex started getting ready to go back up north for the gig. In the dream, Jay lay warm in bed, feeling secure, in control and content, listening to her man moving around the flat.

She was woken by the phone again at two o'clock, immediately conscious that Dex wasn't there with her. It was Gina Allen calling. Gina always went on tour with her husband; a man whose compulsive philandering bordered on psychosis. She explained that the band had driven to Manchester where the next gig was booked. So far, Dex had not made a reappearance.

After discussing the stupidity of men for a couple of minutes, and the fact it was a miracle any male band ever managed to stay friends long enough to achieve anything, Gina said, 'The thing is, Jay, I think Dex . . . well . . . I think there's something badly wrong.'

At that point Jay wished Gina was a stupid woman whose remarks she could ignore, but Gina's stupidity extended only to her choice of men. 'What do you mean?'

'It's – um – just a feeling. I've seen all of Dex's moods and tantrums – even more than you have. But this time it was different. He's not that happy with the new material,

18

and he's blaming the others. I think he's really run away this time.'

'Not happy with the new material?' Jay's mind flashed back to all the long days and nights when Dex had been composing the songs, closeted away in his work-room with banks of equipment, emerging sleepily on occasion to feed and watch half an hour of MTV. Sometimes, he'd stay up for nearly three days, before falling exhausted into bed for sixteen, eighteen, twenty hours, only to wake and repeat the pattern. But he hadn't seemed disturbed or upset, or even dissatisfied. Jay had listened to some of the tapes, and had helped Dex decide which songs to use on the tour. He always wrote at least twice as much material as he needed. 'How do you know this?'

'After the gigs – he's been ranting and complaining. Telling the others they weren't pulling their weight. Slagging off the sound engineers. Everything. He said it was all just crap.'

'Was it?'

'I don't think so, but I'm not a musician, am I. The crowds liked it. When someone pointed this out, Dex just said they were all morons.'

Jay laughed. 'Nothing new there, then. The album'll sell millions next year, and he'll still complain. Don't worry. I'm sure he'll show up soon.'

Gina sighed down the phone. There was a silence that unnerved Jay far more than any words Gina could have said. The room suddenly seemed colder. 'Spit it out,' Jay said. 'Come on, Gina, what else is it you want to say?' Images flashed before her mind. Could it really be another woman – a *serious* other woman?

'I've watched him,' Gina said. 'He's been so nervous, drinking heavily even for him. I found him . . . God, this is difficult . . . I found him banging his head against a wall, Jay, like some kind of nutter. It was hideous. He was bleeding.'

'When was this?'

'Yesterday afternoon. I tried to talk to him.'

'What did he say?'

'He just pushed me away and walked off. I told Dan

19

about it, but you know what men are like. He just ignored it.'

'Did you talk to Tony?'

'Yeah, kind of. Tony said he'd speak to Dex, but I don't know if he did.'

'What has Tony decided to do? Are you guys staying up there or coming back?'

'We'll stay here overnight. Tony thinks Dex'll just cool down and turn up here.'

'But you don't think so.'

'No.'

It was only once Jay was dressed and drinking orange juice in the kitchen that she sensed Dex was not coming back, ever. She was looking out of the window, down across the park, and the afternoon went so still, as if the whole world was watching her. There was an imminence in the sky, as if it was full of unseen thunderheads. My God, she thought to herself, in wonderment rather than fear or sadness. My God.

Dex's disappearance was the talk of the music papers later that week. By that time, the police had been called in. Jay prayed for Dex to call her, make contact. One moment she felt sure he was just about to walk through the door, while at other times, the void inside her felt like a silent scream that went on and on. The rest of the band rallied round her, and it was clear Gina especially thought Jay should not be left alone.

'He'll show up,' she said, on more than one occasion.

'I don't feel him,' Jay would reply, clawing at her own chest. 'Not in here. Not anywhere.'

'You don't know that,' Gina would say, misinterpreting Jay's words.

Jay didn't believe Dex was dead, despite the unspoken suspicions that hardened the lines of Gina's face and the barely covered innuendoes in the press that Dex had killed himself.

On the Saturday, his car was found at a seaside resort, but no one had seen him there. He had really disappeared into thin air. When Jay was informed, she went utterly numb. No hideous images flickered across her inner eye, no instinctive convictions clenched her heart. She just didn't know what had happened, couldn't feel it. Even when people visited her, the flat was too still, too quiet. There was a space in it that only Dex had filled. She closed the door on his work-room and told herself she'd never open it again. Only Dex could do that. When he came home.

Fans kept a vigil at her doorstep. Their silence unnerved her. It felt like a funeral.

How could he do this to her? Had he lied about his feelings? She wanted to feel angry but could only muster an exhausted bewilderment. Had she been so stupid, so taken in? No. He had loved her, *did* love her. Something had caused this, something she didn't know about.

One night, drunk, she threw open the door to his work-room and a smell of him came out at her like an enveloping ghost. 'Are you here? Are you?' She turned on the light. Tapes and papers littered every available surface. It burned her fingers to touch them. She resisted lifting them to her nose. She might find a sheet of lyrics that would explain everything. But the papers were just notes. He'd left nothing personal behind, no hint as to his state of mind.

Gina and the band were no help. They couldn't answer her questions. Whatever Dex had been worried about, he'd kept it to himself. He'd not confided in his friends or the woman he loved. That hurt the most. The silence. The lack of trust. The betrayal.

The police were reassuring, explaining that many men in Dex's age group, with stressful busy lives, disappeared in this way. A great number of them were found, or returned of their own accord. They felt it was unlikely he'd committed suicide. Jay might have to prepare herself for months, if not years, of waiting, though.

Snide articles began to appear in the music press. One journalist suggested that as Dex had been successful for so long, he was afraid his popularity was about to wane. Perhaps this disappearing act was a publicity stunt, engineered to regenerate interest in his work. Jay didn't want to read the piece, but just couldn't resist, and boiled with silent rage as she did so. It made her think about how time had hurried by. She and Dex had been together for seven years. Surely she should have known him better than she had? How could she have been so blind?

Jay was no longer just one of the beautiful people; now she was a tragedienne. Dex's fans converged on the flat, some just watchful, others bearing gifts of condolence. Jay drew the curtains on them. Her grief and confusion were too intense and private to share. A girl in Birmingham killed herself and left a message telling the world that she had followed Dex into the next life. No you haven't, Jay thought angrily. He's not dead.

Still, she felt she'd never see him again. For whatever reason, he'd jettisoned his life, and it wasn't his physical departure that hurt, but the fact she'd never know what had been going on in his mind. She'd been careless, overlooked a crack that had become a chasm. If she'd been more vigilant, he'd still be with her. It was her fault. She saw that in the eyes of female fans who haunted the steps outside. If they'd been his woman, they'd have protected him. Jay hadn't. They had been jealous of her all along and now had an excuse to turn on her. She was a celebrity like him, made more famous by him; cold, calculating and greedy. Someone must be blamed for Dex's disappearance. Jay became the scapegoat. Nobody would believe in her grief. The papers had made sure everyone knew she would not go on tour with him, and that she refused to come when he needed her. Had Tony let that slip, or Dan, or Sammy or Martin? Perhaps even Gina, chatted up by journalists. Messages circulated on the Internet. Some implied wild conspiracies, even to suggest that Dex had been abducted by aliens. Others speculated as to whether Jay herself had engineered his disappearance. Perhaps she had murdered him for his money. It was ridiculous, Jay knew that, but every criticism, every insane idea, shocked and hurt her like a slap across the face. Had people no respect for her feelings? They didn't know her. They couldn't see into her mind, experience the physical pain of her grief.

'You must ignore it,' Gina said firmly. 'It's just the way things are. It'll all blow over in a couple of weeks. People will find something else to focus on.'

The realisation hit Jay like a physical blow. Dex's role in the music world had changed. He was no longer a creative immediate force. New stars would rise to take that place. Dex was destined to become a myth, like Jim Morrison or Kurt Cobain. A rock casualty enshrined on the murky Olympus of shattered stars. When he was remembered, it would be as an obscene, sentimental travesty. She hated that. He was a man, *her* man, and he was lost. People were just too eager to make him a god. They didn't want him to be found. The worst thing he could do now was saunter back into his life.

As one week rolled into the second, Jay became increasingly insular. She didn't want to see any of her friends, or even speak to them. Acquaintances in similar jobs to her own, from whom she hadn't heard for months, were suddenly interested in calling her, ostensibly to murmur their condolences. Jay saw through their thin words of sympathy. She tore the phone from the wall. She wouldn't answer the door. Sakrilege had re-released Dex's last single; it went straight to number one. Naturally. Jay couldn't bear to go out of the flat. It seemed everywhere she looked there were posters of Dex's face staring at her. It seemed like a mockery. So, she holed up like a wounded animal in shrouded daylight. She drank rum: white in the mornings, fiery spice in the amber afternoons, and dark, voodoo ichor through the long nights. She felt as if a thousand horses thundered through her head. She could almost see their flaming nostrils, their wild eyes, their foaming manes and tails. They carried her onward into a grey future that could not form properly, that would never become days and nights, seasons turning. She was immortal in the golden light of a perfect October. This moment would go on for ever.

Chapter Two

Rhys Lorrance was the kind of man who wanted to be seen as a villain. He had a villain's charm, and the savage generosity that threatened an equal measure of cruelty should anyone offend him. It was clear to astute people that this was an image Lorrance constantly updated and refined. Sometimes, they wondered whether behind it, he was a scared and gentle man, fond of kittens.

Lorrance was managing director of Sakrilege, and therefore believed he owned Dex. His property had gone missing; quite an expensive piece of property that had been destined to attract more riches into the coffers of the king. So, in that gilded October, it was likely that Rhys Lorrance was not a greatly happy man. He could not use his frightening generosity to entice Dex back into the Sakrilege fold, because no one knew where he was. Like Jay, Lorrance doubted Dex was dead. He knew Dex better than most, and despite what other people might think, did not see the potential for suicide in Dex's emotional outbursts. Neither did he believe Dex could hide for ever.

Ten days after Dex's disappearance, Rhys Lorrance's sleek limousine purred to a halt outside Sakrilege's office in the West End of London. It was a beautiful morning, the air crisp and even here in the city smelling faintly of wood smoke, the essential perfume of autumn. Lorrance emerged from the back seat of the vehicle, smartly dressed in pale colours. He had the look of an American soap opera actor; his teeth looked very white against his tanned face, and his suavely greying hair was touched with gold. Somewhere in the countryside north of London, his trophy wife sat painting her nails and looking forward to the arrival of her aerobics instructor. Lorrance was not self-made, but his father had been; a man born as Ernest Smith, who had changed his name to match his fortune. Lorrance had inherited the country house from his father, and still had a mother somewhere, declining with frenzied eccentricity in a costly nursing home. He'd been a wild child of the Sixties and had built his kingdom from experience gained as a drug-embalmed guitarist with a psychedelic band called Velvet Gurus. Unlike many of his contemporaries, Lorrance had crawled from his youth with his life-force and most of his sanity intact. He found he'd learned more than he realised during those hazy, smoky years of minor stardom, and utilised this knowledge wisely. He had a nose for potential, and it was rare that any act rejected by Sakrilege went on to find fame elsewhere. In the mid-eighties, Sakrilege had been gobbled up by the Charney empire, known as the Three Swords Group. As well as overseeing Sakrilege, Lorrance was also the prime mover behind *The Eye*, a Three Swords tabloid renowned for its excesses. He knew his overlord was pleased by his work. Lester Charney was a media mogul of mythic proportions. He owned most of the entertainment business in England, and continually added companies to his collection. If Lorrance thought he owned Dex, Lester Charney was in no doubt that he owned Lorrance.

Charney lived in the Caribbean now, but like a never-sleeping spider at the centre of its web, he always knew what went on in the farthest corners of his empire. Slight vibrations along the threads sent him information. Although a horde of faceless people ran Three Swords, Charney kept in touch with the higher echelons of his minions, and a few, such as Rhys Lorrance, he kept very close indeed. A thread had vibrated and informed Charney of Dex's defection. A warning hiss had been directed at Lorrance. He now responded to its directive. Quickly.

It was Lorrance who'd plucked Dex from the ranks of a struggling Northern indie band in the Eighties. But for this intervention, it was likely that, by now, Dex would still possess a surname and, if he was lucky, a mundane job, as well as a wife and children. He would be Christopher

Banner, who lived on a council estate like his parents did, and drank in the pub his father had used, where on certain nights he would perhaps watch local bands strain through their repertoire, while he remembered the days when he'd been up there on the stage himself.

Lorrance knew that Dex owed him a lot, in every sense. He appreciated that the artistic type should be allowed their little displays and that the publicity this behaviour generated did nothing to harm sales. Quite the opposite. Dex was allowed to scarper every now and again – it made news – but he had no right to abscond indefinitely. Perhaps he'd let Dex get too close. Lorrance had been patient, but since the softly spoken call from Charney's personal office the previous evening, he was now annoyed and slightly unnerved. He had come to speak with his own minions about what could be salvaged from the situation.

Zeke Michaels was a senior executive of Sakrilege; an Igor to Lorrance's Baron Frankenstein. Many thought him a brash Lorrance clone, unaware that when alone in Lorrance's presence, Michaels became meek, almost submissive. While Lorrance gave orders, Michaels did the marketing equivalent of turning great wheels and pulling levers that instead of calling down lightning to resurrect the dead, pumped life into already burgeoning projects. Sakrilege was a very healthy creature indeed, but like the monster of Baron Frankenstein occasionally and inadvertently trampled weaker species beneath its feet.

Michaels couldn't help feeling that Lorrance somehow blamed him for Dex's disappearance. It was totally irrational. Most of the time Michaels dealt with Dex's manager, Tony, so he'd done nothing himself to upset Lorrance's fractious protégé.

His secretary announced the arrival of the great man, and Michaels composed himself behind his desk. All his tension was directed into a single finger of his left hand that drummed against the desk top. Lorrance didn't come to Sakrilege very often, and Michaels' regular visits to Lorrance's country estate had ceased. This was because the parties had stopped, and

Michaels knew in his heart that Dex was somehow connected with that.

Lorrance opened the door and sauntered in, saying, 'Hi! Zeke!' as if in surprise.

Michaels' face had set into an expression of weary disbelief and resignation. He shook his head ruefully. 'All right, Rhys.' He sighed to show how distressed he was about the Dex situation.

Lorrance sat down on a huge sofa beneath the window. Outside, tall grey buildings rose towards the pristine sky and a shaft of sunlight, fighting its way between them, fell into the room upon Rhys Lorrance's head, augmenting his gilded appearance. 'Any news about our runaway, then?'

It was a rhetorical question. News was far more likely to come to Lorrance before it reached Michaels. Michaels shook his head morosely. 'No, nothing.' He paused. 'What do you make of all this?'

Lorrance raised an eloquent hand. 'Well, it will of course have its advantages. A pity the album hasn't yet been properly recorded, but I assume there will be tapes at Dex's place.'

'You talk as if you don't expect him to come back.'

Lorrance shrugged. 'It's best to be prepared. Dex takes himself too seriously. There are millions of little Dexes out there in the world, waiting to be discovered. No one is indispensable.'

Michaels felt better already. 'True. We just go ahead with the album then, as planned?'

'Yes. I propose we move very quickly to capitalise on the mood.'

Michaels frowned. 'What if he isn't dead?'

'I'm assuming he isn't.'

'But . . . ?'

'But what?'

Michaels shrugged awkwardly. 'Well, he could be seen as a bit of a loose cannon . . . Who knows what's going through his head? He could . . . say things.'

'He won't.'

The words seemed like an iron screen. Michaels knew

better than to pursue the topic. If Lorrance felt confident in Dex's silence, then so must he. At that point, he wondered whether Lorrance knew more about Dex's disappearance than it seemed. He was so calm about it. Perhaps this was some kind of marketing exercise, and at this very moment Dex was ensconced in a hotel somewhere, swilling expensive liquor at Lorrance's expense. 'I'll call the Samuels woman, then.'

Lorrance nodded thoughtfully, his lower lip protruding. 'Perhaps a visit would be more in order. Take her some flowers.'

'Do you expect opposition?'

'From her? No. But it would be as well to keep her sweet – given her vocation in life.' He hesitated, then gestured sharply at Michaels with one hand. 'None of us must panic, Zeke. We all know Dex had a problem with some of the things he's done, but I really don't think he'll divulge anything. I had a word with him some months ago.'

Michaels nodded.

'So keep your ears and eyes open. Let me know if any information comes to you.'

Again, Michaels nodded, although he didn't really expect to find out anything, other than what might be printed in the music papers.

'I want the tapes by tomorrow night.'

'I'll see to it.'

Later that day, Zeke Michaels drove round to Jay's flat. A couple of photographers were still hanging around, as well as a coven of tear-streaked female fans. Michaels flashed his teeth for the cameras, nodded to the girls. It was doubtful they knew who he was, but the photographers were well aware. He showed them his best side and related that, no, he'd had no news about Dex. After ringing the door-bell for five minutes, he thought that Jay must be out, although one of the photographers was quick to assure him she hadn't left the place for days. He banged on the door with his fist, still smiling, crying in the vicinity of the intercom, 'Come on, Jay, it's Zeke. Open up.

'Women!' he said to the photographers.

Presently, the locking mechanism clicked, and he was able to open the door and walk into the building. A couple of the photographers attempted to barge past him, but despite his sleek build, Michaels was not physically weak and managed to propel the interlopers back into the street, in much the same manner as dog-owners keep large, persistent pets out of the kitchen: a combination of leg manoeuvres and body twists.

Dex and Jay's flat was on the ground floor. She was waiting for him in the doorway, looking horrible. Jay Samuels was far too intelligent for Michaels to like her. He distrusted writers anyway; they were like magpies, always on the lookout for things to steal from people's lives. It gratified him to see her in such a state. What was she grieving; the loss of her man or the potential loss of her privileged lifestyle? He thrust the flowers at her. She stared at them, unblinking. 'What do you want, Zeke?'

'Hey, come on, let's go in,' he said soothingly. 'It's a bad time.'

Without responding, Jay went back into the flat, with Michaels following. He shut the door, dropping the rejected flowers on to a table. The place was a mess; newspapers everywhere and the stink of cigarette smoke and alcohol in an airless space. The curtains were drawn, but every electric light in the place was ablaze. Jay Samuels, in his opinion, seemed to have lost it – big-time. He wouldn't have thought it of her. 'I take it you haven't heard from Dex?' he said, clearing a space on one of the sofas and sitting down.

She stood before him belligerently, apparently wearing only a man's shirt. It was probably Dex's. The thought revolted him. She should be out there on the street with the weeping fans. 'What do you want?' she asked again.

Michaels shifted uneasily. 'Jay, I won't mess with you. As you know, Dex's disappearance has caused us a bit of a problem. The album . . .'

'Yeah,' she interrupted dully. 'His work-room's through there. Do what you want, then leave.'

Her compliance surprised him. He'd expected her to be

more protective of Dex's work. 'Well, thanks.' Gingerly, he rose from the sofa and eased past her. She continued to stare at the place where he'd been sitting. It was a relief to get away from her.

Dex's room was in darkness, heavy fabric over the single window. It had a clean, masculine smell that hung like a ghost in the air. Michaels shivered involuntarily. He found the switch to a small lamp and then turned on the main computer. The light from the screen seemed acidic. Much of Dex's work resided as files on the hard disk, although there were DAT tapes too. Michaels had never had access to Dex's store of material before. He knew there would be a pile of songs the public had never heard, and that Sakrilege had never seen. He was almost salivating as he reverently began his explorations. His mouth soon dried. His eyes widened as he looked through the data. The files were still there – hundreds of them – but they were empty, or corrupted or full of incomprehensible gibberish. Dex, it seemed, had sabotaged his own work station.

Heart beating faster now, Michaels turned his attention to the tapes. Racks of them reared above his seat, all labelled and dated. Michaels' attention flicked over the older tapes. He could see there were treasures there – songs he'd never heard of – but what he was looking for was the recent work. There was none, no tapes younger than ten months. He emerged from Dex's work-room, clutching all the tapes he'd salvaged, looking like a man who has just been told the secret of existence and it hasn't been good news.

Jay was sprawled on the sofa now, the shirt up around her hips. Michaels barely registered the fact that she was at least wearing underwear, which at first he'd thought she wasn't. There was a small, grim smile on her face. 'Found what you were looking for, Zeke?'

He glared at her for a moment. Had she done something to the tapes and the computer? 'What do you think?'

'You don't look very happy, but you do have a handful of booty.'

'I think you know that the cupboard was bare.' He shook the tapes in her direction. 'These are just crumbs.'

Jay frowned a little, an expression blurred by the effects of alcohol. 'What do you mean?'

'There are no new tapes, and the computer files are empty. Dex's recent work just isn't there.'

Jay's pale face seemed to bloom with grey. She sat upright abruptly, although her gaze became unfocused. 'You know what this means?' she whispered.

'Yeah, I'm in deep shit.'

She looked up at him with the eyes of an old woman, her fingers involuntarily kneading the fabric of the sofa. 'No. He must have planned this. Even before he left home, he must have known . . .'

'Of course he planned it!' Michaels snapped. 'What else did you think? He fell over, bumped his head and lost his memory?'

Jay put her face into her hands. 'When did he decide, when?' She expelled a groan.

'Don't blame yourself,' Michaels said stiffly. 'I'm sure it could have happened at any time. Dex was always unstable.'

'Get out,' Jay said dully. He left.

No body was ever found. There were often sightings: Dex was in New York, playing in a punk band; someone else reported meeting him on a train in France; while yet another claimed he was living as a down-and-out in the netherworld of London. Jay didn't believe any of these stories. If Dex was alive, he'd have contacted her somehow by now. It came to the point where her own grief seemed meaningless. Dex had abandoned her. Was she going to sacrifice her own life to him too? Gradually, she regained the ability to function, if only through sheer will, and opened her door to the world again. Gina was first across the threshold.

'By God, girl, look at the state of you,' she said cheerfully, and Jay could almost hear her friend's knuckles cracking at the prospect of sorting her out. For a while at least, Jay allowed Gina to take her in hand.

With Gina's help and encouragement, Jay did all the things she supposed other people in her situation did. She rang help-lines and hostels, seeking a genuine sighting. She gave interviews, hoping that Dex would read her pleas for him to get in touch, just to let her know he was alive and all right. But, if he was alive, he clearly didn't want to be found. Occasionally, she dreamed of him, the worst times being when she dreamed of waking in the middle of the night, the police hammering on her door. They'd take her to identify a body in a stark, subterranean room. Dex would be lying on a slab, beautiful, but bleached of life.

Dex's band dispersed, and most of them drifted out of Jay's life. She still maintained a close friendship with Gina, whose support carried her through the dark days of depression that occurred with less frequency as time went on. Gina's husband Dan formed a new band called 'Planet' and secured a contract for himself with Sakrilege. The record label put a lot of money into 'Planet' and they found success remarkably quickly, which would have surprised Jay, had she been more aware of what was going on around her. Sakrilege appeared to make a point of not beefing up Dan's prior connection with Dex. That was most uncharacteristic.

Jay could not work for nearly a year, but once she emerged blinking into daylight, her old friend Grant Fenton gave her a regular feature spot in *Track*, the style magazine he now edited. It took all her energy just to reach that one deadline every month, but Fenton was patient with her. They went back a long way. Eventually, the pain began to ebb from her heart, and Jay was able to take on more work, freelancing for several publications. She was not blind to the fact that her role in Dex's life had enhanced her desirability as a writer.

Sakrilege released an album, called *Silences*, of the unknown songs Zeke Michaels had found in Dex's work-room, and subsequently a retrospective double CD called *Turn Around*. Both went platinum. Jay was not surprised. Her own dark prophecies came true. Dex became an icon, his haunted face emblazoned on T-shirts, although there was no grave that could become a shrine. Now, it seemed his shadowed eyes had harboured a secret. Jay tortured herself because she'd never known it was there, never mind what it might have been. Why had he disappeared? Had he been murdered? She had to resign herself to the fact that she would probably never know.

Chapter Three

On the third anniversary of Dex's disappearance, a documentary about his life appeared on TV. Jay was hurrying around the flat, getting ready to go to a gig, where she planned to interview the band. One of her favourite boots had disappeared. As she cursed and rummaged through a pile of unironed washing in the utility room, a voice bellowed from the sitting room: 'Hey, Jay! Come and look at this.'

'Can't!' she called back.

'No, really. C'mere!'

Reluctantly, Jay obeyed the summons. Her partner of eighteen months was sprawled on the floor in front of the sofa, a remote control in his hand.

'What is it, Gus? I'm really late.'

He gestured at the screen. 'Lover boy's in the news again.'

A ripple of cold went through her body. 'What do you mean?' She knew, of course.

Dex's face stared at her from the TV; a familiar photo, with his hair falling over his inscrutable eyes. In the memory of the world, he would be forever young. For a few electrifying moments, Jay thought he'd been found. She sat down on the arm of the sofa. 'What's happened?'

Gus cast her a shrewd glance. 'Thought you'd be interested.'

His tone needled her. Dex was a topic of which she normally steered clear. Any mention of him triggered unwelcome responses in Gus, who could not conceal his jealousy about her past relationships.

There was footage of Dex's home town, which Jay had never visited, and his sister, Julie, whom Jay had never met. It seemed odd to think he'd had that other life, long before she'd met him. Dex had never liked speaking of his family; he'd shed that life. At the beginning of their relationship, Jay had wanted to meet Dex's family. She'd wanted to share all of him. But Dex had been cool and firm in his refusal. Jay imagined he'd fallen out with his parents and siblings. She didn't push the issue. After a while, it no longer seemed important.

The sister would not speak to the documentary film crew. She looked hard and tight-lipped; a terrier of a woman who had not belonged in Dex's career world.

The commentator's voice, relishing the words, drifted out into the room: '. . . and to this day, no one knows the true story behind his disappearance.'

These words conjured a tingle of relief in Jay's heart, as well as disappointment. The documentary covered all the supposed sightings of Dex around the world. There was even a blurry photo from Peru, where it was claimed he ran a bizarre religious cult.

'I thought you were late,' Gus said, after Jay had sat hunched up for ten minutes, staring at the screen.

She roused herself. 'Oh, yeah.' She would say nothing more. She didn't want a row tonight.

The documentary left her feeling unsettled. She had to sit in her car outside the flat for a few moments to compose herself. There were no photographs of Dex around her home; she'd discarded all mementoes, but for a bundle of old snaps and articles she kept in a sealed box at the top of the wardrobe. She supposed she might look through it one day, when she was very old and the final stings of Dex's disappearance had been pulled. Three years ago, she'd thought she'd never recover from his loss. The depth of her grief had shocked her; she hadn't realised how much she'd loved him. She'd taken his presence for granted, and couldn't help punishing herself for not sensing something had been deeply wrong with him. If it wasn't for the fact his work had disappeared, she'd have been able to think his escape had been spontaneous. But she couldn't think that. She'd had counselling, and that had helped, although rum and Gina had done more to aid her recuperation. Just the smell of rum now made her feel anxious.

Then Gus had come into her life. She'd met him backstage after a gig. He was a sound engineer, one of the best, who could pick and choose the bands with whom he worked. Jay's friends, relieved to see her with any man, insisted she and Gus were an ideal couple, and in many respects this was true. Gus wasn't the showbiz party type, but he'd made many interesting friends through his work, and now Jay's social life revolved around dinner parties and luxurious weekends at the country estates of ageing rock stars. Gus could be possessive about the past, although strangely not the present (she never had to be careful where her eyes were roaming across a room), but other than that, he was dependable, affectionate and reliable. She had a good life. It was steady and certain, yet spiced with exciting events and foreign travel. If some still backwater of her heart moored the thought that something vital was missing, she ignored it. Dex would always be a sore point for Jay, so she could hardly blame Gus for feeling the same. Their friends knew better than to mention Dex's name in either of their company.

Jay pressed her forehead against the steering wheel, expelling a satisfying groan. She didn't want to cry, it wasn't that, she just had to squeeze out the welling of emotion that seeped from her memories. She shouldn't have looked at the TV. She should have shrugged, made a sarcastic remark, and left. Now she was late *and* in a state. It wasn't good.

Shaking her head, she started the car and backed out of her parking space. Would there come a day when she could bear to see his face on TV or dare to play his music? She had to admit she'd never really liked it, not in the way his fans did, yet she couldn't stand hearing those familiar songs now. She had nailed a lid down over her feelings, but still had to avoid any confrontation with evidence that Dex ever existed. She feared the corpse beneath the lid could very easily be reanimated and rise up to haunt her.

At the gig, she felt as if she'd half stepped out of the world. It was difficult to take the event with any seriousness. Posturing men unfurled their egos about the backstage area like so many peacock tails. The mere sight of them irritated Jay to extremity. You are nothings, she thought, followed quickly by: Why am I here? But it was a job she had to do. 'Kill Force' were a big name, and *Track* wanted an in-depth interview with them. The only redeeming aspect of the evening was the vocalist, Jez, with whom Dex and Jay had had a close friendship, years before. Still, his band were mouthy, full of themselves and confrontational. Even before they went on stage, Jay's jaw was aching from the instinctive gritting of teeth.

Subsequently, the interview after the show was a battle rather than an exchange. It was made worse by the fact that the drummer said, 'You were Dex's chick once, right? No wonder he disappeared.'

Fortunately, she still had enough wits to freeze her expression, raise her brows and say, 'And he'll never be found, believe me.'

Afterwards, Jez tried to make peace by taking her for a meal. It took some persuading, but eventually she relented. She and Dex had once stayed with Jez and his family on one of the rare occasions Jay had accompanied Dex on tour. It had been a hedonistic couple of days.

Over tandoori, in a red-lit restaurant in Soho, Jez, American and into self-development, said, 'You're such an angry woman.'

Jay tensed, stirring lumps of Plasticine-red meat round her plate. 'Oh, come on, Jez, this world is shit. It's all so phoney. Don't tell me you take it all seriously.'

'Are we talking about music, or the world in general?'

She narrowed her eyes at him.

He grinned; he had a very wide mouth. 'OK. Musicians are mostly fuck-ups with identity crises. So what? This world is only as real as any other. You've milked it enough.'

She sighed and drank some wine. 'Maybe I've had enough of it. None of it matters, really. It's all about money, and ego, and dross.'

'Some of us say it's about creativity too, and reaching out.'

Jay laughed. 'Ah, the sweet smell of sanctimony!'

37

Jez's expression took on a pious hue. 'You should let the past go, Jay.'

'Oh, shut up! It's not about that. I watched you tonight, singing all about the kids and their anger and how they should fuck the system. Then you trot off to your stretch limo, five-star hotel and life of privilege. It's a sham, Jez. Get real!'

He nodded thoughtfully, clearly determined not to let her offend him. 'Yes, I hear you, but I was part of the audience once, you know. I understand where they're coming from.'

'But they're not going to where you've arrived, and never will. Write songs about your swimming pool in L.A. Then I might respect it all more.'

He raised an eyebrow. 'So what's bitten your tail tonight, then?'

Jay clawed her fingers through her hair, pulling her eyes into an Oriental squint. 'Bad day. Hormonal or something.'

'Bullshit. What's up? Talk about it.'

She glanced up at him. 'You're so tolerant, Jez. You make me sick. Why don't you go and trash some hotel rooms or something? You're unnerving me.'

He shrugged. 'You know I went through that phase four years ago. I have now moved on and intend to write a book about my experiences in the near future.'

Jay warmed to him: an American with a sense of humour. Despite her sniping, she knew he had integrity and wasn't one of those needy, greedy people that seemed to comprise the greater part of the music world. Jez was in a minority, however. 'So, how are Ellie and the kids?'

'Fine. Anna's learning the piano now.'

Golden children in a golden life. 'Are you happy?'

'Are you trying to make me feel guilty for saying "yes"?'

'Not at all. I envy you.' She paused. 'Dex was never happy.'

'Aha,' said Jez slowly, clearly not daring to say more for fear of invoking the fight or flight response.

'I've not spoken about this for a long time, but . . . well something reminded me of Dex today. And before you start lecturing me about letting go of the past, I have. Mostly. It's just the unanswered questions, Jez. I had no idea he was in a state.'

'You and Dex had a very . . . atypical relationship,' Jez said carefully.

'What do you mean?'

'Now, don't get pissy about this, but well, Ellie and I noticed. It was like you were a picture of a woman to him, perfect and remote. You never saw what he was like because he never let you. When he was with you, I think he was just acting.'

'That's a horrible thing to say!'

He shrugged. 'I know. But would you rather I lied to you?'

'I'd rather you told me what you based that opinion on! You didn't see us together for long.'

'We didn't have to.' He leaned forward a little. 'Tell me something, did you ever fight?'

Jay frowned. 'No, hardly ever, and if we did, it was over stupid things like forgetting to buy milk, or something.'

Jez leaned back again, toying with his wine glass. 'Ellie and I have blazing fights, but then we can both be hot-heads.'

'And that's better, is it?'

Jez shook his head. 'That's not what I meant. Dex fought continually with everyone. Why did he never fight with you? It's what he was. Remember, I went on tour with him. He was a nightmare. But I couldn't believe the way he behaved with you. He was like a different person.'

Jay put down her fork with a clatter, abandoning the pretence of eating. 'Can't you just let me think that I was good for him, then? Why does it have to be sinister?'

'I'm just saying there was more to him than you knew, or perhaps less. I don't know. He was trying to create a marshmallow life with you, perhaps because he believed it would change him, but it didn't.'

No one had been brave enough to say this to Jay before, but sitting across the table from Jez, she realised that other people must have thought it. Some of them must have resented her, too. What had she got that they hadn't? How come she could tame the beast?

Jez leaned forward again over the table. 'I don't know whether you know about this, but Dex called Anton from Surf Sharks a few days before he disappeared.'

'So? Anton was going to produce a couple of the songs on the album.'

'Dex told him not to bother. He said the album wouldn't get made and that he might be retiring. He said any payment for the songs would be blood money. Anton made some enquiries and Sakrilege just said that was Dex being Dex, and not to worry about it. Money was involved. Anton was asked to keep it to himself, and he did.'

'But he told you.'

'Only a few weeks ago, and I suspect just because he was stoned.'

'He'll probably tell others then.'

'I don't think so. To be honest, he seemed kind of superstitious about it, even nervous.'

Jay laughed. 'Oh, come on, Jez. This is beginning to sound disturbingly conspiratorial!'

'All I'm saying is that Dex did drop hints to other people about the disappearing act. I've no doubt you could unearth others. If you want the true story, Jay, use your skills to find it.'

'Oh Jesus, I've woken up in a TV series! The police tried to find the true story, and so did the record company. If there is one, Dex hid it too well. I can't waste time looking for it. As you pointed out, I need to let go, not become more obsessed.'

'Perhaps part of letting go is knowing the truth. Anyway . . .' He leaned back in his chair, 'I'm curious myself.'

'This meal wasn't just about smoothing my ruffled feathers, was it?'

'Mainly. I hadn't decided whether I'd speak to you about this or not. I was waiting to test the water.'

Jay reached out and squeezed one of Jez's hands. 'I do appreciate your concern, but, well, I can't go clawing up the past. I don't think it would be good for me.'

'You know best,' Jez said.

It was past three when Jay got home, and even though Gus had an early start in the morning, he was still awake as she crept into the bedroom. She was glad it was dark, because she had to smile when he demanded, 'What time do you call this?' The Dex episode earlier must have got to Gus more than she'd guessed.

'Three-fifteen, Gus. Put the light on and you'll be able to see the clock.'

'Where've you been? The gig finished at eleven. Four hours for an interview? You said you wouldn't be late.'

'Jez and I went for a meal afterwards to catch up on gossip. Then we went back to his hotel for coffee.'

'I bet.'

'Gus! You're not being jealous, are you?'

An indecipherable sound came from beneath the duvet. Jay sat down on the bed and pulled off her boots. This was all she needed. Sighing pointedly, she stomped into the living room. She knew she shouldn't have another drink – what was the point? She was going to bed in a few minutes – but couldn't resist pouring herself a vodka. She justified it by telling herself it was because Gus had rattled her. The TV was still on, hissing static. Was that another gesture by Gus? She reached to turn on a table lamp, then froze. Dex's face stared up at her from the front of a magazine that lay on the sofa. She recognised it. It was the big interview she'd done with him for *This*, shortly after they'd met. A friend of hers had taken the accompanying photos. The magazine had been stored in her sealed box in the wardrobe. 'Bastard!' she muttered, picking the magazine up.

In the bedroom, she turned on the main light and threw the magazine on the bed. 'You've been looking through my things! You've no right to look through my things!' Ice chinked in her glass.

Gus appeared bleary-eyed from beneath the duvet. 'What the fuck are you talking about?'

'That!' She pointed with her free hand at the magazine, which lay like a broken bird over Gus' legs.

Gus stared at it. 'What are you on about?'

Jay knew, even as she continued to rant and accuse, that Gus' perplexity was genuine. He was essentially a simple creature and not proficient at deception. He stared at the magazine with disgust, too phobic to flick it away.

Once her initial tirade had exhausted itself, Jay sat down on the bed, gulping vodka. There was a strained silence. Finally she said, 'You really didn't put it there?'

'No.'

'Then how did it get there?'

'I don't know. You must have . . . I don't know . . . had it mixed up with some papers or something. Why does it bother you so much anyway?' A prim, pompous tone had crept into his voice.

Jay shook her head. 'Oh, just because of the way you were earlier. I know what you think of Dex, and how you hate the fact we lived together here once. I thought you were trying to get at me.'

Gus laughed coldly. 'I don't want to see that slime-ball's face. I don't want to rake through his ashes in your cupboard. Nothing would induce me to remind you of him.'

'I know.' Jay reached for his foot beneath the duvet, squeezed it. 'I'm sorry. It just freaked me out.'

She got up and pulled a chair away from the dressing table so that she could reach the top shelf of the wardrobe. She had to check, even though she knew what she would find. The memory box was still sealed, the tape brittle across its uneven surface.

Three days later, Jay met Gina for a coffee in the West End. A shimmering Indian summer held the city in warm hands; leaves dropped slowly from the trees in St Giles Circus, gradually revealing the old church that lay behind them. Jay sat outside a bar, sipping espresso, waiting for her friend to arrive. The sun was strong enough to coax lunch-time drinkers from their coats and the fresh, ripe air fermented in Jay's nostrils. Despite the anxiety in her mind, she felt fairly at ease. It was impossible not to be affected by the generosity of the day.

Gina came swinging up on to the patio, her red hair freshly hennaed, dark glasses opaque above her crimson smile. She wore the tattiest jumper, jeans and leather jacket imaginable, yet still managed to look well groomed. She sat down opposite Jay in a cloud of Issey Miyake perfume, clearly in the most exuberant of spirits.

'Considering the curse that has just been pronounced upon me by the cash point, I feel remarkably alive today,' she said, grinning.

'You have a capacity to make me feel dull,' Jay said, pouring Gina a cup of coffee from the cafetière on the table. 'Kindly stop glowing.'

Gina sighed. 'I feel great. I can hardly wait to tell you, and it nearly killed me not mentioning it on the phone, but – guess what – I've sold *Visa Vixen*.'

'That's great news!' Jay said. Gina had been trying to sell her novel for years.

'I know. Pull out the stops. Order extra cream for the coffee!'

'How'd it happen? Did you manage to get an agent after all?'

Gina shook her head, looked a little sly. 'No, I used the influence of friends. Three Swords friends, as it happens.'

Jay raised an eyebrow. 'Sell your soul to the devil, my dear!'

Gina wrinkled her nose. 'Hardly. It's only a *small* publisher, but what the hell. It's a start.'

Gina had been working on her novel ever since Jay had met her. Although Jay felt it had the potential to be a cult success, she'd privately doubted its rather aggressive approach could ever ensure wide sales. Gina described it as a cross between *Hollywood Wives* and *American Psycho*. Shopping, fucking and gutting and outrageously politically incorrect. Jay wasn't squeamish but some of the chapters had still made her wince. Perhaps it would be a best-seller after all.

Gina sprinkled a little packet of sugar into her coffee. 'So, what's happening with you? I had a sense of some kind of "happening" in your voice last night.'

Jay wriggled her shoulders uncomfortably. What she had to say didn't match Gina's mood. 'Oh, it's nothing really. Paranoia, I expect.'

Gina took off her dark glasses, eyes like lasers. 'What?'

Jay's eyes swerved away. 'Did you see the documentary about Dex on TV the other night?'

Gina looked slightly embarrassed. 'Yes. Dan and I watched it. It was bollocks, of course.' She reached out a hand to touch Jay's fingers, which were unaccountably icy. 'Oh, it's upset you, hasn't it. I understand . . .'

Jay raised her hands and Gina's fingers curled away from her. 'Not exactly. Well, yes. No. Oh God, this is going to sound mad, and I want you to be clear that I'm not mad, but there've been some odd . . . coincidences since Sunday night.'

It had begun with the magazine. The outburst with Gus had been a mistake, because it had given him evidence that Jay was still screwed up about Dex. Still, she couldn't take that back now. The next day had simmered with a low-burn brew of hostile hurt. Gus didn't want to feel bad, but he did, and made a heroic effort to hide his feelings. Jay felt scalded, and the pair of them had bounced off one another like opposing magnets. Never had the flat felt so small. Never had polite conversation felt so crude.

Later that day, the phone had rung three times in succession, only for Jay to hear nothing but febrile static on the line. She'd had calls like this before – weird misdiallings, glitches in the system – but perhaps because of her mood she invested them with a certain significance. Almost ashamed of herself, she couldn't help thinking of phantom calls from the afterlife, a breath of a name whispered down the line. In fact, she heard nothing like that, but there was a sense of distance, of more than just space. Jay was no more superstitious than the average woman. She read her stars in the paper and partly believed in them when they presaged good news. She touched wood on occasion, and had a crawly-spine dislike of the dark in old houses, which she supposed derived from occasions in her childhood, when she'd been parked at the abodes of elderly relatives by her parents, so that they were free to enjoy themselves at weekends. Both sets of grandparents had owned creaking, watchful dwellings, where grandmothers had writhed in their beds of birth, and their own mothers had decayed into gibbering strangeness and died. As a child, Jay had been very conscious of the great-grandmothers who had died. She'd had bad dreams about their bedrooms, long after the occupants had left them. Another demented great-aunt had minded her on occasion, and had delighted in regaling her quivering great-niece with tales of the Unaccountable Sounds that had plagued her own childhood, specifically how she had heard a man slowly climb the stairs outside her bedroom door every night. For some reason, she associated this with a beheaded king. Nights spent in this house had been a horror for Jay. Her ears had strained for the slightest hint of a Sound. It had been difficult to sleep.

Now, a whiff of those feelings came back to her. She had never felt uncomfortable alone in the flat before, not even just after Dex had disappeared, but now she felt jumpy. When Gus went out at night, all the furniture flashed into sharper focus, and had a waiting look about it. There were no cold spots, and certainly no Sounds, but twice during the evening following the phone calls, Jay thought she caught the flicker of a shadow in the corner of her eye. She changed any 40 watt bulbs for 60 watt and kept all the lamps turned on.

'I know I'm creating all this myself,' she told Gina, her hands cold around her coffee cup, 'but I just want to talk about it. I want it to go away.'

'It's a reaction,' Gina said. 'Dex's disappearance almost destroyed you, Jay. It's going to take time for you to get over it completely, and that documentary was just a trigger.'

'But what about the magazine?'

Gina frowned, clearly trying to think of a rational explanation quickly, so that her pause would not seem significant. 'Gus was probably right. You had an old copy of it lying around, and it just got mixed up with some other papers, or something. If it was any other magazine, you wouldn't have thought twice about it.'

'But that's just it – it wasn't any other magazine.'

Gina put her head on one side. 'OK, let's get this out in the open. Are you worried that Dex is dead and has come back to haunt you?'

Jay shook her head vehemently. 'No! No! Of course not. But . . .' She raised her eyes uncertainly. 'I do wonder whether these things are not some kind of message. I don't mean from Dex or anything, but . . .' She related the conversation she'd had with Jez after the interview.

Gina listened without expression. 'So, who do you think is sending you these messages?'

'I don't know.'

'Do you think Anton snuck into your flat to plant the magazine, then plagued you with crank calls?'

'It seems unlikely. Sometimes, I think that life itself gives us messages. I'm not talking about supernatural things, but just . . . I don't know. Pointers. Signals. Hunches.'

'I don't think you should follow Jez's story up,' Gina said, lighting a cigarette. She closed her lighter with an emphatic snap. 'It won't do you any good.'

Jay sometimes felt uncomfortable with the proprietorial air Gina had with her, as if she was incapable of running her own life. At one time, she'd needed guidance, but now it just seemed patronising. 'You don't need to tell me that. I'm not a kid, Gina. All I wanted was to tell you about it.'

Gina softened. 'Oh, I'm sorry, honey. I'm not getting at you. I just worry, that's all.'

Perhaps she is right to, Jay thought. She felt unsafe, and scanned the lunch-time crowds, as if by checking and re-checking, she could preserve herself somehow. She took a long gulp of coffee. 'Anyway, enough about my weird paranoias. Tell me more about *Visa Vixen*. When's it being published?'

Gina's face lit up. 'In about eight months' time. I can't wait. We must have a *big* party for it.'

'Yeah! I hope you've got a good sexy cover photo.'

'You bet.' Gina reached out and squeezed Jay's arm. 'It's partly down to you, you know.'

Jay laughed. 'Me? How?'

'You encouraged me,' Gina said, 'when even Dan thought I was wasting my time. I really appreciate that, you know.'

'Look, I'm your friend,' Jay said. 'That's all there is to it. Let's order a bottle of wine and toast your success.'

Later, Jay went home to the silent apartment. The living room was suspended in the glow of the afternoon light, a gush of gold falling between the drapes at the long window in the living-room. Jay took off her jacket and draped it over the back of a chair. She looked around herself, rubbing her hands together, resisting the impulse to call out, *This is my home. I am safe here.* Shivering, she went through into the kitchen and filled the kettle with water. There was a strange smell in there, like burning bread. Dex was always burning toast. He'd put slices under the grill and then forget about them. Sometimes, Jay had been woken up at night by the shrill of the smoke alarm and greasy smoke pouring from the kitchen. Dex would be holed up in his work-room, the door firmly closed, his ears shuttered by headphones. She could never be angry with him though. He just wasn't capable of looking after himself very well. Perhaps, if he'd lived alone, he would have burned himself to death one day.

Jay shuddered and dismissed these thoughts from her mind. Instead, she stared out of the window. She did not feel haunted, or even frightened. It was as if something huge and formless was rolling towards her across the sky; an event, a revelation. Something would happen soon.

Gus came home later in the afternoon, before the light had faded completely. There was no sign of ill temper. He kissed Jay affectionately and then began to talk with enthusiasm about a new job that had come up. He would be leaving soon. Jay smiled and encouraged him, suppressing the sudden, disorienting dive of her heart. She'd be alone in the flat for over a week.

Gus put his arms around her. 'Sorry about the other day.'

She did her best not to stiffen. 'That's OK. It was stupid.'

'Yeah, maybe. I try not to react, Jay, but I do. If I could take a big eraser and wipe out your past, I would. It's just me.'

She laughed feebly, wishing he'd let her go. 'Don't be daft. We're fine.' She could hear the tone in her voice, which meant only that she was trying to convince herself.

The phone call came at five-thirty. Gus sighed and picked it up, mumbling something like, 'What the hell do they want now? Are they that helpless?' But the call was not for him. Jay could tell this before he spoke, because his body tensed. His voice became clipped. 'Right, yeah, she's here. Who's calling?' When he turned to hand her the phone, his face was pinched up like an oyster shell.

She took the instrument from him, announced, 'Hi, this is Jay.'

'Oh, hi there, Jay. Zeke Michaels here.'

Her stomach clenched. Somewhere, there were bells ringing or the sound of hooves. 'Zeke. What can I do for you?'

'Could you drop by the office tomorrow?'

'Why?'

He laughed nervously. 'Oh, I just want a chat that's all. Nothing heavy.'

'Zeke, we don't *chat*. What's this about?'

'I'd like you to come down and we can talk, that's all.'

Jay didn't want to mention Dex's name. If she asked, 'Is this about Dex?' Gus would throw a dark mood around himself like a winter coat. 'OK,' she said. 'Ten-thirty?'

'Yeah. Brilliant.'

She put down the phone, staring at it thoughtfully for a few moments. Was this it? Was this what all the weird feelings were leading to?

'What did he want?' Gus asked, in a voice preparing itself to shout, if necessary.

Jay shrugged. 'I don't know. Must be something to do with the tapes I gave him, or something.' She forced a smile. 'Who knows, we might be getting some money!'

'I don't want money from any of those wankers.'

'No,' Jay murmured dryly. 'Of course you don't.'

'What do you mean by that?' His voice had risen, as had his colour. For a moment, looking at him, Jay wondered how she'd ever ended up living with him. Then, she was chastising

48

herself. Their relationship was good. Dex was the only sore point, and surely that was bearable? Most women had to put up with far worse. *But why should we put up with anything? Dex, for all his faults . . .* With supreme effort, she strangled this thought before it could fully express itself.

'Let's not make a fight of this,' she said lightly, still smiling. 'I'll go and see Michaels, and then it'll be over.'

'He could have written,' Gus grumbled. 'Make him write, Jay. Don't jump when he snaps his fingers.'

'I'm not likely to do that,' Jay said. 'I'm just curious.'

'Is that what it is? Sure you're not hoping for news?'

Don't blush! she warned herself, blushing. 'Gus, there's no need for that. Please don't get yourself in a state.'

'Don't patronise me, Jay!'

She put her hands to her face and rubbed it slowly, up and down. Just the sound of it was soothing. 'Please don't be like this, Gus.' She couldn't stop rubbing. She couldn't stand the sound of his voice, the small, petulant boy that whined through the deeper tones. All the accusations were there in his voice – unfounded, unfounded – but finding their way deep into her heart.

Chapter Four

Samantha Lorrance walked brightly through the rooms of her house, on the way to her morning swim and work-out. Her high-heeled mules tapped across the panelled floors, becoming hushed as they padded across the thick Turkish rugs. Every morning, she felt driven to patrol her territory, her eyes alert for smudges on the gleaming woodwork and faint traces of disarray among the sofa cushions. It was not an obsession with tidiness, but a need to allay certain insecurities, which she could neither name nor fathom. She didn't really know what she was looking for.

Samantha was thirty-five, but seemed to have been perfectly preserved at the age of twenty-six. Her blonde hair tumbled over her shoulders, framing a daintily featured face that some had said would run to fat and jowls, but which hadn't. She looked after herself. Eight years before, Rhys Lorrance had snatched Samantha from the tail-end of a down-market modelling career. Her work had mainly involved displaying her breasts and buttocks for the camera, so that men on building sites could ogle her charms as they munched their breakfasts. Lorrance had met her at a newspaper party; she'd been a regular model for a Three Swords tabloid, in which Lorrance had invested some of his wealth. She knew he liked her simple nature – she prided herself on it. She might not be brainy, but she knew she was kind, level-headed and capable in a practical sense. She'd also known her modelling career wouldn't last for ever, and had been pleased and relieved when Lorrance had asked her to marry him. She was astute enough to realise he didn't really love her. Theirs was a marriage of convenience, but it worked fine. She played hostess and glamour girl when he needed it; he gave her all the material things she wanted. She'd tried to be a surrogate mother to her husband's daughter, Lacey, whose own mother had died when she was very young, but the girl had always been a distant, aloof creature. Samantha had been disappointed by this relationship; they could have been friends. But when Lacey was nineteen, she'd run away. She'd always had peculiar friends, who'd liked to protest about things and sit in trees. Strange how so many of them had come from privileged backgrounds like Lacey's. The girl had visited her the day before she disappeared, but Samantha hadn't liked what she'd had to say. She'd wanted no part in the hostilities that clearly existed between Lacey and her father. Samantha didn't worry about Lacey now. Like all uncomfortable thoughts and ideas, the girl had been brushed under a carpet in Samantha's mind.

In the pool area, a heated conservatory, carpeted in soft green, she took off her thick towelling robe amid the lush palms and threw it on to a recliner. Beneath the robe, her trim body was sheathed in a silvery swimming costume. Before sliding into the water, she tied up her hair in a band. The pool was comfortably warm, like a mother's arms. For a few moments, she floated on her back, probing the thoughts that were troubling her.

Rhys hadn't been himself for the past few days. He was never nasty with her, but sometimes, he just went quiet, as if something was on his mind. He'd never tell her what, though. She knew he must sometimes be under a lot of pressure, and that the operation of big business took its toll, but she also realised his work provided the beautiful house she lived in, the expensive clothes and cosmetics, and because of this she had to put up with his silent moods. It didn't happen often enough to cause her great concern, and usually she just breezed through these cloudy phases, confident of the clear skies ahead.

Samantha sighed, and swam a few leisurely lengths, her sleek, toned limbs cleaving the water. Steve, her personal trainer, would arrive in about half an hour. A strenuous work-out would take her mind off her anxieties, the rush of blood and adrenaline through her body would banish any hint of the vague depression that had hung about her for the last few days. On several occasions, she had walked past her husband's study to hear him talking on the phone in a heated yet muted manner. Something serious must be happening. He'd sounded angry, even distraught. In her company, he'd been distant and distracted. At dinner two nights ago, she'd carefully asked him if everything was all right. He'd just bared his teeth at her in an unconvincing grin and assured her, 'Of course, honey. Just busy.' That must be it. Yet tension hung in the air like washing steaming in a small hot room. It made the house seem smaller. In bed, Rhys had muttered softly in his sleep. Samantha had lain awake beside him, praying that he wasn't in trouble financially. Her lips had worked soundlessly in the dark. And last night: it had been horrible. She had gone to bed earlier than Rhys, and as she'd begun to drift off to sleep, the phone had started to ring downstairs. She lay there, motionless, listening to it, holding her breath. It was so late. Late phone calls always meant trouble, didn't they? 'Answer it, Rhys,' she whispered. 'Please answer it.' It rang and rang, the sound increasing in volume, as if the phone was coming up the stairs. Samantha sat up in bed, called, 'Rhys!' Then the ringing stopped, and she laid back down, her heart beating fast. She waited for him to come upstairs and tell her whatever news had come, but the house was silent. She couldn't sleep. Should she get up? It was so cold. He'd come to her soon.

Later, she'd been awoken abruptly by the clamour of a high wind. It attacked the house like a predatory animal, in short bursts of furious power. Rhys had not come to bed. Beside her the flat duvet was endless and icy. Her mouth was dry, filled with a sour taste. The wind dropped for a few moments, then hurled itself at the house again with renewed force. She heard the front door rattle downstairs. It was as if something was trying to get in. She groped for the switch to her bedside lamp, reassured when a warm honey-coloured light chased the shadows from the room. She was behaving like a child. It was just bad weather. Sitting there, she could not move.

Minutes later, she jumped when the door opened and her husband came into the room. 'Oh, Rhys, it's you!'

He smiled. 'Who else?'

THIN AIR

'The phone went earlier,' she said. 'Who was it?'

He took off his jumper. 'Only business. Nothing to worry about.'

He seemed more like himself now, relaxed.

'I hope that wind doesn't take the slates off the roof,' she said, settling down again. She had nothing to worry about. He'd said so.

'It's not as bad as it sounds,' he soothed.

'I was a bit frightened.'

He laughed. 'Poor baby.'

In bed, he held her close, and she realised the wind had dropped. She could be so silly sometimes, she thought.

Steve bounced into the pool area; a short man, who made up for his lack of stature by his fanatical fitness. Samantha climbed out of the pool. Now that Steve had arrived, she didn't feel like working out. She felt tired. It was most unlike her.

'Morning, Sam,' Steve said, flexing his muscles.

She smiled at him. 'Hi.' She shrugged herself back into her robe. They would share a jug of mineral water before getting down to work. 'Can we keep it fairly low impact, today?' she asked. 'I'm not feeling too good.'

'You work at your own pace,' Steve answered, graciously.

She knew she'd find it hard to keep up with him. Her nerves were still jangling from last night. She tried to concentrate on Steve's conversation about his triumphs down at the gym, but her mind kept drifting back to the wind and the darkness. If Steve sensed she was preoccupied, he didn't reveal it. They went into Samantha's dance studio, and soon the music was pounding, their bodies flexing, stretching, reaching. Samantha felt as if someone she didn't know was standing at the edge of the room behind her, watching her perform. It wasn't a person, exactly, but something else, she couldn't say what. It was as if some terrible event was looming, something she had known would happen, but had forgotten about. The last time she'd felt like this was just before Rhys's daughter, Lacey, had run off. She shuddered, hoping her feelings would pass. She didn't like anything interfering with her routines.

After the work-out, when Steve had left, she took a shower

and dressed herself in her favourite soft leather suit with the fringes, beads and diamond studs. She only wore the palest shades of khaki and cream. In her dressing-room, she re-fluffed her hair, and touched up the curling fingernails, which were a testament to the results of never having to do her own washing-up. She felt a bit better now. The exercise had helped.

In the kitchen, her housekeeper, Mrs Moran, massaged cleaning fluid into the work surfaces. 'Morning, Betty,' trilled Samantha. 'Kettle on?' Her voice was high-pitched, still coloured by an East End twang.

The older woman smiled and flicked a switch. 'Mugs are laid out,' she said. This was a morning ritual between them.

Samantha sat down at the kitchen table. Sighing, she reached for the daily papers – they took only the ones that Rhys owned. She looked at the astrology columns in each one. If only astrologers could talk a bit of sense. Half the time she hadn't a clue what they were on about. 'What's this supposed to mean?' she said to Mrs Moran, who was now busy fussing with the teapot. 'The easiest choices are sometimes the most difficult to make.' She frowned.

'Rubbish,' announced Mrs Moran, then added, 'perhaps it means getting some new curtains or something.'

'Yeah.' Samantha tapped her talons on the table-top. 'Do you ever get funny days, Betty?'

'Funny days?' Mrs Moran frowned. 'What d'you mean, love?'

'Well, you know, when you feel a bit out of sorts for no reason.'

'Oh, we all get those days, love.'

Samantha smiled, reassured, and licked her fingers, before flicking through one of the papers. 'Oh, that's all right, then. Must have got out of the wrong side of the bed.' She giggled, unaware of the rather searching glance Mrs Moran directed at her behind her back.

'Rhys's up in London today,' Samantha said. 'Won't be back for dinner.' Restlessly, she got to her feet and went to the kitchen window. The garden looked so different now; the lawn was a brilliant patchwork of fallen leaves. It looked beautiful. Pity that the gardener would soon sweep them all up. Samantha sighed. She wished Rhys liked animals. Today was just the right kind to go romping through the leaves with a dog.

None of the local women were very friendly – thought too much of themselves – so Samantha often felt lonely, although she'd never admit this to herself. Betty Moran was her only local friend. In the evenings, when Rhys wasn't home, she had the telly. She still had friends who had been in modelling with her – Cherry and Lyndee in particular – but they lived in London. Perhaps she could call Cherry and Lyndee today, and if they weren't busy, get them both up for the weekend. They'd have cosy evenings curled up on the sofas in front of the fire in the big lounge. They'd drink gin and tonics and reminisce, listening to old CDs. Both of her friends were divorced and still spent a lot of nights on the town. Sometimes, Samantha would go and stay with them in the city, have a few nights clubbing. Rhys didn't mind. She'd never be unfaithful to him, anyway. Of his own fidelity, she could never be sure, but didn't think about that. There seemed little point. She knew he'd never leave her. Yes, she'd call the girls. Already, she was planning the weekend menu.

Just as Samantha turned away from the window, she saw movement in the corner of her eye. Someone was walking towards the front door, and by the time she directed full attention upon them, had already disappeared from her view – the kitchen window was on the side of the house.

'Oh, we've got a visitor,' she said to Betty. In the deepest corner of her heart, Samantha still harboured the hope that one day the local women might relent, accept her, and invite her to a coffee morning or something. She tip-tapped out to the hall, waiting for the door-chimes, an elaborate orchestra of bells, to ring. But no one pulled the wrought-iron handle outside. Disconcerted, Samantha stood in the hallway, staring at the door. Should she open it before the visitor rang? It might seem too eager. Eventually, curiosity overcame her. Someone had walked up to the house, but apparently they hadn't intended to visit. What was going on? Slightly annoyed, Samantha opened the door. She couldn't see anybody. Perhaps some cheeky local had been taking a short cut across her land, but it seemed almost *too* cheeky to march in full sight along the front of the house. Anyway, their security man, Terry, wouldn't have let that happen. His alertness to intruders bordered on a sixth sense.

Samantha took a few steps beyond the white-columned fascia. The wind was unfriendly, gathering up the leaves in spiteful fingers. It seemed as if the air was alive with flying colours. Shivering, Samantha went back into the house and closed the door.

Walking into the kitchen, she said, 'No one at the door. I hope it wasn't anybody up to no good.'

'Perhaps it was just the leaves,' said Mrs Moran.

'A leaf person!' shrieked Samantha, laughing wildly. She didn't know why; her remark hadn't been that funny.

The previous afternoon, Rhys Lorrance had called Zeke Michaels to deliver a morsel of news. It did not come blanketed in a sauce, but bare upon its plate. 'Dex has been seen, Zeke.'

This news had been greeted by a short silence, followed by a nervous laugh, and the remark, 'Again? He's always being *seen*, Rhys.'

Lorrance had sighed impatiently. 'I'm talking about a genuine sighting. Would I trouble myself with anything less?'

'Well, no, of course not.' Michaels had cleared his throat. 'Where's he been seen, and who by?'

'That doesn't matter to you yet. All you need to know is that the source is reliable.'

'Right, right . . .' Michaels risked a question. 'But was the sighting in this country?'

'Yes. I would like you to contact the Samuels woman. You must speak to her in person tomorrow. Get her to the office as soon as you can after ten.'

Lorrance had refused to say anything more on the subject, saying only that he would explain in more detail when they met, face to face, in the morning.

Now, at half-past nine, Rhys Lorrance sat very still before Zeke Michaels' desk. Michaels was clearly disturbed. Lorrance had little patience with his underling's discomfort. Situations only became big problems if you believed them to be so. 'What time is the woman arriving?' Lorrance asked.

Michaels looked at his watch. 'In about an hour, like you wanted. How do you want me to handle it?'

Lorrance sniffed thoughtfully. 'Well, I consider it likely Dex will have contacted her, but we can't be sure. I suggest you try to shock her into saying something. Get a reaction. If he hasn't been in touch with her yet, he might well do so very soon.'

Michaels grimaced. 'Why should he? He just walked out of her life. She must have been part of his problem.'

Lorrance laughed; a quiet, disturbing sound. 'Perhaps. But I've a hunch he'll want her services.'

'I think she's just going to laugh in my face,' Michaels said. 'This won't be the first time someone's told her they've seen him, *definitely* seen him.'

Was there a note of belligerence in Michaels' voice? Lorrance fixed him with a meaningful stare. Presently, Michaels' eyes dropped and he picked up a pen from his desk, fiddled with it.

'Oh, come now, Zeke,' Lorrance said. 'I'm sure you can concoct something to wind her up. Break her defences. That's not beyond you, is it?'

Michaels sighed petulantly. 'Even if she has seen him, I can't see her telling me about it. Why should she? We were never exactly bosom buddies.'

'Then assume she already *has* seen him. An outright accusation should provide an unguarded response.'

'She's not that stupid.'

Lorrance sighed patiently. 'Well, let us just say, we are casting bread upon the waters of life. I am curious to discern what may return to us.'

Michaels stared at him with round eyes for a moment or two. 'I don't get it.'

'No.' Lorrance rose to his feet and sauntered towards a door opposite the entrance to the office. 'I shall wait here

57

in the bathroom, Zeke. I should be able to hear everything clearly, don't you think?'

Michaels shook his head. 'This is ridiculous. Hiding in bathrooms? You'd better be quiet. It'll be embarrassing if she susses you. Remember Jay Samuels is a nosy little bitch.'

Lorrance ignored this advice. 'Just speak to her. I'm not asking you to win her trust. Just hook her.'

The summer seemed to have given way to winter when Jay stepped out of her front door. A scimitar of north wind cut down the street, stripping the trees of their autumnal flounces. The air was full of twisting leaves. *Things* arrive on the wind, Jay thought, as she got into her car. When the wind changes, they come. She could not remember where she'd heard this particular bit of folklore, but again it reminded her of her childhood. Perhaps all future events had their roots in the past.

She wasn't sure how she felt about the impending meeting with Zeke Michaels. There was no doubt the summons had kindled excitement inside her – curiosity even – but she was also uneasy about it. It could be no coincidence it had arrived so soon after the peculiar phone calls and the incident with the magazine. Since she'd talked with Gina, there hadn't been any further strange phenomena. Perhaps it had all been self-induced and her confession had somehow cleansed her of it.

The last time she had been to the Sakrilege building, Dex had been at her side, a young prince of the music business, commanding the simpering respect of courtiers, who did all but bob curtseys as she and Dex had made their way to the top floor. Few people here would recognise her now. She steeled herself on the pavement outside, then breezed into reception. The decor had changed. It was all chrome and leafage now. Jay approached the first of the company gate-keepers behind the desk. 'Hi, I have an appointment with Zeke Michaels.'

A surly teenager, a perfect example of the starved, hollow-eyed look cultivated by the kind of magazine Jay worked for, raised her eyes from a computer screen. She wore a name tag that said 'Tara' and looked bored beyond imagination. Jay wondered how often the girl practised the look at home. 'Name?' said the girl rudely, tapping keys.

'Jay Samuels.'

'Take a seat.' The girl flapped her hand towards a group of sofas next to the glass wall that looked out on to the street.

'Thank you so much,' said Jay, flashing her sweetest smile. She sat down amid a jungle of unnaturally green specimen plants.

Of course, he'd keep her waiting. She wouldn't let it bother her. The lovely Tara wouldn't offer coffee either. Her eye was drawn to the large framed photograph on the wall near the reception desk. She'd never liked that print. It showed a group of people standing on the lawn of a large house, which was out of focus behind them. Michaels was there, dwarfed by the imposing bulk of the company fat cat, Rhys Lorrance. Dex was with them, along with a couple of other Sakrilege celebrities and some PR people Jay vaguely knew. They all looked so self-satisfied, apart from Dex, who seemed a bit sheepish. The photo had been taken before Jay had known Dex, and had hung in this office for as long as she could remember. She couldn't help sneering at the image, lifting her lip in contempt. It reminded her of all she hated about the music business.

After ten minutes or so, a bright young woman, dressed in a tailored beige trouser suit, her yellow hair cut in a swinging bob, came bouncing through the double doors that led to the inner chambers. 'Hi there. Jay Samuels?'

Jay smiled and stood up. 'Yeah.'

'I'm Sophie, Zeke's assistant. Would you like to come up now?'

'OK.'

As they walked past the receptionist, Jay couldn't resist pausing to say, 'You could be a model, you know. Here's my card. Call me some time.'

The girl glanced at the offered card, looking mortified. Jay was confident she'd never get through. She never gave out her direct line, and her own assistant fielded all calls. However, it felt good to see the girl realise she might have been rude to the wrong person.

As Jay entered Michaels' office, he leapt up from his chair as if he'd been bitten by something and almost ran across to welcome her. His actions unnerved her, because they were so unlikely. 'How are you keeping?' he asked. 'How's Gus? Work going OK?'

Nodding and repeating the word, 'Fine,' Jay eased past him and went to sit beneath the window. She crossed her legs and let her hands dangle loosely over her knees. 'So – why am I here?'

'Coffee?' grinned Michaels.

She raised a dismissive hand. 'No. Come on, Zeke. Tell me what you want.' Just being in these offices made her feel anxious and short of breath.

Michaels sighed. 'I might as well get to the point. Dex has been seen in London.'

A reflex of laughter expelled itself from Jay's throat. Then, she put her fingers to her mouth. She could not speak. Strangely enough perhaps, she'd not expected him to say anything like that. She felt as if a hard cold fountain of silver waters burst upward inside her, from her stomach to her brain. It was a spurt of dread, hope and joy.

Michaels stared at her, his expression far from sympathetic. 'Have you met him recently, Jay?'

For a moment, she could only stare back at him, too dazed to respond. Then she became aware that in some way she was on trial. She was innocent, but merely being asked the question made her feel guilty. She shook her head, croaked, 'No.'

'Well, that surprises me, because my informant tells me that Dex was sighted in your company.'

'Excuse me?' Jay twisted her hands together in her lap. Astonishment kicked her mind into gear. 'When, exactly, and where?'

'Is it true?'

'No. You know damn well it isn't!'

'If I did, I wouldn't be asking the question, would I? Jay, come clean. Admit it.'

'There's nothing to admit. Dex is gone, Zeke. He isn't coming back.' She was no longer sure of the truth of that.

'Whoever told you that I've seen him is lying, or mistaken. Who the hell was it?'

Michaels blinked slowly and turned his attention to the intercom on his desk. With precise movements, he pressed the buzzer and requested coffee from his assistant. Despite her careful cool exterior, inside Jay felt sick and afraid, yet elated. It was no condition in which to be sitting here with Michaels. She wished he'd told her this on the phone, so that she'd have been ready for him. It was clear to her why he hadn't done that. This inner terror was not good; she must assert herself. 'Tell me what you know,' she said.

Michaels shrugged. 'Very little. All I can tell you is that Dex has been seen with you. Or perhaps it was another woman. If he hasn't already made contact with you, we're sure he will.'

'But he's been seen before,' Jay said. 'This is probably just another hoax, or like I said, a mistake.'

'Perhaps so, but you have to remember he's bound up to his ass in contracts with us. He thought he could just walk away from us, taking all his work with him – work that in part was already paid for. It was a lot of money. This is a law suit situation, Jay. If you're holding out on us, it could mean trouble.' He delivered a smug, meaningful look.

'I see,' she said, in a measured voice. Anger contained her more flailing emotions. Anger always made her calm. 'If it's a law suit situation, you'd better call my solicitor.' She got up from her seat, fully prepared to walk out.

'Sit down,' Michaels said wearily. 'If you say you haven't seen him, then you haven't. I'll take your word for it.'

'Take my word for it?' She sat down anyway. 'I can't believe the absolute cruelty of what you've just said. You order me to come in here and then lay this on me, without any warning. You know what Dex's disappearance did to me. Much to my regret, you saw it. If he's back, it has massive implications for me. I've got my life together now. I don't want it screwed up again. I don't give a fuck about your contracts and money, or whatever!'

'Don't get upset,' Michaels said, as if between gritted teeth.

'I had to ask, Jay. You surely understand that. If you had seen him, would you have called me? I don't think so.'

'OK, OK.' She took a deep breath. 'Let's get this straight. Let's talk. Who's seen Dex, and where?'

'I don't know.'

Jay rolled her eyes. 'Then why am I here? Your evidence is flimsy to say the least.'

'The source is very reliable. I don't doubt them, but I can't tell you who it is.'

'If you want us to work together, you'll have to.'

Michaels seemed surprised by her last remark. 'Well, er . . .'

'At least get more information for me, such as time and place of sighting. You *do* want me to find him for you, don't you?' From his expression, she realised that had not been his intention at all.

'If you hear anything, I'd be grateful if you'd tell me, that's all,' he said lamely. His assistant Sophie came into the room, and handed them both a mug of aromatic coffee. Jay was torn about whether to leave at this point, or drink the coffee, which smelled appetising, and grill Michaels for more information. Sophie smiled at her nicely, which partly swayed her decision. Once they were alone again, Jay took a sip of the coffee. 'You know,' she said, 'for a moment there, I thought you were calling on my professional talents: Jay Samuels, sleuthing journalist. It's not that, is it? As far as you were concerned, I was just Dex's appendage. I can see that sexist attitude hasn't changed.'

'Oh, come on, Jay!' Michaels at least seemed embarrassed.

'But it's true. You've just given me the shock of my life, do you know that? I've read all the reports of sightings in the newspapers, but none of them seemed real. Unfortunately, the fact that Sakrilege is taking this one seriously lends the idea credibility. I'm a professional, Zeke, yet you won't treat me like one.'

He shrugged awkwardly. 'We just thought Dex would contact you.'

'Why? He walked out on me, didn't he?' She took another sip of coffee. 'Oh, I don't know, Zeke. This all seems too unlikely. It's just going to be a wind-up. I'm not going to let myself get wound up by a wind-up.' She laughed, perhaps at too high a note.

'If he has come back, maybe you should stay away from him,' Michaels said.

Jay could only grin at his pompous tone. 'If you know what's good for you,' she added in a theatrical monotone. 'Tell you what, you just talk to your "source" and call me. If in the unlikely event Dex makes contact with me, I'll tell him you want to speak to him. If you want more than that, you'll have to trade – information is currency.'

Michaels nodded, his face closed in on itself. 'I'll see,' he said. He focused his eyes beyond her, as if someone was standing there. Swiftly, she looked round, but saw only a door standing ajar. Was someone listening to their conversation? For an absurd moment, she wondered whether it was Dex.

'So that's it.' Jay put down her coffee, half finished, and stood up. 'Thanks for letting me know.' He doesn't want my thanks, she thought. There's nothing to thank him for. This interview was never for my benefit.

As she left the office, she left the door open behind her. 'Keep in touch,' Michaels called.

She raised a hand, but did not turn round. 'You're such a sweet man, Zeke, so considerate.'

Outside, a moaning wind still hurried high above the city. Jay pulled her jacket collar together as icy splinters of air pricked her throat. In her car, her first instinct was to call Gina, but even as she was pressing her friend's number into the mobile phone, she changed her mind. No, not yet.

She should go home; half-finished features on her computer were waiting for her. Spectres of deadlines pressed down upon her. But the winds rushing across the city whispered to her with impish persistence. She needed to be out, looking for something. The meeting with Michaels had unnerved her more than she cared to admit. She needed to reassert herself, do something on her own, using her journalistic skills. Where to begin? she wondered, starting the car. The trail was now three years old. Don't be stupid, she scolded herself. Don't

even think about this. Go home! But another part of her mind
ignored this advice. It was thinking about how if this story had
been about anybody but Dex, she'd have considered it all more
clearly. She'd have begun at the beginning, with his past, his
home life. Dex still had family, she knew that, although he'd
rarely talked about them with her. He'd met her own parents
a few times before they'd died within a year of each other.
Jay had been a late child in their life. The legacy they'd left
her had bought the flat that she and Dex had shared. Now, it
seemed odd that she hadn't met his family, or at least learned
more about them. Why had Dex kept her away from them?
It wasn't that he'd been embarrassed about his roots. Was
this part of what Jez had alluded to in the restaurant that
night? She knew Dex's family name was Banner, and where
his home town was: Torton; in the north east of England.
It was a coastal town, but not a resort. She could afford a
day or so, couldn't she? Didn't she owe it to herself to delve
into this story? She didn't feel weak or upset, but curious and
intrigued. All she needed was an overnight bag.

Chapter Five

Just as Dex had once intuited, Jay was as guilty as many city-dwellers of thinking that once beyond the nebulous bounds of London, travellers entered a kind of cultural hinterland, a place where people watched sullenly from behind their fences and, in private, might well eat their dead. She drove along the M1, weaving dangerously from lane to lane in an attempt to outwit the ponderous flow of the traffic. The sky above the Tarmac was too big and oppressive; patches of pale but intense blue, a backdrop to a burst of silver-edged clouds. The horizon seemed to be outlined in India ink.

Jay felt as if she was on her way to an assignation fraught with danger and exhilaration; the danger perhaps being the risk of discovery. She'd left a cryptic message on Gus' answer-phone, trying to make it sound as if she was off on some hum-drum job, the details of which were too tedious to relate. She'd be away overnight, but would be back in the morning.

She was driving to the mysterious north; the direction of darkness and cold. She imagined grey-clad people hugging secrets beneath their heavy clothing, like rags against a wound. She was a bright southern spirit, coming to cast her light over their shadows, eager to penetrate and understand. Her mission possessed a mythic quality.

By two o'clock, she'd left the motorways behind, and was driving up an A road, where fields stared away on either side to a flat horizon. She wanted to get a feel of the landscape, move away from the hectic scream of hurry and panic that she felt must be expressing itself silently within every car on the motorway. Light drenched the land, golden as winter soup, ambered with a memory of summer.

She lost herself in back-streets of northern towns, looking for stout women with folded arms on doorsteps, whey-faced children playing in the roads. There was none of that; only the signs that interior decorators had surged across the landscape of back-to-back houses, armed with neo-Victorian wallpaper prints, and paint-strippers, and rag-rolled paint. She was seeking the source: the source of Dex. But she was only at the outer gate of the underworld. He had not risen up from restructured miners' cottages, but the bleak and terrible circle of a mid-century council estate; a place where decorators could arm themselves only with bulldozers and excavators, and tons of salt to sow the land clean.

The afternoon was dying by the time she drove past the sign saying 'Welcome to Torton'; it had a tired, unconvincing appearance, seeing as it was situated near the entrance to a modern industrial estate, where soulless cyclopean buildings bulked without feature against the sky.

The High Street consisted of fish and chip shops, building societies and a depressing array of boarded-up shops, although Jay caught sight of the glare of lights from a modest shopping mall up a side street. She pulled into the car park of a high-flanked old pub called The Ship that advertised bed and breakfast on a shabby, handwritten notice in its front window.

She entered the building through a complicated arrangement of narrow doors and found herself in a dingy bar that smelled of stale beer and cigarette smoke. The interior had a mildly maritime theme, with netting, old life-belts, glass balls and lobster pots gathering dust up in every corner of the ceiling. Jay smiled to herself, wondering whether anyone ever stayed here for their holidays. It seemed unlikely. She imagined the odd couple might book a room for a week. They'd be called something like Ruth and Ernie, and would have a thin, pallid child with a chest complaint. Mainly, however, The Ship had to be a haunt of diminished travelling salesmen, working away from home.

The landlady emerged from a door beside the bar. She was middle-aged, slightly overweight and slightly overdressed but seemed friendly enough. As Jay signed the rather greasy page of a guest register, the landlady did not hide her curiosity as to why a woman of Jay's type wished to stay there. 'I'm working,' Jay answered cryptically, leaving her hostess to draw her own conclusions. Jay was shown to a room decked out in sagging Seventies furniture, with newspaper taped over a hole in the glass above the door. 'The kitchen'll be ready in about half an hour,' the landlady said, adding, 'for meals.' She swept out.

Jay unpacked her bag, imagining what drama might have occurred that broke the glass. Had someone tried to get in, their face pressed against the window, their hands clawing at the smooth surface, until it broke, and shards fell down upon the mean carpet? Had a woman screamed in the bed, or had a man sat upright, swearing softly beneath his breath? Perhaps there had been a couple between the sheets, caught *in flagrante*. Jay smiled to herself as she placed her toothbrush and toothpaste on the edge of the narrow white sink. What tales hotel rooms could tell if they could only speak.

Travelling had tired her, but Jay went down into the bar to order steak and kidney pie and chips, and get a feel of the place. The landlady hovered by as she served the meal, clearly wanting to chat. It seemed an opportune moment to begin enquiries.

'Do you remember the – er – pop star, Dex, who came from here?' Jay asked. 'He used to be called Christopher Banner.'

The landlady smiled eagerly. 'Yes, of course I do. Chris Banner was about the only famous person that came from here. He and his friends used to drink in here sometimes.'

Glancing at the early evening clientele – elderly men and faded women – Jay thought this unlikely. 'I don't suppose you know if his family are still around?'

The landlady frowned a little. 'Can't say. I think they lived over at Shorefields, the first estate out of town on the north road.'

'You've never met any of them, then?'

The landlady picked up a clean ashtray and polished it with her apron. 'Well, yes I have, as it happens,' she said. 'I knew the mother, Cora Banner, when I was a girl – she was Lane then, of course. We went to the same school, although she was a year or so above me. Didn't know her well. She used to sing at the Varsity Bar in the Sixties. Bit of a looker, but I reckon singing got chucked out the window after she married and the kids started coming.'

'Sounds like Dex inherited his talent from his mother, then,' Jay said. Cora must have encouraged him to lead the life she never led.

'Dunno about that,' said the landlady. 'Personally, I always thought she had to strain to hold a note. She had looks, not talent.'

'What about her kids. Did you know them? Do you know their names?'

The landlady laughed. 'Oh, love, it was a long time ago. The last thing I remember of Cora was when she got married. There was a picture in the papers. After that, I heard nothing of the family. Until her boy made a name for himself, of course. Why are you interested?'

'I'm a writer.'

'Oh, I see, you're writing about that Dex. Well, he's certainly done well for himself, but we don't see him around here.'

'Uh-huh. That's probably because he's disappeared.'

The landlady looked surprised. 'Has he? Well, I never!' She shrugged. 'These pop stars. You just never know what they'll get up to.' Her lips pursed meaningfully.

What was big news to some was irrelevant to others. Strangely, the landlady's ignorance pleased Jay. It made her feel relieved. An odd reaction, she thought.

A middle-aged couple came in and went up to the bar, prompting the landlady to sail over to serve them. Jay sipped her gin and tonic. Shorefields. First estate out of town.

After her meal, and some directions from the landlady, Jay sought out the Varsity Bar. It wasn't called that any more. Now, it was 'Stampers', and had clearly gone through a wine bar stage in the Eighties. Some of the decor still existed in the dark green walls and art deco wall lamps, although some Nineties' rustic fashion had insinuated itself via the corn dollies and dried grasses that adorned the walls in between framed photographs of Fifties' jazz musicians. Jay

realised there was no point in questioning the two teenage girls
behind the bar about Cora Banner. They would certainly not
remember her. She doubted the establishment was even still
owned by the same people who'd hired the young Cora to
sing for their customers. Jay got chatting to the girls, which
was difficult, because they were more interested in gossiping
between themselves. They knew who Dex was, but only one of
them was aware he'd come from Torton. New stars sparkled
over the young now. If Jay wanted to find former fans, who
might know where he'd lived, she'd need to talk to people
who were in their twenties.

Jay sat at the bar to finish her drink, staring into the mirror
behind the bar, watching people come through the door. Dex
was more likely to have frequented a place like this rather
than The Ship. She noticed there was still a small stage in
the shadows at the back of the room. He might even have
played here in the early days. Jay tried to imagine him as
he must have been then, mouthy, gangling, the hub of a
fawning group of friends. She wished they could have come
here together. He could have told her stories about his past,
shown her the physical markers of it. If only she'd recognised
the gap between them and questioned his reticence about his
history. Their relationship had seemed whole, but that had
been an illusion. Seven years of make-believe while the cracks
got longer and wider, until no amount of underpinning could
have saved what was left. Don't get maudlin, Jay told herself,
lighting another cigarette. This is just work.

In the morning, Jay was woken by the landlady knocking on
her door to tell her breakfast was ready. She dressed and went
down to the bar, where a few tables had been laid with checked
table-cloths and cutlery. Each table was adorned with a small
glass vase containing a couple of scrawny pinks. They were
at least real flowers. Jay was not the only guest. As she'd
surmised, the others were all men, who looked like reps. Some
of them knew each other, and were huddled round one of the
tables talking about sales figures. As Jay sat down, she noticed
there was a pay-phone on the wall near her table. Beneath it on

a shelf was a dog-eared directory and a new *Yellow Pages*. On impulse, Jay picked up the directory. She was looking through the Bs when the landlady came in bearing a plate of English breakfast.

'Oh, that's a bit out of date, love,' she said. It was: six years to be precise. 'I've got a new one upstairs. I'll fetch it for you, if you like.'

'Thanks. That'd be great.' Six years ago, she and Dex had been together. It felt weird. She had to look at the listing for the 'Banners' of the town. There were about half a dozen.

The landlady came back, directory in hand. 'Here we are. Now, you eat your breakfast first.'

Jay grinned. 'OK. Look, I hope you don't mind me asking, but could you spare me a couple of minutes after breakfast?'

The landlady looked flattered. 'Of course, love.'

'I need to trace these people, and you know the town much better than I do, and . . .'

The landlady raised her hands to interrupt. 'I'll be over after I've got the breakfasts out. Now you enjoy your meal.'

The woman joined Jay just as she was finishing her toast. She now felt familiar enough with her guest to tell her that her name was Bella. She offered Jay a cigarette. The men had all gone off to their work now, and the two women sat drinking strong tea, looking through the new directory. 'I need to know which streets are on Shorefields,' Jay said.

Bella craned her neck, so Jay turned the directory on the table for her to see better. She wrinkled her nose. 'Sorry, love, but none of these.'

'Damn,' said Jay, then smiled ruefully. 'I suppose that would be too easy.' She hesitated, then opened up the older directory again and pushed it across the table to Bella. 'How about these?'

Bella took the book and scrutinised the page. She frowned, then lifted her eyebrows. 'Well, this one. Yes. Milton Close. That's Shorefields. All the roads are named after old writers, you know.' She laughed. 'Tried to give the place a bit of class. Didn't help much.'

Jay peered at the page: Banner, C, 64 Milton Close. Could this be it? 'What was Cora's husband's name?' she asked.

Bella couldn't remember.

'Oh well, it's worth a try. The people who live there now might remember the Banners.'

'Or they could have had their phone cut off,' said Bella.

'Possibly.'

'People from Shorefields don't move much,' the landlady said, lighting up another cigarette.

'Can you give me directions?' Jay asked.

'Best keep your windows wound up, and your doors locked,' said Bella, with relish, adding, 'it's only a five-minute drive away.'

Some years ago, in the depths of recession, Shorefields must have been hideous, a landscape of despair, but now, in between the more run-down houses, some efforts had been made to cheer the place up. There were still a few gardens where old electrical appliances rusted in the unkempt grass and wheelless cars sagged on bricks, but mostly the houses looked fairly neat. There was a shopping centre, where a few shops were still open – or had reopened. The others, shuttered closed and boarded up, were daubed with graffiti. The post office looked like a high security prison, with iron blinds that drooped above its windows like the boozy eyelids of an old convict.

It took Jay about twenty minutes to find Milton Close because the estate was a maze. What would the distinguished dead writers who had lent their names to the streets think of this aspect of immortality? Glancing up Shakespeare Road, Jay assumed that the most literary people around were those who could read the tabloids.

She paused on the corner of Milton Close before turning into the road. Her heart was beating quickly. She realised that a small part of her suspected Dex might be here. For a few minutes, she sat smoking a cigarette, chewing the skin around her thumb nails. A group of young girls with babies in push-chairs walked past, a gaggle of pre-school age children gambolling around them. The girls looked contented enough. They laughed together brightly. Who am I to judge? Jay wondered. She started the car again and turned into the close.

The road was flanked by flat-faced houses. Some had trellising out front, and garish robes of Virginia creepers shed their skirts upon the front doorsteps. Bare clematis strangled itself like incestuous wires. Number 108. Not far to go. A poorer family must live here; the short front garden was overgrown with dandelion and wild, untrammelled tresses of yellowing grass. Number 96. These people must've bought their house. Pity about the fake stone front and the Austrian blinds in blinding pink. Number 70. So near now. Children singing. Not these children, lounging belligerently against the sagging fence, decked out like miniature adults in a temper, but ghost children from the past, from the years of Dex's childhood. Jay imagined an old *Beano* comic skittering down the road. There it is: number 64. The family home. The curtains were dingy, half an inch too short, like an unfashionable skirt, and coloured acid yellow. Never a good colour for curtains.

Jay's hands were damp upon the steering wheel. She felt observed, as if eyes moved behind the dingy nets of number 64 and hands twitched uneasily. What would she say if the Banners still lived there? Hi, I'm Jay. You've never met me, but I lived with . . . Dex. Should she call him Dex? Perhaps it would be better to use the name his mother had given him, the one that had been imprinted upon him at the font? She had a vision of women in their Nylon best huddled in the dusty sunshine of a Sixties-built church, and Dex, a faceless infant, silent in the passing arms. What would Cora Banner look like now? Would vestiges of her former glamour still cling to her?

It was more likely that the family had moved on. Jay realised she should have been more organised and, instead of haring eagerly off, gone to the local library to check the electoral roll. She should have made deeper enquiries, visited the offices of the local paper. Her investigation of Dex must be treated like any other job. Still, she was here now. She would leave her car, walk up the short, cracked pavement to the door and knock upon it: three times, like fate or death.

Her knocking elicited no response, but Jay could feel a stillness about her, which told her someone was watching and listening. The Banners must be sick and tired of people coming to the house. She could understand why they wouldn't open their door to yet another stranger. She took a few steps back and stood with her hands on her hips, gazing up at the bedroom windows, where she sensed the most concentrated area of scrutiny.

A neighbour had also taken an interest. After Jay had knocked again, a young woman emerged from the house next door on the left. 'What do you want?' Her voice was hostile. She was quite hefty and looked capable of flooring Jay with one punch.

Jay adopted a conciliatory smile. 'I'm looking for the Banners. Do they still live here?'

'What d'you want with them?'

Jay hesitated only a moment. 'I'm a friend of Christopher's.'

The woman sneered. 'Yeah? Well, you can fuck off! Julie doesn't want to see anybody. Why can't you people leave her alone?'

'Look,' Jay said calmly, but the woman would hear no more. She trundled aggressively towards Jay, her eyes fierce. Her hands were bunched into fists.

'I said fuck off and I mean fuck off!' An air of violence poured off her like steamy sweat.

'OK,' Jay said, raising her hands. 'I hear you. But just tell them I called, will you?'

'Fuck off!'

Jay got back into her car and moved off swiftly. Glancing into the rear view mirror, she saw the protective neighbour standing on the pavement with her arms folded across her chest and her chin stuck out defiantly. Before Jay could speak to the family, she'd have to get past the guard dog.

Jay drove back into town and went to a beach front café for a mug of tea. Here, in the humid warmth, she reconsidered her tactics. Once she'd got her foot in the Banner door, she anticipated no problem, but how could she do that? Some reconnaissance was in order.

Jay returned to Shorefields and drove around the estate. She found the local junior school and parked up, then walked around for a while to get a feel for the place. In a park area near the school, she sat on a bench, her jacket collar up around her ears. It was not a warm day. Young children yelled and ran about, playing on swings and slides. Young women sat in huddles around the edge of the play area, all chatting animatedly.

At lunch-time, Jay went to a pub called The Albion and had a sandwich in the bar. When she asked the barman if he knew the Banners, his response was guarded. 'Yeah, I do, and they've been through enough.' He went immediately to serve another customer. Jay couldn't help feeling slightly amused by the reactions she was provoking in Shorefields. Was it so obvious she was a journalist, or did people think she was an obsessive fan?

She went to order another drink, and tried again. 'Look, I'm a friend of the Banner family. I really have no sinister motive for coming here. Perhaps you could . . .'

'If you're that much of a friend, why are you in here asking questions?' snapped the barman.

Jay drew in her breath.

'What can I get you?' said the barman.

'Another gin and tonic,' Jay said. He'd tell her nothing.

The pub closed at three o'clock. Jay had sat there for several hours, being observed covertly by the suspicious barman. She went out into the waning afternoon, looking down towards the school. Mothers were gathering at the gates. Jay moved a little closer. This was a long shot, but she had a hunch it would pay off. After a few minutes, she saw the Banners' statuesque neighbour come strolling down the road. She was alone. Jay's shoulders slumped. She'd been convinced Julie Banner would have a young child. Her instincts didn't often let her down. However, this did mean that the Banner house was unguarded. She could at least try to gain entry again.

Jay hurried to her car, hoping she wouldn't be spotted by

Julie's neighbour. She drove the long way round to Milton Close, so she didn't have to pass the school, and then took the precaution of parking a few doors down from the Banner household. A young couple wearing Dex T-shirts were standing on the pavement, and looked at Jay with interest as she approached. Jay didn't speak to them, although she was initially tempted to. She wasn't surprised that people still haunted the house of Dex's childhood. Some obsessions took a long time to wane. She heard the two talking about her as she knocked on the door again. Perhaps they even recognised her.

Jay could hear music inside the house; it sounded like a radio station. Whoever lurked within could not hide that someone was at home, but again they didn't answer the door. Jay sighed impatiently, uncomfortably aware of the curious scrutiny of the fans behind her. She knocked again, repeatedly. Nothing.

Jay took a deep breath, and pushed her fingers against the letter box, which opened stiffly with a squeal. 'Julie!' she called into the house. 'Julie, if you're there, please answer the door. I have to speak to you.' She could see nothing but a narrow wedge of hallway, although she had a feeling someone stood just out of view, very close. A smell of burning pizza wafted towards her. 'Julie, I'm a friend of your brother's. I'm not here to make any trouble or bother you. I just need to talk.' Jay's spine prickled. She was sure that at any moment, another neighbour would intervene, or worse the Amazon from next door would arrive. 'Julie, he talked about you to me. Please let me in.'

She could almost hear breathing now, an oppressive sense of someone stooped just to the side of the letter box. 'Look, I know you've been hassled. You've had to deal with fans and reporters and whatever else, but I'm almost family, Julie.' The fans were laughing now. Jay closed her eyes and leaned her forehead against the door, speaking more softly. 'Julie, I've lived with Dex. I slept with him every night when he wasn't on tour. I've woken up with the smell of his sweat on my sheets. Julie, I . . .'

The door opened a crack, secured by a safety chain.

'Please,' said Jay. 'Please.'

She heard the chain rattle and then the door opened swiftly. The fans uttered excited sounds and were already halfway up the short path. An arm shot out from the hallway and dragged Jay into the house, before slamming the door behind her.

Dazed, Jay leaned back against the door. She felt drained, bleeding. A woman stood opposite her, staring. Jay recognised her from the TV documentary. She was a council-estate archetype; bleached hair lividly dark at the roots; a tired, papery face old before its time; deep lines between the badly mascaraed eyes; a thin mouth rimmed by a trace of lipstick, which had insinuated itself into the fine cracks that laced her skin. She held one hand against her face, gripping a damp-looking cigarette. Her nails were bitten to the quick, panthered by the remains of silvery-blue varnish. A girl child hugged the woman's knees, while in the background, came the peevish cry of an infant. Perhaps Cora was lurking somewhere deep inside the house; a worn-out woman in black, still mourning the loss of her son.

Jay held out her hand. 'I'm Jay Samuels.'

Julie stared at Jay's extended hand, until it felt burned and she had to hide it against her jacket. Jay fixed what she hoped was a pleasant smile on her face. 'Thanks for seeing me. I would have phoned but . . .'

'We haven't got a phone any more. What do you want?'

'I want to speak to you about Dex, about Chris. I used to . . . I was his girlfriend.' The term sounded alien on her tongue, but it was a language she felt this other woman would understand. 'Partner' would sound too urbane here.

The woman drew herself up straight, folded her arms and wriggled her shoulders in a hostile manner. 'He's gone.'

'I know,' Jay said again. 'Are you Julie?'

She nodded. 'You lived with him, you say?'

'Yes, for seven years.'

'That's a bloody long time.'

'It was too short,' Jay said. She paused. 'I feel I should have come here before now.'

Julie shrugged. She pointed to an open doorway. 'Go on into the front room. I'll make some tea.'

Jay did as she was directed and placed herself gingerly on the fragile sofa – which felt as if it might tip up from her weight. The matt black TV and video were large, and clearly quite new – probably rented. A satellite or cable TV box was perched on the table beside the imposing set. Other than that, the furniture seemed temporary and disposable; veneered and flimsy. Beneath her feet the carpet was a hideous riot of colour from two decades before, although it seemed scrupulously clean. The house reminded Jay of all the bedsits she'd occupied in her youth. Her upbringing had been comfortably middle class, but her student days and later band following had been based in rooms like this. Dex had grown up here. Atoms of him must still pervade its walls, its air. Jay's legs tingled. She shuddered. Was there a sense of him here?

Julie came in from the kitchen, carrying a Formica tray. Her young child was still attached to her legs and stared at Jay with the open curiosity of a calf or a lamb. The invisible baby was no longer whining. 'Get off!' Julie said to her daughter, adding, 'She's been off school with a cold. Back tomorrow though. Kylie, get off!' Julie laughed, shaking her leg, and the girl slunk away to perch herself on an armchair. 'She's a bit nervous of strangers,' said Julie.

Jay smiled tolerantly. 'I'm glad I found you. All I had to go on was the address in an old phone directory. Lucky the hotel still had it.'

Julie sat down on the carpet and placed the tray on a coffee table. She did not look up from her tea-pouring duties. 'Yeah,' she said. 'I lost the phone a couple of years ago when Mum left. Couldn't afford it.'

Jay nodded sympathetically. 'You must think it's strange I've come here after so long.'

'A lot of people came before,' Julie said.

'I would have done too, but Dex didn't talk to me about his family much.'

Julie expelled a dismissive snort. 'I'll bet. He just wanted to forget about this lot.' Her eyes swept around the room. 'Bet your place is a bit different, eh?'

'Well . . .' Jay didn't know what to say.

'I hope so,' Julie said wistfully. 'He deserved it.'

Jay fought an sudden compulsion to invite Julie down to see the flat. It would be so easy to suggest it, but she knew this was a move entirely inappropriate and to be regretted at a later date. Julie might accept. 'I've come here because,' Jay began, 'well, because I'd like to know what happened to Dex.'

Julie just stared at her, nibbling a fingernail.

'I know it must seem odd that I've left it so long, but . . .'

'He left you, didn't he,' Julie interrupted. 'Why should you come here? He left us too.'

'It hit me very badly when he disappeared,' Jay said. 'I didn't think to get in touch with you. I'd never met you. Perhaps I should have.'

Julie shrugged. 'Wouldn't have made any difference. You're part of his other life, the one he ran to. He always wanted to run away. I doubt that changed.' She handed Jay a mug of dark tea. 'There's sugar on the tray.'

Jay shook her head. She felt strangely emotional now. *Treat this as a job.* 'Can I smoke?'

'Yeah.' Julie produced a glass ashtray from the fireplace.

'When did you last see Dex?' She noticed Julie's face took on a furtive expression, perhaps the precursor to a lie. Her eyes, however, did not leave Jay's face.

'A long time ago.'

Jay offered her a cigarette, which she accepted, making a sound half of appreciation, half of amusement when she saw its designer label. 'Posh fags,' she said.

Jay lit up. 'When exactly?'

'We was always close,' Julie said, taking a long, expert draw. 'Our mum was never around much, so I sort of looked after him. He was my baby doll. I was only two when he was born. He was a quiet kid. I could dress him up.'

She had said all this before, perhaps to a dozen or more journalists. 'When did you last see him?'

Julie sighed impatiently, narrowed her eyes a little, the fingers of one hand pressed against her face. 'Were you really his girlfriend?'

'Yes. Why?'

'You remind me of all those reporters, that's all. You don't act like a girlfriend.'

'I am a journalist,' Jay said, thinking honesty would work best. 'But I'm not here on a job, Julie. I really want to know about Dex.'

'There was a documentary on telly about him the other week,' Julie said accusingly.

'I know. In a way, that's why I'm here. It made me think. I don't think he's dead.'

Julie stared at her for a few moments. 'No, he's not.'

Jay's heart leapt. 'Why do you think that?'

'Why do you?'

Jay grinned. 'OK, it's a feeling, a hunch.'

Julie nodded. She got out the photo albums.

As Jay pored reverently over the pages of these artefacts, Julie willingly supplied gossip about the family. Cora, their mother, had married their father, Ted, at nineteen. She'd already been pregnant with Dex's older brother, Gary. There were pictures of the wedding that looked historical. Cora didn't look as if she was expecting. Her face, smiling widely above a severe white dress, which clutched at her neck and pinched her wrists, was that of a fighter, a woman who would claim she always spoke her mind, no matter how much she offended people. There was a certain harsh, brassy beauty to her. Her eyes were slanted and accentuated by black wings of eye-liner. Her mouth was firm, not smiling at all. She had been made for another life, perhaps, but had ended up with children and a husband. There were no pictures of Cora singing. In this record, her life began with the imprisonment of marriage. The children began on page three. Looking at the photos of the infant Gary held rigidly upon his mother's knee, her stiff hair framing a cruel smile, Jay could see this was not a woman spilling over with motherly love. Her nails were long and varnished against the baby's tender arms.

Then came Julie, blurry pictures of a gap-toothed girl with her hair gathered into lop-sided bunches; at the seaside, with grandparents, regimented school photos. Jay's heart was tugged by the sight of the well-buttoned cardigans, the little patent leather sandals. An innocent child with all her life before her, a princess who could have been whisked away to enchantment. It was the same for all children. How sad photos were, how terrible.

Jay moved on to another album and turned the pages. As time went on, Cora's initial, brittle beauty became harder. Her face lost its definition, although the long nails and bright lipstick were still in evidence. Her hair was an immovable construction of perm and lacquer. Ted, on the other hand, always seemed out of focus, as if he'd never really existed. He lurked on the perimeters of family groups, if he appeared at all. Perhaps he had taken most of the pictures. Julie pointed out uninteresting aunts, uncles and cousins. There were quite a few weddings in the family, and at three of them Julie had been a bridesmaid. 'Three times a bridesmaid, never a bride,' she said with a laugh. Jay glanced at the child, who was still staring at her, like some kind of eerie oracle. Perhaps she would say something shattering at any moment.

Finally, Dex came into the world. 'Little Chris,' Julie breathed, reaching out with her gnawed fingers to touch the photos.

'Chris,' Jay said. She felt as if she was looking into a tomb.

He rarely smiled for the camera. By the time he was at school, she could see in his face the promise of the man he would become. Julie explained that she had taken most of the pictures. By this time, Ted had faded away completely. Jay imagined that Cora's withering indifference had erased him from existence, but Julie said that he'd taken up with another woman in Crowston and moved away. They'd not seen him since. Dex had been about six when that had happened. 'We never fought, me and Chris,' Julie said. 'He was good with me.'

'But not with others?' Jay tried to keep the sharpness from her voice.

Julie shrugged. 'Well, he used to wind Gary up something chronic. He wasn't as naughty as some lads, but somehow he was always in trouble. I reckon people just didn't know what he was about.'

'What about his mother? Did she encourage him in his music?'

Julie uttered an explosive snort. 'What? She didn't give a toss.' She sighed. 'Mum tried, she really did, but the trouble was she just wasn't very good with kids. We were no angels, believe me. Chris could be a little bugger. He didn't belong here. It was good for him he got away and got into the music and all that.'

'Couldn't have been that good for him, Julie, could it?' Jay said dryly, looking into the woman's eyes.

Julie shrugged again, looked away. 'Want another fag?'

She offered a box and Jay took one, proud she didn't even falter at the lethal charge of nicotine and tar that lurked within it. Julie went out to the kitchen to make more tea, leaving Jay to look through the rest of the Dex pictures alone. He'd been a misunderstood poet struggling to exist among people who interpreted his sensitivity as strangeness. The photos dried up round about the time Dex reached his teens, although there were a few black and white shots of his first band; Dex now recognisably a performer, staring moodily at the camera from beneath a hectic fringe. Photos of Julie's young family were even more scant. It seemed the family had lost the urge to record their history. As she leafed through the last few pages, Julie's daughter came to stand uncomfortably close to Jay, leaning against her legs like a dog. She was an unnaturally silent child. Jay thought most children had the presence of sharp needles and a noise that pierced even more sharply. She flipped back through the album. 'Do you remember your Uncle Chris?' she asked.

The child looked at her with a disturbing expression of incredulity. 'I was a baby,' she said gravely.

After a snack of cheese slice sandwiches, Jay said she'd like to look round the town. 'You can come back later, if you like,' Julie said. 'We could go for a drink.'

Jay had hoped Julie might give her a guided tour of Torton, take her to places that Dex had frequented as a young man, but then she had the children to think about, and Jay shrank from asking them all to accompany her. Like Cora, she was not that good with children. 'That'd be great,' she said, hiding her disappointment. 'I'll come back about eight. Will that be OK?'

'Yeah. I'll get a baby-sitter.'

Julie stood on the doorstep with Kylie to wave Jay off. The fans had gone now, although Jay was keenly aware of Julie's neighbour watching them from the living-room window next door. It was clear that Jay's visit was a real occasion for Julie, despite her initial wariness. She said goodbye as if they'd known one another for a long time.

Driving away, Jay felt disoriented. It didn't seem possible that Dex had come from this place. There was so much about him she hadn't known and yet when they'd been together she'd have called him her closest friend. She'd never known him, that much was obvious now. He was disappearing more for her all the time.

Back at The Ship, Jay reserved her room for a further night. She tried to call Gus at home and on his mobile, but on both occasions was greeted only by answer-phones. She'd have to call him later. It was a bit odd that he hadn't tried to get in touch with her, but perhaps that was for the best.

After a quick drink in the bar, Jay explored the town. Not that there was much to see. In the dusk, she wandered down to the grim sea-front, where old vessels rusted in the brackish water. Gulls wheeled forlornly in the grey sky and the wind tasted of salt. Jay stood on the promenade, gripping the iron railings, staring out to sea. What was the point of this? Dex had been a fairly ordinary council estate boy. Could the answer to his disappearance be hidden here? It seemed unlikely. Recent pressures had brought that on. Yet she had discovered he'd run away before, albeit without vanishing completely. Julie seemed a nice woman, although rather sad and lonely. Why hadn't Dex kept in touch with her, included her in his life? Julie's life, to Jay, was terrible. This whole town was terrible; depressing, run-down, fading away. No wonder Dex had fled from it.

Chapter Six

Rhys Lorrance was with his mistress for the afternoon, in an upmarket hotel in the West End. She had already commented on his quiet demeanour and asked what was bothering him. Part of him didn't want to say. He was naturally secretive, but that wasn't the reason he kept his silence. What he had to say might sound paranoid at the very least. But she was persistent, and eventually the story came out. In the event, he was relieved to talk.

Dex, his disappearing star, was stalking him. When the episodes had first started a few weeks ago, Lorrance had just been angry. It had happened at his country home, on a Sunday evening. He'd been in his study, enjoying a glass of brandy and listening to some CDs on headphones, when he'd noticed a movement beyond the dark windows. Glancing round, he'd seen a dark-clad figure walking up and down in a strangely obsessive manner outside the house. Believing this to be an intruder, he'd torn off the headphones and marched over to the window, upon which he rapped with his knuckles. The figure stopped pacing and turned to stare at him, at which point Lorrance's heart nearly stopped. It was Dex; unkempt and manic.

Lorrance took a step backwards. Surely it was impossible that Dex was out there, but, unable to tear his eyes away from the apparition beyond his window, he could see that the intruder was incontrovertibly Dex. 'You said you'd never come here again!' he shouted, loud enough for Dex to hear.

Dex's expression didn't change. He looked neither menacing nor friendly, but simply watchful.

Lorrance began to undo the window locks. 'What are you doing here? Where have you been?'

Dex began to retreat on to the lawn, stepping away from the light.

Lorrance flung the window open, shouted, 'No!' but Dex had already disappeared into the garden. Lorrance felt shocked and unnerved; shocked because Dex had apparently returned to society, and unnerved because if this was an ordinary return, wouldn't Dex have just rung the front doorbell or waited to talk to his erstwhile mentor through the window?

Lorrance didn't mention the episode to anybody, especially not his wife, Samantha, who presently came into his study asking what all the noise was about.

'Bloody dog on the lawn,' Lorrance told her. 'Had to see it off.'

'Oh.' Samantha frowned, perhaps wondering how the fragments of sentences she'd heard her husband call out related to the presence of a stray dog.

Lorrance knew he wasn't a man given to delusions, so didn't question the reality of what he'd seen that night. If Dex had appeared outside his house, then it had happened, and that was that. What Dex was up to was another matter. Why show himself like that, then run off again? Perhaps he really had lost it, gone completely mad.

Lorrance waited for Dex to appear again, but for some time there were no further visits to the house. Occasionally, driving through London, Lorrance would catch sight of a still, scrawny figure in the buzzing crowds. It often looked like Dex, but Lorrance couldn't be sure. He refused to consider that what he was seeing might be a ghost. Lorrance didn't like to believe in things that he couldn't grab hold of and control, but after a couple of weeks, he felt he had no choice but to calmly consider that he might be the victim of a haunting. The thought amused him slightly.

Then he had to change his mind again. After lunch on Saturday afternoons, Lorrance generally took a walk round his estate, to survey the results of his own success. The ornamental lake was ringed by yellow-haired willows, rapidly balding as the season advanced. The gravel paths were all raked, the shrubs neat and tended by Lorrance's staff of gardeners. An oriental summer-house, thicketed with tall stands of bamboo, resided on a small, man-made hillock. Here, Lorrance liked his wife to take her tea on summer afternoons, when she would wear soft white suede, her pale hair cascading over her bare cinnamon arms. Now the summer-house looked bleak and empty, its door locked against intruders. The garden was closing in on itself for the coming onslaught of frost and dark, but still Lorrance saw beauty and grace in its contained landscape. He crossed a cropped lawn, pimpled with conkers, and passed beneath the outflung arms of the horse-chestnuts. He could no longer see the house. Ahead of him was the boundary to his land, a high, undulating wall; its peaks topped with grey stone pineapples, its valleys with smooth copings. Beyond it rose a hill, partly forested. The hill seemed to cry out for a marker of some kind; a triumphal arch, a tower or a statue. The sky looked immense behind it, owing to the fact the horizon was not in any way obscured by trees or buildings. Any monument would look stark and mysterious against it. Lorrance imagined a statue of himself up there, surveying his lands below, still watchful and protective long after his physical body had left this world. He was aware that this idea was deeply egotistical, but was still secretly thrilled by it. As he walked through his gardens, he often thought about that statue, because he was sure he'd have it one day. He'd even made sketches of it as he talked on the phone in his office. The main obstacle to his dream was the fact that the farmer who owned the land wouldn't sell it. But Lorrance knew that eventually he'd get his own way. The farmer was old, and his sons and daughters, when they inherited the farm, would be more amenable to change.

Most Saturdays, Lorrance would open the narrow gate of wrought iron in the wall and climb up the hill. Then he could look back at his house, and imagine Samantha curled up on the sofa there, reading the Saturday supplements, a cup of Earl Grey tea on the table beside her. She was as precious to him as any of the other embellishments to his domain, and that was not a mean judgement. The nearest Lorrance came to experiencing pure, sweeping love was when he stood on that hill, drinking in the scene below him.

On that day, however, someone was already occupying his space. He could discern a tall figure, a coat flapping around him, standing on the hill, looking down. It took him only a few seconds to realise it was Dex. He didn't appear remotely spectral; there was a definite heaviness about him. Lorrance opened the iron gate roughly and began hurrying up the hill. He was not as fit as he used to be, and by the time he reached the crest he was breathing harshly. Dex still stood there, a half-smile on his face, his hands thrust deep into the pockets of his coat.

'Just what the hell is all this about, Dex?' Lorrance demanded, fighting the urge to droop, brace his hands against his knees. Light boiled in specks before his eyes.

'You know,' said Dex, in his flat, northern tone.

'It can be forgotten, all of it,' Lorrance replied. 'Come home.'

'Oh, I'm home all right,' said Dex.

'What do you want?'

'None of us want to be forgotten. None of us. Not in the way you'd have it.' Dex turned round and walked across the top of the hill. Wind blew strongly here, its voice a hissing yodel.

'Dex!' Lorrance went after him, but his legs were aching, his chest was tight. A curl of his immaculate hair had flopped down on to his brow. He saw Dex disappearing down the opposite slope, which was crowded with trees. Dex was younger; his loping strides devouring ground. Lorrance could not catch up. 'Little bastard!' he said.

Since then, Lorrance had been acutely conscious of the dark outside each evening. He was sure Dex was concealed in it, watchful, perhaps vengeful. What did he want? Surely not the truth.

Lorrance's mistress uncoiled herself from the bed, shaking out her long red hair as she strolled to the window. Outside, traffic hissed in the wet on the Strand. He had told her, but so far she'd said nothing.

'Well, there you have it,' he said again.

She turned to observe him. 'What has Dex got on you?'

'Nothing,' he said. 'Absolutely nothing.'

She nodded, smiling thinly. 'Then you should go to the police. He's harassing you.'

Lorrance's hesitation was brief, but perhaps enough to give him away. 'I don't feel that's an appropriate course. I'm not sure it's a good idea for him to come back.'

'In that case, you'll have to put up with it, won't you, or take the law into your own hands. You're so good at that, Rhys. What's the problem?'

He couldn't say. 'He's got the tapes, though. They would be useful.'

'Well, as he said himself, he doesn't want to be forgotten. Perhaps he'll give the tapes to you. Perhaps that's what he wants in his sick, delusional way.' She paused a moment. 'Actually, this makes sense of something.'

'What?'

'He's been trying to get in touch with Jay Samuels. She's had some crank calls. I bet it was him.'

Lorrance visibly blanched. 'Her magazine would love this story.'

'Wouldn't they! It seems to me you can't just sit around doing nothing. You must act. Jay's ambivalent about Dex, but I don't think it would take much for him to have her firmly back in his ranks.'

'I'd like to hear what you'd do in my shoes.'

She laughed. 'I'm sure I can think of something.'

'You hate him, don't you?' Lorrance grinned at her. 'One that got away, I suspect. Did he never fancy you, Gina?'

She pantomimed a growl. 'He's not my type, never was.'

'Didn't realise that was a criterion.'

'You don't know what any of my criteria are.'

'I know *you*, Gina. You're a she-wolf, one of the tribe.'

She sauntered back to him, stood over the bed, hands on hips. 'Then just be grateful I'm running with your pack,' she said.

Chapter Seven

In the evening, Julie took Jay to The Haymaker, a square modern pub in the middle of the estate, with no hay fields in sight. They sat across from one another at a new table designed to look old and drank gin and tonics. Julie had chattered on about herself, occasionally nodding hello to the regulars. Jay now knew all about how Cora had finally run off with a computer salesman (a considerable rise in status for Cora – and one which she no doubt thought was long deserved), and how she was singing again, in working-men's clubs. Julie confessed that her mother was not a great singer, but if she enjoyed it, so what? Julie saw her perhaps once or twice a month. She then went on to describe her disappointing parade of temporary boyfriends, two of whom had lingered long enough to spawn Melanie and Kylie. Gary was a black sheep, forever haunting the fringe of criminal activity. He was sometimes quite rich, sometimes destitute. Julie discouraged him from visiting the house, afraid the police might look for him there one day and upset the kids. Her father, Ted, had disappeared from her life completely. He could be dead, for all she knew. She avoided the subject of Dex, and for the time being, Jay did not push it. Julie's family were like ghosts; she might as well be alone. Jay considered the Banners were extraordinarily adept at losing people, especially each other. Perhaps, one day, Julie would wander out into the garden, where she had left baby Melanie mewling in her pram, only to find empty blankets, still warm.

Then Dex came into the conversation. Julie's reminiscences wandered into the enchanted fields of childhood. She related what Jay considered to be a stream of fantasies concerning the fierce and indomitable relationship she'd enjoyed with

Dex. Jay, unlike many of Dex's London friends, had few bad memories associated with his character, but even she found it difficult to believe in Julie's primrose vision of the past. Dex, apparently, had been noble, fearless, imaginative and sensitive. These attributes did not quite fit in with the image Julie had painted of her brother earlier in the day. 'We used to play up where the new estate is now,' Julie said, her eyes misty. 'There was woods there, and a stream. I fancied myself as a right little princess!' She laughed. 'Chris'd be a cowboy, or a spaceman, or a knight, but I'd always be a fairy princess. It was best when Chris was the knight because princesses have knights, don't they? They don't have spacemen!' She laughed even more.

Jay felt hollow. She remembered times like that in her own childhood, playing in the sun, wearing a couple of old curtains and believing herself a queen.

'What about your family?' Julie asked. 'I bet yours are all rich, aren't they.'

Jay shook her head. 'No, Julie. Like you, I'm alone. Both my parents are dead now.'

Julie frowned. 'Oh, sorry. Haven't you any brothers and sisters?'

'No. There's just me. I think there are some cousins somewhere, but I'm not in touch with them.'

Julie smiled shakily. 'Well, families can be trouble, can't they? We're probably best off as we are.'

Jay nodded, then shrugged, sighed, and took a drink. 'It's not something I think about, to be honest. I keep busy.'

'What about kids?'

Jay pantomimed a shudder. 'Oh no. That's just not me.'

Julie looked introspective for a moment. 'It would have been nice if Chris'd had kids.'

The idea, which flashed across Jay's mind in a series of shocking and repellent images, seemed grotesque. 'He'd have still disappeared, anyway,' she said.

'Yeah, I s'pose he would, if my situation's anything to go on!'

They shared a conspiratorial smile and Jay went to the bar

to get another drink. When she returned, she asked, 'So, did Dex always have trouble with his brother?'

Julie thought about it for a moment. 'To tell the truth, I can't really remember when it all started. Must have been slow, like.'

'Did Gary bully Dex?'

Julie pulled a face. 'I suppose you'd call it that now, yeah.' Then, it had probably been seen as fairly normal behaviour between siblings. 'What happened?'

'Chris'd run away like a rabbit. That's usually when I got to hear about it. I'd be upstairs or something, then there'd be some sounds downstairs, and the back door slamming, and Gary bellowing down the street. There'd be no sign of Chris by then. I used to wait a bit, then I'd go to find him.'

'How did your parents cope with the squabbles?'

Julie sneered, took a sip of gin. 'Dad'd gone by then, and Mum was hardly ever there. If she saw anything, she'd just clobber the pair of them. It didn't happen much when she was there. We kept our heads down then, all of us.'

Jay had a vision of Cora, her Playtexed bosom jutting fiercely, her mouth a severe slash of red, her eyes like those of a battlefield goddess.

Julie laughed. 'One time, us kids all got drunk. Mum had gone out to the pub. Gary was about twelve then, I was eight and Chris was six. Gary used to look after us when Mum went out. We raided the whisky, and when they got back, there was Chris being sick and us other two pissed as newts. We didn't like the taste much, otherwise we might have had more.' Her face clouded. 'We got a right tanning for that, I can tell you.'

'I can imagine.'

'She wasn't that bad,' Julie said. 'She was unhappy. Got up the duff and had to marry a man she didn't love. Life was a disappointment to her. I don't blame her. I s'pose she's happy now.' Julie went quiet for a moment, then leaned forward. 'Anyway . . . about Chris. He speaks to me all the time.'

Jay didn't know how to react. 'I thought you said he wasn't dead.'

Julie looked puzzled. 'He isn't.'

'Then . . . he *calls* you on the phone?' Jay didn't dare to hope.

Julie shook her head. 'No. It's not like that.'

'Then how is it?'

Julie pulled back, her eyes narrowed. 'I might tell you. I might not.' She paused. 'I like you, Jay. You seem OK. I'm glad Chris was with you.'

Jay felt embarrassed, wondering, with her silent judgements, what she had done to deserve this accolade.

'Tell you what,' Julie said. 'Stay at ours tonight. There's some stuff I could show you tomorrow – if it feels right.'

For a brief moment, Jay felt afraid of staying in the house where Dex had lived. Julie must have misinterpreted her pause.

'Look, I know it ain't the Ritz, but I cook a mean breakfast. You won't get one better in any fancy hotel.'

Jay smiled. 'I'm sorry. Of course I'd love to stay with you. I was just thinking about how I've reserved a hotel room, that's all. I haven't got all my things with me. Still, it doesn't matter. I can get them tomorrow. I'd better call The Ship though, otherwise the indomitable Bella might not be pleased!' She leaned down to pull her mobile phone from her shoulder bag and ferret around for the card Bella had given her with the hotel's address and phone number on. After this quick call, she remembered Gus, which prompted an involuntary sigh. 'I'd better just try my boyfriend again and let him know I won't be back tonight.'

'You've got another bloke now?' There was a slight note of reproachful surprise in Julie's voice.

Jay chose to ignore it. 'Yeah.' She punched in her home number, but Gus still wasn't there. Relieved, she left another short, breezy message on the answering machine, vague about her location and activities. Gus was used to her travelling about, so it shouldn't concern him too much.

Julie was still staring at her suspiciously, as she stowed her phone back into her bag. 'I met Gus eighteen months ago,' Jay said. 'It doesn't mean Dex's disappearance doesn't still hurt me, Julie, because it does, but life goes on.'

Julie nodded slowly. 'Yeah. It's easier to replace a boyfriend than a brother.'

'Dex is irreplaceable, Julie,' Jay said, quite sternly.

Julie ducked her head, waved it from side to side. 'Yeah, yeah. But it's different for you.'

The spare room in Julie's house was chilly and damp. Julie stripped down the bed, swathed it with clean bedding and stuffed it full of Kylie's hot-water bottles, but later that night, when Jay went to bed, she was aware of the cold, clammy breath oozing from the sheet and the duvet. There was a faint smell of must. This had once been Julie's room. Dex had shared a room with Gary, now occupied by Kylie. There were no ghosts in the walls.

Earlier, she and Julie had returned from the pub after closing time, Jay hugging a bottle of wine she'd bought for an extortionate price as a 'take-out'. Jay felt slightly drunk, and could tell Julie was heading the same way. All they wanted to do was keep drinking. Jay thought this might elicit more confidential remarks from Julie, but unfortunately, the baby-sitter – a loud teenager who lived up the road – proved difficult to expel and wanted to share their wine.

The baby-sitter finally left about half midnight, and Julie went to make coffee. Jay sat on the floor in the front room, hugging a cushion against the slight draught that whispered under the door from the hall. The room seemed cosy in dim lamp-light, the gas fire hissing comfortably in the grate. Jay looked around the room and wondered why Dex had never sent money to his sister, his protectress. She made do with very little: benefits, hand-outs, second-hand furniture and charity shop clothes. My God, he could even have bought her a house, Jay thought muzzily, feeling great empathy for a woman she'd met only a few hours before.

When Julie came back in, Jay said, 'It's really weird, but since I've been here with you, it seems like it was only yesterday that Dex disappeared. I don't feel the same pain, exactly, but in a way you've made him come alive for me again.'

Julie pursed her mouth slightly, perhaps feeling Dex should never have seemed dead for her, anyway.

Jay felt she'd committed a faux pas. She had meant her remark to be a compliment. She couldn't really say anything more. To add that everything had been so difficult back then, what with the journalists and photographers, would sound crass, almost bragging. If she'd known Julie then, maybe she would have come here to recuperate and would have recovered so much sooner. Perhaps. Maybe she'd have only seemed spoiled; rich and drunk and with a hundred potential Dex replacements just around the corner. She had always been her own woman. Dex's disappearance had not burdened her with survival fears. The loss of a man could only affect her emotionally. When Julie's boyfriends had enacted their own vanishments, she'd been left with debts and the expense of children, with no way to increase her income. Drink puts a gloss over everything, Jay thought, suddenly completely sober.

The evening ended on a tense note. There were no more confidences, or mentions of Dex being in touch, and because the atmosphere had changed, Jay knew she couldn't broach the subject. She wondered whether Julie was having second thoughts about her. Other than Dex, they had little in common. Perhaps, in the morning, she could repair the damage.

The smell of cooking bacon woke Jay around eight, and shortly afterwards, Julie came up with a cup of tea, Kylie peering round her track-suited knees. To Jay, this hour was obscene, a time when usually she was fast asleep. She was also used to the delicate flavours of orange juice, croissants and continental cereals for breakfast. The heavy, oily aromas filling the house reminded her of childhood weekends at her grandparents', when she'd wolfed down 'one-eyed-gypsies'; fried egg beneath a piece of crisp fried bread with the centre cut out, drenched in tomato sauce.

It was too cold to sit up in bed and enjoy the tea, so Jay dressed quickly and went downstairs. A Radio One DJ hectored the kitchen, and fat spat in the frying-pan. All the windows were misted with condensation. 'Sleep well?' Julie enquired, shovelling dripping bacon on to a plate with a fish slice.

'Fine,' Jay said, smiling. The sunlight beyond the foggy windows was clear and hard. The street seemed full of children and mothers. She wondered whether she should check on her car.

Julie plonked a laden plate down before Jay. She thought she'd feel sick at the sight of it but was pleasantly surprised to find it made her mouth water. 'Sauce on the side,' said Julie, nodding at the cluttered work surface beside the sink.

Her baby, a terrifying gnome, wobbled in a high chair across the table, drooling copiously and staring at Jay with piggy eyes, occasionally emitting an ear-splitting shriek, which Jay supposed was designed to attract attention. She ignored it. Kylie, however, to whom Jay had taken a wary shine, sat quietly beside her, drawing with blue crayon in a school exercise book. Julie noticed Jay looking at it. 'She's got some of Chris in her, bless her,' she said. 'The artistic type.'

Maybe I should do something for her, Jay thought, equally aware of how Julie might view any offer of assistance, financial or otherwise, from Dex's rich, London ex. Perhaps Julie would be entitled to royalties from Dex's work – it was clear she wasn't benefiting at present. Jay resolved to look into it once she got back home. She knew people who worked for law firms.

'So, what's on the agenda today?' Jay asked, forking beans and bacon into her mouth. Julie had not lied about her cooking. The simple fare seemed to explode with flavours.

Julie put a plate down before Kylie, who merely twitched her nostrils at it like a cat. 'I've got to take this 'un to school first. Get on with it, Ky, there's a good girl.'

The child grudgingly began to eat.

'Then what?' Jay asked.

Julie glanced at her, taking a draw from a cigarette. 'Dunno yet,' she said.

Clearly some reparation was in order. 'Is there anything I can do to help?' Jay said. 'I could do the dishes.'

'Eat your breakfast first,' Julie said, but her tone had softened.

Jay went along with Julie and the children to the school where Kylie would spend her day. They were joined by Marie from next door, who now treated Jay like an old friend. It was clear that she and Julie had discussed her late the previous afternoon. Kylie and Marie's daughter, Emma, whispered conspiratorially together, walking a few yards ahead of the women. Occasionally, they'd look back at Jay and laugh.

To Jay, the gathering of mothers and their offspring at the school gates was a culture shock. The women talked mainly about babies, and Jay was unnerved by their screaming older children, who all seemed to be running about madly. This was not a world Jay knew or had ever cared to know. Women were different when they had children, apparently focused entirely on being mothers. All Julie's friends at the gate, like Julie herself, had aged before their time, as if all their energy had been sucked out of them, dragging their youth with it. They cast many a curious glance at Jay, until Julie said, 'Oh, this is a friend of Chris'. From London.'

Then the other women felt free to examine her openly, no doubt weighing up her hunched pose, her hands thrust deep into the pockets of her leather jacket. 'Hi,' said Jay, eager to escape.

Once the army of diminutive hellions had been absorbed into the school, Julie said, 'We'll go for a walk.'

Marie clearly sensed this was family business, and left Jay and Julie alone. They set off up the road beside the school. Houses on the other side were raised up on a bank, and here the gardens were slightly larger, most of them well tended. The gnome bounced in her push-chair; it seemed inconceivable she possessed the flowing, elegant name of Melanie.

'Thanks for putting me up,' Jay said, hoping to re-establish the friendship that seemed to have been forming in the pub the previous night.

''S'OK,' Julie said.

They walked in silence for a while, until they came to the flat play area, fenced by wire mesh covered in green plastic, where a few mothers and below-school-age children were gathered. Melanie had begun to make disturbing bird noises.

How can she stand the noise? Jay wondered, peering at Julie sidelong. They sat on a bench, Julie pushing the baby's chair back and forth, both women smoking cigarettes. Around them, the estate rustled with unseen life; the streets seemed empty now. Jay's phone rang and she fished it out of her bag. She recognised her home number in the display. Gus was calling and this must be a hostile move because at this time she was normally asleep.

'Where are you?' His demand excluded greeting, as if he'd guessed where she was.

'Oh, hi,' Jay said. 'I'm just up north.'

'When will you be back?'

'Oh, I don't know. Soon.'

Her vagueness seemed to irritate Gus. He complained about how he would soon be away; they should be spending this weekend together. She'd better be back by Friday. And what was this job anyway? She hadn't mentioned it. A shiver of anger made Jay say, 'I'm with Dex's family, OK? I'll see you later.' She ended the call.

Julie was looking at her carefully.

'Men!' said Jay, and they both laughed.

'They're all the bloody same,' said Julie.

Inside, Jay was already beginning to fret about her rash honesty. She looked down at the phone in her hands and turned it off. She didn't want any more calls. But what would she go back to now? Rows, moods, sulks. Sighing, she dropped the phone into her bag. Why was she here anyway? What could it possibly accomplish?

'Are you going to write about Chris?' Julie asked.

Jay shook her head. 'No. I told you, that's not why I'm here.' She turned sideways in her seat. 'Look, I want to tell you what prompted me to come.'

Julie stared at her, hardly blinking, nibbling her nails, while Jay told the story of the documentary, the magazine and the calls. For some reason, she omitted the part about Zeke

Michaels. Let Julie think it was her hunches alone that had dragged her northwards. 'It was all the coincidences, Julie,' Jay said, with emphatic hand gestures. 'I just had to come. There's more to Dex's story, I know, and as his partner, well ex-partner, I want to find it. Somehow, I don't think I'll be able to carry on my life properly until I do.' Was this the truth, or was it really her journalistic curiosity that was spurring her on? Ultimately, they were the same thing.

There was a silence, then Julie slowly nodded her head. 'You're not wrong,' she said, in a prophetic tone.

Jay didn't speak, but stared at Julie with wide, and she hoped innocent, eyes.

'He's not dead,' Julie said. 'He's *somewhere else*.'

'Do you know where?'

Julie closed her eyes briefly, shook her head. 'No. He won't tell me that.'

'But he speaks to you?'

She nodded. 'I can't explain.' She put her hands between her knees, her shoulders hunched forward, her head tilted towards the bleak sky. 'There's so much, Jay. It's connections, you see. This causes this, causes that. It goes back a long way.'

'How?'

'When Chris was little, say eight years old or so, something happened. It was big news at the time. A friend of his – we used to call him Little Peter – went missing.'

'Another missing person,' said Jay. She shook her head and smiled sadly.

'Yeah. Peter was never found, but well, I used to think that Chris knew what really happened.'

'You think Chris, Dex, was involved?'

'Perhaps if it hadn't been Peter, it'd been him. But it stayed with Chris.'

Jay shuddered. She could almost see the dark cloud Julie spoke of, the way it had clung to Dex like a mist, overshadowing everything. Was the answer that simple? 'What were your suspicions?'

'This must go no further. And I mean it!' Her eyes were fierce. 'If you say – or write – anything, I'll bloody kill you.'

'You have my word. Please . . .'

'I think it was something to do with Gary, you see, and he's blood an' all. Like I said to you last night, Chris used to wind Gary up. Little Peter was Chris' only friend, really. He was a strip of a kid, right snotty-nosed little article, but he and Chris got on great. When they were together, sometimes the devil just used to get into them. They'd do things that would get to Gary. Sit there at the table, giggling, copying what Gary did. Once he threw his dinner over Chris. Chris was copying him so much I thought he'd go right on and throw his own dinner back, but he didn't. He sat there, with peas and gravy and everything dripping down his face, just looking at Gary. Not angry, not frightened, just looking, like he was thinking of something, a way to get back.'

'And you think he found that way?'

Julie shrugged. 'Dunno. But soon after that, the boys were up to their tricks, larking about outside while Gary fixed his bike. Suddenly, there was this sound like a big dog fight or something. I looked out the window and at first I just wanted to laugh. There they were, scrapping in the street like animals. Chris was getting a bit of a pounding, but he was just laughing. Then Little Peter pulled him away and the pair of them ran off. Gary went after them on his bike. I wasn't too worried. Chris knew how to get away from Gary. He was clever like that. Gary came back for his tea, but Chris didn't. Gary said he'd followed them up to the heath, but they'd lost him there. Swore he could hear them cackling at him from the copses, but he couldn't find them. Anyway, I went out to look for Chris around seven, because I was a bit worried by then. I met him on the street, not far from home. He looked weird, I can tell you that, sort of fierce yet holding something in. I asked him if he was OK and he just said he was. I asked about Peter and he said he didn't know. Peter had run off.' Julie sighed and lit another cigarette. 'Of course, when the police came, he got a bit more questioning than that! Sullen little bugger, he was. Couldn't, or wouldn't, tell them anything. He just said they ran away from Gary, then split up. Chris said he didn't come home till late to let Gary cool off, because he knew he'd pushed

Gary far that day. They never found Little Peter. No one had seen him. He just vanished.'

Jay found she was shaking. 'That's horrible,' she managed to say. 'What do you think happened?'

Julie drew in her breath. 'Oh, now I reckon it happened pretty much as Chris said, only I think Peter must have fallen down somewhere. There're old shafts on the heath. Chris felt guilty because he'd caused all the trouble in the first place that'd made Gary chase them. That's what I think. But,' she fixed Jay with a level gaze, 'at the time, I couldn't help but blame Gary. He was always so nasty with the kids, like a mean dog. There was no excuse. Chris just wanted Gary to like him, really. Looked up to him. Big brother stuff. But it wasn't to be.'

'You don't think Gary caught up with them?'

Julie paused for a moment. 'No. No. I'm pretty sure he didn't. At the time, I did. At the time, I thought Gary had just gone and done something terrible to Peter. Not on purpose, but accidental, like. He had such a temper. One knock, and a little kid could go falling down a shaft, or he could hit his head, and then it might be the only thing to do . . . put him down a shaft.' She shook her head. 'I think I was more cut up than I realised. Gary wasn't any different afterwards. He'd have had to be, wouldn't he, if he'd done something like that? And he helped the police far more than Chris did. We all went looking, calling and looking. Jesus, the state of Peter's mum. A black eye from her old man and a mess of tears. She was no use. Chris stayed at home. He wouldn't go near that heath.' She slumped. 'He wasn't the same after that, for a long time. It must've scared him, or something. He just went more quiet. Sometimes he was his old self with me, but no one else. He didn't really bother with friends any more, until he grew up and then the other lads thought he was cool. He changed then. Someone asked him to sing for their band. He'd never tried before, but he was bloody good. Straight away. Odd, really. He certainly had the face for it. Skinny but pretty. It's what a lot of girls like.'

'Mmm. Did he never go back to the heath?'

'Oh, he got over it. We used to go there a lot. In the early days, I remember the summer, and him with a guitar. We'd take cider and some blow up there and he'd sing his songs to me. I was pretty then, with the old fishnets and spiky hair. They were grand days. I miss them.'

'I miss them too,' Jay said. 'But I'm glad I was young then, and not now.'

Julie said, 'Huh! You're not kidding. All they're into now is burglary and drugs, I reckon, or at least around here. In my day, everyone wanted to be in a band. It was great.'

'Yeah. So how do you think Peter's disappearance connects with what happened to Dex?'

Julie squirmed on the bench. She seemed slightly embarrassed. 'I don't know. It's just that . . .' She stared at Jay for a moment. 'Oh, this is so bloody difficult, because I promised him I'd never say. I'll have to ask.'

'Ask Dex?'

She jiggled her shoulders. 'Just ask, that's all. I might be able to tell you. I might.'

Jay wanted to demand, 'When?' but thought better of it. She reached out and lightly touched Julie's shoulder. 'That's OK. Don't tell me anything you don't want to. I could stay for another night, if you want.'

Julie looked away from her; Jay suspected she was hiding the beginning of tears. 'Yeah, do that.'

'You mentioned you wanted to show me something today,' Jay said, stubbing out her cigarette on the slabs at their feet.

Julie delivered a shifty glance. 'Yeah . . . We could go and see a few things. Places where Chris used to go.'

Jay suspected Julie was now holding out on her, but she'd go along with her. Maybe later, after a few drinks, she'd open up again. 'Sounds great. Can I see the heath?'

'It's a bit of a trek.'

'We can use the car.'

Julie left her baby with Marie, and seemed cheerful at the prospect of a drive out. Jay was eager to get going. She wanted Julie to talk about her claim that Dex still communicated with her. It seemed clear his sister was rather odd, but Jay still wanted to know the details. 'How do you fancy a take-out meal tonight?' she suggested, as they set off. 'We could get some wine and stay in, stuff ourselves stupid.'

Julie looked uncertain.

'I can put it on expenses, it won't cost us a thing!' Jay laughed, and Julie joined in, clearly relieved to learn they'd be running a scam rather than Jay simply offering charity.

Just a short way away from the housing estate, the heath fought what was no doubt a losing battle with development. 'It was a lot bigger when we were kids,' Julie explained as they drove through the labyrinthine roads of a new estate. Eventually the houses dwindled and they came to a cul-de-sac, where an ancient stile could be crossed to reach Ladyhorse Common. The wind cut sharply across the open land and, in the sky, rain-clouds gathered in the north. Bleak sunlight illumined the bare trees, where a few last leaves clung. Other people were walking there, with dogs and children. It was not quite the desolate spot Jay had imagined.

Julie suggested they walk over to the edge of the woods. 'People don't go there as much,' she said.

'Why's that?' Jay imagined some ghoulish yet romantic legend was involved.

'You never know who's wandering about,' Julie answered darkly.

'Is this where you used to play?' Jay asked.

Julie nodded. 'There were pools here, but further back, where the houses are now.' She raised a hand to point to the distant line of trees. 'If we go that way, we'll get to the real heath, not this bit.'

In this place, the Dex Jay had never known had grown up. The thought excited yet saddened her. She was beginning to see children in terms of doomed creatures, unaware of the terrible futures that awaited them. 'We had a forest near where I grew up,' she said. 'I went back there a few years ago, and found that most of it had gone. What was left seemed smaller somehow. I mean the trees weren't so tall, and the little stream I used to play in, that seemed so overhung and magical, seemed hardly more than a drain.'

'Things change,' Julie said, shaking her head as if wanting stronger words to express herself.

'Being a child is such a shining gift, yet we don't know how precious it is until it's worn out and gone away.' Jay sighed.

'I wish I could give my kids more,' Julie said.

Jay was moved to touch the other woman's arm. 'I'm not a mother, but all I can say is that letting someone have the freedom to be themselves is the biggest thing you can give anyone. Think about Dex . . . about Chris.'

Julie glanced at her sidelong. 'I know you mean well, love, but it takes more than that, it really does. Here, let's go this way.'

They left the open land and took a path through the trees. Here, the wind was silenced and stilled, and it was as if they'd stepped into another country. Autumn's disrobing of the forest had revealed the old drinks cans and crisp wrappers discarded in the undergrowth, but still the trees had a certain presence. Julie led the way, her scuffed trainers kicking through the damp, rustling leaves. Her shoulders were hunched; she was silent amid her own thoughts. Jay wished she had a camera with her. In her mind, she imagined the article she could write about this visit, the stark contrast of Dex's life with his humble beginnings.

She jumped backwards as a young boy hurtled on to the path from between the trees. He paused for a moment to stare at Jay with dark, almost predatory, eyes. She took in his grubby face, his ragged jumper and holey jeans. Then he was gone, out of the wood the way they'd come. Jay felt strangely out of breath and reached out to a gnarled tree trunk for support.

'Jay!'

When she looked up, Julie was at least fifty yards down the path ahead of her. 'What's up?' she called, beginning to walk back.

'Kid spooked me,' Jay said. 'Damn near knocked me over.'

Julie frowned. The forest was soundless around them.

'Kid,' said Jay lamely, looking in the direction the boy had taken.

Julie could have said something, perhaps, but she didn't.

She smiled tightly and started to walk again. 'This way, come on.'

The trees became thicker, the path heading downhill. Ahead, it veered sharply upwards again. Jay was panting with exertion by the time they reached the top. Here, ancient beech trees formed an almost perfect circle around a depression in the crown of the hill. Children had made swings on two of the bigger branches with nylon rope and thick sticks, polished to a dull lustre by numerous young thighs. Julie clambered up on to one of the makeshift seats, her legs clutching the rope. She pushed herself out over the steep side of the hill, swinging in a wide, dizzying arc.

Jay felt anxious. The branch creaked; the only sound. She sat down on the springy, damp earth. A strange weight pressed down upon her; she felt slightly disorientated and dizzy. The trees were too immense, too close. In this place, they still dreamed of lost centuries. Humans scurrying between the lichened trunks could be no more than ants to these leviathans of the forest. There was a presence: that was it. Jay felt breathless and uncomfortable, observed.

Julie jumped back to earth. 'There's always been swings here,' she said, her face flushed. 'We used to spend hours here.'

'Doesn't look like the tradition's faltered,' Jay said, pulling her cigarettes from her jacket pocket. Why did she feel so unsafe?

Julie accepted a cigarette from Jay, and leaned back against one of the trees, inhaling deeply. She looked younger somehow, released. 'Chris and Peter would come here all the time in summer,' she said. 'Close your eyes.'

'Why?'

'Just do it,' Julie said. Her own were closed already. Jay couldn't bring herself to do it, but watched the other woman. 'If you concentrate, you can almost hear the kids playing.'

Jay took a nervous draw of her cigarette. Ahead of her, one of the swings twisted on its blue, ragged rope. She shuddered. She didn't want to hear anything. 'I don't believe in ghosts,' she said crassly, standing up. For a moment, the world dipped around her, the crowns of the trees spun against the sky.

Julie's eyes snapped open. She looked reproachful, perhaps even disappointed.

'Sorry,' Jay said. 'I don't feel comfortable here.' She realised her words almost contradicted her previous statement, but Julie just shrugged.

'You wanted to see,' she said. 'So I've shown you.'

'Shown me what?' Jay's discomfort was spilling over into irritation. A headache was starting, somewhere deep behind her eyes.

Julie stared at her steadily. 'You're a strange one,' she said. 'I thought you'd know.'

Jay couldn't be bothered to play games. 'Know what? Do you see ghosts here, Julie? Is that it? Do you know more about Dex and the past than you're letting on? Why don't you just tell me straight?'

Julie looked puzzled and slightly wounded. 'I can't tell you anything,' she said in a low voice. 'You can only see for yourself.'

'There's nothing to see,' Jay said in a softer tone. 'These are your memories, Julie, not mine. I can only hear your tales.'

Julie sighed and nodded. She looked disappointed, as if she'd believed Jay would be a conspirator in her fantasy. 'Not everyone's the same,' she said.

Jay just wanted to get away from the place. 'Let's go now,' she said, smiling apologetically. 'I could do with a drink.'

'Yeah, me too.' Julie pushed herself away from the tree trunk. 'It's not a great day for it, is it?'

'Perhaps we can talk later,' Jay said. 'Thanks for bringing me here, Julie.'

''S'OK.'

Jay's spine tingled as they made the precarious descent down the slippery path. She could hear the branches creaking behind her, but no more; no laughter, no cries.

Before a pub lunch, Jay insisted on driving to the nearest big supermarket store, where she could repay Julie's hospitality by stocking up on a few essentials. 'You've been kind enough to put me up, and I don't want to eat you out of house and home.'

'That's not likely, love,' Julie said. Jay could tell she didn't know whether to feel angry, annoyed or grateful for her guest's largesse, but in the end obviously decided just to go along with it. Her perusal of the well-stocked shelves reminded Jay of a kid in a toy store. Julie would not shop in places like this. Hers would be the cut-price store on the estate, where choice was narrow. She ogled the bright vegetable produce; carrots that were too orange, cauliflowers almost too plump; irradiated produce that would stay fresh for a week. Jay dumped three different nets of fresh fruit in the trolley and Julie just cast her sidelong glances; aghast and almost despising. She bought two loaves of bread, warm from the oven, six different cheeses, olives, avocado. If this was a girls' night in, she wanted her favourite nibbles to hand. 'What's your favourite?' she asked Julie, and when Julie offered 'pickles', Jay dumped jars of spiced onions, red cabbage and gherkins into the trolley.

'Planning on feeding an army?' Julie asked. 'And is this going on expenses as well?'

'We'll eat early so Kylie can have some take-away,' Jay said. 'This little lot is for later.' She added a bottle of gin, some tonic water, and two bottles of wine to their haul.

'We'll be sick,' Julie said, her eyes taking on a feverish gleam as she caught Jay's shopping-lust.

'So what?' Jay answered.

At the check-out, Julie made a disapproving sound at the cost of Jay's purchases. Jay ignored it and flashed her gold card at the cashier. She would not let herself feel guilty.

After the shopping expedition, Jay drove to a pub she'd noticed on the way that offered lunches. She was not surprised when Julie protested. 'We've got all that nosh for tonight,' she said. 'I can't eat that much.'

'Then have a liquid lunch,' Jay said. 'This is my treat, Julie. I want to do it.'

'I can see that.' She paused. 'Don't forget about the birds in winter.'

Jay stopped the car in the car park. 'What?'

Julie was turned sideways in the passenger seat. 'It's what I always used to say to Chris, whenever he came up – which wasn't often, not after he'd left us. He'd start flashing his money about and I'd remind him about people who put food out for the birds. They don't think about how they'll not be living in their house for ever, and what happens to the birds who're relying on them when they're gone? They have to go back to pecking at the hard ground. It's nice, Jay, all this giving, but it's not really fair.'

Jay felt herself blushing. 'Perhaps there shouldn't have been a winter for you,' she said, slightly defensively.

'You don't have to put the food out in the garden of his house,' Julie said quietly. 'I knew Chris better than anybody, and he knew me as well. There's nothing to make amends for. You don't have to.'

'I know, I know,' Jay said. She closed her eyes briefly. 'I'm sorry, Julie. I'm not doing this very well.'

'That's OK,' Julie said. She opened her car door. 'Let's just go for a drink, shall we?'

Julie went up to the bar to order while Jay took a seat in a bay window. It occurred to her that Dex might have come to see Julie while he'd been living with her in London. He'd never mentioned it. Why had he kept his family so apart from his life? Why had Julie never come down to London, or been invited to gigs? Jay imagined Julie's children in her London flat; Kylie drawing at the breakfast bar in the kitchen, Melanie rosy and blooming in colourful infant clothes, scrabbling around on the rug with Early Learning Centre toys. Dex could have given his family so much, but had chosen not to. It seemed absurd, given that he was supposed to have been so fond of his sister, but perhaps she didn't know him as well as she thought she did.

Julie came back with gin and tonics. Jay thought of the groceries residing in the boot of her car. At least now Julie could probably afford these drinks. 'I think you're a bit scared,' Julie said.

Jay took a sip of gin, rolling the flavour round her mouth. 'Scared?'

'You weren't happy out there in the woods, were you?'

Jay twisted her mouth to one side. 'Not sure. It seemed close, that's all, almost claustrophobic. I'm a city girl, remember. The wilderness is a scary place to me.'

'No, you were afraid to open up.'

Jay leaned forward. 'What do you mean?'

Julie laughed, too loudly. 'Oh, I'm a bit weird sometimes,' she said. 'I feel things, but I s'pose most women can. I can always feel Chris around when I'm in the woods.'

'Yet you say he's not dead.' Jay paused briefly, then plunged on. 'How does he speak to you, Julie? Does it happen when you're in places like the wood?'

Julie shook her head. 'Not always. It can happen anywhere. We're so close, see. It's always been like this. If he took a tumble, I'd feel it, like a slap in the face.'

'You do realise what Dex was like before he disappeared, don't you?'

'A handful,' Julie said.

Jay laughed. 'Ye-ess, you could say that. Did you feel any of the things that happened to him then, like when he was angry or depressed?'

'I'd pick up a whiff of a mood now and again,' Julie said. 'I expect you had to cope with a lot.' She was edging away from the subject.

'Dex was never a problem for me,' Jay said. 'What does he say to you, Julie? What does he say now?'

'It's not words,' Julie said. 'Pictures more like, or feelings. He knows you're with me.'

Jay shivered. She could not doubt Julie's word. The atmosphere in the pub had become thick as fog. The diners and drinkers were like figures in a photograph. 'What else?' she murmured.

'Nothing,' Julie said. 'I'll need some time, Jay. You'll have to be patient.'

Jay switched to fruit juice, while Julie drank a couple more gins. 'The world we see is a puzzle,' she said, 'but there *is* more to everything than what we see.'

'Is there? In what way?'

'There are in-between places, you see.'

'In between?'

Julie nodded. 'Yes. Cracks, I call 'em.'

'And is Dex in one?'

'Yes,' said Julie. 'He is.'

Chapter Eight

Jay and Julie spent the rest of the afternoon driving around the town. After they'd visited The Ship so that Jay could settle her bill and collect her belongings, Julie directed her to Dex's old school, then to where his first gig had taken place, and after that a tour of where his friends had lived. Jay could not discern a sense of Dex in these places. The boy that existed within the pages of Julie's photo albums seemed unreal. Jay couldn't fix him into this world. It seemed strange. Finally, they crawled slowly past the drab house where Little Peter had lived. There were no pale faces between the curtains in the upstairs window.

Once the take-away Chinese meal had been consumed and the children put to bed, Jay opened the first bottle of wine. Julie thought it was too dry and, to sweeten its taste, added a generous measure of lemonade to her glass.

'I'm not a big drinker,' Julie said, adding meaningfully, 'not like you.'

Jay smiled. 'Oh, come on, you know all journalists are drinkers. It's part of the job.'

Julie shook her head. 'The ones that drink probably say that.'

Jay sat on the floor, feeling jumpy. She'd finished her first glass of wine before Julie had even got half-way through her diluted drink. Maybe she should cut back on her alcohol intake. But what the hell for? I should have gone home, she thought, and on impulse pulled her phone from her bag. As she suspected, there were plenty of messages from Gus, and a couple from Gina. She must have been mad to speak to Gus like that this morning. She'd pay; he'd make her pay. Perhaps she should phone him now, try to make amends. She could lie, say Julie had contacted her, and that was why she was here. Perhaps she should open the gin instead. 'Oh God!' said Jay, resting the back of her head on the sofa.

The two women sat in silence, with only the gas fire lisping between them. Julie drained her glass and sighed. 'Oh well, I might as well come clean.'

Jay raised her head, reached for the wine bottle. Cold liquid splashed over her hands.

'Chris came to see me three days before he disappeared,' Julie said.

Jay took a drink, could say nothing.

'He told me not to tell anyone, ever, and I haven't, but now, well, I s'pose you should know.'

'What did he say?'

Julie laughed. 'He was in a bad mood, all right. Hated the world and everything in it. I knew he was looking for a way out again. I recognised the signs. It was no surprise to me when he disappeared.'

'You know, don't you,' Jay said quietly. 'You know where he is.'

'No,' Julie answered. 'Only that it's no place you could get to. He never mentioned you, though I saw all the pictures in the papers afterwards. I just thought "poor cow". Didn't recognise you when you turned up here.'

Jay imagined Dex arriving at Julie's house; the car at the kerb, like hers was now. She saw him pacing round the kitchen, full of frenetic energy, unable to sit down. Julie would be at the table, making tea, the kids around her. What had been going through his mind? Would he have told Julie the truth? Jay could not help but feel wounded that he'd made no mention of her. Perhaps, by then, she had already stopped existing for him, as he'd made the decision to leave her and his life behind. But what had he said? Julie offered fragments, like scratched and defaced paintings from the wall of an ancient tomb. Many stories might fit the marks: Dex was ill and unstable and had run away; he'd been afraid of something, or sick of something, or maybe just tired of the life he had made. Maybe it had been something to do

111

with the past, some uncleansed, emotional wound festering away beneath the gloss of fame and wealth. Perhaps he'd had something to run *to*, rather than away from: a person, or a place, or a dream. Julie's memory was imperfect, perhaps because at the time she hadn't imagined she'd never see her brother again. A hope might have fountained within her: Dex had cast off his life in order to spend more time with his family. Had he intimated this? Julie became agitated by Jay's constant questioning. 'He was unhappy, bothered,' she said, 'that's all. Something wasn't going right for him. I thought maybe he'd had enough of all the stupid people he must have to deal with.'

'Is that me you're talking about?' Jay asked. She had finished one bottle of wine herself.

'He walked out on you,' Julie said acidly. 'Maybe you were part of it. You never reached him.'

'Who did?' Jay argued. 'I did everything I could. I treated him like a real person.'

Jay didn't know why she was arguing. Julie was right; most of the people both she and Dex had had to deal with were stupid, or shallow, or selfish and greedy. The industry attracted types like that. None of it was real. Hadn't she said that herself to Jez only a short time ago? She put her fingers against her temples. 'I thought we had a good life, Julie. It was such a shock to me. I'm not like the others. I'm not.' Drink talking. She should stop. But it seemed that only a small, sober part of herself was aware of that. A greater, emotional part spoke with the voice of the wine. There were tears on her face now, broken sentences spilling from her mouth. It had come back; all of it. The pain, the bewilderment, the senseless questions, the frail blue flame of hope deep within.

Julie got down on the carpet and wrapped her arms round Jay's shoulders. She smelled of wine and tobacco. 'I'm sorry, love. Here, come on, don't get upset.' Jay, swimming in maudlin gloom, leaned against her, sobbing. Then Julie's body stiffened against her.

Jay instinctively pulled away. 'What is it?'

112

There was silence, but for the purr of the gas jets. Was Dex there? Julie was staring at the closed door.

'What?' Jay asked again in a low, desperate voice.

Julie turned back. 'You'll know one day,' she said.

'Know what?'

'He'll let you know what happened.'

'How will he do that?'

Julie screwed up her face, shook her head. 'You'll just know, that's all.'

'How? Julie, please. Tell me. Please.'

Their voices seemed to have broken the atmosphere. The room was breathing again.

'Chris just told me,' Julie said.

The next day was sunny, but the air seemed hard in the brightness. After dropping Kylie off at school, the two women drove north out of the town, Julie with her baby on her knee – she could not ask Marie a baby-sitting favour twice in one week. The noises emitted by Melanie made Jay grit her teeth, but she hoped that this time, Julie would not be opaque, that she'd really reveal something tangible about Dex.

While Julie chaperoned Kylie to the school gate, Jay had sat waiting in her car. She phoned Gus. And lied. Even lies weren't enough. She was tired of his whining, carping tone after only a minute. Why should she put up with this? Why not simply break the connection, but she listened, making sounds of denial and placation. She let him rant, then said, 'I'll be back later. Don't be angry, Gus. I had to do this.'

Julie had got back into the car at the tail-end of the conversation. Jay threw the phone into the back of the car. 'God, why do we put up with it?' She banged her hands against the steering wheel.

'Boyfriend being off again?'

Jay made a low, growling noise. 'It's that bloody attitude I can't stand. Snotty. Condescending. That's what it is. Like he's so fucking faultless!'

'There's not a man on this earth doesn't act like that,' Julie said. 'Sod 'im.'

Jay nodded and started the car. 'Yeah.' She managed a smile. 'Today, he doesn't exist.'

She wished she could mean that.

As they drove off, Jay felt anxious. Gus was angry. He was so angry he said to her he might not be there when she got home. She knew this was unlikely. In a way, she'd have preferred his absence. What she dreaded were the sulks and interrogations on her return.

The north road skirted the edge of the heath. Further away from the houses, the landscape seemed more natural. Jay sensed it would not be so littered with the careless detritus of humanity; cans and bottles and discarded wrappers. They pulled on to a narrow, twisting track between high hedges, which expelled them into a flat area strewn with gravel, where people could park their cars. Hills rose softly all around, their contours mellowed by age. The parking area was surrounded by oaks, beech and ash, with paths going off in all directions, their entrances blocked by wooden beams on posts to prevent anyone driving up them. In among the older deciduous trees, pine trees seethed up the hillsides.

Julie indicated where Jay should park the car, at the edge of the trees. Only one other car was there; a woman was unloading a brace of tawny Labradors from the hatch-back. Once Jay was free of the heated interior of the vehicle, the air was crisp and biting. It was scented by pine oil and loam; it seemed alive. Jay's jacket would not keep her warm here. They unloaded the push-chair from the boot and secured Melanie into it. The woman with the dogs had already disappeared up the flank of one of the hills; Jay could hear her high, fluting voice calling to her pets. Julie led the way down one of the paths, pushing Melanie ahead of her. A network of narrow streams plaited through the undergrowth to either side, almost concealed by tangled naked blackberry briar. Their path was straight, it did not rise to one of the hills. Jay followed, wondering what mystical experience Julie had in mind for her today.

They walked down the path for a hundred yards or so, then came upon the wide pool of a natural spring, cradled in a grove

114

of oaks that was surrounded by the dour spears of sentinel pines. The spring had been concreted around the edge, but Julie said that at one time there had just been mud and grass and water; torrential in the spring, fading away to a memory of a stream by mid-summer, but back again in winter. The branches of the oaks enclosed the area, protecting it. It was not oppressive, but somehow soothing. Jay was surprised by the clarity of the water in the pool. Julie said it was drinkable, but Jay shrank from trying it. In such a place, knights would have been offered enchanted swords by mysterious pale arms that sliced without a ripple through the surface of the pool.

The women fought their way through a tangle of sodden dead bracken amid the fir trees. By this time, Julie had hoisted Melanie on to her hip, and Jay carried the folded push-chair. After ten minutes or so, they came upon another oak grove, where the trees shouldered together closely. These trees were more squat than the noble forest lords around the pool. They were like dwarves, their roots rippling over the soil in knotted cables. The grove was situated in a hollow that Julie explained was dusty in summer and a quagmire in wetter seasons. This was Dex's place, his secret den. He hadn't even taken Little Peter there. Only Julie knew about it. It had been his hiding place, and she'd always been able to find him there when he'd gone missing after trouble at home. The trees were bare now, their ancient barks ragged. Some had had their insides gouged out by age and parasites. The spreading roots humped like giant arthritic toes from the damp earth, as if intent on tripping and obstructing invading humans. Here, the air smelled riper, more loamy.

Jay hugged herself as she looked around. Julie stood with firmly planted legs, the baby drooling at her hip, clearly allowing Jay to get a feel of the place, perhaps hoping some deep-seated intuition would be aroused. Could there be a sense of Dex here? Jay was almost afraid to imagine it.

'Did he come here, Julie, last time he visited you?'

Julie shrugged. 'All I know is that there's something here for you,' she said.

Jay went up to one of the trees and touched its heavily furrowed bark. She realised she felt slightly light-headed again, as she had at the beech grove Julie had taken her to the day before. 'What's here for me? A message, a feeling, or a thing?'

Julie pulled a face. 'No idea. Just something. We'll have to look.'

Jay kicked at the brown rotting leaves beneath her feet. 'Where to start?'

Julie had unfolded Melanie's chair once more and now strapped the baby into it. 'Looks like you already have,' she said.

Together, the women turned over the mulchy carpet of leaves with their toes, then their hands. They felt among the geriatric roots, put their fingers into damp, fungal crevices in the tree trunks. Nothing. The trees bowed to the earth. They were easy to climb, with wide laps where the branches splayed. Jay clambered upwards, swinging from tree to tree above the ground. Melanie reached towards her with starfish hands, uttering animal cries.

Julie's face was pale and expressionless below. 'Go on, girl, go on.'

Jay's arms ached, her legs were trembling. She climbed up to a place where a flaking limb bulged in an unnatural way. She reached for it, hauling herself higher and found there a metal box, wedged into an old swollen wound in the bark. Once her hands fell upon it, she felt dizzy. How had she climbed this far? How would she get back down? 'There's a box here!' she called to Julie.

'Get it!'

'I can't. It's stuck.' She didn't want to exert too much force for fear of overbalancing. The ground looked very far away, but probably wasn't. If she fell the mulch would cushion her, maybe. Jay tugged at the rusting artefact. Could Dex have put it here? It seemed to have become part of the tree, to have been lodged there for longer than three years. Clawing at the bark, she tried to pull the ancient fibre away. Fragments fell down. Julie dodged away from them, laughing. Eventually, a huge

116

corky mass broke off in Jay's fingers and the box plummeted down to the floor of the grove. Julie just looked at it.

Jay rested her face against the branch. She was lying along it and dared not look down. She was trembling now, afraid to move. Only with her eyes shut was she able to obey Julie's coaxing instructions on how to reverse along the branch. 'You're nearly there, keep going.'

She came to rest in the throat of the tree, surrounded by thick spreading branches. She felt safe there, caged.

'It's not that far,' Julie said. 'Jump, I'll catch you.'

Jay drew her knees up to her forehead and wrapped her arms around them. She felt so tired. 'In a minute.' It was like being drunk, hanging over the toilet basin, waiting for the terrible nausea to pass so that she could make it back to the bedroom. 'Just leave me.' Crows were calling, rising and falling high above in ragged patterns. The trees seemed to have a sentience that pressed down on her in oppressive waves. She might never move again. Jay took deep breaths, and raised her head. It felt so heavy. The sky was white through the bare branches, dancing with black motes. She would just let herself fall.

It was only a few feet. Julie caught her as promised. 'Thought you were doing a swan dive there!' She pulled twigs from Jay's hair. 'Are you all right, love? Scared of heights?'

Jay nodded and sank to the ground, to lean against the rough bark. She felt very strange. Julie handed the box to her. She held it in her hands, turned it over a few times. 'It's locked, corroded.'

Julie handed her a stone. Jay beat at the old metal until the lid broke free. Now she would know. Now.

The box was nearly empty, but for a DAT box and a curled photograph. There were no pages ripped from a diary, no documents, no letters of explanation. Jay took out the DAT box. This must be the missing tape. No. The box was empty. She threw it aside and lifted out the photograph. Dex's face swam up into her eyes. He was standing in typical moody pose on the lawn of a large house. There were a few people behind him, out of focus. One of them could have been Zeke

117

Michaels, but Jay couldn't be positive. Dex was wearing a T-shirt Jay had bought for him. Whenever this photo had been taken, it had been during his relationship with Jay. It reminded her of the picture in the Sakrilege offices' reception, but there were many photos like that. A lot of music people had big houses and she couldn't remember enough details to be able to tell if this was the same one as in the Sakrilege picture.

Her vision boiled with bright specks. She bowed her head.

'What is it, love?' Julie's arm was firm against her back.

'There's nothing.' Jay looked up, blinking. 'What's this supposed to mean? Was the tape here? Has someone else taken it?'

Julie frowned, shrugged. 'Don't know. He didn't say anything to me about a tape.'

'And this picture.' Jay waved it in front of Julie's face.

Julie took it. 'Do you know these people?'

'I might do. That type all look the same – like big, greedy animals.' Jay sighed, taking the photograph back. 'The picture isn't that clear. Why did Dex leave it here? Did he say anything about it to you?'

Julie shook her head. 'No. I'm not sure he came here last time he visited. He didn't mention it.'

'He must've done.' Jay struggled to her feet. 'Think, Julie. What about all these "messages" you say you're getting from Dex. What are they, what's their point? Can we really learn anything from them?'

Julie looked defensive. 'You don't understand.'

'Then explain, *please*. I'd really like to know.'

Julie wiped one hand over her face, Melanie squirming against her. 'I can't. I haven't got the words. Maybe the words don't exist.'

'Talk to him now. Ask him what's going on!'

'It doesn't work like that.'

'Then how does it work?'

Julie shook her head. 'It's no good, Jay. You'll have to be patient. If I feel anything over the next few days, I'll try and let you know.'

Jay sighed. 'Yeah, right.' She gazed up through the bare branches, amazed that only minutes before she'd been up there among them. Julie took the photograph from her limp hands and Jay watched her scrutinise it.

'Do you think Dex might be at this place?' Jay asked. 'Is that the clue?'

Julie shrugged. 'It says something about him, must do. What does he want us to know?'

'Ask him,' Jay snapped, then in a softer voice, 'next time you can.'

Chapter Nine

The flat had a sullen, brooding atmosphere, as if Gus had left a sour aroma of his bitterness behind. The place was in disarray, the air sweetly stale, the curtains drawn. Jay put her bags down on one of the chairs and stood there for a moment, hardly daring to breathe. Was Gus somewhere in the flat? Would he come slouching out from a corner soon to rant and accuse? All she could hear was the distant sound of traffic, the call of a child in the street. Presently, she relaxed enough to take off her coat and began to tidy up.

After Jay had found the box, she and Julie had returned home in silence. Jay had wondered whether Dex had left the photo deliberately for her to find. He was wearing the T-shirt she'd bought him – was that a message to show he understood and appreciated what she had felt for him? Or maybe the photo hadn't been for her at all, but had been left simply as a bitter message to whoever found it. That time, when he'd known fame and success, had been ephemeral. It was just images and memories now, curling at the edges.

Jay had given Julie her phone numbers, and in return Julie wrote down Marie's number, in case Jay should want to get in touch with her urgently. Jay had asked if she could keep the photograph they'd found, and Julie had agreed. The two women had achieved a comfortable understanding. They were so different, yet linked.

At the doorstep, they'd hugged. 'Don't take any shit,' Julie had said.

Jay had smiled wanly. 'I won't.'

Now that she was home, Jay knew she'd have to call Gina soon, and prepare herself for Gus' homecoming. There were features waiting to be finished, apologetic e-mails to be sent. Work to do.

Gus did not turn up, and Jay shrank from calling him on his mobile. This was ridiculous. It was her partner she was thinking about. Only a few days ago, their relationship had seemed OK. How could it reach this disintegrated state so quickly? And over what? Her own obsession with the past, or Gus'? They should stop this, stop it now, before it got any worse. Steeling herself, she dialled his number, only to find he had his answer service switched on. Jay left a bright, cheerful message and said she was looking forward to seeing him. 'Hurry home,' she said, inflecting her voice with a throaty purr. She spent the rest of the day working, making calls to arrange new interviews and browsing through half-finished features on her computer, making the odd change.

Gus turned up around nine o'clock, and by this time, Jay had hurried round the corner to the 24-hour supermarket and stocked up on Gus' favourite snack food; guacamole, poppy seed crackers, blue cheese. She'd cooked a creamy casserole of chicken, leeks and garlic and the flat, now tidy, was lit by soft lighting, aromas floating through in silky strands from the kitchen. When Gus walked through the door, she thought he could have been under no doubt that what he walked into was a home. Jay herself now felt wholly composed, and had pushed all recollections of the past couple of days from her mind. She had decided she wanted her life back, the life she had built and found comfort in. For a moment, she and Gus regarded each other warily, then he smiled and went to give her a hug. 'Smells great.'

She kissed him. 'It's nearly ready.' She paused and said, 'I've missed you.' She wanted to believe it, even though it wasn't true. She hadn't missed him at all. She was simply afraid of the consequences of not missing him.

While they ate, Gus was controlled enough not to mention her own brief disappearance. They chatted about his work, and Jay listened with unfeigned interest as he regaled her with odd snippets of gossip he'd picked up while she was away.

They drank brandy after the dessert, and then a thread of tension came into the atmosphere. Now, he would speak his mind. Jay sipped her fiery liquor nervously. She lit a cigarette.

121

'Jay . . .' He held his breath, turned his brandy glass in his hands. 'We need to talk about what you did.'

She tried to ignore the unsettling thump of her heart. 'I know. I shouldn't have taken off like that.'

'There must have been something you needed to get out of your system. The question is: did you?'

She shrugged awkwardly, her eyes skittering away from his gaze. 'Perhaps you're right in what you say. Certain things have happened recently to remind me of the past, and – you must believe this – part of my interest was just professional. There's a story, Gus, and I wanted to discover it.'

'Why now?'

Again, a shrug. 'Not sure. I just had to. There's nothing to get out of my system, and that's the truth.'

'But you jeopardised *us*, Jay. Some men wouldn't be as tolerant of it as I am. I appreciate you have to face the things inside yourself and work them out, but remember you have responsibilities. It's for your own good as much as mine.'

He's talked to someone, she thought. These are not his words. He's too calm. He must have gone ranting and raving to someone – and it was probably a woman – and they had filled him full of crap. 'I went up north and stayed with a woman called Julie, who was Dex's . . .'

Gus raised his hands, his face screwed up into an expression of wounded, yet noble sentiment. 'Please, don't tell me about it. I don't want to know. I don't want any names mentioned. All I need to know is that it's over now. You did what you had to do and now it's finished.'

'Yes, it's finished.' She wasn't sure if that was true, but if Gus carried on in that tone, she would get angry. Sanctimonious shit! How dare he speak to her like that?

He reached out for her hands, and it took all of her will not to pull away. She had convinced herself she'd been glad to see him, but now the thought of touching him infuriated her. She pasted a smile across her face.

'Let's just forget it ever happened,' he said. 'I'm going away soon, so we shouldn't argue.'

'You're right.' It was like being in a film; the soft lighting, the forced conversation with its sticking-plaster sentiments. Who had he talked to?

'That Michaels shit kept calling you while you were away,' Gus remarked.

Jay found it easy to mimic his grimace. 'Oh God, what does he want now?'

'Wouldn't say – to me. You should ignore it.'

Jay nodded, took a sip of brandy. 'Yeah. I will.'

That night, when they went to bed, she continued to play her part. She felt distanced from what was happening, because to be otherwise would make her push Gus from her in disgust. She was a shade on the ceiling, looking down. She did not like what she saw.

The following day, Jay completed two features and mailed them off. She contacted everyone she had put off contacting, and called Gina.

'What *have* you been up to?' Gina demanded, laughter in her voice.

'I went to see Dex's sister,' Jay explained. 'It was a strange couple of days.'

'Yes, Gus told us.'

'Oh, you've seen him?'

'Yeah. He came round one night while you were away. He was pretty upset, but Dan and I managed to cool him down.'

Jay felt cold. 'I wondered who the other woman was.'

'Sorry?'

'Well, I guessed he talked to someone, because he came out with a load of stuff last night he wouldn't have thought up himself. So it was you.'

'You sound pissed off. Why?' Gina's voice had become harder. She did not like to be criticised.

'Yeah, I am pissed off, actually. I don't expect my best friend to psychoanalyse me with my insecure boyfriend.'

'Hey, hang on a minute . . .'

Jay scraped a hand through her hair. It could happen again now: another row. She mustn't let it. 'Oh, sorry, Ginny.

Ignore me. I just had a bit of an ear-bending from Gus, and it was too patronising for words. I don't blame you. Of course you should talk to him. We're all friends.' She was surprised though that Gus had contacted Gina himself, because previously he'd made it clear, in a subtle manner, that he didn't much care for her. And Dan was one of Dex's old musicians. Normally, Gus would avoid him. It was all moves in a silly game. 'How about we go for a drink later?'

Gina sounded hesitant. 'OK. Are you all right, Jay?'

'Yeah, I'm fine. We'll talk later.'

Jay got back to work. She heard the phone ring and decided not to answer it, being in the middle of constructing a perfect sentence. She heard the answerphone come on, and presently Zeke Michaels' tense voice saying, 'I'm calling for Jay. Please get her to call me.'

Jay's hands froze above her keyboard. It occurred to her that if Gus had spoken to Michaels, he might have let slip where she'd been. That might be seen as evidence against her. Michaels might believe she'd gone north to meet Dex. She shook her head and pushed the thought from her mind. *Leave it, leave it*, she told herself, typing fast.

When Gus put his head round the door to her tiny work-room, Jay found the first thought in her head was to question him about what he'd said to Michaels, but checked herself in time. Reopening that subject would only cause an atmosphere, if not another row.

'Busy?' he asked her.

She nodded. 'Yeah. Lot to catch up on.'

'Well, if you will go haring off . . .'

Can't resist a snipe, can you? She smiled. 'This is true.'

'Michaels bothered you yet?'

'He called, but I left the machine on.'

'I got us a video and some fine Zinfandel to drink tonight.'

Jay turned to him, her face set into an expression of dis-appointment. 'Oh, Gus, I'm going out.'

'Oh? Where?'

'Meeting Gina, but I don't have to be late back.'

'You don't have to, no.' He left the room.

Jay's fingers were tapping against the edge of her keyboard. She'd been unaware of starting the movement. *Let it all go back to normal, please.* She let her left thumb rest against the Return key, watching the paragraph marks scroll down the empty screen.

Apart from the constant calls from Zeke Michaels, the next few days passed smoothly. Jay's muse was with her, and she sped through all her outstanding work. She interviewed a visiting American rock goddess, Devon Klein, in the Savoy, in preparation for a main feature in *Track* magazine. The couple of days she'd spent with Julie seemed unreal now, as if she'd only dreamed them, or watched them happening to someone else. All that talk of Dex speaking to his sister had to be delusional. Jay had allowed herself to be swept up into it, to share that madness.

The evening with Gina was fairly successful; the main evidence of strain being that they parted company quite early before the pub closed. Jay told her hardly anything about what had happened in Torton, concentrating on describing the estate, and the appearance of Dex's sister. She felt disloyal doing this, laughing with Gina at Julie's expense, but the gossip filled any silences, made it seem as if the conversation was flowing naturally.

Jay was surprised that Gina didn't chastise her for her behaviour. Only a short time before, she'd advised forgetting all about Dex. Now, it seemed the opposite was true.

'Did you see him?' Gina fired at her, grinning wickedly.

'Of course not! Don't you think I'd have told you?'

Gina shrugged. 'He might not want people to know.'

'God, you sound like Zeke Michaels! Sakrilege think I'm in contact with Dex, but I'm not.'

'So what are you going to do about it all now?'

Jay frowned. 'Nothing. There's nothing I can or want to do. It was interesting meeting Julie, and perhaps helped me put things in perspective, but that's an end to it.' She realised then she was afraid. Her life was too comfortable. Now she was back in it, she didn't want it to change. Absurdly, she felt that

Gina didn't think she was telling the truth. Perhaps Gus had poisoned her with his paranoiac jealousy. She tried to steer the conversation back to congenial topics, and Gina played along, but there was something different in the atmosphere. It hung between them; unspoken words. Gina didn't argue when Jay finished her drink and said she had to hurry home.

Gus was gratified Jay came home before eleven, which helped improve relations between them. Perhaps everything was going to be all right. Jay sent Julie a card, thanking her for her hospitality. Now, she wondered whether she'd ever see the woman again. She couldn't imagine how.

On the Friday evening following her return from Torton, Jay went out to buy some wine. Gus was away now, but she did not feel ill at ease in the flat. Michaels hadn't called her for two days; she presumed he'd given up and the whole matter was at rest.

The supermarket was nearly empty, and Jay browsed among the well-stocked shelves, deliberating over which bottles to buy. The shop was brightly lit, but there were only a few other customers.

Jay had lived in the city too long not to be aware immediately when someone was watching her. Without turning her head, or appearing alert, she managed to glimpse a tall figure in the corner of her vision. It was clearly a man; still and watchful. Her brain made quick judgements. She knew it was possible to be attacked by deranged people, even in public. Even though she did not risk looking directly at the man, she could tell there was something wild and unkempt about him. With apparent nonchalance, she began to move slowly towards the till at the front of the shop, where she would alert the staff to the possible danger. Her back crawled as she walked, but she was still surprised when a hand grabbed hold of her arm from behind. Her first reaction was anger. Feeling no fear, she wheeled on her assailant, hissing, 'Fuck off, creep!'

The eyes met hers, clear and vivid in an otherwise unshaven, grubby face. Cold rushed through her body like a drug. 'Dex?' she said.

Chapter Ten

He was there in front of her, real and incontrovertible. He looked as if he'd been sleeping rough. She was filled with relief, horror and the conflicting desires to flee and stay.

'Outside,' he said, dragging her with him.

He led her past the curious cashiers by the door. They made no move to ask if she was all right, and seemed to think it was perfectly normal for someone who looked like a tramp to drag her out into the street. All the time, Jay was asking Dex frantic questions. She had no control over them, and later would not even remember what they'd been. She might as well have been asking him the time. He answered none of her anxious queries.

Outside, he pushed her into a dark side alley that was almost filled with straining black bags of rubbish. For a brief moment she wondered whether he intended her harm. This couldn't be happening. His strange beauty, even beneath the dirt, was electric. Seeing him was like looking into a mirror of truth, he was herself, an invisible part of her in flesh. Had she felt this way about him when they'd been together? Surely not.

'Dex, Dex,' she said. She wanted to hold him, but couldn't. It was as if this wasn't really him.

He reached out as if to touch her hair or her face, then curled his hand into a fist by his side. 'Jay, you must leave it,' he said slowly, as if the words were coming from some sealed, but leaking, part of himself. 'Do you understand? Don't touch it.'

'What?' She shook her head. 'Where have you been. Why didn't you . . . ?'

He put long, dirty fingers against her lips. She could smell earth on him, as if he'd been scratching at soil. He wore a long coat that was too large for him. It reeked of damp places. But for his eyes, he might be a corpse that had clawed its way to the light. 'No, no. Listen. You must let it all lie. Keep safe. Keep your life.' His voice was bitter.

'Did Julie tell you I'd been to see her? You've kept in touch with her, haven't you? Why did you leave me, Dex? Why shut me out and not her?'

He closed his eyes, veiling their light. This was not the man she had met at a party all those years ago. This was some iconic form of him, like a spirit. She was conversing with an image she'd invented, or had been invented by others. 'I won't explain,' he said.

Not 'can't', or even a suggestion she wouldn't understand; just plain refusal.

'Have you been on the street?'

He looked away from her, staring into some distant place. 'No.'

'You look like you have.'

'I've come a long way to see you. Jay, you have to get out of the city for a while. Do something else. Don't let Sakrilege near you.'

'Someone's told Michaels they've seen us together. Sakrilege think we're in contact.'

'They would.'

'And now we are.'

He shook his head vehemently. 'We're not. I just had to see you, warn you.'

'What happened, Dex, what's going on? Why did you have to run away? Maybe I can help. Talk to me.'

'No! You forgot about me, didn't you?' There was a shade of bitterness in his voice. He shook his head, eyes closed. 'No, that was the best thing you did.' He opened his eyes to stare at her again. 'I didn't want to have to come here, Jay, but knew I should. You found the box.'

'There was nothing in it. Just an empty tape box and a photo. If these are clues, they tell me nothing. But they make me want to know more. I'm a journalist, Dex. What else do you expect?'

He smiled. 'Oh, Jay, you don't want to know. You've told yourself you don't want to know. Why lie to me now? I'm not

128

warning you because of anything you'll do, but what others might think you'll do. You are right to forget the past. There's nothing there that's worth remembering. And those who try to bring the past into the present are in danger of making it the future.'

'Why must I leave the city? What will happen if I don't?'

Again, he looked away from her. 'Someone thought they saw us together, and perhaps they did. That's the trouble.'

'That makes no sense, and it's not an answer.'

'You can never know, because you're not the same kind of person I am.'

It was like trying to communicate with a holographic image, programmed only to say certain things. His words too were ambiguous. She knew that essentially they were not communicating. 'Are you alive, Dex?'

He looked at her steadily for a moment. 'In a way. It's always been like that.' People might think his angst was merely arrogant posturing, the behaviour of a spoiled media brat, but it wasn't. It riddled him like cancer. There were others like him, she knew. There always would be; gobbled up and sucked dry by the industry that was the only channel they had to communicate their dreams to the people. Sad shamans. 'What have we come to?' she said.

'Will you leave the city?'

'I'm not sure.' She shrugged. 'I don't know if I can.'

He sighed deeply. 'Try to.' He backed away from her and she realised he was about to leave.

'You're going to vanish again, aren't you.'

He raised a hand. 'Think about what I've said. It's serious, Jay.'

'You can't!' She grabbed hold of his coat, tried to pull him towards her, but he wriggled away from her as if she was only holding air. He was running away from her like a hunted creature. She tried to call his name, but it came out as a wordless shout of grief.

Numbly, she went back into the shop and picked two bottles of red wine at random off the shelf. The assistants at the till eyed her with suspicion and some amusement. When she signed the credit card slip, the signature didn't look like her own.

Outside, she wondered whether she really had just seen Dex or whether it had been some bizarre hallucination. Maybe the shop assistants had seen her marching out of the place on her own, babbling at thin air. She shuddered, increased her pace. Now, the darkness seemed threatening. She wondered whether she should call Gina and ask her to come over. Could she possibly tell her what had just happened?

Ahead, she could see the lights of her living-room through the front window. She was nearly home. It seemed so far. At last, she was at the steps to the door. Relieved, she delved in her jacket pocket for her keys.

Before she reached the top of the steps, the headlights of a car parked by the kerb came on, dazzling her with full beam. Idiots, she thought, but then the car doors were opening, and men were getting out. Jay ran up the last couple of steps, only to hear Zeke Michaels' voice calling, 'Jay, have you been avoiding me?'

She turned to face him, sure that her expression must betray what had just occurred. He stood below her, his hands thrust into the pockets of his flying jacket. 'I've been busy, Zeke. What is it?'

'I'd like to come in and talk to you. Just a couple of minutes, that's all.'

Jay had her key in her hand. She eyed the two other wide-shouldered men standing by Michaels. Could she just open her door and run inside? She made only a small movement towards the lock, but one of the men leapt up the steps and closed a gigantic fist over her hand. He didn't hurt her. He looked as if he had the strength of a lion, but clearly didn't need to exert it yet. Michaels advanced towards her. 'What have you been up to, Jay? You *are* avoiding me, aren't you?'

She was afraid. There was no doubt. More afraid than she'd ever been. It could be no coincidence Michaels was here now. He might even have seen her with Dex down the road. 'Come in, then. Make yourself at home!' She marched ahead of them into the hallway, and one of the lion men gently closed the door behind them.

In her flat, she struck a defiant pose, managed to keep her voice steady, and said, 'This is threatening behaviour. What do you want?' She walked purposefully to the drawer where she kept a corkscrew – one of many in the flat. She turned her back on Michaels, to prove her courage and hopefully, through that, her innocence. Her heart was beating so fast she could hardly breathe. She willed herself to take deep breaths, tried to calm herself.

Michaels laughed, but sounded slightly nervous. This wasn't his style, she knew that. Someone else must have sent him here. 'Oh, Jay, why play this game? It would be so much simpler, much less trouble, if you'd just level with me.'

'Over what?' She busied herself opening wine. 'I think it's about time you told me what's going on.'

Michaels sighed theatrically. 'Where have you been these last few days?'

'Here in the flat, actually, although it's none of your fucking business. You're here about Dex, of course. Who's seen me with him now?' She couldn't look at him, didn't dare, but it might not seem suspicious: she was concentrating on pouring the wine. 'This is all really pathetic. What are you playing at?' Steeled, she dared to turn around, the glass held near her face. She raised an eyebrow at him.

'You've been up north.'

'Yes, last week. That's no secret.'

'You visited Dex's sister.'

She shrugged insouciantly. 'Yes. What's so unusual about that? I was his partner once, Zeke.'

'Gus didn't seem very happy about it.'

'Well, he wouldn't be, would he. In Gus' perfect world, I would never have known Dex.' She sighed, swapped her wine glass to the other hand. 'Oh, for God's sake, Zeke, drop this cloak and dagger stuff. What are you going to do? Trash the flat?' She sneered at the expressionless men standing behind him. Her outrage held her fear by the throat, but she wasn't sure how long it could maintain the grip.

Zeke Michaels' shoulders were hunched towards his ears, his hands still thrust deep into the pockets of his jacket. 'We've received some more information. We know you went north to meet with Dex. He gave you something, didn't he?'

Jay rolled her eyes. 'No! I didn't see Dex up north. Check with his sister, she'll tell you.'

'An undoubtedly reliable source,' Michaels said sarcastically.

'If you have these ideas fixed in your head, how can I change your mind?' Jay asked angrily. 'I'm wasting my time. You'll believe what you want to believe. Search the place if you want. There's nothing here.'

Michaels pointed at her with a rigid finger. 'I don't know what you and Dex are planning, but we're on to you, don't worry about that. If you've got any sense, you'll drop it. Why fight his battle for him? You've got a good life now, Jay. Don't jeopardise it.'

'And what's that supposed to mean?' she asked archly.

'So much of our lives depends on the goodwill of others,' he answered and turned for the door, allowing himself a meaningful pause and a final remark. 'Think how much you have to lose.' They left the door open behind them.

Once they'd gone, Jay allowed the feelings of panic to flood through her. She gulped two glasses of wine in quick succession. Gus, stupid bastard! He'd told Michaels where she'd gone last week. Row or not, she'd have to confront him about this. His petty jealousy had put her in a difficult and, it seemed, potentially dangerous, position. After a few minutes of staring blankly at the wall, she gathered her senses and called Julie's neighbour. Marie seemed far from happy about the disturbance this late at night, but Jay insisted it was urgent. It took Marie over ten minutes to get Julie to the phone.

'I've seen him!' Jay blurted. She felt shaken now and close to tears.

'What? When?' Julie sounded shocked, perhaps believing Dex reserved all his peculiar communications for her.

'Just. Minutes ago. God, Julie, what's happening? He told me to get out of London. Why? Then I have a surprise visit from some record company people, acting like heavies from a spy novel. This is too weird!'

'Just calm down, and tell me everything,' Julie said. Jay could hear her lighting a cigarette at the other end of the phone.

Jay related what had happened in a flat, professional way. She felt better then, more focused. 'What do you think?' she asked.

Julie paused, exhaled, then said, 'I'd do what Chris said, if I were you.'

'What? Walk out of my life like he did? I can't do that, Julie. I have responsibilities, commitment, a life. I don't *want* to do that.'

'He thinks you're in danger, though. And look what happened after you saw him. I don't think you should ignore that. I think you should come back here.'

'That wouldn't be a good idea,' Jay answered. 'Michaels knew I'd been to see you last week. He'd probably follow me up to Torton, and it wouldn't be fair on you or the kids if there was some kind of scene.' She paused. 'Has Dex been to see you too, Julie?'

Her answer sounded defensive. 'You know how it is with us.'

'I'm not talking about that,' Jay said gently. 'Has he visited you in person?'

'No. I didn't think he'd be able to.'

'Why not?'

'Because of where he is – that place.'

'What place?'

'I don't know. I really don't. I just get images, and they're very vague.'

Jay considered for a moment, then said, 'Let's think about the photo we found. It's all we have to go on. It *must* be linked to where Dex is now.'

'I don't know about that. It could mean lots of things. I've not picked anything up about that.' Julie paused. 'Look, think about what Chris said. Call me if you need to.'

'Thanks, Julie. I'll let you know what happens.'

'Take care of yourself. Don't drink too much.'

When she'd put down the phone, Jay realised the conversation had both warmed and comforted her. Picking up her wine glass, she went to sit on the sofa. The photo was still in her bag. She took it out and put it on the seat beside her. Could it be Rhys Lorrance's country house? Was Dex there? In which case, why was Michaels looking for him? Was there a rift between Lorrance and Sakrilege? There were too many unanswered questions.

Jay's first instinct in times of trouble was usually to get on the phone to Gina, but for some reason she shied from doing that. She wasn't sure she could cope with Gina's reaction, her often abrasive way of dealing with things. She could imagine Gina saying something like, 'Well, you were stupid to have visited Dex's sister, weren't you? Think how that looks. It's just made trouble for you.' There was no way Jay felt capable of telling Gina she'd actually seen Dex. *Thought* she'd seen Dex. She still wondered if she'd imagined it somehow. But someone, somewhere kept telling Zeke Michaels she had been seeing Dex. Who and why? It didn't make sense, and there seemed to be an undercurrent of malicious intent to it. Someone wanting to make trouble for her. Now she was getting paranoid. Should she leave town?

Seeing Dex had rekindled old feelings, despite her determination to remain objective. She found herself imagining conversations they might have in which she could purge her anger at his betrayal and disappearance. She'd buried her love for him, stuffed it down into a tight corner of her heart, but she hadn't destroyed it. For three years she'd ignored it, denied its existence, and now it was free again. In her mind, she relived the moments of their meeting in the supermarket, trying to recall every detail, every nuance of his expression. His appearance had frightened and confused her, but despite this she was conscious of feeling euphoric and elated.

That night, she dreamed of taking photographs of Dex in front of a big white house, but none of them would go right. Whenever she looked through the view-finder, Dex was out of focus, and when she tried to correct it, he disappeared completely.

Chapter Eleven

Gus came home the following afternoon. Jay spent the whole morning trying to compose herself. She toyed with the idea of telling him everything. Surely, his instinct would be to protect and help her, rather than fly into a temper about her seeing Dex? She had no idea whether Michaels would really try to damage her or her life in some way. His words could just be empty threats, but there was a secret, and it involved Dex, and therefore, perhaps without her knowing it, might involve her too. She tried to recall Dex's behaviour just before his disappearance. Did some clue lurk unrecognised in her memory?

At two-thirty, Jay heard a key in the door. She tensed.

Gus came into the living-room and put his bags down on the floor. His face looked odd, and the minute she saw him, Jay felt anxious. She knew, even before he spoke, that he was about to say something terrible. He stared at her for a few moments, then sighed and rubbed his neck. 'You're here,' he said.

'Of course I am,' she answered. 'What's the matter, Gus? You look awful.'

'How dare you,' he said in a mocking tone. 'How dare you just sit there and think you can get away with it.'

She blinked at him. 'What? Get away with what?'

He shook his head. 'You make me sick. You're so full of yourself, so smug. But you're not the only one with friends, lady, so you can drop the act now.'

It was like being dumped at sea. She was dog-paddling around, her chin just above the restless surface, trying to see land, in which direction to swim. 'What are you on about? What act? Gus, tell me. I don't get it.'

He looked so emotionless, it was frightening. She knew that

whatever she said now, it would not change the mind-set he had formed for himself. She was about to be accused, and she knew what it would be. 'Look,' he said with exaggerated patience, 'I know now why you went north. I know you met Dex there, and I also know the affair has been going on for some time. There's no point in lying any more, Jay. It's time to face reality.'

'I did not meet Dex up north,' she said, too dazed to put any heat into her voice. 'Who's told you that?'

'Then where did you meet him? I don't know where you were, only where you told me you were.'

'This is Zeke Michaels, isn't it,' she said, standing up. It was clear now. This was how he'd try to hurt her. 'He's told you this crap, and it *is* crap, Gus. There's nothing going on between Dex and me, not since he walked out of my life years ago.'

'You expect me to believe that with all that's happened?'

'What's happened? Nothing. Someone's lying, Gus, but it isn't me. It's Michaels. This has all happened because you were stupid enough to tell him where I went last week. It's him who thinks I met Dex, but I didn't. They want some tape they think he has, or they think I have. If you hadn't blabbed to Michaels, he wouldn't have said this. He's paranoid.'

Gus' expression didn't change. 'I didn't tell Michaels where you were, Jay, and he hasn't said anything to me about you and Dex.'

'You're lying now! It has to be him.'

Gus shook his head. 'No.'

'Then who?'

'That doesn't matter. I believe – that's all you need to know. I thought we had a good life together, Jay, but I was wrong. It's been a sham. You never got over that wanker, and you never will. I presume you're still with me because it's convenient. He can't help you maintain your lifestyle any more, can he? Well, you're going to have to find another dupe, because this one is walking out.'

Jay could only stare at him in stunned disbelief. 'You can't be serious, Gus. This is all over nothing.' It was as if he'd been brain-washed and had become a stranger.

'I've just come to collect some more things, then I'm going.'

'Where? Where are you staying?'

'With friends. I'm sorry this has happened, Jay. I'm sorry you're not the person I believed you to be. We've had some good times, but I can't live a lie.' He walked away from her into the bedroom.

A red fog of rage suddenly swelled behind Jay's eyes. She found herself in the doorway of the bedroom, yelling at the top of her voice. 'You complete and utter bastard! You're so prepared to believe the worst of me, and it's all down to assumption. You know nothing. You just want to believe I'm guilty of these outrageous things because it makes you feel better about your stupid jealousy. It justifies your smug, prim judgement of me. God, you're such a fake, Gus. You come on like some cool rock dude, but deep inside you're just a conservative bigot who belongs in suburbia. You can get out of my life. I don't care! I don't want someone around who's so patently lacking in support for me, who sides with my enemies.'

He turned round from the wardrobe. 'Enemies?' His voice was mocking. 'You have enemies? I wonder why?'

'Get out!' she screamed. 'Just get your stuff and get out. It's your loss.'

His refusal to join in the shouting was maddening. His stiff back oozed sanctimony. At that moment, Jay detested him. He was a quarter of the man Dex was, despite everything. She should never have taken another lover. She should have believed, waited, anything. Now Dex thought she had a decent life and he was wrong.

Gus zipped up his bag. 'I'll arrange to collect my share of the furniture. Of course, we'll have to talk about what will happen with the flat.'

'What? What about *my* flat?'

'Well, as I've lived here for some time, I have rights. I'll have to get my own place. So we'll have to come to some agreement.'

She hated the way he was enjoying this. He'd made her change a lot of the furniture, because he couldn't bear to sit on a chair where Dex had once sat, or sleep in his bed. Now, he'd take pleasure in dismantling her environment. 'You can take it all,' Jay snapped. 'I'll clear my life of you. I don't care. If I have to buy you off, so be it. People have to do it all the time, hand over money to sponging ex-partners. I'm sure my solicitors are used to it.'

'I haven't sponged off you. I've paid my way. I have entitlements.'

'Oh, just fuck off.' She walked away from the bedroom, nearly blind with fury. She couldn't cry. She wouldn't let him have that too. Shaking and cold, she went to get herself a drink. She was free now. She could do anything. It didn't matter.

Gus came out of the bedroom. She could feel him standing behind her, full of righteous indignation. 'I'll be in touch,' he said.

She would not answer, or even turn around. His proximity was repugnant. She wanted him out.

'Can you look me in the eye and tell me you've not met with Dex?'

She raised her head, taking a deep breath. 'I can't be bothered.'

He sighed. 'Thought so. I hope he gives you hell, Jay. You've thrown everything away for a lunatic loser. Have fun.'

As soon as he'd closed the door behind him, Jay went to the phone and called Gina. This was something she'd have to share with someone.

Gina seemed stunned by Jay's rapid outpouring over the line and offered to come round straight away. 'I'll pick up some gin,' she said. 'Would you like me to stay over?'

'Yes. Yes.' Jay felt weak now, drained of energy. She wasn't sure if she was sad about Gus leaving or just sneakily relieved. She felt excited, certainly, and that must be connected with Dex. Should she confide in Gina about that? The story of Julie's strange communications with her brother, Zeke

Michaels' threats and Dex's unexpected reappearance seemed like the concoctions of a deluded mind. Gina prided herself on her down-to-earth nature. Jay could not even guess how she might react to all this information.

While she waited for Gina to arrive, Jay paced around the flat. She'd have to buy Gus off, but that wouldn't be too much of a problem. She could borrow the money if necessary. It was still unbelievable to her that Gus was so quick to judge her. How could he believe she'd been seeing Dex behind his back? What evidence was there? Still, she had to admit that had the opportunity existed, she might have been able to get away with it. Her job meant that she was often out at night on her own, until the early hours of the morning, and Gus' work regularly took him away from home, sometimes for weeks at a time.

I wish I had had an affair, Jay thought. Why didn't I? She sighed. Because I thought I was happy. My life was regular and secure. I had no desire to be unfaithful to Gus.

She flopped down on to the sofa. Only a couple of weeks ago, her existence had been so normal. Now, it seemed she was at the brink of a new stage of her life. Big changes. Perhaps it would be for the better. She'd existed in a cocoon for the last few years, Gus being her shield against the world. She couldn't believe that Dex had just popped back into her life again, only to leave it again for eternity. He would be back. She'd see him again. She just knew it.

Gina threw her arms around Jay as soon as she opened the door. Her leather jacket was stiff with cold and she brought a spicy aroma of approaching winter into the flat. Bottles clanked together in a carrier bag that banged against Jay's back. 'Jay, what the hell's going on?' Gina asked, marching into the living-room and discarding her jacket and scarf along the way. She sat down on the sofa with the bag between her feet, and pulled out a litre of gin. 'Glasses, girl. We have some serious drinking to do.'

Jay fetched two tumblers and sat down on the floor. 'Gina, my life has gone crazy. It's so crazy, I don't know where to begin. All I ask is that you have an open mind, and just bear with me.'

Gina raised her brows. 'You've been holding out on me, haven't you? I knew it. Jay, I've known you for years. I could tell there were things on your mind after you got home last week, and you haven't called me as regularly. Why?'

Jay wriggled her shoulders uncomfortably. 'I don't know. I thought about calling you . . .'

'And the other night, you just weren't there with me in the pub, but miles away. Come on,' she poured gin into the glasses, 'tell me everything.'

Even as she began her story, Jay was still torn about whether she should be opening up to Gina like this. Gina could be very opinionated, and Jay dreaded that she was simply invoking some kind of lecture at the end of her tale. She just couldn't bring herself to mention the incident in the supermarket the night before, but passed it by, taking up the story again when Michaels and his friends had been waiting for her outside.

'It was vile. I don't know what they think I've got. But someone is spreading lies about me. All this stuff about Dex. It's mad. Where's it coming from?'

Gina stuck out her lower lip, looked perplexed. 'It's all very weird, I'll say that. It's got to be something to do with these tapes of Dex's.'

'Obviously, and I think that one of them was in that box Dex hid in Torton. Someone must have discovered it and took the tape.' She frowned. 'And yet when I found that box, it looked as if it hadn't been moved for years.'

'Oh, the weather can do its work in a few months, Jay. Someone must have taken it. What about this Julie? She sounds a bit odd, to say the least. Maybe she took the tape.'

Jay shook her head. 'I don't think so. She seems genuine enough. Why would she want to take it?'

Gina pulled a knowing face, ducked her head. 'Well, it's clear to me that she and Dex must be up to something. You don't really believe that crap about how she's in some kind of telepathic contact with him, do you?'

Jay looked away from Gina's gaze. 'I knew you'd find that hard to swallow.'

'Jay, come on,' Gina cajoled. 'She's either off her head or lying.'

'Perhaps. If it's either of those, I'd go for the former. She doesn't strike me as a liar. I really warmed to her.'

Gina took a sip of gin. 'So, I have to ask this, Jay. Is there any truth at all in the rumours? Has Dex been in touch with you?'

Jay felt her face begin to burn, despite her determination to stay cool. 'Well, this is even weirder. It wasn't true. Until last night.'

Gina's eyebrows shot up. 'You've heard from him?'

'I saw him. At the supermarket down the road.'

Gina laughed. 'Now that's a mysterious venue for a meeting! What did he say?'

'Nothing much. It was a very brief encounter. He warned me though. Implied I might be in trouble – because of him. It is to do with these tapes, I'm sure, but I haven't got them, and I don't know where they are.' She sighed. 'Dex looked like he'd been living in a hedge – a right state. He's not well, obviously.' She rubbed her face with both hands. 'Everyone thinks I'm in collusion with Dex, and I'm not, but now . . .' She stared at her friend through her fingers. 'I can't deny having seen him any more. What the hell am I going to do?'

Gina fished in her bag for her cigarettes. 'Well, the first thing you need to do is forget all about Sakrilege and their shenanigans, Dex, the lot. You need to sort your personal life out, make the peace with Gus.'

'I don't think I want to do that.'

'Oh, come on! A few weeks ago, you were the ideal couple. You can't just want to let that slip away.'

'I'm no longer sure how ideal we were. I think I want to build a new life now.'

'Because Dex is back on the scene?'

Again, Jay felt herself colour up. Only Gina had this effect on her, made her feel sixteen again. 'That's not the reason. Gus is a pompous arse. I overlooked it, because our relationship was safe and convenient, and also, I didn't really have to see that much of him, if you think about it. I can't forgive the way he's spoken to me, nor the fact that he's so quick to judge and believe the worst. A real lover would ask questions before condemning. Gus never gave me a chance. His mind was made up about me even before he came through the door.' Apart from that one last chance, Jay thought, when he asked me to look him in the eye. She pushed the memory from her mind. 'He wants money from me for the flat.'

'Will you manage?'

'Yeah. I might have to work a bit harder for a while, but it won't kill me.'

Gina sighed, shook her head. 'I can't believe this, Jay. It's all happening too quickly. I think you and Gus both need time to think about this. How much have you told him?'

'Nothing,' Jay spat. 'Why should I?'

'Jay, Jay,' Gina murmured. 'Think about what you're saying. Step back. You can't just throw away what you had. It's like you've built up an obsession about Dex again, and some part of you thinks you can yank back the past. But you can't. In my opinion, you should tell the truth to everyone. They'll have to believe you. Dex broke you apart once. Remember that. Don't let him do it again.'

'We don't know the circumstances,' Jay said stiffly, feeling as if she was being backed into a corner. 'Can't you see my point of view? I'm being tried, convicted and sentenced over nothing. How would you feel if it was you?'

Gina held her eyes for a moment. 'I can understand the way you feel, but this is just something you've inadvertently become involved in. It's not your problem, and you should fight to make that clear.'

'How? It's obvious what Michaels and Gus think of me: I'm a deceiving bitch. Nothing I say will make them change their minds.'

'You don't know that, not really.'

Jay disliked the cajoling tone Gina was using. This was her best friend, and she felt as if she was being treated like a fool by her. She should have called someone else. But who? Years ago, Grant Fenton had been her confidant, but even though their friendship had lasted, it was no longer that close. Julie was too far away to just pop round, and their friendship was too new for this. Jay couldn't think of another single person to whom she'd feel comfortable revealing her private life. She had hundreds of acquaintances but, apart from Gina, no real friends. It was this disgusting business she was in, full of husks who looked like people.

I want to run away. Now.

She sipped her gin, full of a yearning for some kind of freedom she'd never known.

Jay was woken up by the telephone ringing at ten o'clock; she was awake immediately, her nerves alert. Rather than let the answerphone take it, she picked up the extension by the bed. Disappointingly, Zeke Michaels' voice oozed down the line. 'Don't hang up,' he said, clearly aware of her feelings for him before he even began to speak. 'I'm sorry about the other night, Jay.'

'Sorry? That's not good enough.'

'Have you had time to think about what I said? Don't you think it would be better if . . .'

'OK, you got to my boyfriend somehow, and you'll no doubt be happy to learn he's left me. Unfortunately, this means you can't use him as a lever any more. Goodbye.' She slammed down the phone.

Gina appeared in the doorway, her hair mussed by sleep, her eyes puffy. 'Who was that?'

'Michaels. Bastard!'

'Did you try to explain?'

'No.' Jay swung out of bed. 'I have some work to deliver today. Better get on with it.'

'I'll make coffee,' said Gina.

Chapter Twelve

Jay drove over to the offices of *Track* in the afternoon. Normally, she'd e-mail her work in, but today, she felt she wanted to see some human faces. She had friends at *Track*, didn't she? She just never bothered to cultivate them. Now was the time. She felt quite optimistic.

Track was situated on the third floor of a new office block, where the immense reception was dominated by a huge statue of naked men wrestling. Jay uttered a friendly hello to the young woman at the desk, who gave her an identification tag. 'Go on up,' said the receptionist, beaming.

'Yeah! See you.' Jay felt cheerful and energetic. Today, the world was a better place. She was glad that Gus had finished their relationship.

In the main office, a vast open-plan room, intersected by fabric-covered boards and specimen plants, Jay homed in on the desk of Lorna Templeton. Lorna was younger than Jay by about ten years; a sleek woman, whose coutured exterior hid a wild streak and a raucous sense of humour. She and Jay had got on quite well at occasional *Track* parties.

Jay dropped her briefcase on to Lorna's desk. 'Hi, how's it going?'

Lorna looked up at her, and for a split second her face seemed closed-in, suspicious. Jay's instincts were immediately alert. Then Lorna managed a smile and said, 'Hi, fine. You?'

'Not too bad. I'm just here to see Grant. Is he in?'

'Yeah. Think so.' Lorna looked back at her computer screen, pressed a few keys on the keyboard.

Jay paused before leaving. 'Fancy a drink later?'

Lorna glanced up again, briefly, and smiled in a tight way. 'Um . . . well, can't really. Sorry.'

It was dismissal, Jay thought. 'Oh well, never mind. See you.'

'Yeah. See you.'

Jay squared her shoulders and walked purposefully down the office. Lorna was busy, that's all, but her guts were telling her something was amiss. She felt as if all eyes were upon her, that whispers lay on the tongue of every person in the office, and yet they all appeared to be working hard, their heads down. Perhaps they'd heard about Gus already, or the Dex rumours. Gossip was passed round like flu in this business.

Jay breezed into Grant Fenton's office, a big smile on her face. 'Hi there!'

'Jay!' He looked surprised to see her. 'What are you doing here?'

'Thought I'd bring that feature in. Needed to get out of the flat for a while.' She sat down on a leather chair opposite his desk. 'You're putting weight on, Grant. Lucky for you you've kept most of your hair.'

Grant frowned, but clearly not at her last comment. 'What feature is this, Jay?'

'You know, the Devon Klein one. I interviewed her a few days ago, and I'm actually before deadline, so don't pretend you don't know.'

Before he spoke, a stillness came into the room and entered Jay's body. She knew, as if she had the power of a psychic, that things were very wrong. Control was being taken away from her. Grant actually cleared his throat, his hand before his mouth. 'Jay, we'll not be needing that piece now.'

'Excuse me? It was high priority a few weeks ago. A scoop, you said.' Her voice was deadpan, but her heart had speeded up.

Grant was not the sort of person to avoid her eyes, but what she saw in his gaze did not reassure her. 'I'm sorry, Jay. Perhaps another magazine can use it.'

'What is this? You wanted that piece, Grant. You asked me to do it, and I did it.'

'I was going to call you. Something else has come up, and we've changed our main feature for December.'

Jay frowned, shook her head quizzically. 'That's a bloody quick change, then! Why didn't you tell me sooner? What do you want instead? It's bloody inconvenient.'

'You don't have to do it. I've asked Tom to.'

'Tom? Why?'

'God, this is difficult, and I didn't want to have to do it like this, but your contract with *Track* isn't going to be renewed.'

Jay stood up. 'Are we talking "fired" here?'

Grant looked up at her, then shook his head. 'Fuck, Jay, I can't do this here. Let's go get a coffee. OK.'

'No, you tell me now. What the hell is going on?'

Grant glanced past her at the door. When he spoke, his voice was low. 'Look, you don't want all that lot listening to this, and believe me, every antenna will be tuned this way. Let's go down the road to Helena's. Give me a chance to explain.'

Grudgingly, Jay assented. She was filled with a cold, incredulous fury, sure there was some mistake, or that she could talk her way out of this.

Everyone in the main office still had their heads down. Jay didn't even look in Lorna's direction. Loyalty meant nothing in this business.

Helena's was a small French café, filled with the aroma of fresh coffee. Before Gus, Jay had spent many lunch-times there with Grant. She shouldn't have let their friendship slip. She'd a feeling this wouldn't be happening if she hadn't.

They sat down and ordered cappuccinos. Jay lit a cigarette as they waited for their order. She leaned back in her chair, folded her arms. 'OK, explain it to me. Why drag me out here?'

Grant rubbed his face. 'Jay, you never know who's listening back there, or how, for that matter.'

Jay pulled a scornful face. 'Bugs, espionage. I never knew *Track* was so hot.'

Grant refused to be ruffled. 'Think what you like. I had your interests at heart.'

'So why did you lie to me? What was all that crap about "what feature"?'

146

'I didn't lie to you. It took me by surprise when you walked in, that's all.'

'What's happened?'

Grant squirmed on his chair. 'There was a meeting yesterday. The directors want to give *Track* a face-lift, and part of that involves taking on new freelancers. I hate having to do this, I really do. Don't even know how secure my position is.'

Jay kept staring at him. 'Who else is going?'

At this point, Grant's gaze slid away from hers. Their coffees arrived, giving him time to formulate a response. 'It hasn't yet been decided who's going and who's staying, but someone's lined up to take over your regular feature already. Carmen Leonard.'

Jay laughed, genuinely amused. 'Carmen Leonard? You're kidding me. She's a great body, granted, but hardly a great brain.'

To Jay's satisfaction, Grant recoiled a little. 'She's a super-model, Jay, and she wants to add another string to her bow. She's just being sensible. Modelling is a career for the young. The directors see her as a big catch, and a big draw.'

'So will Tom be writing her features for her?'

'She can write.'

'I bet she can.'

Grant drank some coffee, put his cup down slowly. 'It's not my choice, believe me.'

Jay leaned forward. 'Can you be honest with me?'

He looked her in the eye. 'Yes. You know I can.'

'OK, I'm not convinced this is just about a face-lift.' She raised her brows, tilted her head to one side, fixed Grant with a stare.

He didn't lower his eyes. 'You think someone has the knives out for you? Have you pissed someone off?'

She shrugged, clicked her tongue. 'Seems to me I can do that simply by lying in bed in the dark.'

'What do you mean?'

She could tell him now, Jay thought, tell him everything. She shook her head. 'Oh, nothing. I just find this hard to believe, that's all. *Track* has been part of my life for years. Stupid of me not to realise I wasn't indispensable.'

Grant reached out to squeeze her hands. 'Look, Jay, this isn't the end of the world. You're a superb writer. There'll always be work for you somewhere, but *Track* is changing. There's so much competition now. We can't afford to stand still, and if sacrifices have to be made, we have no choice but to make them.'

'Would you make that sacrifice?'

He paused, then shook his head. 'No. I'm just given instructions. This decision came as a big surprise to all of us. You know I love your stuff.'

'So does the readership. I hope they love Ms Leonard's wit as much.'

'Jay, we both know it's not always about quality.'

She nodded. 'Yeah, I know.'

Grant rubbed his face. 'I'm sorry about this, I really am. I was going to call you today, arrange to come round. I didn't want to have to tell you like this.'

Jay sighed. 'It's OK. I don't blame you.'

'Look, I'll call you soon. We should have an evening together.'

'Yeah, that'd be good. Gus has just left me, so I could do with a social life.'

Grant tilted his head back, took a deep breath. 'Oh, Jay, I didn't know. Christ, this couldn't have been worse timing.'

She forced a smile. 'Don't be ridiculous. It's clearly time for a change all round. Don't worry about me. I'll be fine. I like challenges.'

Grant escorted Jay back to her car, and gave her a hug before she got into it. 'I'll be in touch soon,' he said.

'Yeah. See you.' Jay pulled away from him and slid into the car. She sounded the horn as she drove off, gave Grant a cheerful wave.

Inside, she was seething.

Carmen Leonard? Jay couldn't believe it. Anorexic, mindless bitch! She didn't need this job. Effectively, Jay now had no work and no income. She'd relied on *Track* and had let other jobs slide. Her lover had left her. She had to earn money to live. Now this. Could Sakrilege have had anything to do with it? Why would anyone want to destroy her like this? It was all too bizarre. Must be a coincidence.

When Jay got home, she found Gina in the living room. 'Oh, you're still here.'

Gina grinned in too bright a way. 'Yeah. I rang Dan, and said I'd stay over with you for a couple of days. I'm going to cook dinner.' She frowned. 'You all right, Jay?'

Jay didn't want to cry, she really didn't. She wanted to throw down her briefcase on the sofa, utter the most vibrant profanities she knew, and reach for the gin bottle. But somehow, instead of that, she was standing in the middle of the room, numb, with tears running down her face in a deluge. She couldn't speak. She felt exhausted.

Gina hurried towards her and hugged her. 'My God, Jay, what's happened?'

After a few moments, Jay was able to say, 'They fired me.'

'What? Why?' Gina steered Jay to the sofa and went to pour her a gin, which she thrust into her friend's cold hands. 'Drink. Breathe,' she ordered.

Jay did so, and then found a lighted cigarette being offered to her. She took a long draw, and then delivered a brief summary of her meeting with Grant Fenton. By the end of it, she'd regained her composure. 'They've hired Carmen Leonard in my place.'

Gina looked outraged. 'That's ridiculous! Jay, they can't do this.'

'Of course they can!' Jay wriggled out of Gina's hold. 'They can do what they like. Everyone can. Except me, apparently.'

'But you're part of *Track*. Everyone loves your work. You help sell that fucking magazine.'

'Not any more.'

'It's their loss,' Gina said. 'They'll regret it. I doubt the lovely Carmen can even write her own name.'

'What will that matter? It's the name that counts, after all.

They could get junior journalists to write all her features. Who'd ever know or care? There's no integrity, Ginny. We already know that. It's a fucking dirty business, populated by soulless automata, the physical representation of figures on a balance sheet.' She gulped down the rest of her gin, then put her face in her hands. 'I've got to find work. Now. I've got a rejected Devon Klein feature, and a mortgage and credit cards to pay, never mind Gus. What the fuck am I going to do?'

'Right.' Gina sat back on her heels. 'We think clearly, for a start. You're going to drink another gin, then a strong coffee. You're going to wash your face, will some metal into your spine, and start making calls.'

Jay shook her head slowly from side to side. 'Gina, I'm too tired and it's too late in the day. I'll have to do it tomorrow.'

'No you won't. Come on, Jay, you know enough people. There must be loads of them that owe you favours. Maybe you should get an agent. Start writing books. Anything. But begin by making those calls. Sell the Klein feature, then start planning the future. You have to.' Gina reached out and squeezed Jay's knee. 'I'm here. I'll help.'

This offer of support invoked the tears again. Jay curled a hand over Gina's, watched the salty drops splash down. 'Thanks.'

Gina squeezed her fingers back. 'Right. Have a good bubble to get it out of your system, then go and splash some water in your eyes. I'll get you another drink.' She stood up and marched to the cabinet across the room.

Jay pressed the heels of her hands against her eyes and sat in prickling darkness. This was all too much. She hadn't the energy to call people. She just wanted to sleep. But Gina was persistent, and Jay could do nothing but obey her instructions. She downed the second gin and staggered to the bathroom, where she immersed her head in a bowl of freezing water. Raising her face, she blinked at her dripping countenance in the mirror. She didn't look good. There were lines around her mouth, and the skin beneath her eyes looked fragile and papery. Decay was setting in. She could write a book about the unbelievable injustice of ageing, yet only a few days ago, she'd never even thought about it.

Gina was sitting in the living-room, Jay's Filo-fax open on her knees. 'That's better. First you call Graham Teale.'

Jay rolled her eyes and groaned. 'No! Patronising little dick-head.'

'Quite. But he's first on the list. *Music Times* is the major music paper. Won't they want a scoop feature on one of America's wild rock daughters?'

Jay sighed and sat down, water still dripping from her hair. 'They've probably already run their own, but give me the phone. I'll try. What's the number?'

'Good girl. Here goes . . .'

But Graham Teale didn't want a feature on Devon Klein. He wouldn't even speak to Jay. Neither would the next two music-paper editors she called. There weren't any more. All the other music papers had died in the Eighties.

'Don't give up,' Gina said. 'We move on to the other style magazines now.'

Time was moving on. Jay could only phone a few before it was clear all the editors and their assistants had gone home for the day. No one wanted to talk to her. No one was interested. They'd all run their own Devon Klein features recently, or had already commissioned them from their regular freelancers.

Jay threw the phone on the floor. 'That was a waste of fucking time. It's too late, Gina. Devon Klein is already old news.'

'Don't be ridiculous,' Gina said firmly. 'Tomorrow, we start calling the teen magazines. You could revamp the piece to suit their style.'

'Gina, you're not hearing me. There's no point. It's too late.'

Gina shook her head. 'Then just make some calls to find other work. Don't worry. Your life isn't going to collapse in a single night. Tomorrow, you'll sort it all out.'

By two o'clock the next afternoon, Jay had realised that the world of journalism had closed its doors on her, despite Gina's constant encouragement to suggest it hadn't. The few editors who'd actually deigned to speak to her personally were polite enough, but certainly not eager to take her on. She couldn't believe it. She had a good reputation. Only a few months ago, other editors had tried to get work out of her. She put down the phone and said, 'No more. I have to face it. Someone is making sure I don't get work.'

'Jay!' Gina scolded. 'You've got to stop being so paranoid.'

'It's not paranoia,' she said. 'There can be no other explanation, unless I've been kidding myself about my skills all these years.'

'We have to make more calls,' Gina said. 'You need to meet people. Make appointments. You could try and get a column in a daily. Other music journalists have done that. You've certainly got the ability. You could do a great, bitchy column. Editors will know that. Jay, please, don't give in.'

She sighed. 'It's OK. I won't give in. I can't.'

'Right, well tonight, we'll get a take-out meal, and a couple of bottles of wine and—'

'No,' Jay said. She patted Gina's arm. 'I appreciate what you've done, being here for me, but tonight I really need to be on my own.'

'Jay, no.'

'Gina, yes.' Jay managed a smile. 'I'll be fine. I'll call you tomorrow, I promise.'

After Gina had left, the flat seemed more at peace. Jay sat for a few minutes, thinking about the day. Perhaps it was time to fight in more ways than one.

Chapter Thirteen

Zeke Michaels was far from happy about what Rhys Lorrance was having him do to Jay Samuels. He did not like the woman, but harboured a superstitious dread that doing bad to people was wrong, and caused horrible things to happen. He'd been greatly affected as a boy by a horror story about someone who killed a spider and then got eaten by a gigantic momma spider. All of Zeke Michaels' small gestures towards altruism were tainted by his broad streak of self-interest. None of his kindnesses came without a price tag, but then neither did his cruelties, and they were costs he had to pay himself.

Consequently, when Jay Samuels fought her way through his layers of staff and marched into his office first thing in the morning, he thought the day of reckoning had come. Personally, he did not believe she was in contact with Dex, nor that she had the tapes. He'd seen the state of her in the first days after Dex's disappearance. She'd let him search Dex's private work-room, where it had been clear nothing had been touched by her. She was a silly bitch, of course, but hardly calculating. Let her stick to her rounds of parties and gigs and her sniping articles in magazines. She should not have been touched, but let to lie. Now, Lorrance, through Michaels, had stirred her up. She was angry, and Michaels could hardly blame her. He was no actor. It was difficult to keep playing the part.

Without any preamble, Jay leaned on his desk and poked her face out at him. He thought her neck looked scrawny. She shouted at him. Clearly, Lorrance's quiet words in the right ears had effectively rendered her unemployed. Michaels didn't know about the boyfriend part, but that was a nasty touch. It occurred to him there was something personal about the way Lorrance was slicing the woman up.

She thrust a folded piece of paper at him, crying, 'You caused this. You pay it!'

It was a letter from a solicitor's office, who were representing Gus Metcalfe, Jay Samuels' ex-boyfriend. Apparently, he was asking her for half the equity in the flat and his share of the furniture. Michaels read it through a few times in order to compose a suitable response. Eventually, he looked up. 'At least he's not asking for maintenance from you.'

Jay's face was set in a feline snarl. 'He could hardly get it, could he? I have no income now, remember! And why? Because you and your bunch of crook colleagues have taken it all away from me.'

'Now, Jay, I don't think—'

'Shut up! You're responsible for this delightful little bill I'm landed with.'

She wasn't entirely wrong, Michaels thought. He twitched his shoulders. 'You must know that there's no way Sakrilege will help you with this, even if *I* wanted to.'

Jay growled and turned in a circle. 'But you don't want to, do you? For some reason, you've decided I have to be destroyed.'

Michaels raised his hands. 'Jay, this is outrageous. Calm down a little, will you?'

'Calm down?' She laughed harshly. 'You fucker! You've made such a mistake about me. I don't know anything and I don't have anything you want, and for that you've tried to ruin my life. Well, I won't let you win.'

'Give them what they want and they'll leave you alone.' Perhaps he shouldn't have said that. He saw the cunning sneak across her anger with tiny, precise paws.

'They? Who are *they*? And what can I give them if I don't have anything?'

'Make something up!' he snapped. He was going too far. He should just laugh like some kitsch villain from a James Bond film and mutter some bad-man clichés. He couldn't. Unfortunately, Zeke Michaels was not all bad.

'Who are *they*?' Jay repeated.

Michaels stared at her wild eyes. He couldn't say, because

he had more to fear from Lorrance than he did from Jay
Samuels. 'The entertainment industry is one big network,'
he said carefully. 'Think about it.'

'Oh, I get it.' She punctuated her next angry words with
hand gestures. '*You'll never work in this town again!*'

He shrugged uncomfortably, aware that Jay's fate could
easily happen to him. She didn't deserve this.

Jay planted her fists on his desk again, leaned towards him.
'I don't know how many times I have to tell you, but there's
nothing I can give you.'

He thought he could see fear behind her anger, the fear that
had driven her to come here. She'd shouted herself out, but
couldn't see a way to escape with any spoils in her hands, or
even any dignity. Her fury had run out of steam. 'In business,
bad things sometimes happen,' he said. 'You know that. It's
a fucking mine-field.'

Jay backed away from the desk. 'I haven't trodden on any
mines. This has all come out of the blue. You make ridiculous
accusations and pathetic attempts to threaten me. Then, by
miraculous coincidence, those threats come true. I don't know
how you can live with yourself.'

'It's called survival. We all do what we can to survive.'

She became still. Perhaps he'd revealed too much by imply-
ing he lived under threat too. 'You know, I think you're as
aware as I am that I'm being punished for something I haven't
done. This will all come back on you one day, Zeke. It's the
way of the world.'

She'd found her exit line. He watched her pick up her letter
and walk towards the door. Not dangerous. Too wounded
to be dangerous. She was a casualty of something that not
even Michaels himself fully understood. Lorrance wouldn't
tell him. He knew he was just a cat's paw. 'Jay, wait,' he said,
as she walked out of the door. She didn't pause. Perhaps it
was for the best. What comfort could he offer her anyway?

Jay drove home, her skin still afire. She felt slightly better
now she'd bawled Michaels out, even though she knew it
had probably been a waste of time. She was pleased with the

last thing she'd said to him. That was Julie Banner's influence; the suggestion there was more to life than she knew, cracks in the world.

Gus had wasted no time. The letter from his solicitors had infuriated Jay. It was doubtful she'd be able to keep her home unless she managed to find work soon. Her credit card bills were through the roof. She'd relied so much on having two incomes to play with, and had taken Gus' share for granted. They hadn't lived beyond their means, but certainly to their limit. Now, if she sold the flat to buy somewhere cheaper, Gus would snatch half the profit.

Back home, she drew the curtains against the grey of the day, and turned on a small lamp. Curled up on the sofa, she sipped rum, its flavour reminding her strongly and achingly of the days following Dex's disappearance from her life. Looking around herself, she wondered how many of the furnishings would be in her possession after Gus had taken his share. She had to admit that some of it she quite liked. How would she be able to afford to replace it now? Jay had never been without money. Income had always come easily to her. It was as if her life had been enchanted, or she'd been born lucky. In brief times of trouble, something had always come up, and she'd never doubted that inevitability. Now, she felt insecure and afraid. Something, some indefinable talent perhaps, had abandoned her. She'd hadn't felt this tired since Dex had left. There were no reporters outside the door now, no photographers, only hungry wolves. Had Dex felt anything like this when he chose to walk away from his life? If so, she could empathise. She had no energy to deal with the mechanics of daily existence. She wanted time to assimilate all the things that had happened to her over the last few weeks, and she needed peace, quiet and security for that. Instead, she was faced with just about every major life crisis, apart from bereavement.

And you can't get me there, world, she thought. There's no one to lose.

That in itself was a horrifying thought. Her life had been so busy, so wound up with talking to faces and hurrying to meet deadlines, she'd never stopped to think that, essentially, she was alone. If anybody else was in her position now, they'd have a family to go back to, somewhere to hole up for a while. The money from her parents' estate had been used to put a deposit on this flat. What a white elephant it was now. Too expensive for what it was; money attached to a post code. She did have distant relatives somewhere, but didn't know them. They were just dim recollections from her childhood. Dex had had a family of sorts, yet it hadn't stopped him slipping away from reality. For a moment, Jay considered going back to Julie. She felt sure that Dex's sister would let her stay there for a while, and eventually perhaps encourage her to find work on a local paper. Jay shuddered. She saw her life withering away in that vision.

She took a mouthful of rum. How was it possible to feel so tired, yet still be awake? Was there anything to carry on for? For a fleeting second, she saw an image of herself, dead on the sofa, the phone ringing and ringing, bills piling up beneath the letter box. No, she thought firmly, that's not your path. Fight! She remembered her conversation with Jez in the restaurant. It seemed so long ago. Impulsively she reached for the phone and her address book. She would tell him what had happened. She imagined the invitation out to L.A., Jez and his wife waiting to welcome her. No visions of empty futures there. She'd make a new start. The phone rang and rang, and eventually their answer-phone clicked in. What time was it there? Oh, who cares!

Jay hurled her empty glass across the room, satisfied when it shattered against the wall. The sound of it was muffled. Her flat seemed full of presences, unseen and hungry, feeding on the energy that bled from her like tears.

'Dex, where are you?' she said aloud. Could he hear her? She needed him now. He was alive in the world somewhere, hiding. 'I'll find you,' she muttered, scrambling to her feet. 'Damn you, I'm going to find you.'

All she had to go on was the photograph. It lay beside her on the passenger seat, its edges curled over as if protecting the image on it from her view. She'd really had too much to drink to be driving, but she didn't care. Like Julie said, she drank too much. She had a tolerance for it.

Driving out of the city, she felt as if she was escaping a dark, sticky mass that had prevented her from breathing properly. Her anxiety sharpened because of it, but it was a pure and cleansing pain.

Sometimes, as she drove through the night, she felt as if Dex was sitting beside her, quietly urging her on to find him. His appearance the other evening might have been a cry for help rather than a warning for her. Perhaps this was what life wanted from her, and had forced her to act. Everything was in the process of being taken from her, except for her past, and Dex was so much a part of that.

She knew that Lorrance's country estate was near a village called Emmertame, because that was the name of the recording studios Lorrance had owned there a few years before. She would go to this place, ask questions, try to confront him. Dex had had a grudging respect for Rhys Lorrance. Jay realised he might be involved in Sakrilege's dealings with her, but then again, he might not. He managed the company, but he managed many. It seemed unlikely he'd keep a track of all that went on. Perhaps she could appeal to him for help. In her heart, she harboured the hope that she'd find Dex there. Why else would he have left the photograph in the box for her to find? It was her only clue, and she had to act on it. She had nothing to lose.

Once she was off the motorway and the A-roads, the lanes were a winding labyrinth of lightless complexity. She followed the old-fashioned road-signs that poked towards narrow thoroughfares, where the hedges leaned inwards and dead grasses were held in stasis by the incisive frost. Even though she saw one or two signs that pointed towards Emmertame, she couldn't find the place. How long must she keep looking? What was keeping her out? As she drove, incidents over the past few days replayed themselves in her mind. Images of Zeke Michaels' face, Gus' and Gina's revolved in her head. She could see their mouths moving, but they weren't speaking.

They were barking and yapping at her. She lit a cigarette, tried to push the images from her mind. Where the hell am I going? She laughed coldly to herself. Dex had told her to leave the city. She was doing it now. But what would happen next? What *could* happen? Her whole reality had become the warm interior of the car, its smells and familiarity. She would drive like this until the morning came, or she ran out of petrol.

The lights came round the corner towards her like the flaring eyes of maddened supernatural steeds. Her reactions were deadened, yet her instincts took over. She turned the steering-wheel frantically, sending the car bouncing up on to the high verge to the left. There was a paralysing moment of hideous scraping sounds and then the impact as her car hit the hedge. Her neck jerked back. For some minutes she just hung there in her seat, shocked and dazed. Then sounds began to filter back into her consciousness. Amazingly, the car engine was still running. She hadn't stalled. Painfully, she looked behind her. The lane was in darkness, but for the wan light of the moon. What had happened? It had looked like another car, but Jay couldn't be sure. The accident had occurred so quickly. Who would be driving through these lanes so recklessly at this time of night? Local kids?

Jay was shaken up, but not injured, apart from the wrench in her neck and a soreness across her chest where the seat belt had cut into her. She managed to reverse the car back down on to the road. There was a disturbing rattle coming from beneath it. The exhaust system must have been damaged. Keep going, she told herself, just keep going. But eventually, exhaustion and shock became too much. She had to stop.

It was around four a.m. when she pulled into a lay-by at the edge of the road. It was thick with mud, scored by tractor tracks. Here, she laid back in her seat and undid the safety belt. She turned on the radio and, rubbing her neck lethargically, listened to a ghostly voice that murmured a chocolate-scented smoke through the darkness. These were the dark hours of the soul, when loners waited for the dawn, kept company by the hypnotic voice of the DJ and the old, nostalgic sounds. 'For all those lonely people out there.' A blues song throbbed smoothly from the speakers, an echo from a lost age, when fields had been more golden and skies more clear.

Jay rested her head against the back of her seat and smoked cigarettes. She'd brought a bottle of syrupy dark rum with her, from which she swigged without even noticing the burn as it slid down her throat. She still felt disorientated from the near miss in the road further back. The whole world was muzzy now. There was no moon, but the land was radiant with a subtle blue-white light. Owls ghosted across the stars and there was movement in the hedgerows, strange gleams like the brilliance of eyes.

Jay only realised she'd been dozing when she found herself waking suddenly, her body paralysed by cramps in her neck and shoulders. One arm felt completely dead and she shook it, banging it against the steering wheel and feeling nothing. Her throat felt thick and dry, her eyes swollen. There was a glow on the horizon; dawn. The radio was silent now; whatever station she'd tuned into had faded away. She stretched as best she was able in the confines of the car, then opened the door. Cool clean air swept in to claim its muggy interior.

Her feet were uncertain upon the uneven surface of the road. She ached all over. Flat fields swept away to either side, punctuated by lone oaks, their branches bare and tangled. In the distance, to her left, Jay could see a hill rising from a skirt of mist, its summit crowned by a monument that looked like a finger of stone. She was drawn towards it.

She locked the car and, carrying only her shoulder bag, climbed over a gate into the first of the fields. She couldn't see any houses because of the mist and the rising sun was a pure red disk within it. She felt strange, detached, but on the brink of enlightenment. She would surrender to it. Her fall, her isolation, her journey through the night and the accident which could have killed her had been a rite of passage. Around her, the world seemed different, reinvented. She had no sense of other human beings around. The landscape was the rolling infinity of the otherworld, where dreams would be made flesh and speak, where the impossible might happen. Perhaps she had gone back in time. Perhaps she was dreaming.

She began to walk, and as she did so, the present drifted away from her like smoke. She entered a new reality in her mind; a vision of what might have been, or should have been, or maybe what was ultimately true.

Part II

Chapter Fourteen

The field was endless. Hay field. It swayed hypnotically, the rubbing grasses whispering together. She did not feel tired, hungry or thirsty, even though she had walked for a long time. She remembered that the previous night she had slept in a barn; corrugated iron, the smell of oil, old machinery, rust. In the night, she had heard an owl, and became enveloped by its feathery whiteness. In her mind. The cry of the owl was a mantle. Perhaps there was no owl at all.

But no, hadn't she slept in her car last night? Her memory was indistinct, conflicting recollections overlapped.

She thought she must be dead, killed in the road accident without realising it, although she could not be sure. If she was alive her stomach would be craving food; her body, fluid. Her limbs would ache. She felt nothing. What would it be like to be dead? No one knew. Perhaps this was how it was; confusion, unsureness. Eternity. This might be it.

She waded through the field and the grasses surged around her. A solitary tree, leafless, reared against a bruised sky, but the land was seared and yellow beneath it. The air was hot and perfumed with dust and freshly cut hay. Should it be summertime? There was an inconsistency about the landscape, something dreamlike. The colours were pure and clean, yet somehow watery, like a hazy memory of an idyllic season. She found herself thinking of tropical storms, of rainbows, but there was nothing around her other than a susurrating emptiness.

Ahead of her, some distance away, an enormous statue crowned a wooded hill, where all the trees were in full leaf. The monument reared above the trees, its arms held wide, gesturing. Summoning. She walked towards it like an

165

infant taking first steps: stiff-limbed, her arms held away from her sides.

Grass dust had invaded her throat, her eyes. She was drying out. In more ways than one. She remembered the bottle of bourbon she had consumed in that last hotel. The memory, like the landscape, was oddly inconsistent. It had happened to her, yet it hadn't. She could recall the soulless neatness of the room, how she had wondered at the fact that so many people had stayed here without leaving any trace of themselves behind. People must have wept themselves to sleep in the bed, raged at lovers, thrown things at the wall. The heights of ecstasy must have permeated the furnishings; a woman's soft sigh, a man's groan. Nothing had been left behind, as nothing of herself would remain there once she had left. So she had drunk heavily to cushion her despair. Why bourbon? She had never liked it. And where had the hotel fitted in between leaving her car in the muddy lay-by and walking this field? How had she come to lose this time? But the memory of the car journey through the night, and the decision to walk seemed illusory now, like a story someone else had told her. The memory of the hotel seemed more real. Bourbon in her throat. Despair. She had thought that the world expected people like her to drink bourbon, to steep themselves in it, until it dribbled from their mouths and noses, leaked from their pores in toxic steam. She remembered that, before the hotel incident, she had been drunk for several weeks and the decision to call a halt to her life, as it was, had been lubricated by delirium. She was sober now, but she didn't want to go back. It must be forgotten, all of it, so that she could be dead and perhaps reborn. A muted tremor of fear thrilled through her body. *These are not my thoughts. This is not my past. It is him. He is with me.*

She came to the end of the field, and the hunched shade of an ancient hedgerow. It was on a raised bank; she had to climb up to it and even then could not see beyond the tangle. An archetypal gnarled, wooden fence was partially hidden among the spiny branches. She found a gap where she might break through. But into what? She was tired now and needed to sleep, but felt she had to reach some kind of completion before she dared close her eyes, otherwise there might be no awakening.

For several yards, she crawled along the hedgerow, surrounded by a cacophony of tiny sounds: the click of beetles, the munch of chitinous jaws, the thin shrieks of pain, the rustle and sigh of creatures who had no shape. She came upon a rose bush that dominated the hedge: dog roses. A mass of small blooms hung heavily out in a shady arc that hummed with bees. Their song was Morpheus' call, the summons to endless sleep or death. Looking up through the shivering pattern of leaves, she saw the sky, pregnant with storms, was the purple of Morpheus' cloak. A heron cut across this royal stain, bearing some unknown omen, its wings a pale slice against the dark. She peered through a tunnel of leaves that seemed to have opened up near her face, like a pathway through the briars that might lead to an enchanted world. She saw a picture at the end of the leaves: a church; grey, and mottled with yellow lichen.

She rolled on to her back and laid in the prickly grass at the edge of meadow. Thistles beneath her, thorns above, and the flowers; scent mingled with the stable aroma of cattle dung. This was a moment, a moment of England captured in time. The sky, the air, the music of summer. It was a ghost around her.

I will stay here for ever, she thought. The skies will change above me, brindle me with patterns of light. In her brain, a tune shivered like a skein of smoke from a distant cigarette. Faces crowded upon her inner eye, their mouths working ceaselessly. Demands, lies, flattery. *Give me one honest tongue and I will save this Sodom from destruction.* A short but distinct peal of unrestrained laughter came out of her, and she rolled on to her stomach. Beneath her cheek, the warm earth pulsed with life. She could hear the heartbeat of the world.

'We are nothing to you, are we,' she said aloud. 'We are your children, but you just spawn and spawn without regard for quality. Vomit us out, sickly progeny. Our peevish wails fill your ears, the trees. What's left of them.' Her mind was beginning to work again now; she could think in pictures. It had not been so for some time. But it was not her mind. It was his.

She rolled over on to her back once more. Years were sloughing away from her into the soil. She had lived too many lives, her energy had been scattered, sucked up by social vampires. She wanted to be nothing, because then they wouldn't want her, and she would prove them to be what she'd always known they were. There is nothing worth keeping in this world, but me, she thought. But then, everyone must think that.

Her memories were fading. Hard to recall now the people who belonged to the faces, the speaking heads. She had felt mad recently, but now knew she was purely sane. It was necessary only to walk away from the madness for its infection to leave the system.

In the far distance, a growl sounded in the sky and almost simultaneously, the hay stalks became agitated; their hissing rose to a rattle as the wind started up.

I can't stay here. I'm being moved on.

She clambered to hands and knees, reached through the gap in the hedge with blind fingers, her eyes closed. It was as if a hole opened up and sucked her through, scoring her body with thorns.

The field beyond was cut roughly, like an over-sized lawn. Its prickly length led to the half-fallen wall of a graveyard, which encompassed the old grey church. It was a plain building, devoid of gargoyles, yet ivy had been allowed to swarm over its walls. The graveyard was full of high ancient trees in full leaf. The green of the foliage was so intense, it burned her eyes. The barks of the trees were soft with moss and a mass of flowers sequinned the lawn between them. Behind the church, a careful gout of lightning scribbled across the sky. The air was full of the smell of ozone and the echo of long-dead choristers. All was the present moment. No past. Nothing moved at all. It was like a gold-tinted photograph.

She staggered towards the church like a drowned thing cast up by a storm. Religion had never interested her, yet she had once been afraid of the idea of God. Now, the walls of the church seemed comfortingly solid. She craved permanence.

Inside, the church was dark, yet some freak break in the storm clouds outside allowed a few diminished beams of light to filter through the high stained glass. She felt she must be like a stooped revenant at the doorway, gazing into the house of God. It was a bare, functional place, smugly pious in its simplicity. She saw a figure by the altar; a young girl, arranging white flowers in a tall brass vase. The girl's legs were bare; her dusty fair hair hung lankly over narrow shoulders. As Jay watched, the girl became aware of her presence, her scrutiny. The girl's thin body stiffened; gradually, she straightened up. When she turned her head, it was sudden; a flickering movement. Lightning lit up the nave, rendering her child's face horrible. It was like a scene from a film; a director could not have composed it more concisely. Jay staggered down the aisle, leaning on polished pew backs for support, expelling belches of perhaps blasphemous laughter. The girl watched her warily, flowers in her hands. Her skin looked green, lightning washed. Jay knew the girl was afraid, but felt too weak to reassure her. She must only see a cackling form lumbering towards her, like something from a bad movie. Inside, Jay wanted to stop herself, but her limbs worked independently, their strength draining, even as they propelled her forwards.

Before she reached the altar, she fell to her knees, unable to feel her legs, never mind move them. Laughter turned to sobs. A cool inner self observed these excesses of behaviour with disdain. The girl took a step away fastidiously. One of her flowers dropped on to the cold flagstones between them, bleached of colour like a funeral bloom. She appeared to be one of those intense, humourless children; her face pinched into a maturity beyond her years. She would bolt away now, Jay was sure of it.

But no. The girl seemed to summon her courage and approached. She held out one paw-like hand over Jay's head, her face solemn. Then she nodded and hunkered down, peering intently into Jay's face. Jay could not speak, although clichés fought in her throat to express themselves. 'Help me.' 'Where am I?'

The girl reached out and touched Jay's tears lightly, then grabbed one of her arms with both her hands. 'Come on. Get up.'

Jay scrabbled around like a crippled dog in the girl's hold, as if her spine was broken.

'Get up!' the girl repeated. 'You must come home with me.'

Somehow Jay found the strength, but maybe it had been there all along.

Outside, it had begun to rain, hard, the water coming down in rods; it seemed to bruise her skin. The earth had released an ecstasy of smells; damp soil, hay, animal musk, ripped petals. A horse galloped across the field beside the church, its rider erect upon its back.

The girl came up beside her after carefully closing the church door. She wiped her hands on the front of her thin, cotton dress, then eased her fingers through Jay's right elbow. 'Not far,' she said. 'One step after another. Not far.'

Chapter Fifteen

Jay woke up to a sound like whale-song that ebbed from her conscious mind even before she opened her eyes. A white flare of light bleached the world, just for a second. It cleared and she found herself lying in bed in a strange room. The next thing she noticed was the ticking of a clock. Everything resolved itself as ordinary. The furniture looked old, and reminded her of childhood weekends spent at her grand-mother's while her parents had lived their social lives of minimal debauchery. There was a smell associated with old women; lavender powder, a kind of damp, soapy undertone. She did not like the room. It was cramped and dark, and when she moved, the bed creaked beneath her. She was lying under a wad of blankets, her arms lying by her sides outside the covers, resting on a cold eiderdown. She had had sunstroke once, while staying at her grandmother's. She had been confined, like this, to bed in the afternoon, feeling light-headed and unreal. From the quality of the light, she could tell that outside it was still raining. The summer trees would be vibrant and refreshed by the water, a chaotic palette of greens. The leaves would be precise against the bruised sky, fluttering. Somewhere, a rainbow arced. But where had the rest of winter gone, the spring that followed? When she'd left her car behind, the world had been cold and bare. What had she been doing?

She tried to move and realised then that she was not alone. A presence moved beyond her line of sight. Her neck ached. She could not lift her head.

The girl from the church wafted into view. She looked both concerned and excited, as if savouring her guest's vulnerability. Jay felt momentarily afraid, wondering what the girl had done to her, why she couldn't move.

171

'You're awake,' said the girl, and once again reality see-sawed into normality. Jay wasn't afraid at all. She didn't even have to speak, explain herself. The girl sat beside her on the bed, her hands laced demurely in her lap. 'You need to rest. You need to eat. It's all over now.'

What was all over? Jay tried to move again and found she could. She struggled to support herself on her elbows and a flash of light constricted her head once more.

'Perhaps you shouldn't sit up just yet,' said the girl. 'Ida is making you some soup.'

Jay's nose filled with the smell of fatty meat; she retched.

'Oh no,' said the girl, frowning. 'Don't be sick. I haven't got a bowl or anything.'

Jay laid down again, blinking at the ceiling, identifying patches of damp in the yellowed wallpaper. When she spoke, her voice sounded scratchy and thin in her own ears. 'I'm not sure where I am, how I got here . . .'

'You were lost. You found *me* in the church. I had to bring you home. You needed looking after.'

'Why are you doing this?'

The girl shrugged. 'Someone has to. You're here now.'

'And where is here?'

'Journey's end. Lestholme. Where we live.'

Jay sighed, swallowed. She was thirsty and touched the outside of her dry throat. She wanted to submit to the sensation of illness, desiring pity and comfort, yet some part of her fought against it. It seemed strange to her. Hadn't she given in, fallen backwards into the arms of fate, when she'd walked away from her car? Why not simply flow with it now, whatever happened to her? But no, wasn't that someone else's life? She couldn't remember. Memories were muddled.

'What's your name?' asked the girl. 'I'm Jem.'

'Jay,' she answered.

Jem nodded. 'You're here now.'

Presently, a woman came into the room. She wore a frilled apron, like a character out of a Fifties' sitcom, and carried a steaming bowl of soup, from which the handle of a spoon extended. Her face was round and smiling, cheeks rosy. She was an archetypal mother. Jay experienced another moment of disorientation. From beyond the open door, she heard the unmistakable sound of a radio, a woman's voice, shrill and metallic. She was taken back to the time when her mother would listen to women's programmes on the radio while Jay played on the floor at her feet. She could smell cold gravy, rancid greens. She imagined a winter day outside, greying in on itself. Jay shivered in the bed.

'Cold, are you?' enquired the woman bearing down on her with the soup.

'This is Ida,' Jem said. 'She looks after me.'

'Get on yer, saucy minx!' exclaimed Ida. She put down the soup on the bedside table. Her arms were huge, made for wringing out laundry and then pegging it out on a line to flap in a stiff wind. Her body as she leaned forward was mountainous; ancient mountains eroded into undulating hills of flesh. Jay couldn't help thinking of Ida striding along a hilly sky-line trailing clouds in her hair. She forced her body upright in the bed, her brain splashing around her skull. The tray was placed across her knees. She looked down into the green gel of the soup, wondered how she could eat it, yet the smell rising in waxy steam from its surface was inviting, faintly redolent of onions.

'You'll feel so much better after you've eaten,' Jem told her. 'Ida's soup is . . .' She paused to smile. '. . . life-giving.' A woman much older than Jem seemed to speak through her body, smile through her smile.

Jay felt unnerved again and an involuntary question came out of her: 'Am I dead?'

The woman and the girl looked at one another, a glance difficult to interpret. It might have contained sympathy or collusion. 'No,' said Jem. 'I don't think you are.'

Jay rubbed her face with one hand. 'I feel so strange. I had an accident . . .'

'You'll feel right as rain in no time,' said Ida.

'But I can't . . .' Jay shook her head. She wanted to say, 'I can't stay here,' but realised there was no reason not to. She was clearly more shaken by the accident than she'd first thought. She needed to recuperate. Yet shouldn't she contact somebody? Who?

'My car,' she said.

'Don't you go worrying about that,' Ida said.

'Will someone get it for me? Can you do that? Can I give you the keys?'

'All's taken care of,' Ida murmured. 'You just stop your fretting and eat your broth.'

Once she had eaten the soup, Jay was overwhelmed by tiredness.

'You'll sleep now,' Ida said, patting the eiderdown with plump motherly fingers. Her voice, though soft, contained a command. She seemed the Mother of Sleep.

Jay welcomed the approaching cloud of slumber. She could almost see it rolling towards her; white, thick, enveloping. Before it claimed her, she experienced a brief recollection of how she had felt before she'd come across the church. The hotel room, the bourbon. She was sure now those impressions had been images of Dex's life, and the way he'd felt as he'd walked away from it. She had experienced *his* journey, *his* turmoil. Did that mean he was also here in Lestholme? Perhaps this was the place Julie had spoken of. For just a moment, Jay was enveloped by warmth. After all her searching, she had finally experienced some kind of bond with Dex.

In the evening, Jay went downstairs. She did feel refreshed, though tender throughout mind and body. She wandered dark passages, floored by tiles that were covered by thin runners of faded Persian carpet. In an overstuffed living-room, she came across a man, who she imagined must be Ida's husband. He sat in a cracked leather armchair in front of the television. His face was heavy-set and melancholy, his body huge and inert. The picture on the set before him looked old somehow, a transmission from the past. Footballers ran back and forth across a field, grainy imps of grey and white. The air in the room was solid, slow-moving, gravid with aromas of yesterday's meals. Heavy chenille curtains of orange were drawn against the evening sun, which would otherwise intrude across the man's line of vision. On the table, linen-draped, a cracked bowl was filled with soft-looking apples. A wasp, antennae absorbed, climbed over the aged mound, round and around.

Jay noticed an old woman, dressed in black, sleeping in another armchair near the window. Her wispy white hair flapped a little as she exhaled, and her marbled hands lay along the chair arms, the nails astonishingly well shaped and smooth. Apprehension came with a serpent slide up Jay's spine. These people were eerie.

Jem came into the room, and brought life and energy with her. She bounced up to the man's chair and leaned upon its back where the man's hair had left oily stains. 'Arthur, this is Jay,' she said. The heavy faced man in the chair glanced round, stared at Jay through oyster eyes for a moment, then twitched his loose lips and resumed his scrutiny of the TV screen.

'This is your family,' Jay said, her voice lame.

Jem was still bouncing at the back of Arthur's chair. 'Yes.' It was said with defiance, as if challenging Jay to make an uncomplimentary remark.

I can't stay here, she thought. Whatever Jem thinks, whatever she meant by what she said upstairs, I don't belong. I must move on. I have to find Dex.

Ida came into the room, bearing a tray laden with small, dry-looking sandwiches and slabs of Madeira cake. A smell of fish paste filled the air. At Ida's injunction, Jay sat down at the table beneath the window, across from Jem, and nibbled at a sandwich. Its taste took her back to her own childhood again. Uncannily, these people strongly reminded her of her grandparents; not particular individuals but a kind of composite aura, as if Ida, Arthur and the old woman in the corner were somehow the essence of her memories. As Jay bit into a moist hunk of cake, someone scored a goal on the TV, and a thin roar erupted from the televised crowd. She had lived this moment before. The only thing lacking was the deep red jelly, cold from the fridge, that her grandmother Ruperts, her mother's mother, would always lay out for tea on Saturdays. Perhaps this was all coincidence. She was looking for her childhood, because then she had been ignorant and therefore happy. Those gilded days, filled with rich, imaginative games, seemed like some lost Arcadia now. This place, and these people, might exist only in her imagination. Perhaps she was lying in a drunken sleep in her car at the lay-by, only dreaming she was here. It might be that she was looking for Dex only in the labyrinth of her own mind, and her inner wandering had brought her here. But how could she wake up? It all felt so real, while at the same time illusory. She laid down her half-eaten cake on her plate, rubbing soft crumbs from her fingers.

'Jem, I'm looking for someone.'

Jem looked up at her, her face both wary and enquiring.

Is she me? Jay wondered. *The person that I was?*

'His name is Dex. I think he might have come here before me.'

'Lots of people come here,' Jem answered. 'What does he look like?'

'He's tall, and quite slim. About my age. Dark brown hair. Dark eyes.'

'A lot of people look like that.'

'It would have been a few years ago now. He disappeared, and I think I might be here because of him.'

Jem shook her head. 'You're only here because of yourself. That's what happens.'

'Perhaps, but I still feel he might be here too. I have to look for him.'

Jem shrugged and pulled a wry face; a weirdly adult gesture. 'I don't know everyone here. How could I? I've never heard of anyone coming here to find someone else though.'

'I have to look.'

'You should rest. Eat, sleep, relax. There's plenty of time. I'll take you out into the garden.'

Jem led Jay out of the room. Jay felt almost blind in the passage-way beyond, but then the light was dim. From the kitchen came the clatter of pans, the sound of slippered feet on bare tiles. Jem steered her out of the front door into the evening, where the aromas of grass and carnations rose in a wave and enwrapped her body. She expelled a sound, 'Aaah,' her head thrown back.

Jem's small hand pushed firmly against the small of Jay's back and she stumbled on to a square of lawn, precisely groomed, where a bird-bath on a pedestal stood empty of water. The garden hugged the house in an L-shape. A strip of narrow lawn and a path led down to a shaded area beyond, where bean plants seethed up sloping poles. What would it be like to walk beneath that arched green walk-way, surrounded by the smell of the creeping tendrils? Once, she must have done that. One of her grandfathers had grown beans in his garden.

'You will feel better soon,' Jem said.

Jay smiled uncertainly. 'I feel better already.' She looked around herself, feeling oppressed by the gigantic beech tree that spread fluttering arms over the lawn. She had been here before, long ago, yet she hadn't. It was all wrong. She had to find Dex, but she also had to find out what had happened to her, where those lost months of winter and spring, perhaps years, had gone.

'I know what you're thinking,' Jem said.

Jay glanced at her. 'I need to use the telephone.'

'We don't have one.'

That didn't really come as a surprise. 'It's very kind of you to look after me, but I need to make contact with people. I left my car somewhere. After I've looked for Dex, I'll have to go back.'

'But where to?' Jem danced around the lawn, came to a standstill with the bird-bath between them. It was too small for any but the tiniest of birds to flutter there. 'You came here. People only come here when there's nowhere else to go. It's such a long way to anywhere from here.'

'Look, I need to find out . . .'

Jem's sigh interrupted her. 'This is your home now. The place of all rest. You must stay, Jay. You wouldn't have come here if you hadn't wanted to.'

Jay shook her head. 'I didn't know what I was doing. I was lost.' She could walk away now, step by step to the garden gate and beyond. Jem was only a child; she couldn't stop a grown woman from doing what she wanted to do. The others, in the house, seemed only part of its structure, to have no life beyond its walls. This place could not be real, or perhaps her senses were still playing tricks on her, making strangeness where there was only normality.

'It's very simple,' Jem said. 'You called to the town and it pulled you to it. That's what happens to everyone. It's a special place.' She looked fearsome in the sunset, a mad child. Jay saw then that Jem had assumed responsibility for her, perhaps simply because she had found her, rescued her. It was a game, and Jay must not collude in it. She must get out of here, find a bank, find a phone. She could call Gina, or Julie. She was afraid of discovering how long she'd been away, but realised it was essential to snatch reality back. She must deal with whatever happened next. With this resolve, she went back into the house, leaving Jem on the lawn.

In the kitchen, she found Ida carrying pans from cooker to sink and back again, seemingly without purpose. 'Is there a hotel in the village?'

Ida looked at her blankly, as if she'd spoken in a foreign tongue. 'Have some soup,' she said, smiling roundly.

Jay shook her head. 'Thanks, but I don't want any. I need to find a hotel, a cash point . . .' She heard a sound and turned to see that Jem was slinking into the kitchen.

'It's no use,' the girl said. 'You can't hang on to the past. It's let you go.'

Jay felt dizzy, trapped. The house was closing in on her, dream reality or not. She pushed past the girl and ran down the hall to the front door.

Outside, she went towards the gate, her sight pulsing painfully with dark spots. Beyond the gate was a lane, but she could see a cluster of buildings further down; what looked like a pub, shops. She ran as in a nightmare; slowly, hardly covering ground. Her feet slipped from beneath her and the landscape around her was motionless, as if painted on reality.

She came to a staggering halt next to a village green. People walked there, up and down, arms linked. It looked like the lawn of a lunatic asylum. All her energy leaked out of her, into the surroundings. She collapsed on to the parched green, her sight occluded.

Then Jem's paw-like hands were upon her shoulders. 'You mustn't fight it,' she said softly.

Jay clenched her fists against the earth. 'No! This is not my future; it's not!' A shiver of heat passed through her.

Jem put her arms around her and whispered close to her ear. 'You were hurt and came to hide. You were abused and came to heal. You took the step and the sky heard you. In this place are your dreams, and dreamless sleep.'

Jay raised her head and opened her eyes. She felt herself slipping, her will fading. Around the edge of the green a crowd of people stood in a ring, staring at her. Some faces were devoid of expression, others seemed concerned, others still appeared faintly hostile. They were not a community though; she could see that. They were freaks, misfits, the creatures of nightmares. Dex was not among them.

'You are one of us now,' Jem murmured.

Chapter Sixteen

No hotel. No phones. Lestholme was truly a lost place, and a home of the lost. Jay knew instinctively that Jem was wrong about her. She did not belong there. But she had been drawn to it, allowed ingress, and she was sure this was connected with her search for Dex.

Jay had run away from her life, albeit without quite the same sense of leaving it for ever that Dex had felt. She was still not entirely convinced that Lestholme was not a figment of her imagination. Although she'd been imaginative as a child, she'd grown into a rational, practical person. The peculiarities of the village and its inhabitants did not belong to the world Jay had created for herself. For one, they seemed caught in a sort of time loop, inhabiting a reality comprised of the rosier aspects of the Fifties and Sixties. The air had the strange feel of summers past. It was like continually being reminded of a past event that perhaps never actually happened. Kitchen windows were thrown open to emit the fragrance of home cooking from the redolent depths of the houses and cottages. Women hung out cracking sails of pristine washing upon lawns where the grass was the green of youth. Men strolled in the lanes with walking sticks, cravats at their necks, dogs at their heels. Children romped singing in circles upon the village green, and long skipping ropes whipped the air, accompanied by rhythmic mantras. Radios all played old tunes, and the broadcasters talked in the plummy accents of earlier decades. The radios themselves were old fashioned. Jay saw them, because she began systematically to call on every household in the village on her quest for information about Dex. Everyone welcomed her in unreservedly, but did not respond favourably to direct questions. They were vague, as if too enwrapped in their own dreams to care much about hers. They were not a community as such, but more like survivors of a disaster, brought together by the camaraderie of troubles shared. And they'd all had troubles.

Jay had spent a fretful first night in Ida's house, unable to sleep. She'd finally drifted off at dawn, only to be woken what seemed like minutes later by Jem telling her breakfast was ready. Downstairs, Ida glided from cooker to table to sink in repetitive motion, her face set in a beaming smile. There was no sign of Arthur or the old woman, but Jay suspected that if she should venture into the living-room she'd find them sitting there, just as she'd seen them the previous evening.

Jem and Jay ate toast, spread with home-made marmalade. Jay could sense that Lestholme might close over her like a fleecy gloved fist. If she wanted to, she could release her past into the air, let it float away from her. She did not want that. She still wanted truth, to find Dex, and she would begin by investigating. She was also determined to discover what Lestholme actually was, and how its inhabitants had ended up there. The mere decision to begin work in this way made her feel more stable, more in control. Jem seemed willing to conspire in Jay's plans. 'I've never heard of anyone trying to find a friend here,' she said, 'but it should be easy to look.'

Jay sipped from a cup of Ida's strong tea. 'So where do we start?'

'Next door, with Sally Olsen.'

Next door was actually around fifty yards up the lane. As Jem and Jay strolled slowly along, Jem told Sally's story. When Sally was seven years old, she'd been kidnapped by a woman whose own daughter had died. Sally had not been ill treated by her captor, and in fact had enjoyed the biggest spoiling of her life. Not that she could really remember it. She just knew. For a while, her picture had been in all the papers. Her mother had believed her dead. Subsequently, after the police raid that had resulted in Sally's release, her mother had closed Sally away from the world. She'd been a lonely child, because friends had been discouraged. At an early age, she had been in the nation's spotlight. Photographers had come to take her picture, and women's magazines had run stories

181

on her. Then the interest had gone away, and Sally had been left with her neurotic mother and the slowly closing walls of a shrinking world.

'I wouldn't normally say these things to a newcomer,' Jem said, 'because everyone's story is their own, but I feel it's OK with you.' She reached out and took Jay's hand. Jay was touched by Jem's words and gesture. She wondered what the girl's own story was, but felt that now was not the time to ask. They had reached the cottage gate.

Sally's home was surrounded by a well-tended Old English garden, complete with spires of hollyhock and foxglove, banks of climbing roses and dense purple tuffets of lavender. The cottage was thatched, with overhanging eaves. Wind-chimes tinkled in the shadowed porch, where muddied wellingtons lolled beneath a bench covered in gardening implements. This might be a dream home, but it was real and immediate. Sally worked in her garden; here was the evidence.

Jem went to the open door and leaned into the house, calling Sally's name. Almost immediately, the occupant hurried out of the dim interior.

Sally was a bright and nervous young woman, with long fair hair. She was dressed in jeans and a T-shirt and her hands were scratched, and gritty with dried soil. Jem introduced Jay, saying nothing of why they were calling. 'Lovely to meet you,' Sally said to Jay, wiping her right hand on her jeans before offering it to shake. After the introductions, she ushered her guests round the back of the cottage to a grey-flagged patio where rustic furniture burned in the sun. Jay found herself yearning to walk in the garden, investigate the tunnels of yew, the briar-covered walkways. Even in the bright sunlight, Sally's back garden was a wonderland of shadows and hidden corners, starred by flowers of glowing colours.

Jay and Jem sat down on a warm bench, and presently Sally came out of the cottage with glasses of home-made elderflower cordial on a tray.

'Jay's looking for someone,' Jem said, and Sally sat down, her expression alert, her attention fully focused on Jay.

'Oh, that's different,' she said.

Jay smiled and sipped her drink. It was ambrosial, slipping down her throat with refreshing coolness. 'I'm not quite sure how I ended up here,' Jay began.

Sally interrupted her, nodding earnestly. 'Oh, believe me, I know how you feel. But don't worry, all the strange feelings will pass. When I got off the bus here, I thought I was dead!' She laughed.

Jay couldn't help feeling slightly chilled, despite the generous warmth of the day. 'You got off a bus?'

Sally nodded again. 'Oh yes. Some of us come by bus.'

'How did you hear of Lestholme?'

Sally shrugged. 'Well, we don't do we? Did you?'

'Er – no. I didn't intend to come here at all.'

'Nobody does. That's the beauty of it.'

Jay took another drink. 'Happy coincidence.'

Sally just laughed. 'We are lucky, very lucky, blessed by God, his mercy.'

Her last remark made Jay uncomfortable. 'So, anyway, as Jem told you, I'm looking for someone. His name is Dex.'

Sally stuck out her lower lip. 'Dex. I don't know anyone of that name.'

Jay described him, and Sally said she could think of a couple of people that might fit the description, but that she'd not spoken to them. 'You have to realise that some of us are more – well – *private* than others. We all have to respect that. Some people keep themselves to themselves. That's OK.' She reached over the table and patted Jay's hand. 'It's important you know that you can speak to any of us at any time,' she said. 'Most of us like to talk. It helps us.' She put her head on one side enquiringly, and Jay realised Sally was waiting for her to start purging herself of whatever tragedies had impelled her to find Lestholme. Perhaps Sally thought the queries about Dex were merely a smoke-screen to cover distress.

Jay smiled. 'That's very kind of you, but in some ways I feel like an intruder here. I don't think my troubles compare with yours. I'm really here to find Dex.'

Sally's eyes narrowed slightly in concentration. 'This Dex is part of your story?'

'You could say that.'

'Then you might not find him in quite the way you expect,' Sally said.

'Finding him in any way will do fine,' Jay answered. She noticed Sally exchange a glance with Jem. They must think she was terribly damaged, unable to speak of the pain that really filled her. Their pity annoyed her. She drained her glass. 'Well, if you don't know Dex, I suppose I'd better move on and try to find someone who does.' She stood up.

Sally and Jem stared up at her. Jem didn't look as if she was about to move.

'I can't sit around, Jem,' Jay said, rather sharply.

Jem ducked her head. 'Then keep looking,' she said. 'Ida will call you when tea is ready.'

Jay turned away from them and rolled her eyes in private contempt. Ida would call her! She shook her head. 'See you later, then.'

She walked round the side of the cottage and out into the lane, slightly put out that Jem hadn't come with her. Ahead of her, the houses were closer together. She'd just knock on doors. Why not?

It was easier than she imagined. All she had to do was say, 'Hi, I'm new to Lestholme,' and she'd be invited into whatever house, bungalow or cottage she'd approached. Everyone was welcoming and friendly. Many lived alone, but others shared houses so that they appeared to be families, although none of them were related. The children that Jay saw playing in the gardens were lost children. Somewhere, parents must be grieving for them. The thought sickened Jay. Her search for Dex became almost eclipsed by her curiosity about Lestholme. How had all these people come here? Although they answered her questions with apparent sincerity, she noticed they were adept at skirting facts. Some spoke of arriving by bus, as Sally had done, while others murmured vaguely of walking into the village. No one, it seemed, had arrived by car. The village didn't appear to have any cars. That alone was bizarre enough. Everyone was able to recall their past existences with ease, but not one of them was without a murky patch of memory that involved the time immediately prior to their arrival in Lestholme. If Jay pushed them on this subject, they became slightly agitated, and would start blurting out their 'stories', as if to shout down the discomforting topic. Jay was surprised that she recognised some of the people she visited. Once, they had been fairly famous, or their painful stories, which should have remained private perhaps, had been emblazoned across the tabloids.

One example of this was Terry Mortendale, who had been an infamous football star in the Seventies. He had burnt himself out with booze and women, and after being flayed by a gleeful and gloating media, had faded from public view. He'd ended up in Lestholme.

At three years old, Lindy Trent had pushed her own baby brother into a canal, where he'd drowned. She was only nineteen now, and Jay could vaguely remember the case that had dominated the papers for a while.

Father Bickery had run away with one of his female parishioners and, allegedly, a certain amount of parish funds. The Sunday papers had loved that story. His life had been ruined.

There were many more people like these: runaways, adulterers, embezzlers, failures, the bereaved, the fuddled and the stars of five minutes of fame. Apart from the common denominator of being traumatised by what had happened to them, all the villagers shared another trait: they had been the subject of intense, if sometimes brief, media interest and they hadn't been able to cope with it. Their lives had been invaded, ripped apart, revealed to all, and some innate weakness within them had made their realities crumble. They couldn't deal with it any more, so they'd escaped. While some individuals might thrive on media attention, to the villagers in Lestholme it had been a scourging fire, a catalyst that had brought out deep-seated frailties. Jay felt uncomfortable with how she could be seen as a wolf in disguise amongst these sorry sheep, but she had to admit that Lestholme, with its media casualties, was the place where someone like Dex might end up. She had always known that in some way Dex had craved attention, which was why he'd chosen the career he had, but like the villagers he sometimes hadn't been able to handle it, hence the occasional attacks on photographers and cold indifference to fans. But Jay would never have believed being a celebrity had affected him so badly he'd had to jettison his entire life. Was this simply another aspect of his personality she'd never identified? Had he heard of Lestholme before and therefore found his way to it?

How *did* people get here exactly? She knew instinctively that nobody arrived by accident. Supposing she was not imagining the place, how could this have happened? Was it the result of carefully worded adverts in the property section of a local paper, or merely word of mouth? Evidence seemed to suggest some kind of invisible benefactor, but the villagers spoke only of God in this respect. Jay thought it unusual that so many people in a community had a religious life. Were they some kind of Born-Again Christian set-up? But they didn't have that fanatical edge she associated with such converts, and there was never any mention of Jesus. Their god, to them, was as much a part of their life as the sky above them. It, he or she was a permanent presence, but they were not fervent about it. As to how and why they were in Lestholme, they seemed to find Jay's enquiries mystifying. They were simply there. They had found their place. What more was there to it than that? Everyone accepted their position with relief. They felt they had found respite from a cruel world. As for people they might have left behind, they might as well have been dead. Lestholme was a focus, a fountain of life; nothing else mattered other than to be there. Jay was intrigued about how the village functioned economically. No one seemed to work. Was it possible they were all living off the state in their hideaway idyll? It seemed unlikely, but what other explanation was there? There were a few shops in the village that provided just about everything that people required – and she had to admit their requirements were minimal in comparison to people outside – but again all her enquiries as to how merchandise came into Lestholme were not answered. All the shopkeepers would answer obliquely. 'God provides for us,' they said, as if faith alone stocked their shelves.

Jay tried to keep an eye on the time, but her watch had stopped. The afternoon seemed endless; she was awash with tea and cold drinks, filled to bursting with cakes and biscuits. Her mind was a whirl.

Late in the afternoon, she paused to smoke a cigarette on the village green, and was joined by an old woman, who despite the heat wore a heavy overcoat and a headscarf. Jay gave her a cigarette, and asked, 'Is there a pub here?'

'Up there.' The old woman pointed up the narrow main street. 'But it won't be open until after tea.' She paused. 'Fancy a drink, love?'

Jay sighed. 'Yeah.'

The old woman pulled a small, battered Thermos flask from the pocket of her coat that had sticky marks all over it. 'Drop of Scotch in there. Help yourself.'

'Thanks.' Jay took the dubious receptacle and unscrewed the top. The whisky smelled warm, smoky and earthy. She took a sip, but it didn't burn her throat. She suspected it wasn't alcohol at all. 'Do you know a man called Dex?' she asked, without much hope.

The old woman giggled girlishly. 'The pretty one. Oh aye.'

Jay nearly choked. 'You do? Great! Do you know where he is?'

'He's around,' said the woman, taking her flask back.

'Where can I find him?'

The old woman shrugged. 'Don't know about that.'

'Has he got a house or a cottage?'

'Dunno, love. Only seen him a couple of times.'

She knew his name. She must have spoken to him. 'Tell me about it.'

'Can't rightly remember. He was handsome, that's all. And his name was Dex.'

Jay leaned back on straight arms, turning her face to the late afternoon sun that was now dropping behind the branches of the trees around the village. She felt elated and tired. There was a point to being here now.

A mournful sound came drifting towards her, wordless, yet summoning.

The old woman beside her took a quick sip of her whisky, smacked her lips together, then said, 'Sounds like your tea's ready, love.'

'Yes,' said Jay, standing up. She knew the call. 'That's Ida.'

'Best go home, then.'

'Yes.' A cool breeze had started up, as if to sweep away the day. Everything was so quiet. 'See you,' said Jay. She walked back the way she had come, until she reached Ida's cottage. There tea was waiting for her, and this time there was red jelly too.

Chapter Seventeen

Days passed like dreams. The scented air was like a drug. Golden light poured down, colouring everything with warmth. On the occasional days of rain, there were magnificent thunderstorms, and the green of the trees and verdure burned against the purpled sky.

Jay spent her time meeting with and talking to the villagers, staying for meals with them whenever she could. She made friends. The stories she heard, which now seemed more important than how the village functioned, were like myths of some long-forgotten pantheon. The people she met were the heroes and heroines of archetypal tragedies. Perhaps Lestholme was some bizarre Olympus, where they could hide themselves among the clouds.

Jay met the old woman with the whisky several more times. Her name was Ada Blunt, and the reason she came to Lestholme was the aftermath of being raped by a gang of muggers. When Jay heard this story, which Ada delivered with astonishing sang-froid, Jay felt sick and light-headed. Ada lived with four cats in a surprisingly modern bungalow at the edge of the village. Sometimes, Jay visited her in the evenings. On one occasion, Jay couldn't help mentioning that she imagined Ada would be more at home in a setting like Sally Olsen's.

'Oh no, love,' said Ada. 'I like my modernities. Can't be doing with all that dust.'

So Ada had her dream home, too. Jay questioned her carefully about how she'd come to the village, but Ada seemed more fuddled than any others Jay had spoken to. 'It's my real home,' she said. 'It's where I came to. An answer to my prayers.'

'Can you remember leaving your old life?' Jay asked her.

Ada frowned. 'It's all too dark,' she said. 'Sunlight started here.'

'How did you get this house? Do you rent it, own it, or what?'

Ada shook her head. 'It's mine,' she said. 'It was ready for me when I got here.'

Questions such as these upset the villagers, some more than others. Jay didn't like to press too much. In her past, Ada had suffered, and Jay respected that. It was clear that here in Lestholme, Ada was very content.

The old woman expanded slightly upon the meetings she'd allegedly had with Dex, but as time went on, Jay wondered how accurate Ada's memory was. Still, she had recognised Dex's name. Nobody else in Lestholme, however, appeared to have seen or met him. Jay did catch sight of a couple of shy young men, who looked a bit like him, but they were more like fairy-folk than burned-out rock stars. They would not talk to anyone, and lived among the trees, out of sight.

Jay spent as little time as possible in the shadowed rooms of Ida's house. Ida, Arthur and the perpetually sleeping old lady, Meg, disturbed her more than anyone else in Lestholme. She never learned their stories. They never offered to tell. The only thing that stopped her seeking somewhere else to stay was that Lestholme might then become just too comfortable for her. Jay wondered why Jem had chosen to live with Ida and the others, when she could probably have moved in with someone like Sally or Ada, who were both much more companionable. Their houses too were far more homey. Jem insisted she liked her surrogate family and felt comfortable in their house. 'I know they're a bit strange,' she confessed, 'but that's part of what I like about them.' She was an imaginative girl.

One morning, Jay went back to the church where Jem had found her. People worshipped here, but exactly *what* did they worship? There were no crucifixes, no images of saints, and even the stained-glass windows were just of pastoral scenes. They appeared to be of local places, because one of them showed the hill with the monument on top. She resolved to return when people were present, to see what kind of service was held there. But when she asked Jem about it, she discovered there were no services. People went into the church as and when they felt like it. They would sit in silence there, thanking their god for all he had given them, contemplating the happiness they had found.

One day, walking alone around the village, which had become as familiar to her as her old flat in London, Jay decided to walk away from it. She had been there for three weeks, and apart from the scanty information from Ada, had turned up no further evidence that Dex had ever been there. It was not that she was desperate to leave, but she needed to test a theory. She did not consider herself to be the same as the villagers, the kind of person who ran away from reality because it was too painful to bear. She'd always faced up to life's traumas, and was disturbed by the thought she might be in Lestholme because she'd lost that strength. She wanted to taste the outside world once more, even if she only put her toes over the invisible boundary that must somewhere exist. She needed to know that she could return to reality if and when she wanted to.

She walked and walked, seemingly for hours, but somehow every lane that she took led her back to the village. She must be walking in circles. She did not want to think that she *couldn't* leave. Still, the walk was pleasant and the balmy air drugged her senses. It no longer seemed important to find a way out. Jay strained her ears to detect any noise of cars or machinery, but there was none. The fields on the left side of the road were perfect, and cows and sheep grazed there, but she had never actually seen any sign of agricultural activity around the village.

There was no doubt that the village had, in many ways, healed and comforted her. She had no immediate desire to take up the life she had left, which she guessed must be the same for everyone around her. All that frantic worry and hurry seemed ridiculous now. Real life was experiencing the world in its raw state, breathing in its scents, bathing in the life-giving light of the endless summer sun. Real life was lazy afternoons and evenings spent with gentle companions, drinking tea together, laughing. There were so many things to talk about that had nothing to do with money or deadlines or social events. She no longer had a desire to drink alcohol; she didn't even miss it. She could sit in a comfortable lethargy, listening to someone talking about the habits of foxes, or how to lay out a garden, or how to make jam. It was strange how the questions and mysteries that had been so important when she'd first arrived now seemed irrelevant.

Father Bickery had taught her about art, and in his large shadowed house, she had made her first tentative efforts to paint. Mrs Cambourne, a trim middle-aged lady of the most genteel type, had lent her books, old classics Jay had always meant to read, but never had. After she'd devoured them, Jay had sat with Mrs Cambourne in her neat garden, analysing plots and characters. She'd sung songs in the hazy evening, with a household of confirmed bachelors, who all looked as if they should be someone's favourite great-uncle. She'd pricked her fingers learning to embroider in the kitchen of Sally Olsen, wrapped in the scent of vanilla and baking currants. This was life, surely? What had people like Gus, Gina and Zeke Michaels got to do with what was really important? All that bitching, all that keeping a tenacious hold of her position in a hostile, uncertain world; it held no attraction for her now. Yet, despite this, Lestholme was not enough for Jay. She sensed it deep within herself, a restlessness. Perhaps some cynical, hard-bitten part of her could not believe in the village's Utopian perfection and found it cloying. Ultimately, she knew that she still did not really belong there. But the lanes would not release her. They twisted and twined, drawing her ever back to their heart. In some ways, she was relieved, in others anxious.

Realising that she either had no sense of direction, or was being deliberately thwarted in her attempts to leave the village, Jay sat down on a milestone and lit a cigarette. She smoked less now, too. Of the two packets she'd had in her bag, one was still almost full. She faced a wood, where coins and bars of golden light made treasure among the lush ferns. Sitting very still, she saw a tawny doe glide between the sunbeams some yards from the road. Jay's feet were firm against the gravelly road. Her fingers could feel every texture of the lichened stone she sat upon. The air itself entered her lungs with the surge and thickness of water, filling her body with energy and the greenness of her environment. The landscape was so real and so perfect, it was like the template for all idyllic spots on earth.

She saw someone strolling towards her and recognised the erstwhile footballer, Terry Mortendale. Jay raised a hand in greeting, and Terry increased his pace to reach her.

'Great day,' he said, his hands in his pockets. He was a tall, heavy man, past the peak of fitness perhaps, but relaxed and healthy, a far cry from how he'd last appeared in the papers.

'I have yet to experience a bad day here,' Jay said.

Terry laughed. 'It's funny, but you never get tired of it, do you? Years ago, I'd have said you would, that you'd get bored with a place like this.'

'It's a different slant on life,' Jay said, stubbing out her cigarette on the road. She stood up. 'I'm going back to the village now. Are you heading that way?'

'Sure am. Want company?'

'That'd be nice.'

They strolled along in easy silence for a while, until Jay said, 'I was trying to leave, you know.' She expected Terry to ignore her remark or change the subject, but he didn't.

'Oh? Why's that?' He didn't even sound surprised.

Jay shrugged. 'I just wanted to see whether I could.'

'You can't mean that,' Terry answered, 'otherwise you wouldn't be here now.'

Jay smiled. 'Perhaps. Can people leave here?'

Terry stuck out his lower lip thoughtfully. 'Don't really know.' He paused, then said, 'I'm not sure how big "here" is. I did used to wonder about it, because Lestholme never seems crowded.'

'When did you stop wondering?'

Terry laughed, but there was a strained undercurrent to it. 'The day I did what you did.'

'How did you get here?' Jay asked him.

'My life, everything I was, everything I had, was all gone.' He glanced at her rather sharply. 'People don't ask here. It's up to us to tell. You're a journalist, aren't you?'

Jay wondered how best to handle this. 'Well, kind of, but . . .'

Terry laughed. 'Even some of you end up here. That's rich!'

He did not like the press. He blamed them for the break-down of his marriage, the disintegration of his life.

'But didn't you have responsibility, too?' Jay asked carefully, aware of feeling defensive. 'You can't blame other people for all of it, surely?'

'It didn't help,' he said.

Jay thought momentarily of Dex, of the stories that ran in the music press, week after week, when he was on tour; the reports that relished his bad behaviour. We all do things we regret occasionally, she thought, especially when we're drunk, and the next day we might feel embarrassed about it, but the memory fades after a while. What must it feel like to know that you won't be allowed to forget it, that everyone will be reading about your indiscretions a few days later, making judgements, voicing their own opinions? Failures and weaknesses would be emblazoned in headlines, fixed in the minds of those who read them.

'That's exactly what it's like,' Terry said, and Jay realised she must have been thinking aloud.

'Are you happy now?' Jay asked.

He nodded. 'It's more than a word, or a passing pleasure. I *am* happiness.' They had reached his cottage gate. 'Call in sometime,' he said.

'Thanks.'

'But no more talk like today, OK?'

'Yeah. Sorry.'

He smiled in reply and sauntered up to his open front door.

Jay carried on into Lestholme and met Jem coming out of one

of the village shops. She was sucking a lollipop and carried an old school satchel over her shoulder. 'Hi, Jay, I knew you'd come by. I was waiting for you.'

'I've been for a walk,' Jay said.

'I know. Fancy another?'

Jay sensed immediately that Jem had something to say, and assumed this would be associated with Dex. She agreed readily.

'Let's climb the hill,' Jem said. 'You've never seen it. Ida's packed me some sandwiches.' She patted her satchel. 'We can have a picnic up there.'

'Sounds great,' said Jay. 'Lead on.'

The hill was surrounded by ancient forest, thick with lush bracken, threaded by narrow tracks. Its smell was powerful, almost overwhelming; a composite of leaf and mould and flowers. The path they followed was steep, covered in loose stones. Sometimes Jay had to grasp tufts of bright green grass at the side of the track to keep her footing. Beside them, a narrow stream tumbled down the hillside, splashing from pool to pool in a series of rocky waterfalls. Ferns hung over the water and, in places where sunlight came down through the trees, the air was iridescent with spray. Jay realised how out of condition she was. Jem climbed steadily ahead, her bare legs streaked with bramble scratches, her sure feet encased in scuffed leather sandals.

Eventually they emerged from the woods on to the crown of the hill, which was blanketed in purple heather and gorse bushes in flower. Elderberry trees, laden with heavy white blooms, dipped their branches towards the ground. The air was full of the hum of bees and the flash of quick insects. There were ruins on the hill, now covered in dog rose. Jem said that once a house had stood there. She and Jay sat down on the warm stones of the ruins and ate their picnic. Jay could see the ghost of a garden in the profusion of bushes and flowers. Wild strains had strangled many of the cultivated plants, but tall, unruly rose trees still stood, gnarled and wild, draped in purple clematis. And some distance away, looking out over the valley, stood the soaring monument. The figure on its summit had its back to them, its arms outflung.

'You can climb up it,' Jem said, noticing Jay's study of the ancient stone. 'There are steps inside. But it's dangerous at the top. There's no safety rail or anything.'

Jay shuddered, imagining the beating of the wind at the head of the monument, how a person could spread-eagle themselves against the statue's stony flank, and be pressed against it or plucked away and flung to their death below. 'I bet you come here a lot,' she said. 'It's a lovely spot.'

'Yes, I like it,' Jem said.

They munched in silence for a while, then Jay said, 'Do you have any friends your own age?'

Jem frowned at her, then smiled. 'My own age? I have friends. We're all friends, but I like to come here alone.'

'Then I'm honoured, am I?'

'I thought you might like it too.' She paused. 'I have noticed your *difference*, Jay.'

'Difference?' Jay bit into a sandwich carefully. She would not push Jem because she'd already learned how flighty the villagers could be, how the wrong question could send them off at a tangent into their pasts.

'Yes. You are in the present, very much so.'

'Hmm. Do you think you're the same?'

Jem nodded, her face grave. 'Yes. I think it's because I didn't give everything up, and neither have you.'

Jay sensed she must be careful. 'I'm not sure I understand.'

Jem took an apple out of the satchel and bit into it, talking with her mouth full. 'People here don't want to question things, but I did – like you do.'

Jay held the girl's gaze with her own. 'I think it's good to question things. It's how we expand our knowledge.'

'I know, but it's not quite the same here. Part of coming to Lestholme means letting go of the questions and simply "being".'

Jay made sure she asked no questions, but just offered suppositions. 'The people here were damaged. They were all running away.'

'They are the missing,' Jem said. 'Except that for many of them, no one has missed them at all.'

Jay sighed. 'Well, I guess it's time I told you my story, if you want to hear it.'

Jem touched her arm. 'Of course.'

Had all those things really happened to her? Jay felt removed from it now. Admittedly, her story was far less traumatic than the majority of those she'd heard in Lestholme, but now, speaking it aloud, her former life seemed so bleak and empty. Jem listened without interrupting, her brow furrowed.

'I felt I'd lost everything,' Jay said in conclusion. 'So I drove out into the countryside, looking for Dex. Or at least I thought I was. It was winter time. I left my car and walked into a field, then it all gets muzzy. Somehow I walked into summertime, into Lestholme, and met you in the church. I don't understand it, Jem. How long had I walked, or had I been somewhere else for a while? You can appreciate why I thought I might be dead and this was some kind of after-life.' She risked a laugh. 'I still wonder whether I'm dreaming all this.'

'It's not any of that,' Jem replied. 'At least, I don't think so. But how can we tell?'

Jay told Jem about her meeting with Terry Mortendale earlier, and now she had to start asking questions. '*Does* anyone ever leave here, go back?'

Jem contemplated this for a moment, then said, 'I think they must do – or else they go somewhere else – otherwise Lestholme would be a city, not a village.'

'That's what Terry implied. Have you ever seen people go?'

Jem shook her head. 'No. This is a different life. You have to accept that things don't happen the same way as outside.'

'But how did we *get* here, Jem? Who runs the mysterious bus – which incidentally I've never seen – that brings some people to Lestholme?'

'People say it's God's bus.'

Jay laughed. 'Some fiery chariot!' She sighed. 'Come on, Jem, there has to be a rational explanation.' She paused. 'Do you want to stay here for ever?'

Jem wrinkled up her nose. 'It's not a case of wanting or not wanting, it simply is. I used to think about it, and how it must have involved a choice at some stage, but I must have forgotten that moment. There's nothing outside that calls to me. I'm here, and this is everything.'

'Is it happiness?'

'I'm not sure that exists for me any more. I'm not unhappy.' Jem rested her cheek on her raised knees, her skinny arms clasped around her shins. 'Days pass, and sometimes I can't remember them. I come up here to think, and it's always the same.'

'You seem older than you look,' Jay said. 'You must think a lot.'

'I have no age,' Jem answered. 'None of us have. Time is different here.'

Jay laughed uneasily, feeling the firm contours of her reality beginning to wobble again. 'This must be a dream!'

'I had the same thoughts as you once.' Jem twisted her mouth to one side, frowning. 'People like to talk about the things that happened to them, but I don't. That's why I'm different. And you, you don't have the same kind of thing, at least I don't think so. When I found you in the church, you were a ray of light, a mind that had come to me. If this is a dream, maybe I conjured you up.'

'You were lonely? You wanted to talk?'

'Yes, that might be it.' She looked Jay directly in the eyes. 'When I lived in the outside, I saw something, something awful. It happened to my mother and little brother. That's why I'm here.'

'God, Jem . . .' Jay reached out and took one of Jem's hands in her own.

Jem returned the pressure. 'It's OK. I want to tell you about it. A man came into our house one morning. Broke in. I remember it was a beautiful day. I was upstairs, and I heard my mother yell out. When I came down, she was dying, bleeding on the floor, all stabbed. He was just a black shape, formless almost. The strange thing was, I wasn't scared. I didn't feel anything. I just stared at him, and to this day,

I can't remember what he looked like. Maybe he wasn't a man, but something else. Surely a man couldn't do what he did? It made no sense. He didn't know us. My brother – he was barely more than a toddler – was screaming, in a terrible high-pitched, desperate way. The man must have hated that sound.' She paused, put her head in her hands. 'I can't tell you how he killed little Ben. I can't.'

'Ssh,' Jay soothed. 'You don't have to.' She was crying, tears running freely down her face.

Jem raised her head. Her face looked old, full of despair. 'I ran outside, trying to scream, but only this weird, thin sound would come out, like in a nightmare. He must have come out behind me, hit me with something. But he was on his way really, by then. He just sat down in the middle of the road, apparently, and started honking like a pig or something. People came pretty quickly. I'd have been dead probably if they hadn't.'

Jay felt sick. A story like that didn't belong in this golden world of perpetual summer. But of course, Jem's experience, and everyone else's here, were part of what made Lestholme. They were its core of darkness. 'Jem, that's . . . oh God, there are no words to say what it is.'

Jem made a visible effort to control herself. 'I know. I survived, and people wanted to know me because of it. It was very strange. For a long time, I was in the papers, like Terry and the others. The stories said how brave I was, what a wonderful person, but eventually all that interest faded away and I was alone again with what had happened.'

'And that's when you came here?'

'I can't remember properly. My father had died a year or so before, and I ended up living with my aunt, but I don't think she knew how to deal with me. She wasn't unkind, but just constantly awkward and embarrassed. Too cheery, if anything. Then there'd be days, whenever she looked at me, when she'd set her face in this puppy-dog, sympathy expression. I hated it.'

'How long ago was this?' Jay asked tentatively.

'I can't say. I told you time is different here.'

'But roughly: a long time – like years – or a short time?'

'It feels like a long time,' Jem said. 'But I haven't changed.'

Jay stared at her. 'Jem, are you saying that time stops in Lestholme, that you've grown no older?'

'That's what I'm saying.' Her head sank to her knees once more.

'That can't be.'

Jem didn't answer.

For a few moments, the only sound was that of the wind, then Jem raised her head from her knees and gazed up at the monument, her profile looking like that of a much older girl. 'Did you ever wonder what happened to all those people, the ones who were famous for a while? For just a short time, everyone's interested in them, but it doesn't last. That interest is like a big wave of energy that's constantly moving, seeking out new prey. And the people: sometimes, they are lost and empty. Their lives have been changed, they have been picked up by the wave and carried along in it for a while. The wave can be good or bad. It didn't hurt me as much as it hurt Father Bickery, even though what happened to me was far worse than what happened to him.'

Jay spoke softly. 'What *is* this place, Jem? You know, don't you?'

Jem stared at her for a few moments, and Jay wondered whether she'd answer. 'It's somebody's conscience,' she said at last.

Jay frowned. 'What?'

Jem stood up. 'Come on, I'll show you.'

They walked through the heather until they came to the foot of the monument. Close to, it was bigger than Jay had thought. The tower was quite wide, and spiralling steps could be seen beyond the doorway, disappearing up into blackness. 'Do we have to climb it?' She didn't relish the thought.

'No. It's dangerous.' Jem took hold of Jay's arm and led her past the monument to the edge of the hill. On this side, the ground fell away precipitously and the wind was strong. Trees were more sparse too, and smaller; clumps of feathery birch. Beyond them, on the plain below, fields, forest and occasional lakes were laid out in a patchwork. Lanes threaded between them, but Jay could see no cars. For as far as the eye could see, there were no telegraph poles or electricity pylons. There was just countryside, with a river running through it. If she squinted, Jay could perceive what looked like mountains far away through a shimmering haze, but no cities, no towns. Nearer, at the foot of the hill, cupped by dark woodland, was a great, white house. It had pillars at the front and a sweeping drive that led to a lane beyond. Jay gasped, then held her breath. 'Whose house is that?' It looked like the building in the photograph she'd taken from Dex's hidden box.

'It is the house of a god,' Jem said. Her voice was dry. She pointed up at the statue on the monument. 'And that is the god looking down at his house, protecting it.'

Jay threw back her head and shaded her eyes to stare at the statue. 'Does this god have a name?'

'Yes,' Jem said. 'Sooner or later, we all learn it.'

'What is it?'

'Lorrance,' Jem murmured.

It took a moment for the implications to sink in, then Jay snapped, '*Rhys* Lorrance?

Jem shrugged. 'Don't know. He is known to us simply as Lorrance.'

'Have you seen him? What is this? Does he own Lestholme?' Ideas were racing through Jay's mind. Lorrance: music industry man, but media man too. Media casualties, village of respite. Was he somehow responsible for Lestholme? Jem had already said it was somebody's conscience.

'I've not seen him,' Jem said. 'I don't think people do. Gods don't appear to people.'

Jay gripped Jem's shoulder. 'He's not a god. I know of him, Jem. He's a real person. He owns the recording company Dex used to be with. We must go down there! Dex might be there!'

'You can't go down,' Jem said. 'You can look on the house of god, but you can't reach it. Not that people often try.'

'Have you?'

Jem looked away. 'Yes. Several times. I wanted to meet

god and ask him questions. The hill is endless though, and wherever you walk, you end up back in Lestholme. I've tried lots of different ways, using markers and thread, all sorts of things. It never works. We're kept away. We're not meant to get to the house.'

'How is Lestholme Lorrance's conscience?'

'The god commits many acts that shame him, but he cannot turn his face to them. That is what we are told. He created Lestholme as a sanctuary, but it was only one aspect of him that did it. All his other aspects are unaware of it.'

Jay shook her head, her mind reeling. 'Do you know what Rhys Lorrance is out in the real world?'

Jem shrugged. 'It is of no consequence to us whether he exists in the outside or not. Here, it is different.'

'He's a very powerful man, Jem. He works for a corporation that owns newspapers, record companies, magazines. It virtually runs the entertainment industry.' She shook her head again. 'He must be mad, creating this place, making everyone think of him as a god. I can't believe it!'

Jay wanted to take this knowledge outside immediately. Everything was making sense to her now. If a part of Lorrance abhorred that some people were crushed by fame, their lives irrevocably changed by media attention, perhaps he had bought this village up, and somehow, through some vast conspiracy, arranged for people to be brought here, should they need an escape from their lives. It stretched credulity, but had to be more possible than the more mystical, supernatural explanations. Maybe Jem hadn't stopped ageing at all. She sometimes looked older than she appeared. Perhaps she simply dressed and acted young, because in her mind, she remained at the age she was when she'd left home. Yes, it made sense now. Jay was filled with excitement, feeling as if she'd somehow reached familiar territory. If her suppositions were correct, Lorrance could even arrange for everyone to be fed and housed; they wouldn't need state assistance. The villagers might be odd in their ways, because they were fed some kind of euphoric drug, designed to make them feel content. It was fantastic, in the literal sense, but what a story.

'Dex *is* here somewhere,' Jay said. 'I just know it now. I have to get to that house.'

Jem laid a hand on her arm. 'You can't.'

'I'm going to try,' Jay said firmly. She laid her hand over Jem's. 'Try with me.'

As they walked back to Lestholme, Jay began to make plans for the forthcoming foray. Jem listened, a slight frown on her face. 'It all adds up,' Jay said fervently. 'All that stuff about people saying "God will provide for us." They obviously mean Lorrance. We have to think, Jem. We have to try and remember what happened to us, how we got here. We may have been drugged.'

Jem looked glum. 'What about your lost months, then? How do they fit in?'

Jay made a sound of irritation. 'Drugs again. It must be. And my coming here must be connected with Dex.' She frowned. 'Some things don't add up, though. Why would Lorrance bring *me* here? Unless Dex asked him to, of course. He did want me to get away from London. Perhaps I'm here for my own safety. I have to find out what I'm being kept safe from. And the only way to do that is confront Lorrance himself.'

Jem sighed, hitting out at the lush grasses of the hedgerow with a thin stick. 'It doesn't feel right. You don't understand, because you haven't been here long enough. I used to wonder about the explanation, but I've come to accept that Lestholme simply *is*; a special place for the lost. It isn't just down to someone buying the village and putting people in it. It's not about drugs. I know it isn't.'

Jay ignored her remarks. 'You've tried getting to the white house by going down the hill. There must be another way through the lanes. We'll try tonight. We can use the stars to keep our bearings.'

'I've tried that way. All roads lead back to Lestholme.'

'That's impossible, Jem. You've got to stop believing in the fantasy. I know my ideas sound fantastic, but at least they are possible.'

Jem sighed. 'Do what you have to. Then you'll see I'm right.'

Chapter Eighteen

They set off after sundown; two adventurers, one fired with energy, the other somewhat reluctant. Jay noticed Jem dragging her heels. 'You don't have to do this if you don't want to.'

Jem's face was very white in the moonlight. 'I thought you wanted me to come.'

'I do. And I think you want to know the truth, but you mustn't come if it worries or scares you.'

'I'll come.' Jem's voice was low. 'It doesn't matter if I'm scared.' She glanced up at Jay. 'I feel I have to keep an eye on you, anyway.'

Jay laughed. 'It'll be fine.'

The expedition had begun with another sortie to the hilltop. Here, Jay examined the position of the moon and the few constellations she could recognise, and even made a rough map of what she could see below. The house of Lorrance looked chalky and insubstantial against the shadowy, blue backdrop of its cup of forest. No lights burned in the house that she could see. Perhaps the owner lived in the other side of the house, where the windows faced the trees. 'The river cuts through Lorrance's land back there,' Jay said, 'perhaps we should follow it.'

Now, Jem directed them towards the willowy banks, where the slow-moving flow slunk through the night. It was like the essence of all rivers, tangled with tall reeds, iris and bullrush. Occasionally, some slick-backed creature would break the surface. The water had a low, murmuring voice; as if naiads were gossiping softly together. Bats flirted with the river, skimming it with their wings. Jay and Jem walked along the footpath that wound alongside the water. It was overhung with ancient willows so immense that sometimes two trees on opposite banks would be entwined with one another. Jay was sure in her estimations of the landscape. 'We can cut across the park land here, by this spinney.'

Jem offered no resistance, said nothing. They tramped away from the riverbank, through tall grasses. Surprisingly, on the distant horizon, a fork of lightning shimmied down the sky. Then a wind started up, smelling strongly of ozone.

'Jay,' Jem said in a warning voice.

'It's OK,' Jay murmured. She would not surrender to signs and omens. Rhys Lorrance was a powerful man, but only in the sense of money and position. She did not, could not, believe he wielded any higher force. But as much as she chose to ignore the phenomena, she still felt that in some way they signalled she was getting close.

Jem put a hand on her arm, forcing her to stop. 'Listen.'

Jay cocked her head on one side. 'To what?' Why were they whispering? She could hear the wind shushing through the grass and perhaps a sound like rain, though none fell.

'I think we should go back,' Jem said. Fear oozed out of her infectiously.

Jay refused to allow it to touch her. 'We're all right,' she said. 'It's just superstition.'

Jem exhaled; a soft, whining sound of anxiety. She was lagging a few paces behind.

Jay noticed the movement in the grass before Jem did, but said nothing. It could be the wind. Then sounds came: yelping, panting, the thud of feet. The canopy of the trees ahead was waving wildly now, and between the branches could be glimpsed the white shimmer of stone. 'The house,' Jay said. She knew there was something between them and the building ahead, but kept moving. It was not far now.

Then she saw them. Dark shapes leapt and bounded towards them: dogs. Jem screamed Jay's name.

Jay reached out for the girl's arm. 'Stand still! Stand still!'

The dogs were of all breeds and sizes: dark Labradors, shaggy Alsatians, lean red setters, bouncing terriers. They did not look like typical guard dogs, more like family pets, but there was no doubt in which direction they were headed.

'There must be over two dozen of them,' Jay said. 'Lorrance must really like dogs.'

'Let's go, let's go!' Jem urged, pulling against Jay's hold.

'If we run, we'll have had it,' Jay said. 'They're not snarling. They might be friendly. Just stand your ground.'

Jay was thinking quickly; what should she do if the animals attacked? Could they keep running forward and make it to the house? They had no weapons on them, not even a stick. *Don't show them your fear*, she thought. *They'll smell it.* Her body felt drenched in cold sweat.

Then a voice came out of the night. 'Don't be afraid.'

Jem uttered a short, low screech, and Jay jumped sideways. A figure had appeared beside them, as if it had manifested out of the air. It had one arm raised towards the dogs, who now seemed to be soaring towards them, tongues lolling, pelts rippling. For one hellish moment, Jay thought the animals were upon them. She was surrounded by movement and noise. Then, she realised that the pack had simply leapt past them, in a flurry of paws and fur and panting. Jay could smell their dog aroma, feel the warmth of their passing, but already their yelping had diminished with distance. They had been like a phantom wild hunt, hurrying through the night.

'Bloody hell!' she said, bracing her hands against her knees. She felt out of breath.

'Jay, they wouldn't have hurt you.'

She looked up and saw a familiar stranger. 'Dex.'

'It's an angel of the god,' Jem said, her voice still full of fear.

'It's Dex,' Jay answered slowly. 'Isn't it?'

He folded his arms. He looked different now, less haggard and wild than when she'd seen him in London. He was dressed in a long jacket, dark trousers, heavy boots. His hair was tied back at his neck. His features seemed translucent in the pale light. Jay was torn between wanting to hug him or utter a sarcastic remark.

He took a step towards her. She could see a strange light reflected in his eyes. 'Are you all right?' he asked.

She nodded. 'Yes. Confused, but all right.' She brushed her

fingers through her hair. 'What the hell were those dogs?' She glanced over her shoulder, but there was no sign of the animals. 'They seemed . . . almost unreal.'

'They are the sad hounds,' he said. 'You shouldn't let them frighten you off.'

'They didn't look particularly sad to me.'

'But they are. Their owners followed them on to thin ice and drowned, or tried to push them from the path of an oncoming lorry, or train. They are lost and alone, so they are here. The dogs run at night together. They love, like humans do, and for them the kiss of fame was short but penetrating.'

This was not the Dex whom Jay had known. He talked with the hollow voice and opaque words of a prophet or a holy man. Was that what he had decided to become, here in the land of the god, for whom he worked? Or was this little speech merely to fend off more personal and perhaps painful conversation?

'I came to find you,' Jay said. 'I knew you'd be here.'

'You couldn't find me. I found you.' He came closer, and Jem cringed away.

Jay wasn't so intimidated. 'No, I think you knew I'd find you.' She held Jem against her.

Dex smiled; a reflex. 'Perhaps some part of me did want to be found, but I'm not aware of it.'

'I don't believe you.'

'Let's go back to the village. We need to talk.'

'We do, but not yet. I want to see Lorrance, find out what the fuck's happening here.'

Dex shook his head. 'You won't. You can't. It's a waste of time.'

'I have to try.' Jay took a firm hold of Jem's hand and marched forward towards the glimmer of stone. It wasn't so much that she wanted to confront Lorrance. Jay needed to see the house close up. She had a feeling no one was at home, anyway, but in the circumstances, that might be better. She could take a look around.

Dex watched her for a few moments, then relented and

caught up to walk beside them, some feet away. 'You shouldn't be here, Jay.'

'I know,' Jay said. Her heart was beating fast. 'But I am.' In a way, she couldn't accept Dex was there beside her. She had looked for him, asked questions, but now that he'd shown himself, he seemed like a dream. She knew him, yet she didn't. 'Have you been here all the time?' She couldn't imagine him co-operating in the simple, idyllic routines of Lestholme.

'Mostly.'

Jay shook her head. 'It doesn't seem likely somehow. Are you telling me the truth?'

'Yes.'

'Why didn't you come to me before? Why wait until now?'

He shrugged. 'I wanted to, but sometimes I didn't. I felt I shouldn't involve you. It's not fair.'

Jay laughed. 'Involve me? I'm involved whether you or I want it or not, aren't I?'

He smiled. 'I know I shouldn't be glad you're here, but I am.'

'You must have been lonely . . .'

He frowned. 'Please, Jay, not now.'

She could tell her words hurt him. 'So,' she said, in a more brisk tone, 'are you here because of Lorrance, or through him?'

'Both.'

Jay sighed. He'd said he wanted to talk to her, yet his answers to her questions offered little. 'It's obvious Lorrance has set himself up here as some kind of feudal lord,' Jay said. 'Will you tell me how I got here? Did you arrange it somehow?'

'No,' Dex said. 'You created your own gateway, which means things must have got tough for you. I did warn you.'

'Warn me? You didn't warn me of this. I drove off into the night, then ended up losing some months of my life. What did they do to me? Was it a tranquillising shot from across a field?'

'It didn't happen like that. You've lost no time. In fact, you've probably gained some.'

Jay made a disparaging sound. 'Dex, please! I can't accept that. I'm not gullible like those poor creatures in Lestholme.'

'I couldn't have explained any of this to you when I last saw you,' Dex said. 'You wouldn't have believed me, and I can see you still don't believe, even though you're living it. I'm amazed you got in here. You must have been temporarily desperate. What happened?'

'Didn't Julie tell you?' Jay asked.

Dex paused before answering. 'The communication I have with Julie isn't like speaking on the phone,' he said. 'I knew you'd been to see her, and that you'd found the box, but not what happened afterwards.'

'My life fell apart,' she answered, 'courtesy of Sakrilege, I think.' She explained all that had happened, a story to which Dex listened without commenting, but she could still feel his anger on her behalf. 'So, I'd lost my main avenue of work, my lover and was in danger of losing everything else.'

Dex shook his head. 'God, Jay, I'm sorry you went through that. You shouldn't have. You really don't belong here.'

'Tell me about it.'

They walked through a thin fringe of tall firs and then the house was before them. Close to, it looked odd. There were no pathways around it, no garden. It just stood in a field. Jay couldn't even see a driveway now, and the windows were depthless black holes, reflecting no light, even though the moon shone full and bright.

Jem said, 'I don't want to go near that place.'

'It's safe,' Dex said. 'You're in no danger. You'll soon see why.'

'Jay,' Jem said. 'I'm not sure.'

'It's OK,' Jay answered. 'I don't feel there's any threat.'

Dex led them up to the gleaming frontage and then disappeared through the front door, which must have been open. Jay could see nothing beyond but darkness, and for a moment she too was nervous of venturing forward.

Dex's voice called to them from the other side. 'Come on. There's nothing to be frightened of.'

Gripping Jem's damp hand firmly, Jay stepped over the threshold. For a moment, she stood in utter stillness, then said softly, 'What is this?'

The house was a white shell. There was nothing inside; no rooms, no roof, only a lawn from wall to wall and the moon shining high overhead. It did not even look as if it had ever been a proper dwelling. Looking up, she could see no sign that floors had once filled it. The white walls were flawless. It was like a stage set.

'You see now?' Dex said, gesturing around him.

'It's a folly,' Jay said.

'I don't like it here,' Jem murmured.

'It's not a folly, but an impression,' Dex said. 'A signpost between the reality of Lestholme and the outside world.'

'The house of god,' said Jem.

Jay pulled a sour face. 'Lorrance built it so that the villagers think he lives here, keeping an eye on them.'

Dex smiled wanly. 'No. It is a house, Jay, and under different circumstances, in a different location, you could visit it, climb its stairs, look into its rooms.'

'*Where* is it, that other house?'

'It's the same one, and it's here, but not here. Lestholme is nowhere, Jay, and to get here you have to want to *be* nowhere. Some people kill themselves, some people disappear, and of that latter category, some end up here.'

'You're telling me this is some weird reality shift or something?' Jay uttered a caustic laugh. 'I can't buy that, Dex. It doesn't happen outside of books and films.'

Dex shook his head and smiled. 'Always the sceptic. Believe what you like. It makes no difference to what is. There are different levels of reality, and they can be accessed by altered states of mind.'

'That brings me back to my earlier suggestion,' Jay said. 'Drugs.'

'It's not that, but concentrated emotion or will.'

Jay went to examine the walls close up. They were like porous marble, glittering under the moon. She rubbed her fingers over the stone. It felt rough beneath her touch, as if weathered. 'What has Lorrance got to do with it? Why is he seen as a god by the people here?'

'It's complicated, and I don't think you'll readily accept the explanation.' Dex sighed through his nose. 'Come back to the village now – we'll talk.'

As they walked back across the fields, Jem said, 'I can't believe we did it. We got into the house.' She sounded excited now; relieved and proud of herself.

'You can enter it if you believe you can,' Dex said. 'Most of the villagers don't want to see the empty shell, but that of course has always been the problem with religion.'

They went to the small pub in the centre of Lestholme, and here Dex bought pints of beer. It was the first time Jay had visited the place. At one time, she'd almost always had a drink in her hand, but now the urge to seek that temporary oblivion had left her. She didn't even think about it.

While Dex was occupied at the bar, Jem and Jay went out into the garden at the back of the building, which was surrounded by colossal trees. The ambience was that of a Doré engraving; the foliage had the immensity and stillness of a far earlier age. Jay sensed there was water near by, perhaps a pool or small lake, hidden among the trees. She sat down beside Jem at a wooden table, which was streaked with lichen, and spongy beneath her hands.

Dex came out to them carrying a tray. It seemed such an ordinary scene; a man, a woman and a young girl sitting in a pub garden. Jay had to struggle with disorientation.

'So, tell me what's going on,' Jay said. 'If anyone can, I'm sure it's you.' She sipped the ale Dex had bought her. Like Ada's whisky, it was full of flavour but not any Jay associated with beer. 'How did you get here? Can you remember?'

Dex sat down beside Jem, who wriggled slightly away from him. 'Always the journalist,' he said. 'Asking questions.'

Jay shrugged. 'I've always asked questions. I'm a journalist because of that rather than the other way around.'

Dex nodded. 'I got here because there was no other place to go. If I wasn't here, I might be dead. I'd had enough.'

Those last few words hurt. 'Why didn't you tell me?' Jay demanded. 'For God's sake, Dex, why just walk out? We could have worked out whatever problem you had. What you did was so cruel. Didn't you even think about what it might do to me?'

Dex dragged his fingers over his face. 'I know I should have, but . . . People in my state of mind don't think about others, Jay. It's never so neat as that. I loved you, I really did.'

Jay herself would not admit to Dex she might still love him, but his use of the past tense still stung.

'I thought about killing myself,' he said, 'but lacked the guts. So I walked. And ended up here. But I wouldn't collude in it. I haunted this place, explored its dark corners. For a while, I lived with some people, and time passed by like water. I did a lot of thinking and came to the conclusion that, despite everything, I belonged here.'

'Then why come out to find me?'

'Because, despite what you might think, I do care about you. I didn't want you to get hurt. I wanted to warn you.'

She held his eyes for a moment. This was so difficult. Neither of them really knew how to behave with the other. They'd had no formal ending, yet it was impossible to carry on from where they'd left off. 'Other people don't seem to come out of Lestholme,' she said. 'Why are you so different?'

He shrugged, placed his beer carefully on the table. 'I'm different, because I'm part of Rhys Lorrance's world. I have a foot in both camps.'

'Rhys Lorrance,' Jay said softly. 'Exactly what part does he play in this?'

'Lorrance has friends even more powerful than himself. They help him get what he wants, and a by-product of that is Lestholme. It's his. That's all there is to say.'

Jay smiled wryly, shook her head. 'No, Dex, it's not. This is me sitting here. Talk to me.'

Dex tucked a stray lock of hair behind his ear. 'Lorrance works for Three Swords, owned by Lester Charney. The higher you go within any corporation, the more concentrated

213

power becomes. Boards of directors are controlled by cabals – men with the most power and money. Because of their position, they understand more about the way the world works. They exploit it. Lester Charney is such a man. And Rhys Lorrance is his creature.'

'You're saying Charney created this place for Lorrance?'

'Not exactly. It's a product of what Charney has done for Lorrance, what he's taught him. I don't think Lorrance's even aware Lestholme exists. He's a symbol of what created it. It's his curse, perhaps, but unacknowledged. He doesn't take responsibility for it.'

'What has Charney taught Lorrance exactly?'

'The ultimate. The extreme. How to grow fat on the life force of others.'

'This doesn't make any sense to me.'

'I'll tell you my story,' Dex said. 'As you'll already have learned, it's the tradition of Lestholme, and it might help you understand.'

Chapter Nineteen

From the first days of their working together, Rhys Lorrance had singled Dex out for attention. Perhaps he had seen in Dex some thread, some link, that advised him his protégé might have the same hunger for power he did, as well as enjoy the same avenues of pleasure. After three years of Dex being with Sakrilege, Lorrance had told him about a select group of friends, who would meet every month or so at the Emmertame estate. 'In this business, with all its pressures,' Lorrance said, 'we need our release. And you'll meet people there, people who will be useful.'

Rhys Lorrance was not the sort of person Dex would normally consider befriending, but there was something compelling about Lorrance. When he gave Dex his attention, Dex never doubted he was the whole focus of it. Lorrance might be a hard-headed businessmen, but he was always good company. If anything he seemed to have great empathy with people, to know their secret selves, upon very short acquaintance. Perhaps that was part of why he was so successful.

Lorrance's elite club included various trusted members of the Three Swords empire, certain celebrities, and shadowy individuals who were unknown to Dex, but to whom Lorrance seemed almost subservient. They were businessmen, clearly, but they were different from all Lorrance's other friends. They had a disturbing observant quality, lurking at the edges of every gathering, as if what transpired there was a kind of tax they considered their due.

Dex himself was now unsure why he had become so involved with Lorrance's party set. He had always felt a gruding gratitude that Lorrance had plucked him from obscurity and paid to make him a star, but in the beginning, Dex had been an idealist, scornful of big business, eager to attack it from the inside. A weakness must have drawn him in, a desire for gratification in its most fleeting, shallow forms.

Dex had started attending Lorrance's gatherings long before he'd met Jay. It had been a secret then, and one he'd kept throughout their relationship, though at times it had gnawed at him like gall. The parties always took place at Lorrance's country house. Sometimes Dex drove up there with Zeke Michaels, although Michaels did not attend every event. Lorrance would send Samantha away shopping in London for the weekend, and make sure his daughter, Lacey, would not be approaching the family home.

The first time Dex visited Emmertame, he'd been astounded by the luxuries; the best food, the best drink, the best drugs. The parties took place over long weekends when Jay had believed Dex was at the studio recording, or else rehearsing with his band.

The evening always began with a sumptuous meal. It would be eaten off the long mahogany table in the room that on more sober occasions served as a boardroom, where Lorrance would hold meetings of a different kind. There would be presents for the guests at every place-setting: wraps of coke, a few joints, colourful little sweets. Lorrance seemed to want the meetings to have a mysterious flavour. He would toast the powers of the universe that had given him his wealth and position, and invite his guests to petition these same powers for boons of their own. The strange shadow guests, in their dark suits, would sit there apart from everyone else; watching, perhaps supervising. Dex called these people ghosts; all they did was haunt. Lorrance said they were business colleagues, but what kind of business? Dex sensed that Lorrance too was wary of these people. He rarely kept his eyes off them for long, as if afraid they might slink off into some corner of the house, perhaps to plant bugging devices or poison the water.

After the meal, the drinking would continue, spiced with whatever narcotics were available. Even now, Dex could only recall impressions of those times; the sado-masochistic shows in dim red light, the press of hot flesh against his own, reeking breath, the scent of abandon, beyond all care. Young women would stagger drunkenly through the rooms, clutch-ing half-empty bottles of vodka or whisky, giggling together, falling upon whichever famous bodies they could find. And for those with alternative tastes, there were beautiful youths, with knowing, hard eyes and skilled hands. Dex had no doubt that every forbidden desire could be gratified in that house. Lorrance would pride himself on it.

On Sunday mornings, the revellers would come to, puffy-eyed and sick. Lorrance, on the other hand, was one of those people who seemed to shrug off the effects of drugs and alcohol. Perhaps his body was pickled in a cocktail of substances that generated energy. He never looked ill, and would take his breakfast at ten o'clock – in the garden in summer, or in the heated conservatory in winter. His guests would mill round the house dispiritedly, departing gradually in their cars. By midday, the house would be empty, although Dex might sometimes stay until Monday morning, when he would return with Lorrance to the city.

'Look at them,' Lorrance would say as his guests drifted away. 'So easily sated and depleted.'

Dex would not comment, for he felt he was the same. And slightly soiled. He was relieved he could never recall the weekend's events in detail.

It was inconceivable that Samantha and Lacey Lorrance could even be a remote part of this world. Samantha would invariably return late Sunday afternoon. After a moment's frowned contemplation, during which she might have sensed a strange taint in the air, she would shrug off whatever bothered her, smile brightly and chatter on in her high voice, attempting to groom out her East End inflections.

'Oh, look at this, Rhys,' she would say, fluffing out some fragile garment from her purchases. 'Innit lovely?'

'Charming.'

Lorrance would kiss her on the cheek and offer her a gin and tonic and she'd always say, 'All right, though it's a bit early.'

She would supervise the staff while they cooked dinner, unaware that since dawn a battalion of cleaners hired from the city had been scraping and sweeping the remnants of the two-day party from the rooms. Dex had even known Lorrance call in a decorator at short notice, after an unfortunate episode of projectile vomiting from one of the guests.

Samantha twittered about the house, bringing with her a completely different atmosphere, a kind of innocence. Dex was at once repelled and fascinated by her. She had a healing presence, albeit one that grated on his nerves.

Lacey might sometimes appear on Sunday evenings. Samantha went out of her way to curry favour with the girl, attempts to which Lacey seemed oblivious. Lorrance appeared uncomfortable around his daughter, perhaps because he realised she was far more astute than his wife, and might therefore spot evidence of what went on in the house. The situation couldn't have lasted; that much was obvious. It was almost as if Lorrance was dicing with fate, pushing to the limit the risk of exposure.

The weekend began as any other. Music throbbed from various rooms, interspersed with high-pitched laughter and drunken shouting, and the sounds of running feet. Dex lay in a drugged stupor on a sofa in the main lounge, while a faceless person – and he couldn't even remember if they were male or female – expertly fellated him. Dimly, he was aware of a pulsing roar outside that sounded like a helicopter. That might be possible; he'd seen the dark men arrive that way.

Shortly afterwards, Dex heard a commotion in the hallway; shouting then, unmistakably, screams.

Dex struggled out into the hall, and at first saw only a mêlée of people and buzzing activity that made no sense. Then he realised they were all milling around something on the floor: a male body, lying face down, its limbs in an eerie approximation of a swastika. A couple of girls were screaming, repeatedly, monotonously, with hardly a pause for breath. Others were talking fast, gesticulating wildly, but no one, for some reason, knelt down to check for a pulse.

Lorrance appeared at the head of the stairs. He looked terrifying, like a vengeful god; tall, golden and powerful.

'Shut up!' he roared and everyone did. He descended the stairs slowly. He wore a long, striped silk dressing-gown and leather slippers, but otherwise seemed perfectly groomed. His eyes were cold. At the bottom of the stairs, he shouted, 'Move!' and flapped his hands at the crowd. 'Get out of here!' They backed into the rooms whence they'd come; chastened demons. Only Dex remained. He and Lorrance stared down at the body on the floor, a young man Dex did not know, but felt he should recognise. 'Who is it?' Dex asked eventually.

'Some tart,' Lorrance answered.

'He looks very dead,' Dex said, wobbling on his feet.

Lorrance nodded. 'It would appear so.'

'Should we . . . call someone?'

Lorrance fixed him with a gaze that seemed at once blazing and icy. 'Who, his fucking mother?'

Dex winced away from the blast of words, shrugged helplessly.

'He's just a little slag off the streets. We dump him. Can you drive?'

Dex laughed, a nervous reflex. 'Drive?' He couldn't say any more.

'Just a couple of miles down the lane. We'll take it slowly. There's no police around here who aren't good friends of mine.'

'But what will you tell people?'

'That we took him to hospital. He's only dead to us, Dex.'

'No, Rhys, I can't.'

'You can.'

'No, this isn't right.'

Lorrance fixed him with a stare. In his eyes, Dex saw infinity stretching back; a relentless void. 'You have no feelings,' Lorrance said quietly. 'Not about this.'

Dex looked down. There was a body on the floor; they'd have to deal with it. The dead boy had always been dead for Dex; he possessed no personality and no past. Whatever he'd thought or felt a moment before had vanished.

Between them, Dex and Lorrance lifted the body into a

soft approximation of standing. They arranged the limbs, so it looked as if they were supporting the boy tenderly for the short, slow walk to Lorrance's car. It was possible to believe he was only unconscious. A couple of the floor tiles were cracked where the body had hit them; they were smeared with blood. The rooms were hushed around them, as if every party-goer was afraid and holding their breath. Sounds echoed hollowly. The body weighed heavily against Dex's shoulder. He told himself, 'this is a dead person', but could feel nothing in his heart.

In the car – a sleek silver Mercedes – Lorrance sat in the back, his arm around the body. Dex backed the vehicle out of the garage, and saw two tall, indistinct figures standing in the driveway, illumined only by the crimson glow of a cigarette. 'Who are those people?' Dex asked. He could not see their faces.

'They are friends of ours,' Lorrance answered. 'That's all you need to know.'

The two men appeared to watch the car as it left the estate, but it was difficult to tell. In the rear-view mirror, Dex could see only shadows. There was no sign of a helicopter on the field before the house.

Out in the lanes, Dex found it surprisingly easy to drive. 'Where to?' he asked.

'The forest,' Lorrance answered. 'I'll direct you.'

They drove along in silence for a while, and all Dex could see in his mind was those two shadowy figures on Lorrance's driveway. The image eclipsed even that of the body sprawled on the floor. Dex swallowed with difficulty. He glanced in the mirror and saw Lorrance's face. He was gazing placidly out of the window at the passing countryside, apparently without a care in the world.

'Somebody might find the body,' Dex said. He wanted reassurance.

Lorrance shrugged. 'Unlikely. The place where it will lie for eternity is on my land. My land is private.'

'Someone from the party might say something.'

Lorrance laughed coldly. 'About what? The ones who

remember anything clearly in the morning won't want to be involved. They know better than to try and make trouble. Don't worry on my account, nor your own.'

Dex was unnerved by Lorrance's insouciance. He had always believed that truth leaked out eventually, that it was an unwritten law of life, no matter how long it took.

'Turn off here,' Lorrance said, indicating an old five-bar gate. Dex turned the car's nose towards it. The headlights illumined a wide track, leading between a high avenue of elms. A chain hung heavily from the gatepost. Dex could see a padlock.

'Have you got a key, Rhys?'

'Nowhere is out of bounds to me,' Lorrance said. He opened the car door, got out, and the body slid heavily into the vacant seat.

Dex drummed his fingers against the steering wheel. Lorrance had his back to him. He could not see what happened with the gate, but how could Lorrance have had keys on him? He was still wearing only a dressing-gown.

Once Lorrance got back into the car, they drove a short way into the woods, taking a left turn to crawl up a narrower track. Then Lorrance directed Dex to stop the car. Outside, the night was still and fragrant, although there seemed to be noises in the distance that Dex could not identify: heavy sounds, like muffled booming.

Carrying the body between them, the two men walked for some minutes along the track, until they came to an old ruin on their right, which had once been a lodge of some kind. Perhaps a gamekeeper had lived there. Moonlight picked out few details, other than the bulk of the crumbling walls, the slick shine of ivy. The roof had gone, but the ceiling of the ground floor ensured the lower rooms were in darkness.

'There's a cellar under the lodge,' Lorrance said. 'Take my torch and put the body down there.'

Dex did not appreciate the suggestion. 'Aren't you going to help me?'

'No. Hurry up.'

Dex studied the ruins. They seemed watchful, slightly

malevolent. He suspected Lorrance might have made use of them before.

'Get on with it,' Lorrance said coldly. 'Don't waste time.'

Reluctantly, Dex began to drag the body towards the shadows. Piles of masonry covered the ground near the open front door, and littered the floor of the interior. Dex shone the torch around. Sticks of furniture remained, and unidentifiable rags hung from the rafters. He couldn't just throw the body down the dark stone stairs. If this boy must die without a name, without mourners, it seemed the least Dex could do was carry his remains into the cellar. He still wasn't convinced this was a good place to conceal it. Kids might come here. But there was no sign that anyone had visited the place recently.

Dex's feet slipped on the damp steps, but he kept the torch beam directed straight ahead. He didn't want to look around this place. The atmosphere pressed down upon him, watchful, perhaps scornful. He hastily arranged the body on the floor, which was covered in rubbish he didn't investigate. This was Lorrance's problem, not his. He was just helping out.

But you're part of this, a sharp inner voice reminded him. You're a conspirator.

'Shit,' he said aloud. For a few moments he squatted, hunched, on the floor, his elbows resting on his knees. It was as if he'd been floating in a dark ocean, and now it had closed over his head. He'd always known Lorrance was ruthless, but this was something worse. Why had he agreed to help Lorrance dispose of the body? He should have walked away, yet back at the house, Lorrance's compelling gaze had overridden his own feelings. Someone will find this body, he thought, someone will. Then someone might say something, someone with a conscience. Did anyone at Lorrance's parties have consciences?

A voice came out of the darkness, 'They never found *me*, Chris.'

Every hair on Dex's body stood up. For a moment, he could not move, then adrenaline flooded his body and he was up the stairs like a bird, fumbling his way through the dark ruins. It was Little Peter's voice he had heard. Little Peter, a ghost who had never been laid to rest.

Back in the car, Lorrance had just rolled and lit a fat joint. 'Took your time,' he said as Dex flung himself, panting, into the front seat. 'What's up? Saw a ghost?'

'Fuck!' Dex put his head in his hands. 'I fucking heard something.'

Lorrance leaned forward over the seat, making the leather creak. 'What did you hear?'

'A voice. It's nothing. I was hallucinating. It was creepy down there.'

'And did you complete your task?'

Dex rubbed his face with his hands. 'Yeah.' He glanced over his shoulder. 'Is it safe, Rhys?'

Lorrance leaned back. 'Quite safe. Join me in the back here. We can't return to the party yet – not enough time for us to have driven to a hospital.'

Dex clambered over the seats, and took the joint from Lorrance's hands. 'I need that. Give it here.'

Lorrance observed him coolly. 'You're the one I trust, Dex. You have done well tonight.'

A cold fist seemed to close on Dex's stomach. Had this been a test? 'What happened? How did he fall?'

Lorrance laughed. 'Very easily,' he answered.

Dex narrowed his eyes. 'What . . . ?'

'He said he would die for me. And he did.'

Dex sucked furiously on the joint. 'This is bad, Rhys, very bad. I don't want any part of things like this. It's all getting out of hand.'

Lorrance reached out and stroked Dex's hair. 'No, it's just time for a change. Life is a series of cycles, each different from the last.'

'You can't trust those people who call themselves your friends. You don't know one of them won't talk.'

'I do know. Don't worry. You must learn to trust me. Haven't I always been right in the past?' Lorrance laughed softly to himself.

When they returned to the party, it seemed as if nothing out of the ordinary had happened. The music was up again, the laughter, the shouting. People had walked across the smear of blood on the cracked tiles, which was the only evidence of the young man's demise. Dex felt nervous, sick, afraid. He went out into the garden and sat there for over an hour, smoking dope and swigging from a bottle of bourbon. His mind was curiously devoid of images, although the words he thought he'd heard in the cellar of the old lodge occasionally flashed across his consciousness. 'They never found *me*, Chris.' Dex knew that somewhere, the body of Little Peter lay hidden from view. It had to, didn't it? People didn't just disappear.

Around two a.m., Lorrance came out of the house and swam into Dex's field of vision. He was dressed in a soft cream jumper and dark jeans. He looked young, his golden hair catching the starlight. Dex stared up at him, blinking. 'I can't live with this, Rhys. I . . .'

Lorrance made an irritated gesture. 'Dex, there's someone who wants to meet you, someone important.'

'I don't want to meet anyone.'

Lorrance sighed, grabbed Dex's right arm and hauled him to his feet. 'Pull yourself together, there's a good boy.'

'Rhys . . .'

'Come on.' Lorrance's gaze was steady, commanding.

Sighing, Dex followed him into the house. 'What is this, Rhys?' He felt in no condition to meet anyone, let alone someone who was important to Lorrance.

Lorrance said nothing, but took Dex into his study, which he always kept locked during parties. The room was lit dimly; a fire burned in the hearth. A large, florid-faced man sat in the high-backed chair at Lorrance's antique desk. He was smoking a pipe, and his eyes, within their wads of flesh, were like an eagle's, as if they could see for miles or through walls. Dex had never seen the man in person before, but knew who it was: Lester Charney. Behind him stood a tall, attenuated dark figure, whose posture was slightly hunched. This second man looked foreign, being dark-skinned, but Dex could not place his nationality.

'Well, Les, here he is, our golden boy. Dex, this is Lester Charney.'

'Golden goose,' said Charney, appraising Dex with his aquiline gaze. He was surrounded by a sweet smell of perfumed tobacco. His body was ponderous, but Dex had the impression it could move very quickly. He had never been afraid of anyone in his life, not even his brother Gary, and he wasn't afraid now. The feeling went deeper than that, to evoke a primal instinct for survival. You could not flee from this man, and you could not fight him; the only choice was to serve. Such ideas were alien to Dex, who prided himself on his autonomy. Even in his stupor, he recognised that he had been brought before the dark heart of the empire; its emperor.

'All right,' he said by way of greeting.

Charney blinked mildly. 'You are a great asset to us,' he said. 'And perhaps will be greater still. A pity you abuse yourself, but that can be changed.' He signalled to Lorrance, who went to a cabinet and returned carrying a very small glass of a milky liquid, which he offered to Dex.

Dex laughed uncertainly. 'What's this?'

'Drink it,' said Charney. 'I want to talk to a functioning mind.'

The dark man behind Charney neither moved nor spoke, but kept his attention wholly upon Dex. He looked like a vulture, waiting for something to die. Dex, realising he had no other choice, took the glass and swallowed the contents. The taste was indescribable, yet not entirely unpleasant. It sent a rush to his brain that made him stumble backwards, but sobered him almost immediately. He was sensitively aware of his surroundings, the three men who observed him.

'That's better,' said Charney. He took a long draw on his pipe. 'You push yourself to the limit, in body and mind, but just how far are you prepared to go?'

Dex brushed his hair from his eyes. 'What do you want?'

'An answer to my question: how far?'

'I've got where I want to be.'

Charney laughed softly. 'So little ambition? You're not even on the first rung of the ladder. You're praying at its feet.'

Lorrance put a hand on Dex's shoulder. 'You're being given a chance,' he said. 'You must take it.'

'A chance for what?' Dex squirmed away from Lorrance's touch.

'A chance to be more than just a minor celebrity who will be burned out within a few years,' Charney said. 'Rhys is very pleased with you. He has spoken to me about you.' He chuckled, in a disturbingly avuncular manner. 'I think you remind him of a younger, more idealistic form of himself. Is that right, Rhys?'

'He has fire,' Lorrance said softly and turned to Dex. 'You have anger. You despise the world, and your music has power. That can all be honed into something greater.'

'We are always alert for people such as yourself,' Charney said. 'We are a select group, and extremely particular about whom we involve in our operations. We are the hub at the centre of the wheel. You are being invited to put the hectic spin of life behind you and sit at the centre of stillness, where all is controlled. Do you understand this?'

Dex nodded. 'Money runs the world. I know where you're coming from.'

Charnely nodded. 'And are you with us?'

'Why me?' He displayed his palms to Charney. 'I'm not like you. I'm not part of your world.'

Charney grinned. 'You are. And Rhys believes you are more like us than you know. You're just the raw material, which it is our job to shape and polish. Now, answer me. Are you with us?'

'I'm not into this kind of thing.' He shuffled his feet uncomfortably.

Charney drew in his breath slowly. 'There *are* fates worse than death. What you saw tonight was nothing. Now, are you with us?'

Dex glanced at the dark man standing behind Charney's chair. He knew then that should he answer in the negative, he would be destroyed. Nothing so crude as murder, or even a fatal accident, something worse. This was what his weekends of gratification had led to. He had walked into

226

the hot and humid jungle, hungry for sensation, and had inadvertently wandered into the territory of the lions. They had been watching him all along from the shadows.

'Whatever,' he said. At that moment, all he wanted was to escape that room. 'Whatever you fucking want.'

Lorrance and Charney exchanged a glance. Charney was expressionless. 'I generally trust your judgement, Rhys, but have to confess I do not find this candidate entirely suitable.'

'He *is* the right raw material,' said Lorrance. 'He must learn.'

'Then teach him,' Charney murmured, 'and bring him to me when you're done.'

Lorrance bowed his head.

'I appreciated your gift tonight,' said Charney, leaning back in his chair. 'It was the sweetest thing.' He kissed his fingertips. 'I feel utterly sated.'

'My pleasure.' Lorrance put a hand on Dex's back and steered him towards the door. Dex felt chilled inside. He was sure that in some way Charney had drawn strength from the anonymous boy's death. He glanced back at the desk. Charney and his dark man were conferring. Lorrance and Dex had been dismissed.

Outside, Dex said, 'What the hell was all that about?'

Lorrance stroked his cheek. 'Can't you guess? You're being admitted into the club.'

'Like the fucking masons, or something?'

'Something,' said Lorrance. He leaned forward and kissed Dex on the mouth. 'Don't let me down. Charney will be disappointed.'

Dex was surprised by the kiss. Lorrance had never touched him in that way before. 'What do you want of me?'

'Commitment, truth, courage. In return, you'll learn about power. You'll have what you want from life, whatever that may be.'

'Rhys, you shouldn't have done this to me,' Dex said. 'Why didn't you ask me first? I don't want this.'

'It's too late.'

'I fucking realise that. You had no right.'

'No right?' Lorrance laughed in genuine amusement. 'I made you, Dex. I can do with you what I like. If you think otherwise, you're far more stupid than I gave you credit for.' He stroked Dex's hair. 'Be angry, if you like, for that is part of you. Live it. But know you can trust me.'

He left Dex standing in the hallway of the house, the party tumbling around him. Dex felt nauseous now, and confused. What had just happened might have been a dream. If only it had been. The effects of the potion he'd swallowed were diminishing; his senses were fuzzy, his limbs prickled. He needed to sit down.

In the drawing-room, he collapsed on to a sofa, his mind curiously blank. For some time, perhaps hours, he stared at the ceiling. Sounds rose and pounced like waves; music, voices, the purr of fabric against flesh. He could smell the sweat of everyone in the house. He could smell their dissipation, their lack of awareness, their self-centred terror. On the other side of the gate was truth, and the gate was the word 'whatever'.

There were no weekend parties at Emmertame after that. If any of Lorrance's guests or staff mentioned to friends or family what they'd seen that night, it never leaked out. They were all conspirators. Zeke Michaels had not been a guest that weekend, and Dex doubted he'd ever been told what had happened there.

Dex knew that something had marked him, something beyond what he understood about the world. He waited for a summons from Lorrance, for the education that Charney had spoken of to begin. He lived in dread of it. When the accident had happened in the hall of Emmertame, Dex had not felt that affected by the young man's death, perhaps because of Lorrance's influence, but afterwards this was not the case. He was haunted by it, and sickened by the callous way in which Lorrance had dealt with it. Dex had become part of this world, and had come to hate it. He was not the person Lorrance believed or wanted him to be. In his youth, all Dex's songs had been full of fire against the very things he now did himself, the world in which he moved. He had become part of all he had despised, and worse. It had happened insidiously, crept up on him, bit by bit, until he was fully in the thick of it.

Often, Dex thought of confiding in Jay about what had happened that night at Lorrance's, but couldn't bring himself to. Despite her sassy worldliness, she now seemed innocent to him. He couldn't involve her. It wouldn't be fair. She was part of the sacrifice he must make to cleanse himself. He wrote songs about that night, every detail of it, lashing himself and the world he inhabited, the world run by people like Charney and Lorrance, to whom life meant nothing and power meant all. Dex had lost sight of any spirituality in his life, and now yearned to rediscover it. This would be the new album. Through music, he would tell the world a few truths, albeit concealed in parcels of words that only a few might unwrap. Words came more easily now. Language was a tool he could wield with mordant precision. If this gift came from Lorrance and his overlords, Dex would use it to expose them. He was withdrawing his consent to Lorrance's schemes. Dex knew the path he had chosen might mean his own destruction, but he could see no other way. Unless he fought now, he would be lost. He knew his weaknesses.

Lorrance must have sensed Dex's withdrawal, but undoubtedly viewed it as a temporary reaction. He would, after all, be confident of his power over his protégé. A month or so after the party, he called Dex on his mobile (he never liked Jay to know when he'd called), and asked how the tracks for *Songs to the Shadow* were going. 'I'm exorcising ghosts,' Dex had said.

'Nothing too gloomy, I trust,' Lorrance replied.

Dex was filled with the urge to rebel, which had often been his undoing in the past. 'Perhaps you should hear them.'

A pause. 'Yes. Come to dinner this Sunday.'

After he'd broken the connection, Dex considered he might have spoken unwisely. Before Sunday, he made a few changes to the lyrics, encoded their meaning more cryptically.

* * *

Lacey was at Emmertame that Sunday night; a cold, sullen presence at the dinner table. She had dyed her fair hair different colours of red and green, which had faded. Her clothes were a jumble of ethnic styles that hid her body. She reeked of patchouli. Dex wondered why she ever bothered going home, as the experience clearly brought her no pleasure.

'Good of you to dress for dinner,' Lorrance said.

Lacey shrugged, disinterested in his opinion, and drank some wine. She glanced at Dex with what appeared to be despising. Dex could tell she considered him to be simply her father's creature.

Samantha yacked her way through the courses, leaving no space for other voices, which was perhaps fortunate as Dex felt he had nothing to say. Lacey kept directing penetrating glances at her father, which sometimes he would return. Dex was puzzled about their relationship. Lacey hardly spoke, but a conversation took place, Dex was sure of that.

After dinner, he and Lorrance went into the oak-panelled music room, and Dex produced a tape of his recent songs. Lorrance poured brandy, and they both sat in leather, high-backed chairs as the music spilled out of the hi-fi. Lorrance said nothing, sipping his drink steadily. Dex had sought to wrap his statements up in metaphor and innuendo, but now it seemed all too obvious what he sang about. At the end of it, Lorrance rose slowly from his chair, put his drink down deliberately on a side table and moved to the stereo. With careful, precise movements, he took the tape out of the machine and began pulling it from its case. It tumbled out like shining entrails.

'Hey!' Dex half rose from his chair, but was paralysed by a glance from Lorrance.

'I presume this is not the only copy,' he said, still pulling tape. The spools screeched softly.

'No.' Dex was stunned. He had meant to say he would tone down the sentiments in the songs, but it seemed Lorrance had already made up his mind about them.

'Are you insane?' Lorrance inquired gently. 'You must

destroy these songs. The music is good, of course, but the rest must go. I do this only for your sake, Dex.'

'I told you, it was an exorcism,' Dex said. 'I can only write what's in my head.'

'Whip yourself in private,' Lorrance said. 'I can't believe what you've done.'

Something in his tone made Dex crack. 'Can't believe what *I've* done?' He laughed coldly. 'Have you never thought about what happened?' For a brief moment, Dex's mind was filled with the image of a forgotten, rotting body, lying in a cellar, half eaten by rats and insects. He had to put his fingers against his mouth, afraid of retching.

'No, I don't think about it,' Lorrance replied. 'There's no point. It happened, and the occasion marked the end of our parties for a while.'

'Did you kill that boy, Rhys?'

Lorrance stared at him. He didn't seem angry or affronted. 'He killed himself. It was unfortunate, and something to be put behind us. It certainly should not be shouted about in songs. Do you understand that?'

Dex closed his eyes. So far, nobody appeared to have searched for that boy, not like people had for Little Peter. Nobody cared. The evidence was slowly disappearing into the quiet, listening forest, until nothing would remain.

'You are learning,' Lorrance said, 'and I appreciate this blood-letting is part of the process, but it's time for you to rise above petty human codes.'

Dex glared at him. 'I'm not interested. You conned me into something, and I don't even know what it is. I don't want to know.'

Lorrance smiled kindly. 'You are part of it now. There's no going back. Whatever your view of morality is, rest assured it's only a product of human limitation. True power is beyond morality. Sanctimony and righteousness are for the weak and ignorant. I have hauled you out of the masses. You are awake now, Dex. Get used to it. See the world as it is.'

'I've always been awake.'

Lorrance shook his head slowly. 'You've been dozing,' he said. 'Dreaming.'

Dex stood up. 'I have to go.'

Lorrance nodded, clearly at ease. 'Very well. I will see you again soon. Make a new DAT, Dex. Take off the vocals and write something snappy that the kids will like.' He smiled and tapped his brow. 'Let your true songs, your essence, play up here. Eventually, you will communicate them, but only once you've achieved a certain level of understanding. This will take time, I know, but I am not concerned about you, Dex. I can see your soul.'

Dex shuddered inside. 'I'm not what you think I am.'

'You have no idea what I think you are.'

Lorrance walked with Dex to the front door. There, he put a hand on Dex's shoulder. 'Did you hope to reach me with those songs, make me feel remorse?'

'No. It was just for myself.'

'Just as well. Good-night, Dex. Drive carefully.'

Out in the night, Dex stood in the driveway and stared back at the house. It was an evil place and it had touched him intimately. If he stayed around Lorrance, perhaps all that was good within him would die, and he'd become like the others, like Charney. Three Swords. They pierced the heart of the world.

Dex got into his car, and turned on the CD player. Songs from his last album, *Memory Drift*, surrounded him. Songs that had meant something. He knew Lorrance wanted him to write vapid confections about drugs and partying and shallow sex. Feed the masses what they want. Help them stay asleep. He remembered his original vision and what he'd hoped to achieve. He'd wanted to throw cold water over people, wake them up to reality. How far he'd strayed from the path. Perhaps the only way to escape whatever Lorrance had decided for him was to sacrifice himself. The songs he'd written should be released. He should be honest. If they weren't, perhaps nothing should be released at all. People might wonder, then. As he put the car in gear to set off, a ray of light spilled out of the house, then disappeared.

The front door had opened and closed. Dex peered out at the drive, and saw a slim figure approaching. It was Lacey. She leaned down to look into the car, her face impassive. 'Drive me somewhere,' she said.

'Sure,' Dex answered. 'Get in.'

She walked around the car, her feet crunching on gravel. Once she had climbed in, she filled the interior with her earthy patchouli scent.

'Where do you want to go?' Dex asked. She had no bag with her. Her hands, with their multi-coloured fingernails, were clasped loosely in her lap.

'Just drive.'

Dex set off down the driveway. Lacey said nothing, staring out of the windscreen. He wondered what she wanted from him. 'I'm going back to London,' he said. 'You want to go there?'

She shook her head. 'You can stop in a moment.'

'Why? What is this?'

She glanced at him. 'Stop now.' They were only a short way from the gates to the estate. Dex pulled on to the grass at the side of the road. Bright moonlight shone into the car, illumined the landscape around it without colour.

'Well?' Dex said.

'Don't be a fool all your life,' Lacey murmured.

Dex stared at her. 'I'm no fool. What do you want?'

She smiled bitterly. 'You are a fool. You shouldn't give in to my father. He didn't make you, he just used you.'

'You listened to our conversation.' Dex leaned back in his seat, his arms folded.

'Yes, I listened,' Lacey said. 'I have no interest in you, that's not why I'm talking to you now. I care only about truth.'

Dex expelled a bark of caustic laughter. 'Truth?' He shook his head. 'Get out of the car, Lacey. Don't try to involve me in any family feuds.' It was not inconceivable Lorrance had sent his daughter out here himself.

Lacey raised her eyebrows at Dex, spoke coldly. 'I'm not involving you in anything. All I'm saying is be true to yourself.' She opened the car door. 'I know what happens,' she said, and walked away from the vehicle, leaving the door hanging open.

Dex watched her walk back on to the driveway to home. Had that been another test? Dex could not tell. Perhaps Lacey had acted from her own impulses, in which case, how much did she know?

It was shortly after this that Lacey Lorrance absconded from university and ran away. Dex found out about it from Zeke Michaels. 'She's gone to join a hippy commune or something,' he said. Dex privately wondered if this was true.

Dex pretended to work on the new material, but spent all of his time thinking. When the time came to go on tour, he was terrified. He had made the decision to perform the songs as they should be performed. He would sing the truth. Then, after the first gig, he realised an incontrovertible truth. He stood up on stage, watching the audience pulsing to the music, their hands held aloft. He sang to them – really sang to them – projecting into his voice all the feeling in his heart. The applause came, the baying, but it was no different from the response to any other concert. They still howled for the old familiar songs. Dex realised then that his fans never really heard him. His painful revelations, about himself and the world, had washed over them. He expected too much from them. Their adoration was his life-blood, but for them to adore him they had to be ignorant. He could not have their understanding and their blind faith, for faith dies in the glare of awareness. At that moment, as the lights dimmed, and he left the stage, he realised he had gambled with the commitment of his audience, but had misjudged them, over-estimated their intelligence. He was no guru to them; he was a star. Gurus might speak, and people might learn from them, but stars merely glowed; beautiful, but remote. The audience would never respond in the way he'd like. They'd never come to their senses and say, 'Yes, he's right. We must do something about this.' But he sensed the power he had over them, the sort much prized by Lorrance and his kind.

Gina Allen was standing in the wings, chewing the inside of her cheek. Dex felt scorched by her glance. She looked predatory.

He brushed past her. Backstage, Dex began to fret. He knew that Lorrance would soon discover he'd dared to sing the forbidden songs, because he'd noticed earlier on that a half dozen or so dark-suited ghosts had been stationed around the edge of the venue. What would be the consequences of his actions? He'd be punished in some way. Jay might even be in danger, or Julie and the kids. And for what? The audience hadn't even noticed his message. They adored him, but not Dex the person. He wasn't real to them. They didn't want him to be real. Neither did the carrion-eaters that hung around the scene, the social climbers, the wannabes.

Dex had sensed the power in his voice, a force that became stronger every day. His education had been taking place whether he co-operated with Three Swords or not. He was changing. And nobody would notice. He could charm people, influence them, direct them, and like drugged sheep they'd comply. What value did these people have, anyway? Men like Charney and Lorrance existed because the masses were too lazy and self-centred to care. There were fates worse than death. Dex could wait for it, or walk away from it all, deny them their victory. Ultimately, it had not been a difficult choice to make.

Chapter Twenty

Jay sat with her head in her hands, her elbows resting on the worn table-top. 'I was a fool not to sense anything was wrong with you,' she said. 'I was too wrapped up in deadlines and that shallow, horrible life.'

Dex moved uneasily. 'Don't blame yourself, Jay. I was deeply in the shit before I even met you. You gave me respite, you gave me love, but ultimately it was not enough.'

'Thanks.'

Dex ran his hands through his hair. 'By the time I left you, I was hardly myself any more. I had to go, just to try and recapture what I'd been. Jay, if I'd stayed, I don't know what would have happened. Leaving you was the kindest thing I could do. You found a new life . . .'

Jay leaned forward. 'Dex, be quiet. I loved you. You should have told me what was going on. We could have got out of it together. I would have stood by you. We respected one another.'

Dex was silent for a moment. 'I didn't want to put you in danger. I thought you'd get over me.'

'Some people you never get over,' Jay said. 'I learned to live with it, that's all. I'll never meet anyone like you again.'

Dex pulled a rueful face. 'I'm not that special, Jay, not really. I'm an ordinary northern bloke, who got lucky. You wouldn't have looked twice at me otherwise.'

Jay shook her head in exasperation. 'It didn't matter to me about the fame, the adulation. Can't you understand? You could have been a bricklayer. It was never about that.'

'We wouldn't even have met if I wasn't what I was.'

'But we did meet. It happened. It was precious.'

He took her hands and rested his forehead on them. 'I'm sorry. I'm so sorry.'

Jay kissed his hair, inhaled that familiar smell. She wanted to hold him, absorb his pain, cleanse him. Perhaps there would be a time for that. She withdrew her hands from beneath his. 'Dex, you have to tell me now: what stirred it all up again? Why did Sakrilege take an interest in me after three years? Why did someone say they'd seen us together?'

He raised his head. 'It might be partly because I showed up at Lorrance's house. I let him see me. I wanted to fucking spook him and I did. He probably thought I'd decided to return to my old life and that I'd make contact with you.'

'Would you have done, if Sakrilege hadn't taken that interest in me?'

He paused. 'Jay, I don't know. I thought about you a lot. But I was screwed up with self-pity. I thought I was bad news for you.'

'Dex, shut up. We were good for each other. Whatever the consequences, you should have confided in me. I'd have faced death for you. Didn't you realise that? My life without you was so empty. If you were trying to spare me, you didn't. I'd have been happier being with you, whatever we had to face. I could have been your strength.'

'You were,' he said. 'And I was wrong to do what I did. But at the time, there seemed no other way.'

'So where do we go from here?'

He might have misinterpreted the question, or simply didn't want to answer it. 'All I can tell you is that I feel a movement in the world. It's as if big clouds are gathering in the sky. Power resides in the songs I wrote, power that Lorrance gave to me. They were worth more than anyone knew. I might not have been able to release them, but I wrote them, Jay, I sang them. Something is going to change. I can sense it. Three Swords have enemies. Not everyone with power in the world uses it for selfish reasons.'

'How do you know? Who are these enemies?'

'It sounds crazy, but I think they're a kind of force for balance. I've never met any of them, but I've felt them.' He frowned. 'It all goes on above us, Jay. Silent unseen wars and power struggles. It's happening all the time, and most people never know. I think it's happening now. Lorrance's enemies want the tapes, because they'd give them access to his power. Then, they would be able to pierce Three Swords' weak spots. The songs are like spells. It's hard to accept, I know, but it's the truth.'

'I can accept that people might believe that,' Jay said. She narrowed her eyes. 'Someone must have thought I'd lead them to you – and the tapes.'

Dex looked at her bleakly. 'There are no tapes, Jay.'

'What?' She'd been through hell for nothing.

'I destroyed them,' Dex said. 'That's why I left the empty box back home. I thought you'd realise.'

Jay's eyes were wide. 'You must let Lorrance know this, Dex. Wouldn't Sakrilege leave me alone, then?'

Dex pulled a scornful face. 'I don't think it would make much difference. Lorrance will be furious I slipped away from his hold. He's quite capable of punishing you in my place and is probably already doing so. I think he enjoys destroying people. He's powerful and he's amoral. His mind is strong, and his life force, and his will. He despises people, because he thinks they are beneath him in every way, and perhaps most of them are. He's not all bad, Jay, because if he was, he wouldn't be able to affect people the way he does. I'm sure he's convinced that what he does is right, perhaps even inevitable. You don't have to like him, but you can almost admire what he is. He, and people like him, run the world.' Dex put his finger into a pool of liquid on the table top, stirred it round. 'People who control the media control the thoughts of the people, their desires and aspirations, even their opinions.'

'Don't believe everything you read in the press, right?' Jay made a scornful sound. 'Dex, I'm a journalist. My work is about truth.'

'Your *work*?' Dex asked archly.

There was a silence. 'I still have my work,' Jay said. 'Lorrance can't stop me writing, or influence my opinions. I could publish stuff myself, sell it on the street, post it on the Internet.'

'You could try,' said Dex. 'But now you're here, in Lestholme, where the lost ones hide.'

'OK, let's talk about this place, shall we?' Jay said. She gestured widely with her arms. 'I still want a rational explanation.'

Dex glanced at Jem, who so far had remained silent. 'I want to know, too,' she said.

'Are you sure?' Dex asked her.

She nodded.

'OK, there is no rational explanation. Lestholme is a fantasy place, a land removed from ordinary reality that perhaps has no boundaries.' His gestures became more emphatic. 'Most of us exist on one level of reality, but under the right circumstances, it's possible for us to enter another layer or level. The people who come here make a decision to leave their lives, in whatever way. Dark light falls from the monument on the hill. It attracts them, because despite its power, it provides succour. People can be ghosts here.'

'Dex,' Jay said warningly. 'I can't accept that. It sounds like the ramblings of an addled mind.'

'But that's it! You can't accept it because you've lived all your life in the mundane world. People like the higher echelons of Three Swords know there's more to existence than that. Their ability to accept the unbelievable is what gives them their advantage. Charney is the real god here, Jay, not Lorrance. He's the one with the greater knowledge and understanding.'

Jay wrinkled her nose, rubbed her face. 'Supposing, just supposing, I can suspend disbelief and take in what you're saying. I still don't understand why Lorrance should be seen as a god at all. Surely, he should be the devil for the people here?'

Dex considered this. 'He's not really a god, just a symbol. To be a god, wouldn't he have to be aware of Lestholme? Lorrance runs *The Eye* tabloid for Three Swords. If you like, the villagers are the sacrificial victims of *The Eye*, the eye of god. Charney is the dark light behind all gods.' Dex made an earnest gesture. 'People need symbols. It's how they understand the things they cannot see or even perceive. In your reality, Charney and Lorrance are simply powerful men, perhaps evil, but here, and maybe in other levels, they become their aspirations.'

Jay stared at him, her mind reeling. She did not doubt his sincerity. If she believed him, she had her explanation, rational or not, but she still found it hard to accept. 'Whatever this place is, however it exists, I don't want to stay here for ever. How do I get out, Dex? How do I get back what was mine? Do you know?'

He paused, then nodded uncertainly. 'I think all you need to get out is the true desire to return. You can go back when you're ready. Are you ready?'

Jay took a deep breath. 'Yes. I am. I couldn't leave before, because I hadn't found you, and I think some part of me knew instinctively I'd find you here. Now, I want to face what's out there, not hide away.' She paused. 'Will you come with me?'

He stared at her steadily. 'I'll take you out, yes. There's something I'd like to demonstrate to you.'

Jay sensed the reticence in his words. He would not stay out there with her, and she would not beg. She sighed through her nose. 'OK, so how are we going to do it? I've tried to leave before, and I thought I really wanted to, but it didn't work.'

He smiled. 'We'll catch the bus.'

Jay was unsure of how to say goodbye to Jem, because she didn't know whether she'd ever see the girl again, but Jem did not appear to be upset. She held Jay's hand as they walked with Dex through the dark lanes beyond Lestholme's heart. 'What do you think about what you've heard?' Jay asked her.

Jem shrugged. 'It makes a kind of sense, doesn't it?'

'Of a kind.' Jay paused. 'Jem, do you want to come with me?'

Jem shook her head emphatically. 'No.'

Jay felt slightly offended. 'But I might not come back.'

Jem glanced up at her. 'You will.'

'You don't know me that well.'

Dex had halted ahead of them, and was gazing up the lane into darkness.

'I'll have to go home now,' Jem said.

Jay thought she was afraid of seeing the bus, perhaps anxious that she might be compelled to climb aboard. 'OK.' She leaned down and hugged Jem. 'We're friends,' she said.

Jem kissed her cheek. 'I know. Take care.' She began to skip back down the lane into Lestholme, pausing only once to turn back and wave.

Jay's heart felt heavy. Was she doing the right thing? She had many friends here, and now she was walking away from them, without so much as a farewell. Back to what? The selfishness and betrayal of people who cared only for themselves; a mountain of debt; all the problems she'd left behind.

'Ready, Jay?' Dex asked.

Jay turned back to him. She saw a wavering radiance, as of headlights, approaching them. 'Yes.'

The single-decker bus looked ordinary in the extreme, as it squeezed between the high hedges of the lane. It pulled to a halt alongside Jay and Dex, and the doors slid open. Jay looked up into the face of the driver; a man in a smart uniform. He smiled a greeting, and beckoned them up. What kind of creature could he be? Was this just a job to him? Did he get paid, have a wife and family somewhere to whom he returned when his work was done? Or was he like the people who lived in Lestholme, living a shadow life?

There was no fee to pay. Jay and Dex climbed aboard, into the yellow green light within.

'You'll be going to London, then,' said the driver. The doors hissed shut behind them.

There was only one other person on the bus, huddled up against the window near the back, muffled to the ears in a dark great-coat. 'He never gets off,' Dex murmured.

Jay sat down, gripping the shiny rail of the seat in front of her. 'This is too weird,' she muttered.

The bus did not go into the centre of the village, where it would have been able to turn around with comparative ease.

241

Instead, the driver executed some complicated manoeuvring involving a farm track. Jay felt light-headed. She was leaving, going back to what she'd left behind. Was she mad?

'How did the driver know where we wanted to go?' she asked in a whisper.

Dex shrugged. 'He knows, that's all. It's his function to know.'

Jay narrowed her eyes at him. 'This is all too Lovecraft for me. Is the driver an ordinary man?'

'I expect he was. Once.'

Jay sighed, shook her head. She knew she'd get no clear answers, perhaps because there were none. She'd been used to gathering facts, putting them into an order that made sense, revealed the story. 'So what happens when we get back to town?' she asked. 'Will I be able to go straight to the flat?' It seemed the obvious course of action.

Dex shook his head. 'Well, you could, but there's a party I'd like to take you to first.'

'A party?' Jay laughed scornfully. 'Great! Just what I need.'

'It's an information-gathering foray,' Dex said.

'How do you know there's a party?'

He shrugged, and Jay growled in exasperation. 'Look, just forget all the secretive stuff now,' she answered. 'Why a party?'

'Primarily, I want to show you why I can never return to reality completely, but I also think you might find out some interesting things. I can't tell you what, because I don't know. It's just a hunch.'

'How intuitive of you.' He was not the person she'd known. It was as if she was talking to a relative of Dex's, whom she'd heard all about, and had perhaps talked to on the phone, but had never actually met before. Glancing at him sidelong, it seemed inconceivable to her that once they'd shared a bed and a domestic life. But, despite this, she felt easy in his company.

Jay dozed for a while. When she opened her eyes again, they were on the motorway, and a glorious sunset stained the sky. Had she slept for so long? It couldn't take a whole

242

day to drive from Lestholme to London. She experienced a slight shock at finding Dex beside her. It was still strange to her that he'd reappeared in her life. Her head had lolled on to his shoulder as she slept, and his arm lay loosely along the seat back, not quite touching her.

They drove into the West End, and here the bus came to a stop. Traffic blared, people scurried, lights blazed from every shop. Even in the bus, Jay could smell the air; the indescribable aroma of London. She felt stiff as she stood up. 'Are we really going to a party?' she asked.

Dex nodded.

'But we're hardly dressed for it.' She indicated her jeans and jumper, her leather jacket.

'That won't matter. Trust me.'

Jay stepped down on to the pavement. It was raining hard. 'I'm not sure about this,' she said.

People hurried around them, staring straight ahead, armed with umbrellas, their collars up around their faces. Jay felt absurdly vulnerable; she had become used to the calm and tranquillity of Lestholme. Dex took her arm and she did not protest. They wandered into the narrow streets of Soho that smelled sweetly of cooking meat. Here, Dex led the way to a narrow doorway. Music spilled down a stairway towards them, and a bored-looking cashier sat behind a metal grille just inside the door. She was talking to a huge bouncer. Both conversed in soft but aggressive tones.

'Here we are,' said Dex.

Jay rubbed moisture from her face. 'Do you think we'll get in?' Her jacket and jeans were soaked, her hair plastered against her forehead and neck.

'Oh yes,' Dex replied, flicking his own wet hair from his face. He pulled her across the threshold, and they walked straight past the cashier and the doorman, up the red-lit stairs.

Chapter Twenty-One

Jay knew at once it was a record company party, because a pyramid of CD covers was arranged on a table near the door. Whose release did it celebrate? Was it just a glorified press conference? Whatever the reason, rent-a-mob were there in their hundreds; rilling and trilling and flashing. Some things never change. Outside the night air had been chill, but in the dim-lit club, it was humid and hot. Jay's clothes were steaming; she felt very uncomfortable. She saw faces she recognised: their bright grins and eyes. Her nostrils contracted against the mélange of perfumes, while her ears felt over-sensitive to the shrill squawks of laughter and gleeful bitchy asides. Here was her world again. It was as if she'd never been away, and yet at the same time she felt removed from it all, as if she'd never been a part of it. She stood at the threshold with Dex, and for perhaps the first time in fifteen years felt nervous about joining a social gathering. What else had Sakrilege done to her reputation while she'd been away? She still did not know how long she'd been in Lestholme. It could be days or weeks. Not yet Christmas, she noted. The trees outside had still been coated with a stubble of last leaves. November, perhaps, but which year?

'I can't,' she said abruptly.

Dex's hand pressed the small of her back. 'Yes, you can. They won't notice us.'

'Dex, no . . .' She tried to turn away, but he propelled her into the crowd. It was as she feared. Everyone ignored her, even those who only a short time ago had wanted to know her. Social climbers. Now she must have dropped off the ladder completely. 'This is awful,' she said.

'For them, perhaps, but not for us.' Dex steered her further into the press of bodies, all in their bright, tight clothes. 'Jay, we are the lost. It's our highest card. It takes a while for us to rejoin society. It's not just like coming out of prison or hospital.'

'What do you mean?' They had ended up pressed against the bar, clearly in several people's way, yet these people did not complain or cast scorching glances.

'Look how long it took me to get your attention,' Dex said. 'I still have a key to the flat, you know.'

Jay stared at him, slightly disgusted. 'I don't even want to think about that!'

Dex grinned at her. 'Don't worry. I didn't abuse my ability. You just don't have to worry about being recognised. We're eavesdroppers here. They can't see us.'

Jay sighed. 'Then that makes me a lost soul too, doesn't it?' She realised that in some ways Dex relished what he had become. He appeared more relaxed than she'd ever seen him.

'There's dear old Zeke,' said Dex.

Jay couldn't suppress a shudder of alarm. 'Where?'

Dex pointed. The Sakrilege man was surrounded by a group of people, but didn't seem to be in a party mood. His face looked drawn, and there were puffy dark shadows beneath his eyes. Jay hoped he was suffering. Perhaps he blamed himself for her disappearance. She hoped so. 'He can't see us?' she asked. 'You're sure of that?'

Dex nodded. 'Come on. Let's join our friends.'

A woman was speaking. She wore a transparent lace dress over slight underwear and had the glazed, famished look of a model. After a few moments, Jay recognised her. It was Carmen Leonard. She looked different from how she appeared in all the glamour shots; bonier and more startled. Despite her rather manic eyes, her voice was a monotonous gabble. 'Well, of course Dex is in Brazil. It's the most reliable sighting. The columnist, Rita Akeland, told me, and you know she's a real scavenger for facts. He's in Brazil, I'd put money on it. Working with an ethnic band.'

Jay felt suddenly very cold. Of course these people would be talking about Dex. Perhaps it was because he was hidden among them, his essence somehow touching their memories.

'It's all just supposition,' a man in a lime-green suit said scornfully. 'I reckon he topped himself and that's that.'

Carmen Leonard gibbered in pique, taking a sip of champagne.

'I heard he's in Barcelona,' said a youth in baggy clothes and a baseball cap worn back to front. 'Getting wrecked and all that.'

'Who gives a fuck where he is?' snapped a young, scorched-blonde, American vocalist, decked in tight zebra-print pants and a cut-off fluffy top that revealed a tangle of surgical steel through her navel. 'He's a fucking has-been, so why are we even talking about him?' It was clearly her party.

Zeke Michaels, unexpectedly, rallied to the defence, although it was clear he was very drunk. 'Perri, my dear, what would you have us talk about? You? You might call Dex a has-been, but I've no doubt his next album of releases and remixes will outsell yours by the thousands.'

'Hope he enjoys the royalties,' the girl shot back, her cheeks slightly red beneath the eyes. It must have been a furious blush to fight its way through the pan-stick. 'Just who *does* get all the cash if a musician absconds, Zeke?'

It was a good question, Jay thought. She wanted to ask it too. She'd have liked to mention Julie and her children. Perhaps Zeke Michaels didn't even know they existed.

'Why worry?' Michaels said, smiling coldly. 'You'll have enough pennies to play with yourself when *Karma Crash* hits the stores.'

Green Suit, Baggy Boy and Carmen Leonard all tittered and the young American looked cornered. She might be a spoiled brat, but Jay felt for her. At least she had the guts to ask awkward questions, and even more importantly think those questions up in the first place.

'You might think I have an empty, pretty little head,' snarled the singer, 'but without me, and people like me, you parasites wouldn't have a job. I keep you in coke and Armani suits. I pay for parties like this.'

'Oh yeah?' Michaels looked annoyed now. He swayed a

little, and champagne slopped over the rim of his glass. 'Without people like me, you'd be a nobody. Married with two kids when you're twenty-three, and dreams of fame while you watch pop stars on the TV. What is given can very easily be taken away.'

The girl laughed, even though her heart must have begun to beat just that bit faster. 'Oh, Zeke, you can't ever see inside me. I could be married with kids, but music's in my soul. You can never take that away. I'll write and I'll play until I wave the world goodbye. I know success is ephemeral. It's a joke. Don't expect me to be grateful. You people gnaw away at artists, and we eat from your gilded bowls. You can make us and break us, but without us, there'd be no industry. I think you should remember that more often.' With dignity, she stalked away.

Jay applauded, laughing. 'Good for you, Perri!'

'Prima donna,' murmured Green Suit, rolling his eyes.

'Temperament,' added Michaels, shaking his head and grinning. 'Think they know it all. She's just a kid.'

Dex made a noise of disgust. 'Pompous, sexist git. He would never have dared to speak to me like that.' He shook his head. 'Still, little Perri's wrong, isn't she, about how the music industry needs musicians?'

Jay nodded, her mouth set in a grim smile. 'Yeah. They can be grown in vats nowadays, and their music born in the circuits of computers.' She chuckled. 'Maybe dear old Zeke is thinking this very moment whether he can offer that naked model a recording contract.'

'Perhaps, when Perri is on the scrap heap, they'll pay her to provide the voice – anonymously, of course.'

'Computer graphics could see to the video performances.'

They held each other's glance for a moment, then slapped palms. 'It's a deal!'

Dex put his hand beneath Jay's elbow to move her away from Michaels' clique. 'Find Perri, one day, Jay. Don't let the plague get her.'

Jay glanced at him. 'What do you mean?'

He smiled. 'Those of us with integrity should stick together.'

'Then you find her,' Jay said.

Dex did not respond to this. 'Well, this little knees-up is just about perfect for what I wanted you to see.'

'Which is?'

'My actual presence is not required in the world for Dex to exist in it. I have become virtual.'

'And so have I, it seems.'

'You're already returning, Jay,' Dex said. 'I'm sure that by morning, you will have adopted this old familiar reality as your own again.'

Jay's shoulders slumped. 'It's bizarre, but now I'm not even sure that's what I want.' She looked up at Dex. 'I want to keep a bit of Lestholme in my life, the peace, the pace of life.' She paused. 'The people.' Jay sighed. 'They live in delusion, in a bubble, protected from the realities of life. Yet it's something that all of us crave at some time.'

'Perhaps you don't have to step out of reality to find it,' Dex said.

'Why say that? You did.'

He shrugged. 'I'm not as strong as you, and never will be. I think your Lestholme lives inside you, Jay. That's the way to find your own Utopia.'

Jay smiled sadly. 'If only you'd thought that when you made the choice to walk out of my life.'

'I made a decision not to involve you in my problems. Perhaps that was unfair to you, but we can't undo the past.'

'No.' Jay narrowed her eyes and looked around the room. It was time she found out what had happened in her absence. If Dex was right and she'd soon be a part of this world again, she must call Gina as soon as she was able. Face the music.

She turned to tell Dex her decision, but found he was no longer beside her. She scanned the crowd, but could not see him. Had he vanished for her already? She couldn't believe it. There was so much they'd yet to discuss, not least Julie's future, never mind Jay's own. 'Dex,' she hissed. 'Are you here? Dex?'

It was like waking from a dream to discover she'd been sleep-walking to a strange place. The noise of the party rose around her in a hungry roar. Everyone appeared to be moving faster than normal. Jay fought a sudden dizziness, and began to move towards the door. She didn't want to manifest in front of these people.

The door was in sight. She had only a few feet to go. Outside, she'd be able to breathe more easily, consider what she should do. Two people came to stand in the doorway, looking around the room before they joined the party. It took Jay a moment to recognise them, then a current of shock fizzed through her. It was Gina and Gus. Together. Jay stood only inches away from them, yet they paid her no attention. Gina's hand was tucked through one of Gus' arms. 'Gina!' Jay exclaimed, and Gina turned in her direction, frowning, but clearly couldn't discern who'd spoken her name.

'What's up?' Gus asked her.

'Someone called me,' Gina said, her face perplexed. 'Weird, but it sounded like Jay.'

'Jay?' He sounded horrified.

Gina shrugged. 'It's OK. It can't be her. I must be imagining things.'

'Why can't it be her? You don't know . . .'

'Relax, babe,' Gina said, licking her teeth. 'She won't be here.' She kissed Gus on the cheek and began to drag him into the room.

Jay could not assimilate the implications of what she'd just seen and heard. She was filled only by crimson anger. Lurching forward, she screamed, 'Bitch!' and slammed her fist into Gina's face. Gina jerked backwards, pulling Gus with her, who cried, 'What the fuck?'

People around them smirked knowingly. Someone said, 'Peaked too early, Ginny?'

Gina picked herself up, bewildered and furious. Her face was crimson.

Jay dashed past her, down into the lobby of the club. She didn't look back, but ran into the lane and from there to the busier street beyond. Traffic hissed up and down damp Tarmac, lights dazzled. Overhead, the high buildings of the city seemed to rock like the masts of moored ships. Jay felt sick, furious. How long had the relationship between Gina and Gus been going on? Images flashed through Jay's mind: Gina, the epitome of concern after Jay's trouble with *Track*; Gina solicitous and caring. A lie? Jay hugged herself. She felt so cold, and now a soft, icy drizzle was falling. What now? She couldn't look upon Gina as an ally. The only person she felt she could call upon now was Grant Fenton but, even if she could make her presence known to him, she didn't relish having to explain her situation. He would tell people. She didn't want that. But what other choice did she have, alone in London at night, with no place to go?

Jay began to walk down the street, her mind awhirl. She felt she could no longer rely on her memories. Had Dex ever been with her? Was Lestholme real? She shook her head and uttered a soft groan. She wanted to go to Julie, but Dex's sister lived so far away. Still, Jay could catch a train, even if it meant hanging around Euston all night. Would her credit cards still work?

The street was crowded, despite the weather. Jay moved instinctively in the direction of the station. People pushed her without realising it. Somebody grabbed her arm, and for a moment, Jay thought she must be visible again. 'Wait. Where are you going?'

She looked up into Dex's face. 'I thought you'd gone,' she said. 'I couldn't find you.'

'I went outside. You were following. Then you just took off up the road.'

Jay shook her head, confused. 'No. That is . . .' She paused. 'Gus and Gina were there.'

'I saw her,' Dex said. 'Did you try to speak to her?'

Jay shook her head. 'No. She was *with* Gus, Dex. This puts a different slant on things.' She put her hands on his arms. 'Please don't disappear for me again. Right now, you're the only friend I trust.'

'I didn't mean to,' Dex answered. He frowned. 'But if I did, perhaps it means I have no control over it.'

Jay released his arms. 'We won't let that happen. If it requires will-power, we'll give it will-power.'

250

He smiled uneasily. 'OK. So, where were you headed with such purpose? Is there something you want to do?'

Jay considered. 'I was thinking of trying to get to Julie, but something else has just occurred to me. You said you still have a key to our flat. Have you got it with you?'

He studied her. 'Yes.'

'I want to go there. I want to see what's happened.'

'OK, if that's what you want.'

Jay glanced at him. Did he suspect this would be as fruitless a task as trying to find Lorrance at Lestholme? 'Of course, it might have been sold. Other people could live there now.'

'That's a possibility.'

'But I want to find out.'

They used the tube trains like any other people, except they didn't have to pay. They clambered over the barriers at each station, beneath the eyes of station attendants. There were certain advantages to living the life of the lost.

Jay felt strange walking back up the familiar street. She thought it should look different somehow, but it didn't. Lights still shone reassuringly from behind blinds and drapes. Empty milk bottles stood on porches and cars slid by, their windscreen-wipers working furiously. Jay and Dex were soaked with freezing rain.

Jay spotted Gus' car, a fashionable four-wheel-drive vehicle, parked outside the flat. At least it appeared he hadn't sold the place and had most likely moved back in. Jay stood at the bottom of the short flight of steps while Dex went to open the door. After a few moments, he turned around. 'Looks like the locks have been changed.'

Jay slumped against the iron railings. 'Fuck and damn! We might have guessed.' She straightened up. 'In that case, we'll have to go round the back, break in. So what if someone hears? They won't see us.'

The alley between the buildings was in darkness, although when they reached the rear of the building a security light came on. Clearly, they possessed some degree of solid presence in the world. Jay picked up a discarded wine bottle from top of an overflowing dustbin, and broke one of the flat's back windows with fierce, precise blows. Dex stood with folded arms, a few feet away. Jay suspected he didn't think this was a good idea, although he offered no opinion.

Jay hoisted herself up on to the window-sill. 'Are you coming?' she asked.

Dex hesitated, then came forward. 'OK.'

One after the other, they dropped into the warm, dark silence of their old home.

It smelled different. Jay didn't want to turn on a light, but by the dim radiance of the outside security lights, she could see that her kitchen had changed. For a start, it was a mess, and there were new bits of crockery stacked on the draining board unwashed. The smell was of stale food and strong perfume. Issey Miyake. Gina's scent.

Growling beneath her breath, Jay stalked into the living room. Coats, magazines and newspapers littered the chairs and sofas. There were more dirty plates on the floor and the coffee table was smeared with sticky rings. Jay recognised items that belonged to Gina: a pair of shoes, a pool of silver chains and pendants on the table. She made a low noise of disapproval and anger.

Dex came into the room behind her, exhaled slowly. What must it feel like to him, coming back here again? How many times had he been here before, unseen?

'This is vile,' Jay said. 'I feel like I've been burgled.'

Dex said nothing. Jay went into the bedroom, cast her glance over the unmade bed, wrinkled her nose at the smell of sweat and unwashed socks. Her Japanese kimono, which Dex had brought back from abroad, lay in a careless, crumpled heap on top of the bed. Gina must have been wearing it.

Jay felt beyond emotion. She marched out into the hallway and hauled out a large canvas bag from the cloakroom. Then she returned to the bedroom, where she began stuffing some of her possessions into the bag. Dex still said nothing. Jay was unsure whether he felt awkward on her behalf or his own. 'Go into my work-room and see if there's any money lying around,' she said, 'or my passport, anything. Check the desk drawers.' She wanted to claw something back from them, take what was hers.

Dex left the room without speaking.

Jay stood still for a moment. She moved to the untidy dressing table and picked up a gigantic bottle of Gina's perfume. She weighed it in her hands. It oozed an odour of betrayal. Tight-lipped, Jay emptied its contents over the bed and threw the bottle on the floor. Then, she picked up one of Gina's bright red lipsticks and scrawled 'Friend' on the mirror. From the wardrobe, she took an elegant black evening gown that she used to wear at only the most glitzy functions and arranged it on the bed, so that it looked like a deflated body. *Diamanté* on the single shoulder strap glittered coldly in the blue light.

Dex reappeared in the doorway. 'Bounty,' he said, holding out a foot-square wooden box. 'All your personal effects appear to have been stuffed in here, bank statements and so on, even a replacement credit card, and also your passport. Oh, and three pounds fifty in change.'

'Surprised they didn't burn everything,' Jay said. She stood, hands on hips, looking down at the bed. 'I feel like that bitch has tried to steal my life.'

Dex put down the box and curled his arms around her. He didn't say anything. It reminded Jay painfully of the time when they'd been together. He'd never been a great talker. Gus had always been full of opinions, but Dex had simply been a pair of arms, a sense of empathy that needed no words. For a moment, Jay let herself rest her head on his chest. Then she raised her face to him. 'I don't know what to do now. Do I go to Grant or Julie? Do I try to tell people what happened to me? Apart from Julie, everyone will think I'm mad.'

Dex's gaze was steady. 'There's something *I* want to do.'

'There is? What?'

'You're not afraid to face reality, Jay, or the past. It's not just about guts, but about caring. I want to go back to the forest.'

Jay knew at once what he meant. 'You want to find that boy's body, don't you?'

He nodded. 'Yes. And when I do, it will be evidence you can do something with.'

Jay took a deep breath, held it. 'I see.' She sat down on the edge of the bed. 'Dex, the body is pretty useless as evidence without your testimony. Would anyone believe me if I said the information had come from you? Where's the proof?'

'Maybe that doesn't matter. He should just be found, that's all, buried properly.'

'That would ease your conscience, I can appreciate that, but perhaps you should think more about exposing Lorrance. Face this thing with me. I'd help you, you know that, and your presence and support would help me. If we go public, surely it would give us a kind of immunity? If anything happened to us, it'd be too obvious who was responsible.'

Dex turned away. 'You don't know those people. They're capable of anything – and of getting away with it. They'd most likely find a way of discrediting us.'

Jay sighed, slightly impatient. 'Dex, we should take back our lives. I'm prepared to face up to things. Why can't you?'

'You don't know those people,' he said again.

Jay stood up, went to him. 'You're afraid of them, I know that.'

Dex pulled away from her. 'Don't humour me. I was there, Jay. You weren't. Charney is untouchable, I'm sure of it. I don't want to risk stirring him up. You don't know what might happen to us.'

'You said yourself that things are changing,' Jay reminded him gently. 'Charney and Lorrance have enemies. Perhaps we wouldn't have to make a stand alone.'

Dex stared at her in incredulity. 'You're prepared to take that risk?'

She lowered her eyes. 'Dex, I only have your word these men are all-powerful. They intimidated you when you weren't in your right mind.'

'Jay, don't say that!' Dex snapped bitterly. 'You've seen Lestholme. You know what can happen.'

'I've seen people living in a sanctuary,' Jay said. 'I haven't seen a fate worse than death.'

Dex rubbed his face. 'I don't know,' he murmured. 'I don't know.' He looked at her. 'After the forest, I could think about it.'

'OK,' Jay said. She rubbed his arm. 'That would be a start. So, let's think about practicalities. How do we get there?'

Dex grinned sheepishly and dangled some keys in front of her. 'More bounty,' he said. 'I suspect these are keys to the poncy little four-wheel job outside.'

Jay took them from him. 'They are.' She frowned. 'It's stealing, of course. Gus will report it. Then what?'

'By then, it won't matter,' Dex replied.

Chapter Twenty-Two

It was an hour or so before dawn when Dex turned the vehicle into a winding lane, very similar to the one where Jay had left her own car perhaps months before. He swerved off the road and crashed through a five-bar gate into the forest. Tall, skeletal trees hemmed the track, dripping moisture. It was an eerie place, like the land of the dead: no greenery and nothing moved.

Jay had been dozing. She woke up and murmured, 'This is it, isn't it?'

'Yup,' Dex said, crashing the gears. The vehicle, clearly four-wheel drive in a cosmetic sense only, bounced uncomfortably along the rut-scored track. Jay felt sure the car would roll at any moment.

Grey light was seeping through the black branches as Dex brought the vehicle to a halt. Jay looked in the glove compartment for a flashlight, and was relieved to see Gus still kept it there. She handed this without words to Dex. Then, they both got out.

Jay stood shivering in the misty pre-dawn air. 'It's a haunted place,' she said.

'Are you up to this?' Dex asked. His face was shockingly white.

She nodded. 'Lead the way.'

They plodded along a narrow track hemmed by the drooping spars of dead bracken. Unlike the woods near Julie's home, there was no evidence of human visitation around; no Coke cans or wrinkled crisp packets. This was pristine forest, heavy with ancient presence. Jay felt light-headed, although weirdly detached about what she soon might see. It was almost too grotesque to accept as reality. She knew that when she saw the remains, she wouldn't be able to think of them as human.

The corpse would look vile, terrible, but her senses wouldn't react. She felt driven, concerned only with evidence. If the body existed, it gave credence to Dex's story. She wanted to believe him.

Dex halted and pointed ahead. 'There,' he said softly, as if they had come upon some gingerbread house, or a rare animal; something wondrous.

The first red stain of the dawn made silhouettes of the naked trees, and now birds were singing. Jay felt her heart lift. It was unaccountable, but perhaps a human instinct to be heartened by the dawn, symbolic of renewal. She saw the ruins; the lower storey appeared to be mostly intact, but there was no roof, and the walls had crumbled down to reveal the first-floor rooms. Rubble was strewn around the entrance, and the floor inside. Stepping over the threshold, Jay looked up and saw there was no ceiling now. A flight of stairs led up to nothing. The place reminded her of the ghost of Lorrance's house at Lestholme, only this was dark, dank and decayed, where the white house was flawless and light.

Dex turned on the flashlight and swept its beam around the room. He seemed reluctant to proceed.

'Let's get it over with,' Jay said. 'Where's the cellar?'

Dex directed the light at the stairs. Beneath them was a door, wedged open with lumps of broken plaster. He moved towards it. Neither of them spoke as they made the difficult descent of the ancient stone steps, which were slippery and wet beneath their feet. Jay tentatively sniffed the air. She smelled mildew and damp earth, but no particular reek of decaying flesh. Perhaps it was too late for that now. She kept her balance by pressing her hand against the slimy wall. It seemed to writhe beneath her touch. This must be done, she told herself. Her jaw was clenched tight.

At the bottom of the steps, Dex paused while Jay caught up with him. The cellar was low-ceilinged and littered with piles of bricks and what appeared to be broken wooden boxes. Dex slowly cast the beam of the flashlight over the rubbish. Jay came to stand beside him and took his arm, watching the probing eye of radiance. What would they see first: a skeletal white hand against the earth, a skull? She swallowed painfully. This must be done.

After a few moments, Dex expelled a wordless question, and broke away from Jay's hold. He climbed over some bricks, casting the light around quickly, this way and that. The beam swayed drunkenly.

'What is it?' Jay asked.

Dex didn't answer, but hunkered down in the rubble. He began casting bricks about, pieces of damp wood, rags of rotten sacking. Jay approached him. She knew already what he would say next.

'It's not here. There's no body.'

'Perhaps you're not looking in the right place.'

Dex glanced up at her, his face spectral in the beam. 'Jay, believe me, it's something I'll never forget. I know where I put it, and it's not here.'

'Perhaps animals . . .'

'Lorrance must've come back and moved it. Fuck!'

'Somebody else might have found it.'

'Who? Grave-robbers, Satanists, skull collectors? Don't you think it might otherwise have been reported?'

'Perhaps it was. I don't read the papers every single day or watch the news, and you've been hiding from the world.'

Dex shook his head. 'No. I just know it hasn't been found. I just know.' He stood up. 'Lorrance couldn't have trusted me that much. He probably came back some time afterwards and buried the boy. The body could be anywhere. This was a stupid place to put it in the first place. Too open.'

'Then we have no evidence.'

'No, we don't.' Dex sighed.

Jay stepped forward and took his arm again. 'Dex . . . I have to ask this. Are you absolutely sure about what happened that night? You said yourself you were off your face. Could it have been a dream or a hallucination? You know how reality and dreams can get very mixed up when your mind's in an altered state. What exactly had you taken that night?'

Dex stared at her angrily. His mouth twitched, but he did not speak.

'I'm not judging you,' Jay said gently. 'We have to look at every angle.'

Dex released his breath in a hopeless gasp. 'God, I don't know. I haven't lived in reality since I walked out of it.' He shook his head. 'No. It *did* happen. I couldn't have imagined it. The screams, the way the poor kid was lying on the floor, the blood, the heaviness of the body as we dragged it from the house. It still had a *smell*, Jay, like a living thing. Those images will stay with me for the rest of my life.'

Jay squeezed his arm. 'We need to talk about what we're going to do,' she said. 'We need a breathing space. Can you take us back to Leastholme for a while?'

He smiled weakly, ran his fingers through his hair. 'OK.'

They walked back to the car, and now the forest was transformed by daylight. It had seemed so dead on the way there, but now Jay could see ivy crawling around the wizened tree trunks, many of which were stained with lichen and moss, and in places where the bracken hadn't spread, the ground was vividly green with short, wiry grass. Holly bushes bore bright red berries, and the leaves beneath their feet were a palette of autumnal colours; yellow, duns, oranges.

There is more colour in the season of death than we remember, Jay thought. Perhaps we colour it in our minds with the hues of our own grey lives. When we live in winter, we forget that spring inevitably must follow.

Before they resumed their journey, Jay took Dex in her arms. They neither spoke, nor made any move to change the embrace with a kiss.

All the decisions I've made in my life, thought Jay, have brought me to this moment. We stand in the wood in the dawn. What makes sense and what doesn't?

'Remember the story you told me,' she said.

Dex pulled away from her slightly, looked down into her face.

'You said that when you first brought the body here, you heard a voice in the cellar.' She fixed his eyes with her gaze,

259

wouldn't let him look away. 'What really happened to Little Peter, Dex? Do you know?'

'He was the biggest influence on my life,' Dex said.

Jay did not interrupt, just stroked his arm.

'Nobody knows what really happened. Did Julie tell you about it?'

Jay nodded.

Dex sighed. 'Pete had a difficult life. His dad was fond of using his fists, his mother was a drained wreck. Pete strained at the leash of life. He had a great sense of hope. I envied him that. Nothing would get him down. On that day, when my brother, Gary, tried to kick the shit out of us, it was like something got into Pete. He was wild, ecstatic, as we ran away. On the heath, he jumped and twisted in the air, like a mad stoat. "Watch me, Chris," he said, "just watch me." I couldn't keep up. There was a strange feeling all around me, like things weren't normal any more. I followed him into the trees, and I could hear him laughing – it was a low, cackling sound. Then everything was quiet, like someone had turned off the sound to the world. Too silent. I called his name, and looked for him, but there was no sign. I thought something had taken him, I didn't know what. I walked around for a long time, and the place no longer looked familiar. I had a feeling I could follow Pete if I tried hard enough. Maybe I had to surrender to that strange feeling, jump up in the air, twist around and . . . vanish.'

'What do you think happened?' Jay asked. 'Did he choose to disappear like the people in Lestholme?'

'Yes, I think he did,' Dex said. 'I've only realised that recently. Back then, I was convinced something sinister had happened; a human monster, or a forest monster, or a deep hole in the ground. I felt responsible, because it was my brother who'd chased us off, and me who'd started the argument with Gary. I knew no one would ever find Pete. He was as surely gone as if the fairies had taken him. At the time, I believed that to be a feasible possibility.' He smiled sadly. 'Now, I know different, because of what's happened to me.'

'Why should you hear Peter's voice in the cellar, though? Why then? Haven't you ever wondered about it?'

Dex gazed off through the trees. 'I was doing something that marked a major fork in my life. I shouldn't have done it. I should have run from Lorrance before I ever met that creature who pulls his strings. Maybe Pete wanted to speak to me, warn me . . .' he glanced back at her, 'like I tried to warn you.'

'Could he be somewhere in Lestholme? I noticed a few strange men who don't come into the village much. They appear to live in the forest.'

Dex shook his head. 'I don't feel that, Jay. He's somewhere, and sometimes I can swear he's close, but he's not part of Lestholme. I've a feeling the village couldn't contain him. It's too static.'

Jay opened her mouth to speak, but Dex interrupted her, 'Please don't ask me to explain that. I can't. They're feelings.'

'It's OK,' Jay said. 'Thanks for telling me. I'm trying to understand all this too, Dex. I need as much information as I can get.'

He took her arm and began to lead her to the car. 'I love your clarity, Jay. You're like a beam of light sweeping round the darkness.'

I could always have been that for you. She didn't speak the words.

Jay got into the car and buckled her seat belt. 'Can we just drive into Lestholme? Can it be that easy?'

Dex turned on the ignition. 'I've been in and out several times. Lestholme knows me. It'll let us back in.'

After driving around the countryside for half an hour or so, without any sign of the village, Dex was not so confident. 'Perhaps it's because you've been back to London, Jay. Perhaps you can no longer enter the village. I've a feeling it won't let us find it.'

'It will,' Jay soothed, hoping she was right. 'We have to believe it.'

'I'm not sure. Perhaps we should be on foot.'

'Just keep driving,' Jay said. 'We must *will* it to happen.'

Jay closed her eyes, and visualised Lestholme as strongly as she could; the church, the narrow streets, the peculiar, damaged villagers. It was just around the corner, very close. They could just step into that world, because it was there next to them all the time. They had carried it inside them to London, and now they must externalise it again.

They drove beneath an old viaduct that turned a corner. For a while, they were in darkness. Dex turned on the headlights, and then, on the other side, they found summer. Strangely, it was night-time, like the moment they had left the village, but it was a night of balmy warmth. Jay opened the window on her side, and a perfume of mown hay filled the vehicle. She breathed it in deeply, relaxing back against the head-rest. It was like coming home.

Dex parked in the pub car park. 'Well, this is one stolen vehicle that will never be found,' he said, turning off the ignition.

Jay laughed, and climbed out of the car. She stretched her body. 'This is weird, but it feels good to be back. Lestholme is all the gilded memories of childhood. It spooked me at first, but after what happened last night, that awful party, Gus and Gina, it feels like heaven. I think it's my ideal holiday resort.' She smiled ruefully. 'Would it ever let itself be that for me, do you think?'

Dex did not answer. 'Looks like someone's been waiting for us,' he said.

Jay turned round and saw that Jem was sitting on the low wall next to the road. 'Hi!' she called.

Jem climbed down. She smiled widely, then made a clear attempt to appear more composed. 'Welcome back. Despite what I said, I did wonder if you'd return.'

Jay mussed the girl's hair. 'It was a possibility I wouldn't, but here I am. Was I gone long?'

Jem shook her head. 'No. Someone's been walking up and down beside the pool back there. They've been waiting for you.'

Jay frowned. 'Who?'

Dex had joined them. 'What's this?'

'A woman,' Jem said. 'She won't speak. She's a white lady, walking up and down.'

Jay and Dex exchanged a glance. Who could it be? Jay looked back at Jem. 'Are you sure she's waiting for us?'

'Yes. It's very clear. I can see her link with you, like a light around her.'

'Could it be Julie?' Jay asked.

'Let's go and see.' Dex marched off ahead of them, towards the garden at the back of the pub.

Jay took Jem's hand. 'Is she a ghost, do you think?' The question was only half light-hearted.

Jem wrinkled her nose. 'Well, that's very difficult to tell, isn't it?'

When Jay caught sight of the pale figure, which seemed to hover at the water's edge, she felt more apprehensive than when she'd stepped into the cellar looking for a decomposing body. There was something alien and otherworldly about the figure; it seemed to shine with its own light.

'Dex,' Jay said in warning. She didn't want him to get too close to the woman. 'Stay back.'

Dex turned to look at her. 'It's OK,' he said 'I know her. It's Lacey Lorrance.'

Chapter Twenty-Three

Lacey's long, white summer dress and pale hair were spectral in the star-light, yet close to, she was no unearthly creature but a woman of flesh and blood. Her dress was ragged, and her features were set in a determined expression. She clearly had something to say.

'You've always been here, haven't you?' Dex said softly. He stood with arms folded some distance away from the girl. 'Part of your father, yet not part of him.'

Lacey shook her head. 'I am not of this place,' she said, her voice low and husky. 'But I knew you were here. You didn't listen to me all those years ago, did you, Dex?'

Jay stepped towards the girl. 'Do you know who I am, Lacey?'

Lacey narrowed her eyes slightly. 'Of course.'

'Did you know I was here, too?'

'Yes,' Lacey replied. 'You are part of what is happening. Dex involved you the moment he caught your eye.' She glanced at Dex. 'You didn't mean to, but it was inevitable.'

'How did you know we were here?' Jay asked. 'Have you been watching us? Did your father tell you?'

Lacey shook her head. 'I knew for sure when you came to the house.' She came closer. 'That place is a nexus point of many realities. I can't cross into Lestholme, but because of your presence at the house, I became aware of you.'

'You're here now,' Jay said.

'You enabled me to come. None of the villagers dare approach the house of their god, but you did. I could follow in your footsteps. I know it must be hard for you to understand, but you left me a kind of trail.'

Jay rubbed her chin briefly. 'Right, so here you are, and here we are. Let's forget about the technicalities of that for a minute. What is your part in what's happening, Lacey? Why do you want to speak to us? What can you tell us?'

Lacey glanced at Dex. 'We both want to know the same thing,' he said. 'How much did you know of what was going on with your father and me? Why didn't you speak more plainly when I came to the house that night?'

Lacey sat down on the grass, and beckoned for the others to do likewise. Jay noticed that all her fingernails, and the skin around them, were gnawed raw. She couldn't be as assured as she appeared.

'First of all,' Lacey said, 'I was wary of speaking with you, Dex, because I wasn't sure of you. You seemed unhappy with what you'd become involved in, but as my father said that night, an initial state of uncertainty was part of the process. He wanted to make you one of his people, utterly and completely. You were balking, but how strongly? I couldn't be sure.'

'You knew about Charney?' Dex asked. 'And his cabal?'

Lacey nodded. 'Yes. I couldn't help but know, because I am my father's heir. You must have realised he wanted me as part of his group too, has always wanted me. I was conceived to have a role in what he did, but like you, I rejected it.'

'I didn't know that,' Dex said. 'He never mentioned it.'

'He wouldn't.' Lacey raised a hand to her mouth, nibbled the corner of a fingernail. 'I'm not totally innocent. As a young teenager, I did as he asked, acted as a channel for the powers he appealed to.' She examined her fingers, then glanced up at Jay defensively. 'From your face, I can see what you think of that.' She leaned forward. 'Yes. My father deals in the occult.' The words were delivered in a defensive tone.

'Lacey,' Jay said, shaking her head. 'I find it very hard to accept alternate realities, never mind this. It's going too far.'

Lacey shrugged. 'Whether you believe in it or not is irrelevant. The important thing is that my father believes in it, and so do the men he bows down to. They believe it gives them the power to rule others, and their belief makes it so.'

Jay nodded slowly, her mouth pursed. 'That I can accept. It makes sense.'

'What happened to you, Lacey?' Dex asked. 'Did you disappear voluntarily?'

Lacey smiled grimly. 'Partly. I wasn't spirited away by my father, but what I knew and what I saw pushed me through to the shadowlands.'

'The shadowlands,' said Jay. 'What are they?'

'I'll show you,' Lacey said. 'That's why you've returned.' She touched Dex's arm. 'You could never have found the body.'

'What happened to it?' Dex asked.

'It walked,' Lacey replied.

Jay and Dex exchanged a glance. 'Then the boy wasn't dead,' Jay said.

Lacey got to her feet, and brushed down her dress. 'Now is a changing time,' she said. 'In the shadowlands, they are moving, they are restless. I want you to come with me there. You have nothing to fear. It's quite safe.'

Jay stood up. 'Will we get all the answers there, Lacey?'

'I don't know what all your questions are. I can only show you what is. That may be enough.'

'Do you want to come?' Jay asked Jem.

The girl stood up and took Jay's hand. 'I'm scared, but I know I'd regret not seeing what she wants to show you. I'll come.'

Lacey led the group through the trees, along a well-trodden ancient trail. The night was silent, but for the occasional plaintive mew of a little owl. After a few minutes, the trees thinned out and the path led on to a stretch of heathland.

'I've never seen this place before,' Jem said. 'It was never here.'

Lacey looked back. 'I'm your key into this layer of reality,' she said. 'Ordinarily, people from the village wouldn't be able to walk this path.'

The heath reminded Jay of Ladyhorse Common, which she'd visited with Julie. But here, there seemed no limit to the landscape. Purple heather stretched for miles, interspersed with swathes of sweet vernal grass and clumps of sheep's bit. The ground was mazed by earthy tracks, sometimes curling around spinneys of birch and oak. An eerie wind blew over the land; its moan was a thousand soft complaints.

Jay's skin prickled. She walked more quickly to catch up with Lacey, leaving Dex and Jem a few yards behind. 'Tell me about the layers,' she said. 'I don't understand what you mean by them, or how people can move between them.'

'Through our five senses, we live in one world,' Lacey said, in a matter-of-fact voice that perhaps challenged Jay to ridicule her words. 'We live in one aspect of reality. We believe that what we perceive is all there is to it. We forget that we're limited by our senses, and in our arrogance cannot think that anything might exist beyond what our eyes can see, our ears hear. But reality is not as simple as that. Our senses filter it for us, so that we can exist within it as the primitive beings we are. We're unaware of all the different layers of existence that are around us all the time.' She gestured carelessly with one hand. 'Once we're free of this delusion, we can begin to sense those other realities – see them, smell them. We can explore this new faculty through concentrated meditation, or sometimes we might be flung without our realising it into a reality, or layer, beyond the one we know. That's what happened to me.'

Lacey's ideas might seem outrageous, but they still plucked an unexpected chord within Jay. It was true that the only tools people had to interpret the world, or the universe, were their five fragile senses. She had to agree it was arrogance to suppose those tools were perfect, the best of the range. 'If what you say is correct,' she said, 'it's like we're trapped within our bodies, using faulty equipment to look outside.'

Lacey nodded earnestly. 'Yes, the equipment might pick up fuzzy pictures and incoherent sounds, but because it's all we know, we assume it's the full picture.'

Jay shook her head, laughing softly. 'I can't believe I'm even considering accepting this and yet it does provide an explanation.'

'It isn't magic or make-believe,' Lacey said, 'it's an aspect of nature or science that has yet to be fully explored. Philosophers have known about it for millennia, but who outside of academia wants even to think about it?'

'Mystics,' Jay said, 'people who are looking for answers. They wrap the ideas up in woolly, spiritual terms. I hate that sort of thing. I can't help it. I'm a burrower, a ferreter for facts.'

'Mmm,' Lacey said. 'A lot of people feel that way, which leads to the ideas themselves being discredited. Quite convenient for people like my father, who don't want others to see the truth.'

Jay rubbed her face. 'My instinct is to question, yet here I am, walking these other realities, accomplishing something that serious mystics only dream about. Why has it happened to me?'

Lacey inclined her head to one side. 'On the one hand, you're a journalist, concerned with truth, but the other side of that is your curiosity, a willingness to venture into unknown territory to obtain that truth. Perhaps that's the answer you seek.'

Jay nodded. 'It's feasible, I suppose.' She paused. 'So what did happen to you? Do you mind telling me?'

'No, I can talk about it. I'd grown up accepting what my father said to me as truth. When I told him I wanted to study psychology and philosophy at university, he probably thought it could only enhance my usefulness. What he didn't bargain for was that my studies woke me up. I began to question his actions. He knew so much, yet used it for selfish ends, gathering material wealth and power. He had the knowledge, but not the wisdom. Eventually, things came to a head. He had embarked upon a very dark path, where human life other than his own meant nothing.' Lacey's face became closed-in, hard, her posture tense. 'I knew what he got up to at his weekend parties, even if his own wife forced herself to remain ignorant. I knew about the accident, and for a while just kept my distance. I thought it was the only way to keep sane. It seemed so hopeless. The world was contaminated by these men of power and knowledge. They were invincible. Then someone contacted me, and I realised that my father and his kind weren't without their adversaries.'

'These must be the shadowy enemies Dex told me about.'

Lacey's shoulders relaxed a little. 'Yes. I'm not saying they're wholly good – because who is? – but they at least put a curb on the activities of Charney's cabal, make things difficult for them.'

'You joined them,' Jay said, 'didn't you?'

Lacey drew in her breath. 'Not at first. Stupidly, I confronted my father. I suppose I wanted to give him a chance to redeem himself. Needless to say, that was pointless. He made a great show of "casting me out", as if that would scare me. I tried to speak to Samantha, but she was deaf to me. So, like you, I got into my car and drove.'

'Like me?' Jay put her hand on Lacey's arm. 'How do you know so much about me?'

'We have points of empathy,' Lacey said, 'I've been trained by people who know how to recognise such things. I perceive certain things within you, and they resonate with things inside me.'

'Are you telling me you can read my mind?'

'No,' Lacey said impatiently. 'I'm just in tune with some parts of you.' She dismissed the subject with a brief gesture. 'As I was saying, like you, I drove off into the night, except I was blinded by tears of frustration rather than full of alcohol. I drove around for a while, then headed back home, not even sure what I wanted to accomplish. I think mainly I wanted to show my father he didn't have the power to banish me. He'd done that because he wanted to bring me to heel, make me sweat for a while. I wanted to make him see he couldn't do that. But the home I arrived at wasn't the one I'd left.'

'What do you mean?' Jay asked.

'You'll see very shortly,' Lacey answered. 'We're almost there. Look around. Absorb this place. You might learn something.'

At one time, Jay would have felt slightly affronted by such a patronising remark, but Lacey's even tone soothed the sting of the words. Jay dropped back a few paces to walk beside Jem. 'Are you OK?' she asked. Jem took her hand. It was clear she hadn't been speaking much to Dex.

'I'm fine.'

'Find out anything interesting?' Dex asked.

'Oh yes,' Jay answered. 'I'll tell you later. For now, I just want to experience this place.'

Dex raised his eyebrows, but Jay had the feeling her comment had pleased him.

They walked along in silence, following Lacey over the undulating landscape. A nightjar lifted from the heather to utter its haunting, chirring cry high above. Out of the corner of her eye, Jay sensed a movement, but when she turned her head, there was nothing there. The stillness of the night had become condensed and hard. Jay felt she could sense the overlapping layers of reality all around, just beyond her perception. But how could she see them? She felt it might be similar to the way the eyes could focus on a computer generated 'magic image', and perceive a shape in a chaotic pattern. If she concentrated hard enough, she was sure an image would suddenly loom before her, clear and definite.

Jem squeezed her hand. 'Jay, I think there are other people here, lots of others.'

'I sense something,' Jay answered. An indistinct shape flickered past her. Experimenting, she focused her eyes beyond it. As she'd suspected, it helped her to see what was hidden; sheer will did the rest. Shadows surrounded her, human in shape, becoming more substantial with every moment's study. She no longer had to concentrate on perceiving them, they were just there, although she couldn't see precise details of their features or bodies. The shadows did not appear to be aware of Jay and her companions. They were wrapped in their own dramas. Some walked with leaden steps, their shoulders hunched. A few of them were wringing their hands, or pulling at their hair. Others flitted about as if seeking something. They made no sound.

'Where the hell are we?' Jay murmured. 'Can you see them, Dex?'

He took her arm. 'Yes. And I don't know where we are.'

Lacey stopped to wait for them. 'Don't be afraid of the shadows,' she said. 'They're just thought forms or memories.

If they distress you, don't look at them. Dismiss them from your perception.'

Now that she'd trained herself to see the forms, Jay didn't think she'd be able to reverse the process. The images were too strong. 'Where are we?' she asked, trying to keep her voice even.

'A node,' Lacey said. 'A between place. I know that won't mean much yet, but just bear with me.'

They had come to the crest of a rise. Wind hissed through the grass around them. Below, down a gentle slope, was the house. Unlike the one Jay had seen near the river at Lestholme, there was evidence of activity within it. Dim lights glowed at the windows, in odd colours of murky green and purple. All around it, indistinct shadow figures wandered with shambling steps. It seemed to Jay as if the house somehow kept them in its orbit.

'This is the home I came back to that night,' Lacey murmured. 'It's the ghost that forever hangs around Emmertame.'

Jay remembered Dex's story, when he'd told her he'd once looked at Lorrance's house from the outside and seen it as evil. Jay could empathise with his feelings now. The house was white, its architecture graceful, yet an invisible and oppressive miasma hung around it, reeking of despair and soulless joy. Her instincts balked at approaching the place. She wanted to turn round and run away, fast. Her inner self feared contamination.

Lacey took Jay's hand. 'You will come to no harm,' she said. 'If there was any risk of that, I wouldn't have brought you here.'

Jay found it difficult to swallow. Her heart was beating so fast, she feared it might stop completely at any moment. 'You know we want answers,' she said in a weak voice. 'Show us what we came here for.' She glanced at Dex. 'Are you OK with this?'

His face was unnaturally pale. He managed a brief nod.

Jem reached out and took Dex's hand. Linked together, the four of them walked slowly down the slope.

* * *

The house was full of people, yet any noise was strangely muted. A party was in progress, but the music was only a dull, rhythmic thump and voices a listless tide of sound. The deep glow of red and indigo light turned human figures to blurred shadows. Jay felt she must be moving more quickly than they were, or else much slower. They were vaporous ghosts, leaving trails of ether in their wake. Jay glanced at Dex. His face looked livid in the odd light and his eyes were wide, the whites glowing unnaturally.

'This is the soul of my father's house,' Lacey said, 'what he has made it.'

'It's that night all over again,' Dex said hoarsely.

Lacey shook her head. 'No. We are not in the past, Dex. This place exists in no time. It's just a representation of all that happens at Emmertame, the soul of the place. That night is part of it. You'll see for yourself.' She turned away from them slowly and gazed up the sweeping stairs that disappeared into a purplish darkness.

Jay's skin was still crawling, and she took deep breaths to maintain control over her screaming urge to flee. Her eyes were drawn against her will to the top of the stairs. It was too dark up there to make out any details, but she sensed movement, violent movement.

The body fell in slow motion. It seemed to pour itself over the shadowy banisters above, like smoke. Jay saw its limbs flapping like empty sleeves. When it hit the floor, quite near to their feet, it bounced a little, bonelessly. Jay stared down at it in a kind of fascinated horror. This isn't real, she told herself, but another voice whispered cruelly inside her: *but it happened once. You're looking at death.*

Jay put a hand to her mouth, which had filled with nauseous saliva. It wasn't a young man lying on the floor in front of them, but a school-age boy. This was like a nightmare, when the most bizarre and frightening things can happen, and the dream self just experiences it without judgement. Jay felt entirely in the present moment; she had no past and no future. She was pure experiencer.

At her side, Dex expelled a tight whine, as if his jaws were clamped involuntarily together. Jay heard Jem utter a soothing sound, but was incapable of turning round herself. She was compelled to look away from the body, up the stairs. A tall pillar of darkness hovered on the landing. It had blue lights for eyes and exuded an almost palpable smell of malevolence.

'That is my father,' Lacey said. 'The true form of his soul.'

Jay was immediately concerned this apparition might come down to them, threaten or attack them in some way, but before she could ask Lacey for reassurance on that point, Dex uttered a choked groan behind her. Jay turned and saw he'd flung both forearms before his eyes. Jem was reaching up to him, murmuring, 'It's OK.'

'No, it isn't!' he cried, and pointed a shaking finger at the body on the floor. 'It's him!' he said. '*Him*!'

Jay frowned. 'Who? Dex, this isn't real, none of it. You must see . . .'

'Little Peter,' said Dex. He swallowed, his throat convulsing visibly.

Jay looked back at the body. The shock of Dex's words made it seem more real to her. Had Dex brought his own demons with him to this place? The body moved feebly against the tiles, its fingers scratching the polished surface. Jay did not want to see it lift its head. She wanted to turn away, deny what she was seeing, but was powerless to move. Lacey's voice was a wordless murmur at her side.

Little Peter looked up. For one dark moment, Jay was horrified, but then her body flooded with a tide of relief. This was no hideous horror, but a little boy. He did not look injured and he was smiling.

'Chris, they never found me,' he said, and got to his feet.

Beside Jay, Dex was rigid, but had lowered his arms from his face. 'Are you dead, Pete?' he said.

The boy laughed. 'Dead? No! I knew when I was in the deep green place that I had to escape, and I did. I disappeared. It was so easy.'

'What is the deep green place?' Jay asked.

'The underforest, the place beyond all shadow.' He held his

arms out to them, clenching and unclenching his fists. Jay was reminded of Julie's baby Melanie, her starfish hands. She was back there, crouched in the ancient oak, looking down into Dex's secret hideaway. Only she was no longer Jay. She was witnessing this through someone else's eyes: Peter's.

It was not terrible anger, it was not hurt or fear. The thing that made Peter run was a yearning. That day, after the incident in the road with Gary, Peter had felt merely tired of all the senseless altercation, the smallness of everyone's lives. He lacked the knowledge or the words to describe this disappointment, and could only experience it as pure feeling. He wanted to get away. He wanted to reach a place where he wouldn't feel this way, where life was different. He knew it existed, for hadn't he dreamed of it so many times? Images had come to him as he'd swung on the old frayed rope at the top of the hill in the wood. He would go there alone, often. As the twilight fell and the wood breathed silently around him, the green would condense in his head, until he was surrounded by a viridian mist, shot with purest spring yellow. Peter had swung faster and faster, feeling the air whoosh around him. Forest colours whirled and spun behind his closed eyes. His swing was a pendulum, ticking into another time. He dreamed of jumping from the swing out into the air, running back through the forest to emerge on to a common devoid of human litter, of people, of dogs. There would be no houses in the distance, no telegraph poles, only endless landscape. On the swing, he was so sure he could make this happen, but it never did.

Not in the way he imagined.

He was running through the drooping, prickly grass on the skirt of the wood. Somewhere behind, Chris was shouting his name, but Peter could not stop. His legs had gone mad; they had become a blur beneath his body. Stupid Gary with his stupid, ugly face. His eyes had nothing in them, they were just jelly, and his mouth was a red hole of anger. Peter laughed as he ran. Everyone was stupid: his stomping father with his dark, closed-in face; his mother who fluttered like a limp handkerchief on the wind; even Chris, who made trouble with people on purpose. Peter knew he did not belong with any of them. The trees were beckoning to him, urgently, shaking their branches, as if to say, 'Hurry, hurry.' Peter ran beneath their shadow and the sounds of the outside world faded away, as if the summer-laden branches were a shutter that snapped shut behind him. He could hear only birdsong and the tramp of his own feet. Spears of light pierced the trees, illuminating the grass below, making it radiant. Among the tree roots, bright red fungi bulged out of the ground, covered with fairy spots. Peter ran up one hill and down another, further and further away from the common. He did not feel tired or out of breath. He was a young stag bounding through his domain, the sun warm against his hide. The trees were unbelievably tall around him; he would not have been surprised to see a dinosaur lumbering out of them. This was an ancient time; he could feel it.

He came to a pool, where willows dipped their lissom bony branches in the water. Behind him now he thought he could hear the crash and rustle of pursuit; the hunt. He was caught in a dream state, where half of him believed he really was a stag and that hunters with dogs would bring him down. Another part of him knew it was only Chris, desperately searching, perhaps with Gary somewhere behind him, lumbering and hollering. Peter ached to escape. He did not want to talk to anyone. He did not want to go home.

He saw her among the willows, a pale arm raised against a pleated tree-trunk. She could have stepped out from the heart of the tree, a willow maid in soft green robes. Closer to, she looked like a real woman, wearing a faded summer dress covered in sprigs of green leaves. She held out her hand to him, 'Come here, little man. Come here.' It was as if she knew he sought a hiding place and she could show it to him. She did not wait for him to take her hand. Once she saw he was following her, she ducked beneath the willow branches and scrambled into the undergrowth. He could hear her moving ahead of him. Her trail was easy to follow. He came to a nest in the ferns and found her crouching there. She beckoned, saying nothing. He went to her arms and she held him down against the earth. She breathed as the forest did, silently but immensely. She smelled of mown grass, of mushrooms.

Someone crashed past them. Peter felt heat, smelled sweat, shied away from the chaotic motion. Then whoever it was had dashed away, further into the forest.

Peter lay against the strange woman, who had her arms loosely around him. She did not speak, but lightly caressed his hair, humming in an oddly tuneless way beneath her breath. Peter felt totally at peace. Tales of his earlier childhood drifted through his mind. Was this some fairy queen come to claim him? Would he ever go back now?

After a while, the woman stood up, pulling Peter with her. He offered no resistance – did not even want to. Instead, he took her hand and walked with her from the woods. Her name was Effie. She lived in a small house at the edge of the common, where there were no telegraph poles, no urban sprawl and the only dogs belonged to her. At night, they could hear the sea as if it was only yards away. He lived with her for nearly ten years.

Jay came out of a daze to see the grave face of the boy looking up at her. Was he a ghost or just an illusion? He still looked like a ten-year-old boy. 'Why are you here?' Jay asked him. 'If you disappeared from the world, did you go to Lestholme? Was that where Effie lived?'

Peter shook his head. Jay realised that as she'd been speaking, he had changed. She didn't notice the transformation until it had occurred. Before them stood a young man, dark hair falling over his face, whose features were sensitive, the eyes large. It appeared he could be whatever age he chose.

'It was a place like Lestholme,' Peter said, 'and maybe it's even on the same layer, but it was different too. It isn't near here at all.'

While Jay and Peter had been speaking, Dex had crept forward like a cautious yet curious cat. Now he drew in his breath sharply, grabbed Jay's arm and pointed at Peter with a rigid finger. 'That's *him*,' he said, his voice full of wonder.

'Yes, I know,' Jay soothed. 'It's Peter.' She wondered whether Dex was losing his mind.

'No, you don't understand,' Dex said, his face screwed up. 'I mean this is the person who Rhys Lorrance killed. I saw him *dead*.' He turned to Lacey. 'This is a hideous thing to do – show me images of Pete – then this. What are you trying to do to me?'

'Hold on,' Jay said. 'Calm down, Dex. We're here to find answers. You don't know who this person is yet.' She addressed the young man before her. 'Are you Peter, whom Dex knew as a boy?'

'Yes. I was him.'

Jay glanced at Dex. 'You see?' She turned back to Peter. 'Right. And are you also the person injured in Rhys Lorrance's house?'

'He tried to hurt me.'

'Dex thought you were dead.'

'He *was* dead!' Dex cried.

'Hush!' Jay said. 'Why were you there, Peter? Had you followed Dex?'

Peter smiled. 'No. Effie taught me things. I learned about the world, the secrets behind it. Effie gave me a responsibility. When I grew older, I met friends of hers. These people are *aware* in a way that most are not. They offered me training, and I took it.'

'Dex was offered a similar thing,' Jay said, squeezing Dex's arm, 'but from the other side, so to speak.'

Dex rubbed his face, uttered a sound of anguish. 'I can't take this. I really can't.'

Peter took a step forward, although he did not touch Dex. Jay thought she could see a luminous blue glow emanating from Peter's body that poured over Dex like smoke. 'You must find peace, Chris. Like I did.'

Dex closed his eyes, surrounded by a caul of blue light. 'Tell me how,' he said in a low voice. 'I can't see how.'

'Acceptance,' Peter said. 'That is the beginning of it. When I returned to the real world, as you would call it, I knew things that most people didn't. I knew how to traverse the layers. I had an eye for truth and for the evil that lurks in a human heart, I could smell it, and when a stench came to me, I would have to find it.'

'You are one of Lorrance's enemies,' Jay said. She turned to Lacey. 'Was this who contacted you?'

She nodded. 'Yes. It was after what had happened at Emmertame. Peter had sought to disempower my father . . .'

'I failed,' Peter said. He clenched his fist before his face, and to Jay it felt as if he pulled upon invisible strings that were attached to her mind. The images were not so vivid as those of Peter's childhood.

She saw shadowy forms around her. Peter had waited a long time to come to Emmertame. He had worked carefully, speaking to the right people, to infiltrate Lorrance's party crowd. Effie had said to him, 'This man is an enemy of the world,' and Peter had pledged himself to destroying this evil. Jay saw that although Peter and his kind worked against the powers of anti-life, they themselves were not above killing. She saw the moment when Lorrance realised it was no cheap little whore he held in his arms, but something more powerful, more dangerous. He had been afraid, for just a few short moments, but fear turned quickly to rage. He had acted rashly, perhaps out of a sense of knowing his nemesis had smelled him out. It was true that he hadn't pushed Peter over the banisters. That had been the result of a battle of wills, a battle Peter had lost. Jay felt the sickening impact as his body hit the tiles; she felt the ruin in the flesh, the broken bones, the burst organs. But Peter had survived. She was with him in the cellar, felt him drawing upon the energy of the forest to heal him. It had taken a long time.

Now, Jay looked into his face. She did not know if he was more or less than human. This world around her was not her world. 'Lester Charney thought Lorrance killed you for his benefit.'

Peter smiled bitterly. 'Rhys Lorrance would have happily let him believe that. He dares not display weakness to men like Charney. I had got too close. Charney would have been furious if he'd known.'

'Why didn't you get in touch with me?' Dex said angrily. 'For fuck's sake, you could have helped me, warned me, got me out of that mess . . .'

'I couldn't. You were too close to Lorrance. He had a certain amount of control over you and we couldn't risk exposure.'

It wasn't just that, Jay thought. People like Lacey and Peter, who were perhaps just small fry in the cabals opposed to Charney, considered themselves superior to someone like Dex, or herself for that matter. They weren't that different from their enemies. She sensed they were capable of using people just as dispassionately.

'I tried to frighten Lorrance,' Dex said. 'I wanted him to think I was dead, that I could haunt him.'

'Then don't you see?' Peter said. 'He lost his power over you. You visited his house, invaded his domain, yet he could not compel you to act according to his will. That is your evidence of freedom. You escaped him the moment you made the decision to slip out of reality.'

Jay found Peter's tone patronising. He knew that Dex's fear had kept him shackled, and part of him despised that weak human emotion. Peter directed his attention towards her, clearly able to perceive her thoughts. 'People like Lacey and myself, we are rare. You cannot judge us. We have chosen to see beyond the safety nets, and that gives us freedom. We can meet in all places of the world, all the layers, and there are many.' Before Jay could respond, he reached out and curled his fingers around Dex's hands. 'You were not responsible for anything that happened to me. Perhaps, in a way, the reverse is true. If I hadn't been who I was, and you hadn't known me so well when I was young, perhaps this world, the unseen, would never have touched you.'

'I didn't recognise you,' Dex said, his voice bewildered. 'When you were lying there. I just did what Lorrance said.'

'Don't punish yourself for that,' Peter said. 'I want you to know that you will be free. I can help you cast out your demons.'

'How?' Dex asked, frowning. 'Join with you and your people?' He sneered. 'That's not the answer I want.'

Peter shook his head. 'That will not be necessary. You need to finish what you started. Release the songs.'

'Yeah, right, that's easy,' Dex snarled.

'But it is. Release them here. Release them from your heart, your mind. Sing them.'

Dex glanced at Jay, who shrugged. 'Try,' she said. 'It can't do any harm.'

'You must do this,' Lacey urged. 'It will make things happen.'

'What things?' Dex asked.

Lacey clenched her fists at her sides. 'It will smash my father's nest to pieces. He'll lose his power.'

Dex hesitated. Jay could almost hear his thoughts. He was wondering whether by handing Lacey and Peter what they wanted he was merely shifting the balance of power from one undesirable group to another. Like Jay, he was not convinced Lorrance's opposition was any better than he was.

'I want assurances,' Dex said. 'I want Jay and me to be safe and free. Jay must be given back everything that was taken from her.'

Peter and Lacey did not move, but Jay sensed that in some arcane way they had exchanged a glance. 'Jay will have what she wants,' Peter said and looked Jay in the eye. 'But be careful what you ask for.'

'Yes,' Jay said, 'I don't want to wake up and find myself in bed beside Gus, for example, as if none of this ever happened. I've been through shit, but some of the changes have my approval.'

Peter smiled, in a totally human way that made Jay feel better about him. 'Precisely.'

'Sing the songs,' Lacey said to Dex. 'Sing now.'

He sighed. 'I haven't sung since I walked away from my life.'

'It doesn't matter,' Peter said. 'You don't have to give the vocal performance of your life. It's the intention that counts.'

Dex nodded thoughtfully. 'OK.' He closed his eyes.

Jem reached for Jay's hand.

His voice was shaky at first, slightly out of tune. Jay had heard these songs a hundred times, but had never known their true meaning. Now, her skin prickled as she listened to them. The words seemed almost irrelevant, what was important were the feelings that expressed themselves in Dex's ragged tone. She could almost see his bewilderment and fear, his self-disgust, his anger. It was not a comfortable experience being surrounded by those emotions. Dex's voice became stronger, louder as the lyrics to 'Losing Me' burst out of him. He could almost have been singing about a failed love affair: 'You can't make me into you, you can't keep me near, because I've seen the truth of your heart, I've seen inside your fear.'

Jay felt as if she was shooting up out of her body to look down upon the scene below. Sounds had become colours. She could see them flaring out of Dex's body, glittering beams that reached up towards the sky and rayed outwards to touch the world around him. The songs were truly being released. They were breaking away from him, becoming free, like sentient spirits. She had no doubt that this event must have some effect on the real world. It was too intense not to.

Lorrance had been wrong to get Dex to change the words, because ultimately, they'd meant little. It was the feeling inside the music itself that counted. When Dex disappeared, he should have left the songs behind, because then Sakrilege would have released them. They would have been played on millions of CD machines all over the world. The sentiments, and the power they contained, would have become free so much sooner. If only Dex had realised. Jay found herself laughing, back in her body. Beside her, Dex was silent, staring at her.

'I'm sorry,' she said, 'don't stop. I'm not laughing at you.'

'I've finished, Jay,' he said.

She put her hands to her mouth. 'My God,' she murmured.

Peter smiled at her. 'You see, don't you?' he said quietly.

She nodded. 'Oh yes. I see perfectly.'

'Now you must go from this place,' Peter said. 'Lorrance is not your concern. You have my word he will no longer harm you.'

'Are you sure of that?' Jay said. 'How long will it take for the songs to take effect? We have practicalities to deal with.'

'His downfall has already begun,' Lacey said.

'If we return to reality,' Jay said, 'how will things work out? Lorrance was not my only enemy. There was a woman, Gina, and my ex, Gus.'

'Don't worry about them,' Peter said. 'They are confined to one place, and because of that, you have the upper hand. The woman acts in ignorance. She is a void within, and has no concept of consequence. You should not blame her. She is caught in the tide.'

'Lorrance and his underlings will have other things to worry about now,' Lacey said. 'You will no longer seem so important to them. Trust us. We're not lying.'

Peter inclined his head gently. 'You are free to go home.'

As soon as he uttered these words, it seemed to Jay that the shadow world of the house began to grow dim. They had been shown what Lacey wanted them to see, Dex had done what was required of him, and now that reality was fading. 'Did Lorrance put me in Lestholme?' Jay asked urgently. 'I have to know. How did I get there?'

'You followed an instinct, that's all,' Peter answered. 'You followed a story, and the story was partly your own.'

Lacey went to stand beside him and linked one of her arms through his. They looked like archetypal characters: the Queen of the Elves and her gallant knight. 'Peter and I have work to do,' Lacey said. 'You will see the results of it.'

Unexpectedly, Jem jumped forward towards them. 'Touch me,' she said. Lacey reached out and gently placed her fingers against Jem's outstretched hand. Jay saw nothing unusual; no visible exchange of energy or flare of light. Jem sighed and stepped backwards, her shoulders pressed against Jay's chest. Peter and Lacey did not speak again. Behind them, the pillar of dark smoke still hovered on the stairs, but now it did not appear quite so looming and threatening.

Jem took hold of one of Jay's hands and tugged it. She said nothing, but Jay knew she meant it was time to leave. She linked her arm through Dex's and pulled him gently. Then, somehow, without seeming to move, they were outside the house. The great front door slammed shut in their faces. All was silent now and the house was in darkness. Jay glanced round. The wide heathland was empty of presences. A fat moon hung low above the horizon and Jay's hair was ruffled by the passing of a silent wind. When she spoke, her voice sounded muffled. 'Are you all right, Dex?'

He nodded, his face set in an expression of shock.

'Let's go back to Lestholme.'

They walked back towards the distant line of forest.

Chapter Twenty-Four

They heard the sounds of merriment long before they saw its source. Walking back through the beech and oak at the edge of the village, Jay heard singing and the music of a fiddle. The sky ahead was ruddy with a fiery glow. They emerged from the trees by the side of the pub, next to the village green, and here a celebration appeared to be in progress. A huge bonfire had been built in the middle of the green and was now burning savagely; glittering streams of orange sparks spiralled up towards the stars. Women were dancing around the fire, hair lashing, skirts swinging. Men stood in a circle around them, clapping rhythmically. One of them, perhaps one of the confirmed bachelors Jay had visited, played a hectic jig on a violin. It was a pagan scene, filled with ancient power.

Jem began jumping up and down, tugging at Jay's hand.

'What's going on?' Jay asked. Unaccountably, her heart was immediately filled with hope and joy. She felt she had undergone a rite of passage, and now it was time to dance and celebrate.

'I want to dance,' said Jem.

'It's a kind of madness,' said Dex, 'called freedom.'

Sally Olsen whirled out of the group of women, and came skipping up to them. Her face glowed red, and tendrils of her damp hair hung over her brow. She sang a greeting, apparently unable to keep still.

'Sally,' Jay said. 'What's this party for?'

Sally reached to clutch Jay's arm briefly. 'The era is changing,' she said excitedly. 'Oh, Jay, can't you feel it? Isn't it wonderful?'

Jay raised her hands in puzzlement. 'I feel something.'

Sally made an expansive gesture with one arm, as if reaching for the stars. 'New feet walk across the sky,' she said. 'New gods are coming. She has flowers for feet and diamonds beneath her tongue. She is clad in woven rays. He is the herald of truth.'

Sally sounded as if she were hallucinating, yet her mood was infectious. Jay found she couldn't stop smiling.

Then the night was filled with the sound of a mighty booming crash. It seemed to shatter the sky and the stars rocked against their velvet backdrop. Jay winced against Dex, who curled an arm around her, staring wildly about himself.

Sally only clapped her hands. 'Look! It is time!'

Jay broke away from Dex and followed the line of Sally's pointing hand. She gazed up at the hill, where it seemed a multitude was rampaging, far more people than she'd imagined inhabited the village. As she concentrated upon this scene, her vision became telescopic. She could perceive every detail. Some of the crowd carried burning torches, which they waved about their heads. Children wove in and out of the dancing figures like sprites, followed by the dogs Jay had seen in the field by the river. Their tails were wagging and they barked excitedly. Above them all, the monument of Lestholme's god and its tower were crumbling. Great chunks of lichened masonry broke away from it and seemed to fall in slow motion to the ground. The people cavorted around it, dodging the plunging debris. 'They'll be crushed!' Jay cried.

Sally laughed. 'No. Not on this night of all nights.' With these words, she wheeled away, her skirt flying round her flashing calves.

Jay felt a thread of unease worm through her mind. There was a tugging sensation within her, as if her consciousness was being pulled from her. 'No,' she murmured and clutched on to Dex's arm. 'No.'

'Jay,' he said. His eyes looked panicked. They were being pulled away from that place, but Jay would not let them be separated. Not again. She refused with all her will and wrapped her arms around Dex's body. A sudden confusion of crashing sounds, of glass shattering and mountains exploding, seemed to engulf her body. Her eyes were clenched tightly shut. Then, there was only silence. For a moment, she could not feel anything, but gradually became aware of the rough texture of Dex's coat against her cheek, the pressure of his arms around her. She opened her eyes and pulled away from him. 'Where are we?'

Dex groaned. 'Fuck. How the hell?'

'Dex, *where are we*?'

'Lorrance's house,' he said.

Jay looked around herself. They were standing in a spotless white hallway, which she recognised as the one where they'd met Peter in the shadow world. 'What does this mean?' she asked. 'Is he here? Did they lie to us?' For one hideous moment, she considered that Lacey and Peter had delivered them into Lorrance's hands. Had they been working for him all along?

'I think it's OK,' Dex said uncertainly.

'There's a car coming,' Jay said. 'I can hear it outside. I think we should hide.'

'OK.' Dex took her hand and led her into the house.

'This could be just another layer,' Jay hissed. 'Something else we're meant to see.'

'Possibly,' Dex answered.

'Where are we going?'

'I thought we should make for the back door. The kitchen's this way.'

Suddenly, a tall figure loomed out of a doorway to their left. Both Jay and Dex couldn't help cursing and jumping backwards. 'Rhys!' Dex cried.

Rhys Lorrance stood before them. Jay had never been this close to him before, even though she'd occasionally glimpsed him across rooms at various events and seen his photo often in the papers. Perhaps because of her recent experiences, and the knowledge she'd gained, she immediately felt the heat of Lorrance's power radiating off him. He didn't seem to be in any state of decline other than appearing slightly anxious. Dex uttered Lorrance's name again, but it was clear that he could not see his visitors. He strode past them, back into the hall.

'Why are we here?' Jay said. 'Are we back in our own reality or not?'

'I don't know,' Dex said.

Outside, car doors slammed. Dex and Jay remained immobile, Jay straining her ears for any sound from Lorrance. There was none. She sensed he was waiting in the hall, as motionless as they were. After a few moments, the doorbell chimed. Silence. The bells chimed again. Then came a more threatening sound. The front door creaked open, without any noise of footsteps or other movement. Curious, Jay went back towards the hall, Dex following. She saw Rhys Lorrance standing tall and powerful before the door, braced as if for an attack. A man stood in the doorway, while another was visible loitering outside. Dark men, clad in black.

'Ghosts!' hissed Dex. 'Jay, come back here. They'll be able to see us. I know it!' He grabbed her arm.

Jay resisted, drawn by an uncontrollable impulse to witness what happened. She heard Lorrance utter some unintelligible words. He began to raise his hands. Then came the gunshot. Lorrance staggered backwards, a hole blown through his torso. He fell to the ground. Jay could not move. She saw the gunman walk into the hall and calmly direct another bullet through Lorrance's brain. Then the assailant raised his head and looked Jay full in the eye. She couldn't even cringe away from his dead-eyed stare. What she saw in it was an utter soulless and icy implacability. She was irrelevant to him, no more than a powerless phantom.

The gunman turned round quickly and walked from the house, leaving the door open. Jay buried her face against Dex's chest. 'Oh my God,' she whispered. She had begun to shake. The world around her was shaking too. She clung to Dex and he to her. They were being wrenched away again, drawn through a void of terrifying crashes and roars.

They did not find themselves in silence this time, but surrounded by the merry tune of fiddles and joyous voices. Jay opened her eyes to Lestholme, and above her saw the final chunks of masonry fall from the statue. Her body flooded with relief, although her limbs were stiff yet shaking at the

Storm Constantine

same time. It was difficult to pull away from Dex. He had crystals of ice in his hair.

Dex shook his head slowly, as if coming out of a trance. 'It's happened,' he murmured. 'They said it would. We saw it, Jay.'

'A scene I could have done without,' Jay said, swallowing thickly. 'A vile dream.'

'Are you OK?'

She nodded. 'Yes. I think so. God, Dex, was that real what we saw? Who killed Lorrance and why? Was it Peter and Lacey's people or Charney's?'

'It might not have been literal reality,' Dex said, 'but a representation of it. Charney might see Lorrance as a security risk now, or maybe someone else has taken the law into their own hands, but somehow I doubt their method for dealing with it will involve murder. That's not often their style. You know that. They have a thousand different ways to ruin people.'

'But it felt – and looked – so real.' Jay shuddered, trying to expel the image of Lorrance's falling body, and the blank eyes of the gunman, from her mind.

'These things often do,' Dex said in a cynical tone.

'Part of you doesn't want him dead, does it?' Jay said.

Dex shrugged uncomfortably. 'He did a lot for me, but if a part of me still cares about him, it's a very small part.' He stroked her face. 'You're the one, Jay. Believe it.' He smiled uncertainly, as if he hadn't smiled properly for a long time. The expression, in its boyish naiveté, wrenched at Jay's heart. She was filled with a certainty that it was time for her to take back control of her life. She had seen things that few people saw, been given an insight into the complexities of the universe and how nothing might be how it seemed. 'Dex, it's time to make a choice,' she said.

He closed his eyes, breathed in slowly. 'I know.'

'Come back with me.'

He looked down at her, cupped her chin in one hand. 'I don't know,' he said. 'Will you give me some time?'

'Some,' Jay said. She reached up and curled her arms around his neck.

*   *   *

288

Samantha Lorrance considered herself to be a practical, rational person. Even though she read her stars in the paper, she'd never admit to being superstitious. Life had felt very odd over the last few weeks, but she put this down to the pressures of her husband's work. As his wife, she couldn't help but be sensitive to his moods and even though he wouldn't confide in her, she knew he was anxious about something. Samantha didn't like some of the people who'd been coming to the house. The men in dark suits looked like gangsters to her. She hoped Rhys wasn't involved in anything dodgy. Still, she was prepared to stand by him, whatever happened. She was his wife. He cared for her. Loyalty was very important.

One morning, after her work-out, Samantha went up to her bedroom. A song was looping through her mind. It was an annoying tune she could not dispel and she found herself singing the words beneath her breath. 'I've seen the truth in your heart, I've seen inside your fear.' Not very nice words. How did she know them? It wasn't the sort of song she liked. Must be something Rhys played.

As she changed from her leotard and leggings, the wind slapped furiously against the window. The frame rattled so much, Samantha thought the catch couldn't be fastened properly. She went to investigate. Down on the lawn, the untidy leaves whirled and swirled around the bare tree trunks. The garden seemed so huge, seen there from the top of the house. Dark clouds belched across the sky, promising a deluge. The lawns were still green, although the gardeners had been busy in the flower beds, which now looked empty, the rich earth newly turned.

She heard a voice call from the garden, a woman's voice calling her name. It sounded like Lacey. What was she doing out there?

Samantha felt impelled to open the window. Once she did so, a surge of wind broke over her, bearing into the room a scent of smoke and loam. Samantha leaned out of the window, letting the wind dishevel her sleek hair. She could not see Lacey in the garden. Perhaps she'd been mistaken about the voice.

289

There was something exciting about the autumnal smells and the chill, rushing air. Samantha could see the hill at the far side of the estate, its bare crown stark against the white sky. It seemed two figures were standing on it looking back at her, but when she looked again there was no one there. The leaves filled the air. They confused her sight. Some of them even came in through the window and stuck to her face. Suddenly repelled, Samantha slammed it shut. Immediately she was cocooned in stillness and silence. She could still see the violence of the elements, but could no longer hear it. It was almost like a tornado out there, everything being whipped around, the trees leaning and swaying. She was worried one of them might fall on the house. Then, quite suddenly, the wind dropped. It was so sudden, Samantha wondered whether what she'd just seen was some kind of minor twister wriggling across her land. She glanced down at the lawn.

The leaves had fallen into a perfect formation: a message. Not the face of a demon, nor an omenic pictogram, but simply a number: eleven digits. Samantha studied it in surprise for a moment. It was a London telephone number. How could that happen? Then, a low breeze scudded across the grass and the leaves twisted into it, becoming a chaotic scatter once more.

Samantha found that she could remember the numbers she'd seen quite easily. She was a rational, practical person, but because there was a phone in the bedroom, she acted impulsively. She punched in the number and it rang about three times. The voice that answered was her husband's.

She said, 'Rhys?' Perhaps her voice sounded odd.

He barked, 'Who is this?'

She answered, 'Me.'

The phone slammed down at the other end, leaving Samantha with a silent line.

She sat down on the bed, the phone in her hands. She felt boneless. Where was Rhys? How had that number appeared to her? What did it mean? She picked up a pen and wrote the digits down on the notepad that lay on her bedside table. For several minutes, she just looked at it. Then she rang the number again, just to check, just to see. It rang and rang. No one answered, although she could almost feel the eyes that watched that ringing phone, willing it to stop.

For an hour or so, she pottered around the house in a daze. Was it a woman's number? Was Rhys having an affair? Her stomach felt hollow at the thought of it. Maybe there'd been no number in the leaves at all. Maybe it was her own mind that had made her think she'd seen it. It could have come from her memory.

Rhys's office was always kept locked when he was away from the house, so Samantha had to ask the security man, Terry, to break in for her. She would pry into Rhys's desk, see what she could find out, look for the number. Rhys would not expect something like that from her, and neither did Terry. He was not suspicious of her request, and accepted her excuse of having left a sheaf of bills in there that needed paying urgently.

'Thank you,' said Samantha in a dismissive tone, once Terry had forced the lock. She stood at the threshold, looking at him, until he went away.

The study was dark and watchful. Old ashes in the hearth gave off a bitter smell. Samantha went to the desk, which was empty of papers. Only an old-fashioned blotter and a black telephone lay on the gleaming surface. Samantha pulled the handle of the wide central drawer of the desk. It was locked. She hesitated. Should she break into the desk? Oh, why the hell not – she'd already have to explain the forced door. Terry wouldn't do it, though. He'd think that was too much of a liberty.

Samantha marched into the kitchen and took a large cook's knife from the draining board. Mrs Moran was at the sink. The moment she saw Samantha, she said, 'What's the matter?'

Samantha gave her a fierce glance. 'I'm going to find out,' she said, her mouth unusually firm.

Mrs Moran, wiping her hands on a dish towel, followed Samantha back to the study. Samantha didn't stop her. The housekeeper looked on in bewilderment while her employer attacked the desk drawer lock with the knife. 'Be careful,' she said.

Samantha ignored her. The more the lock resisted her, the angrier she became. Certainty was settling within her: Rhys had betrayed her; Rhys had secrets.

Finally, with the wood around it scored and splintered, the lock gave way. Samantha threw the ruined knife on to the red carpet. Mrs Moran still stood at the doorway, her eyes round. Samantha sat down in her husband's leather swivel chair. She started to pull all the contents of the drawer out on to the desk. Most of them were just receipts, but she did find an address book. Too convenient. As she suspected, the number she'd seen in the leaves wasn't there. Rhys would have another book, one he kept on him at all times. Private numbers would be written in it.

'What are you looking for?' asked Mrs Moran, walking gingerly towards the desk.

Samantha looked up at her. 'I don't know. Where would you find evidence of infidelity?'

'No!' exclaimed Mrs Moran.

Samantha couldn't explain about the leaves. Mrs Moran would think she was mad. She stood up and stalked into the living-room, where there was an extension of her own telephone line. She called an old friend, who she knew could find someone to gather information for her.

Rhys didn't come home that night. She didn't hear from him. That alone told her something was amiss. He'd been due back for dinner. She resisted calling him on his mobile and whenever she tried to call the number the leaves had given her, there was no reply.

The next morning, a man named Jones called her and told her how much it would cost to hire him. Samantha engaged his services immediately. Jones said that normally he would expect to receive payment in advance, but as a favour for a friend of a friend, he could give her an address now.

'What address is this?' asked Samantha.

'Of the number I was given,' he replied, rather smugly.

'That was very quick,' said Samantha. 'Thank you.' She wrote the address down as he dictated it. The address belonged to a man named Gus Lyons. Then Jones asked her what further requirements she had.

'I may not need anything else,' she said. 'Send me a bill.'

Jones laughed. 'That's not the way it works.' He sounded displeased now, sorry he'd given her the address.

'Where shall I send the cash?' Samantha said impatiently. He gave her a PO box address.

After she'd ended the call, Samantha dressed herself with care, cancelled her personal trainer for the day and went out to her car. The wind was not blowing today, and the sun shone harshly on the garden. Samantha looked back at the house, suddenly sure that she would not be living there for much longer. A sense of ending hung over the bare trees, and enveloped the stark white walls of the house. Samantha tossed back her hair and got into her car. She was going to London.

For a few hours, Samantha went shopping. She drew out some cash from her account, and posted it to the address Jones had given her. That was dealt with now. She wouldn't have to remember it. Late in the afternoon, she went into a café, where she studied her A–Z street guide of the city. The address she'd come to find was in a fashionable area, expensive. It belonged to a man, yet Samantha was sure a woman was involved. She could almost smell an alien perfume. I may be wrong, she told herself. Strange men had been coming to the house for years. This Gus Metcalfe could be any one of them. Rhys might have been at the flat because of business. Yet still she couldn't dispel her suspicions. She'd have to go there to see for herself. Samantha sipped her cappuccino, her face numb. She would do this thing, then, depending on the outcome, she might contact one of her friends. So far, she'd called none of them.

Samantha walked down the street, looking up at all the lit windows. She could see houseplants, wall hangings, paintings, book-cases. Why didn't people close their curtains, draw their blinds? The door she was looking for looked like all the other doors; painted black, set in a cream façade. Steps led up to it.

Samantha didn't pause. She went right up to it and rang the bell of the appropriate flat. She knew, even before the call was answered, that a woman would respond. Samantha rang the bell again, and eventually a woman's voice oozed out of the intercom; husky and confident. 'Who is it?'

I have to get in, Samantha thought. 'Mrs Lorrance,' she said. Her heart had increased its pace a little.

'I don't know any "Mrs Lorrance",' said the voice.

Samantha hated that voice already. 'I just want a moment of your time,' she said. 'It's a personal matter.' Her own voice was light and friendly. She wasn't stupid enough to go pounding in with anger and accusation. That would get her nowhere.

'I'll be out in a minute,' said the woman and the intercom went silent.

You don't know anything yet, Samantha told herself as she waited on the doorstep. This might all be explained. She stood with her back to the door, looking down the street.

The door opened and Samantha turned round. She noticed the bright red hair first, then the face with its puffy eyes, the look of someone who'd just woken up. The woman had a striking appearance, but there was a slyness to her expression. She said, 'Yeah? What is it?'

Samantha smiled. 'Hello, I realise you don't know me, but I called my husband here the other day – Rhys Lorrance.'

A small smile played subtly around the woman's mouth. She said, 'Did you?'

'Yes. Would you mind telling me what he was doing here?'

The woman's smile became more blatant. 'Why don't you ask him?'

At that point, Samantha knew she was looking at her husband's mistress, a woman who was enjoying this encounter. 'I'm asking you,' she said.

The woman shrugged. 'And maybe I don't want to tell you.' Her smile became a grin. 'Bye bye, Samantha. Just you go on home, now.' She began to retreat into the hallway, and then a man's voice called out, 'Gina, what is it?' He appeared behind her, wrapped in a bath robe, his hair wet.

Samantha saw the woman's expression become furtive. 'Nothing,' she said and tried to shut the door. Samantha wouldn't let her. She stepped forward, her hand flat against the wooden panels. 'You're screwing my husband,' she said.

The man came forward, his face set into a puzzled frown. 'What the fuck is this?'

'This woman's mad,' said Gina.

'Mad, am I?' Samantha's voice had become more strident, her accent less refined. 'How long has it been going on? Just tell me that.'

'Just go away.' Gina flapped her hands in Samantha's direction. 'I don't appreciate hysterical women accosting me on my doorstep.'

Aspects of Samantha's wild East End youth reared up within her. She grabbed hold of Gina by the hair, felt the satisfying rip of roots. 'You're a whore!' she screeched, throwing Gina back against the hallway wall.

The man hurried forward and tried to intervene, so Samantha kicked him on the shin. 'What's all this about?' he demanded as he hopped backwards. 'Who the hell are you?'

'Rhys Lorrance's wife,' screamed Samantha. 'That's who I am.'

'Rhys Lorrance,' said the man. 'Gina, what the hell's going on?'

Gina had managed to pull herself away from Samantha, who now stood clutching only a handful of red hair. 'Get rid of that fucking bitch, Gus! Get rid of her!' Gina ran back into the flat.

The man faced Samantha. 'Would you mind telling me what's happening?'

Samantha pointed a shaking finger at the flat door. 'You can tell *her* that I'll be citing her in my divorce, OK? I'll be taking Rhys to the fucking cleaners, so she needn't think she'll end up with much.'

'That's my partner you're talking about,' said the man.

'She's my husband's whore,' said Samantha with satisfaction. 'She's had him here. I know. I spoke to him on the phone while he was here.'

The man's face closed in like clouds over the sky. Samantha saw jealousy there, like a bruise beneath the skin. She knew that look in a man's face. She knew what came with it. 'It's true,' she said. 'It was yesterday. We've both been had.'

She turned to leave and then paused to say, 'Oh, what's her full name?'

'Virginia Allen,' said the man. He was staring at the door to his home.

Samantha walked away. She felt buoyant, released. She wouldn't divorce Rhys. She wouldn't have to. She had a feeling Ms Allen's affair with her husband had just ended. Rhys didn't like mess. He didn't like trouble. She'd tell him what she'd done, of course, and act hurt and upset. He'd make it up to her.

Instead of contacting any friends, Samantha drove straight back to Emmertame, full of confidence. Her instincts had been right, she'd acted on them, and now, in her opinion, the matter was closed. She was prepared for a couple of days' unpleasantness at home, but that was a necessary by-product of her action.

As she'd expected, Rhys's car was parked outside. He'd have found out about the forced locks by now. He might be angry, but she had enough ammunition to counter any attack. Her break-in had been justified. Hadn't she proved that?

The lodge at the gate was in darkness, and Terry's car wasn't there. Mrs Moran would have gone home for the day, so Samantha would have the privacy for her encounter with her husband. She felt fired up, ready for it.

As she parked her car next to the Mercedes on the drive, Samantha noticed the front door of the house stood slightly open. Light spilled out into the driveway. Puzzled, she hurried from the car. Wind hissed high overhead, but at ground level, the air was still. Samantha shivered. She felt frightened. An open door on to the night was not a normal thing. She wanted everything to go back to normal now.

Samantha reached the threshold. She pushed the door open wider.

He lay there on the floor in the hall, his limbs in an eerie approximation of a swastika. Blood ran out of him in a wide, thick line, almost to Samantha's feet. She could tell immediately that he was dead.

Samantha was a rational, practical person. She did not rave or weep, she did not collapse or scream. She swore softly beneath her breath in a relentless monotone as she knelt over her husband's body. There was an enormous wound in the back of his head, where the blood had flowed from. A small, corresponding wound on his forehead suggested he'd been shot. His chest was injured too. Her hand hovered a few inches above his head. His eyes were opened, but filmed. Did she know this person? She couldn't feel anything inside. She was completely numb, and yet some deep part of her was not surprised by what she'd found. How could that be?

When she stood up, she felt a bit light-headed, but was capable of making her way to the living-room and dialling 999. Then she sat down on the sofa and spent the time until the police and ambulance arrived crying. The tears were silent, cleansing, a kind of release. It was so strange. She was shocked by what she'd seen, but couldn't feel grief.

Chapter Twenty-Five

Jay and Dex spent two days staying with Sally Olsen. Sally said to Jay, 'It must be like when you first met,' but it wasn't. Jay and Dex were completely different people now. She could lie in his arms, breathing in that old, familiar scent, and feel sure that she was beginning to really know him. There were no secrets between them now. She knew he was afraid of returning to the real world, but like her, he'd never belonged in Lestholme, and it would never be enough to satisfy him. The previous night, after they'd made love, Dex had said to her, 'I'm ready now.'

Jay's eyes had filled with tears. She kissed his eyelids, his forehead, his cheeks. They did not have to repeat history. They had a different awareness now, and could create a new life for themselves. Jay felt serene and supremely confident. Things that had once mattered to her seemed irrelevant. 'It'll be good,' she said.

When Jay went out into Sally's garden on the morning of the third day, she could smell autumn in the air. Summer would fade for Lestholme, she thought, but no doubt in their new time, they would have equally idyllic winters.

Sally came out of the house behind her. She folded her arms and stood next to Jay on the patio. 'You're going to leave today, aren't you?'

Jay nodded. 'I think so.' She smiled at Sally. 'We all have to find the place that's right for us.'

'You'll be missed,' Sally said, then frowned a little. 'Funny. I've never noticed anybody leave before.' She paused. 'It feels different here now, doesn't it?'

Jay detected a slight note of anxiety in Sally's voice. 'It'll be better,' she said. Although she would not voice her thoughts, she felt that Lorrance's influence had gone, and the villagers might not live in quite so much of a dream. Perhaps Lestholme would become more of a retreat, where people could rest temporarily from the world.

'You've all been good for me,' Jay said, and hugged Sally tightly. 'I've learned such a lot.'

'You've affected us too,' Sally said.

Around lunch-time, Jay and Dex went back to Gus' car at the pub. Some of the villagers had gathered to see them off. To Jay, it felt as if she'd been on a long holiday, where she'd met friends whom she'd probably never see again. Intense relationships can form on holidays, but they rarely last beyond that capsule of time. The person it would hurt most to leave was Jem. The girl hadn't been around much for the past few days, no doubt aware that Dex and Jay had needed time together. Now, as they strolled to the pub, Jay looked for Jem among the people around them. It wasn't until they reached the car that she saw the girl sitting on a low wall next to the road. Jem stood up as they approached.

'I wondered where you were,' said Jay.

Jem smiled.

Jay realised she was going to find it very hard to say goodbye. She hoped that within Jem some healing process had begun to take place. 'I'll miss you,' she said.

'No you won't,' Jem answered.

'Jem, I will!'

'No you won't.' Jem took her hand and spoke gravely. 'I'd like to come with you. If that's all right.'

'Jem! Is that all right? Don't be stupid. I'd love you to come.' She looked at Dex. 'We both would.'

Dex just shrugged. 'I don't mind.'

Jem reached down behind the wall and picked up a battered canvas bag, which clearly contained her entire possessions. 'I can't hide from what happened to me,' she said, 'but I can make the decision to let it go.'

Jay nodded. 'Well, let's go, then. No point in waiting.'

Jay got into the driver's side of the car, Dex beside her, while Jem scrambled into the back. 'Technically, we're car thieves,' Jay said. 'Do you think we're likely to be stopped on the motorway by police?'

Dex fastened his seat belt. 'I don't think that will happen,' he said.

They set off down the road, in the direction the bus had taken a few days before. Villagers waved goodbye, then drifted back to their homes. Jay felt slightly disorientated. It was difficult to believe she was actually going back.

'What do you want to do when we get back?' Dex asked her.

She sighed. 'First, I want to go back to the flat. There are a few things that need resolving.' She glanced round at Jem. 'What about you?'

The girl shrugged. 'I don't know yet. I want to see what it feels like first.'

Jay turned a corner in the lane. When had the trees lost their foliage? She hadn't been watching for the moment of transition, but it was clear they were back in the world they'd left behind. She saw a tractor making slow progress up a ploughed field. They had to pull in to the side of the lane to let another car pass.

'And what about you, Dex?' Jay asked. So far, he'd said nothing about his intentions.

He glanced at her. 'I feel much the same as Jem,' he said. 'How can I know yet?' He exhaled slowly. 'I don't want to take up where I left off. You don't expect that of me, do you?'

Jay reached out to squeeze his knee. 'No. I don't think any of us should do that.'

They drove into London near dawn. Dex had taken over the driving, so that Jay could doze. Jem had also fallen asleep for the last stage of the journey. Early morning traffic rushed around them, the faces of the drivers intent and faintly hostile. Jay woke first and glanced round at Jem, perhaps to check that she was still there. She found herself looking at a young woman who appeared to be in her early twenties. 'Dex, she's changed,' Jay said.

Dex took a quick look, then shook his head. 'Lestholme might be a hole in time, but London's very much caught up in it.'

'Perhaps she's always been that way,' Jay said, 'only we just couldn't see it. She never stopped growing up.'

'We're back,' Dex said. 'What else should we expect? If Jem is to function in this world, make contact with her relatives, she must be part of it.'

Before they turned on to the road where Jay had lived, Dex stopped the car, so that Jay could nip into a newsagent's and buy a paper. She had to know how much time had passed. The date on the paper was 28 November. She felt as if she'd been away for months, but it was only weeks. Such was her eagerness to discover this information, the headline hadn't grabbed her attention immediately. Now, she saw it, and quickly scanned the story. 'Dex,' she said in a low voice. 'What we saw was real. Lorrance is dead.'

Dex nodded slowly, but didn't appear that shocked. 'OK. What's it say?'

'Just that he's been shot.' She read the story out to him. The police had no suspects, although the wife of the dead man had spoken about shadowy business associates that she'd always suspected of dirty dealings. Perhaps later the wife herself would be accused. That could happen. 'So, who do you think did it now?' Jay asked Dex. 'Charney's mob or Peter's?'

Dex shook his head. They had come to Jay's old road and he parked the car a short distance from the flat. 'It could be either,' he said, 'or even Samantha, as you suggested, or Lacey, or Michaels, or anyone Lorrance ever damaged. I don't care. I'm glad he's dead now. I really am, Jay.'

She reached out to squeeze his arm.

Jem stirred in the back seat. 'Are we here?' she asked, brushing hair from her eyes.

'You slept like a log,' Jay said. 'Yeah, we're here.'

Jem yawned and stretched. 'I'm stiff all over.'

Jay turned the rear view mirror towards the girl. 'Look at yourself,' she said.

Jem did so, rubbing her face with the fingers of one hand. 'I look terrible, like I've slept in a ditch.'

'You're a woman, Jem. A young woman.'

Jem looked puzzled. 'I know, Jay. What's the matter with you?'

Jay and Dex exchanged an amused glance. Then Jay said, 'Oh well, time to get this over with.' She opened the car door.

'Do you want moral support?' Dex asked her.

Jay shook her head. 'No, but get out of the car. There's a café down the road. You could wait there for me.' It was then she noticed, with some surprise, that her own car was parked outside the flat, its flanks dull with a muddy patina. 'That's mine,' she said to Dex, pointing at the vehicle. 'At least we'll have transport.'

Dex paused, then said, 'Jay, I think we should go to Julie's after this.'

Jay nodded. 'Yes, that's a distinct possibility. But let's take things one step at a time.' She kissed Dex on the mouth. 'Please go, now. Give me the car keys. I'll see you shortly. The café's called Anna's, it's down there, not far.'

Dex was clearly reluctant to leave her, but Jem linked her arm through his and dragged him off down the street. Jay watched them go. The love she felt for them would sustain her through whatever happened next.

She glanced up at the windows. The curtains were drawn. It was still very early. Perhaps Gus wouldn't be there. What would she do if Gina answered the door?

Jay pressed the buzzer for her flat. She had to press it several times, on each occasion leaving her finger there for longer. Eventually, she invoked a grumpy sounding Gus. 'Who the fuck is it?'

'Hello, lover,' Jay said lightly. 'Are you going to open the door or do I break another window?'

There was a stunned silence, then the soft word 'Jay' and the sound of the lock being activated. Jay opened the door. Her heart was beating fast.

Gus was unshaven and sheepish, wrapped in a dressing-gown at the threshold of the flat. He tried to say something, but Jay just pushed past him and marched into the living-room. The flat was in the same squalid condition as the last time she'd seen it. She turned and saw Gus standing in the doorway, rubbing the back of his neck. He looked awkward in the extreme. Jay folded her arms. 'Well?'

Gus shrugged. 'Jay, I . . .'

'Where is she?'

'Where's who?'

'You know damn well who. The virginal Virginia. Is she hiding in the bedroom?'

Gus frowned. 'No . . . She's not here.'

'Lucky for her, then. Would you mind explaining to me what you're doing here? I presume you broke in and took possession. How long ago was this?'

Gus ventured forward. 'Jay, you just disappeared. Gina told me what had happened, and how you'd gone to that wanker's sister . . .'

Jay nodded slowly, her eyes narrow. 'Did she now. Was it her idea for you to come back here?'

'Well, you just left it, didn't you? It would have been repossessed. The mortgage was still going out of the joint account. What did you expect me to do? Just let the place rot? How was I to know you'd change your mind and come back?'

'How long ago?' Jay asked.

He wriggled his shoulders in embarrassment. 'About four weeks ago, a few days after you'd told Gina what you were going to do.'

'Right.' Jay took a deep breath. 'For the record, I never told Gina of my plans. She obviously had her own agenda through all this. Perhaps we were both dupes.'

Gus yawned and laughed bitterly. 'You could say that.'

'Oh?'

Gus sat down on the sofa, his hands dangling between his knees. 'Well, you might as well know. There was a bit of a scene last night. Some woman turned up here accusing Gina of having an affair with her husband.' He rubbed his face. 'She was doing the dirty on me. We're finished.'

Jay laughed coldly. 'Poor you.'

Gus nodded, seemingly oblivious of Jay's tone. 'Yeah. The

woman who came – it was that Rhys Lorrance's wife. Can you believe it?'

Jay contained her reaction, and spoke softly. 'You'd be surprised to know how much I'd believe.' She paused. 'And was Gina having an affair with Lorrance?'

Gus sneered. 'She tried to deny it, but I could tell she was lying. She'd had him here. Bitch.' He looked up at Jay, his expression bewildered. 'She said it was a business friendship, to do with her book. Lorrance was helping her, she said. Stupid fucker actually answered my phone while he was here. His bloody wife was on the other end. She knew what was going on all right.'

Jay thought he looked pathetic. She almost felt sorry for him, but her main concern was the information he'd just given her. 'What did Gina say about me, Gus?' Jay asked. 'How did she convince you I was seeing Dex?'

Gus' expression took on a mulish cast. 'She told me the truth, that's all.'

'The truth!' Jay laughed coldly. 'You still believe that?'

Gus ran his fingers through his hair. 'Oh, I don't know. You were up to something though, Jay, you can't deny that.'

'I wasn't,' she said. 'Whatever happened was a direct result of Gina's betrayal and your lack of trust.'

Gus leaned back on the sofa. 'Oh, that's right, blame me.'

'I'm not. I'm just saying it was a result. That's different.'

'So what happens now?' he asked. 'You want to come back?'

Jay laughed again, this time in incredulity. 'That's not why I'm here,' she said. 'I just wanted to get everything sorted out.'

'This place is still half mine,' Gus said.

Jay nodded, smiling. 'I could dispute that actually, but I won't. You wanted me to buy you off, so try this on for size. Give me my half instead. You can have the place.'

Gus stared at her. 'You *are* back with that wanker, aren't you?'

'That's none of your business,' Jay said.

'I knew it!'

'Yeah, you know it,' Jay said, 'you know it all, don't you? What do I care? If you want to think I was seeing Dex before, then believe it. It doesn't matter to me. You and I weren't right for each other. Surely you can see that now?'

Gus sucked his lower lip for a moment, then seemed to crumple inwardly. 'You came here a couple of nights ago, didn't you? Gina didn't want to believe it. Said it was kids that had broken in. But I knew it was you. I'm not that surprised to see you now. You took the car, right?'

'Yes, and now I've returned it.' She threw him the keys. 'It's outside.'

'Where have you been?' He frowned. 'Jay, it's been weeks. Your car was found abandoned out in the middle of nowhere. I thought the worst, until Gina explained everything. What possessed you to do a thing like that? Didn't you consider how people might worry?'

Jay set her mouth into a sneer. 'What people? You? Gina? As if you cared!'

Gus showed her his palms in an open gesture. 'I know we had an ugly scene. I was wound up, but that doesn't mean I wasn't concerned about you.'

Jay sighed and sat down in a chair opposite him. 'I needed to get away to think about my life,' she said. 'It was time for a change all round. I don't want to fight now, Gus. Gina's been a cow, obviously, and even now I'm not sure how much of one. I don't really want to know. In a way, her betrayal did me a favour. I've had to sort myself out.'

Gus shook his head slowly. 'This has been one weird time.'

'It has. So, anyway, what do you think about my suggestion? Can you buy me out?'

Gus fixed her with a meaningful stare. 'Is that what you want?'

'Yes. It is.'

There was a short silence, then Gus said, 'I didn't want any of this to happen, Jay. I was content, then suddenly my whole life was falling apart.'

Jay didn't feel capable of comment.

Jay couldn't give Gus a contact number, but told him she'd be in touch in a day or so. He wanted to know where she was going, but she wouldn't tell him. He also asked her if she was going to confront Gina. 'You just call her and tell her what's happened,' Jay said. 'I'm sure she needs a friend at the moment.'

Gus began to grumble and swear, but Jay interrupted. 'Of course, you won't have seen the papers yet. Lorrance was killed last night.'

Gus raised his eyebrows. 'Get away! How?'

'Shot,' said Jay. 'He was involved in all kinds of shady business.'

'Who isn't, in this fucking industry?' said Gus.

Jay nodded. 'True. Still, his death will probably be a great shock to Gina.'

'Well she deserves it,' Gus said coldly.

'Who are we to judge?' Jay said.

She went out into the street, unsure of what she felt about Gina. It was hard to accept someone she'd looked upon as a close friend could have behaved in the way she had. She must have known what Lorrance was doing, even as she offered the hand of comfort and support. What made someone do a thing like that? It was grotesque. Jay strolled down the road to the café. She must cast off all the unwanted baggage from her past life. Anything was possible now. Anything.

Chapter Twenty-Six

Samantha Lorrance walked through the bedrooms of her house, deciding what she would keep and what she would sell. Later that morning, an estate agent was coming to value the property. Samantha couldn't live there any more. She'd been staying with her old friends in London for a week or so, and now planned to move back there. She had become a very wealthy woman, and could afford to buy somewhere to her taste in the city.

Mrs Moran was in the kitchen as she had been every morning since Samantha had moved in as a new bride. Samantha could hear the comforting clatter of cutlery and crockery. Perhaps whoever bought this house would keep Mrs Moran, Terry and the gardeners on. Samantha didn't like to think of them losing their jobs. Strangely enough, letters of sympathy had arrived from several neighbours, women who'd never bothered with Samantha before. I needed you more in the past, Samantha thought as she read the letters. She would reply warmly, because she liked to be polite, but she didn't really care about them.

Samantha was eager to leave the house. She had a dinner date with Cherry and two male friends later on. She hoped the estate agent wouldn't be late. She'd go and have a cup of coffee with Mrs Moran until he arrived. Sometimes, she cried about Rhys, especially at night, but it was just because she felt sorry for him. She didn't miss him particularly. Being his wife had been like living in an enchanted castle. It hadn't been real life and she realised now she'd had no deep love for him. She'd thought that marrying him would secure her future, and despite what had happened, it had.

Samantha came down the stairs. The hall was a horrible place to her now and she always hurried through it. She wasn't afraid of seeing a ghost, but shied from recalling the sight of her dead husband. She resisted the urge to close her eyes and run blindly for the passage to the kitchen. At the bottom of the stairs, Samantha uttered a short moan of horror. There was something on the floor there, just where Rhys had died. For a moment, she was frozen to the spot. Then she saw that it was just a shadow, cast by someone standing in the living-room doorway.

'My God,' Samantha said. 'Lacey?'

'Hi.' Lacey came out from the room and looked up at her stepmother.

Samantha skipped down the stairs and gave the girl a hug. 'You poor love. Oh, sweetheart, how are you?'

'I'm fine,' Lacey said. She kissed Samantha on the cheek and withdrew. 'And you?'

'Oh, mucking through. It's been . . .' She shrugged. Any words would seem inadequate. 'You missed the funeral. I'm sorry. I didn't know how to contact you.'

'I knew about the funeral,' Lacey said. 'It's OK. You know how it was with me and Dad.'

'Come and have a cup of coffee,' Samantha said firmly, slipping her hand through Lacey's elbow.

'I will,' Lacey said, 'but first, I have to ask you something. It's very important.'

Samantha felt uneasy. 'Well, yes, of course. What is it?'

'The house,' said Lacey.

'The house?'

Lacey pushed a few strands of hair from her face. 'Mmm. This isn't easy, but it is important. I want to come back here.'

Samantha frowned. 'Here? To live?'

Lacey nodded. 'Someone has to. I can't explain, but I need to be here.'

Samantha sighed. 'Oh, love, I'm so sorry. I'm putting the house on the market today.'

'Please don't,' said Lacey.

Samantha stared at the girl for a few moments. 'I can't live here, Lacey.'

'I know.' Lacey closed her eyes briefly. 'Something's left here, Sam. It can't be left alone, or passed on to anyone else. It has to be me.'

Rhys had left his daughter nothing in his will. At the time Samantha had discovered this, she'd wondered what would happen if Lacey ever did make a reappearance. For this reason, she'd been half expecting it. 'Look, we can come to some arrangement,' Samantha said. 'I'm not mean, Lacey. I'll make sure you get something.'

'No, you don't understand,' Lacey said. 'I don't want money. I want this house. Remember when I came to you and tried to explain what Dad was into? You wouldn't listen to me, but now you must know in your heart I was right. You don't ever want to know what went on here, but it was bad, Sam. Someone has to take that legacy on, do something about it. You don't know what I'm talking about, really, so how can that someone be you? And strangers don't deserve to live with what's here. Could you just sell this place and let that happen? What if the new owners have children? Would that be fair?'

Samantha paused, uncertain. She felt as if dark wings were closing around her.

'Please don't make me show you what's here,' Lacey said quietly, her face set into an expression of anguish. 'I can do that, and I really don't want to, but if you won't let me have the house, I'll have no choice but to show you.'

Samantha thought of numbers appearing in swirling leaves, of shadows that walked to the door of the house. The hall felt incredibly cold. She did not want to know and she did not want to see.

'You're a good person,' Lacey said. 'Please accept what I say. It's not about money.'

'You couldn't afford to run a place like this,' Samantha said. 'Could you?'

'That's not your worry. I have my resources.' The hall echoed with her voice, its walls white and chill.

Samantha felt a responsibility hanging over her, something she didn't want. The decision, ultimately, was easily made.

Immediately she felt lighter, and giggled. 'Oh, what the hell. I have more than enough for my needs. Have the house, Lacey, if that's what you want.'

Lacey threw her arms around Samantha and hugged her tightly. 'Thank you. You've done the right thing.'

'I don't envy you,' Samantha said, leading Lacey from the hall towards the kitchen. 'This place has a bad feeling.'

'We can change that,' Lacey said.

With Jay's half of the equity in her old flat, she and Dex bought a dilapidated farmhouse in the north of England, to be nearer to Julie. Music was in Dex's blood; he couldn't abandon it, but the pieces he composed now were very different from anything he'd done before. Sakrilege fought to keep him, but lost the fight. It was almost as if Dex wasn't meant to be on that label any more. Zeke Michaels lost his job in a major staff reshuffle after Lorrance's death. Life, Jay thought, had certainly given him part of what he deserved. She suspected Michaels' personal life wouldn't be going too well either.

Dex signed up with a new company and began to work again. His music had matured, moved on. He would appeal to an older audience now, which was only right because he too was older. The music papers made a meal of his return though and the fan letters came rolling in. Jay thought Dex would be snide about them, but she could tell that he was secretly touched by his old fans' loyalty. He played a private, acoustic gig for the fan club in London and for the last time sang the songs from the unrecorded album. The audience neither bayed nor howled, but listened silently as if they too were aware there was more to the music than it appeared. At the end of the gig, there was a moment's almost rapt hesitation, before the entire club exploded into applause, whistles and catcalls. The response moved Jay to tears.

Jay thought she might write a book at some point, but for the time being was content to renovate her new home, experimenting with the crafts she'd begun to learn in Lestholme. Jem re-established contact with her aunt, but lived with Jay and

Dex. She had decided to go to college next year, but until then would help Jay with the house.

Jay sometimes thought to herself, as she sat in the evenings before the old range in the kitchen, 'This is the life we always should have had.' She'd never experienced real contentment before, but even so, was not afraid of losing it. She felt she'd earned what she'd got. In the beginning, she'd considered contacting Gina, just to see whether she could glean the truth from her, but ultimately decided she didn't want to know. That was all behind her now. Gina's book came out and was very successful, not really to Jay's surprise. But the woman who appeared in the Sunday supplement articles to accompany the book's release was not the one Jay had known. She looked so much older, and a certain fire had gone from her eyes. Jay did not want to feel smug about that, but still couldn't dispel a slight sense of satisfaction.

Julie, Kylie and Melanie were now regular presences in Dex and Jay's lives. Dex had offered to buy his sister somewhere else to live, but for some reason, Julie didn't want to move out of her home. Jay insisted that she at least accept some financial help though and advised Dex on setting up a trust for the children.

'There's not going to be a winter,' Jay said once, as Julie was trying to protest about the arrangements. 'This isn't crumbs for the bird-table, Julie, but consistent support from family.'

'You can be a right bossy cow, do you know that?' Julie said, but she was laughing.

One Sunday afternoon, as Jay, Dex and Jem sat watching an old movie on the TV, the telephone rang. Jay and Dex exchanged a glance. They both confessed afterwards they'd experienced a sense of premonition.

Jay got up to answer the phone. A voice said, 'Jay, it's Lacey Lorrance.'

Jay had believed Lacey was no longer a part of this world, and to hear her voice was chilling. 'What do you want?' Jay asked, unable to keep a slight frostiness from her voice.

'Who is it?' Dex asked.

Jay raised a hand to silence him.

'I'm living at Emmertame,' Lacey said. 'I'd like to see you.'

'What for?' Jay demanded.

'To talk.'

Jay paused. 'No,' she said. 'We've let go of the past. Please respect that.'

Lacey's voice was urgent, pleading. 'His own people killed him, Jay. It wasn't us. Don't think that. We must talk. You're important Jay – you, Dex and Jem. What you lived through has made you different, and that difference gives you responsibilities . . .'

'Lacey, please!' Jay interrupted. At the mention of that name, she sensed both Dex's and Jem's bodies stiffen behind her. 'You live your life the way you see fit, we'll live ours. That's it.'

Jay was prepared to argue more, but found she was listening to a dead line, just silence. Slowly, she replaced the hand-set of the phone.

'They want us,' Dex said.

'They can't have us,' said Jay.

'This might just be the beginning.' Dex raked his hands through his hair. 'We know too much. They're hungry for recruits, Jay.'

'Hush,' Jay said.

Jem was curled up like a scared cat in her chair, her eyes wide. 'Are we safe?' she murmured.

'Yes,' Jay said in a low, cold voice. 'We're safe. I won't let anything get to us, not after all we've been through. I promise you.'

Jem smiled uncertainly and Jay reached out to stroke her hair.

Dex shook his head. 'I can't believe that Lorrance girl's nerve,' he said.

'She's obsessed,' Jay said. 'We have to deal with obsessive people all the time, Dex. Lacey's no different. We mustn't lose sight of that.'

She walked to the window and looked out at the orchard.

Bright yellow leaves skittered among the fallen apples. The sky was dark. 'Play your games,' she murmured. 'Don't think you can involve us. We're finished with it.'

'Is there someone out there?' Jem said, her voice high.

'No.' Jay closed the curtains over the greying afternoon.

Acknowledgements

The author would like to thank the following:

The three unofficial editors who gave me a hard time with this book, but whose constructive criticism helped shape it, Paula Wakefield, Debbie Benstead and Eloise Coquio; my official editors, Andrew Wille and Antonia Hodgson, for their thorough and helpful editorials; my agent Robert Kirby for being my Jerry Maguire; my partner, Jim Hibbert, for bringing light into my life even in the darkest days; Vikki Lee France and Steve Jeffery of my information service, Inception, for everything they continue to do so well; Yvan Cartwright for creating my web site; my closest friends who bear with me through the hard times and celebrate with me in the good times, Deb Howlett, Karen Townsend, Freda Warrington, Adele Stanley, Steve Chilton, Paul Kesterton, Mark Hewkin, Andy Collins, Simon Beal, Adrian McLaughlin and Phil Plumpton; Mikey Clarke, Max of Little Pink Cat and Nick Thorndyke for their unbelievable patience and donation of time when sorting out my computer problems. Finally love and thanks to my dad and step-mum, John and Norma, for being who they are.

Storm Constantine Information Service:
Vikki Lee France and Steve Jeffery
Inception
44 White Way
Kidlington
Oxon OX5 2XA
E-mail: Peverel@aol.com
Web site: http://members.aol.com/peverel/inceptio.htm

Storm Constantine's official web site:
http://members.aol.com/malaktawus/Storm.htm